24.95

Cadillac Beach

Cadillac

Beach

a novel

TIM DORSEY

wm WILLIAM MORROW *An Imprint of* HarperCollins*Publishers*

This is a work of fiction. Names, characters, places, and incidents either are the product of the author's imagination or are used fictitiously. Any resemblance to actual events, locales, organizations, or persons, living or dead, is entirely coincidental and beyond the intent of either the author or the publisher.

HarperCollins books may be purchased for educational, business, or sales promotional use. For information please write: Special Markets Department, HarperCollins Publishers Inc., 10 East 53rd Street, New York, NY 10022.

FIRST EDITION

Designed by JoAnne Metsch

Printed on acid-free paper

Library of Congress Cataloging-in-Publication Data

Dorsey, Tim.
  Cadillac Beach : a novel / Tim Dorsey.—1st ed.
    p. cm.
  ISBN 0-06-052046-9
    1. Storms, Serge (Fictitious character)—Fiction. 2. Grandfathers—Death—Fiction.
  3. Miami Beach (Fla.)—Fiction. 4. Serial murderers—Fiction. 5. Psychopaths—Fiction. I. Title.

PS3554.O719C34   2004
813'.54—dc21   2003054135

04 05 06 07 08 WBC/RRD 10 9 8 7 6 5 4 3 2 1

For Lee Barnes

Too much is never enough.

— MORRIS LAPIDUS

Acknowledgments

P

ROFOUND THANKS AGAIN to my agent, Nat Sobel, and my editor, Henry Ferris. I also owe a tremendous debt to Michael Morrison for believing in the books, Lisa Gallagher for watching my back, Debbie Stier for her much-needed calming influence and David Brown, the man behind the curtain of those insane tours.

Prologue

IN 1964 THREE champion surfers committed the biggest jewel heist in U.S. history, knocking over New York City's Museum of Natural History in a daring midnight burglary. They made off with scores of famous stones, including the Star of India, the world's largest sapphire. Within days federal agents and local police tracked the trio back to Miami Beach. The sapphire and almost all the other priceless gems were recovered. Almost.

A dozen large diamonds remain missing to this day.

IN 2004 A phone rang in the back of a limo. A salesman answered. A tag on his jacket: HI, I'M DOUG.

"Yes, dear. . . . Yes, dear. . . . No, dear, no, I haven't been drinking. . . ." He looked at the bourbon in his hand like a bloody knife and set it on the wet bar, as if she might see through the phone. "Ice cubes? No, that wasn't ice cubes you heard. . . . I told you, I'm not drinking. . . . I swear I'm not. . . . Not a drop. . . . Maybe I'm *technically* drinking. . . . Yes, dear—I mean, no, dear. . . . I'm sorry, dear. . . ."

The other salesmen in the back of the limo mocked and giggled. *"Yes, dear. No, dear."*

The man on the phone swatted the air in front of them for quiet. "No, dear. . . . No, that was the other guys. . . . No, they weren't making fun of you. They're making fun of me. . . . What did they mean by 'whipped'? They're just saying I'm working hard and really tired. . . . No, they are not bad influences. . . . I do not always get in trouble every time I'm with them. . . . That's just twice . . . three times. . . . You've made your point. . . . We're on the way to the airport right now. . . . We're picking up Dave, then straight back to the hotel for the training conference. . . . Right, no lap dances this time. . . . I promise I'll call. . . . I promise. . . . I said I promised. . . . I'm pouring out the rest of the drink right now. . . ." He held an empty hand in the air and turned it over. "I did so really pour it out. . . . Look, I gotta go. . . . I really gotta go. . . . I love you, too. . . . What do you mean, 'You do not'? . . . Okay, and I'll remember to call. . . . Bye."

He hung up. They were all staring at him.

"What?"

"Jeee-zusss!" said Keith, who weighed three hundred pounds and still had lipstick on his cheek from the lap dances. They all wore the same plastic-straw convention hats: UNITED CONDIMENTS.

"Doug, man, you're going to have to do something about that ball and chain," said the one with the RUSTY name tag. He handed Doug his drink back. "And the first thing you need to do is kill that right now!"

The limo sped west across the causeway toward the sparkling Miami skyline. Water all around, harsh orange sunlight in the haze. A departing Carnival cruise ship out the left windows, passengers waving at the world in general. To the right, private islands, armed guards, yachts, helicopter pads. Rusty grabbed the bottle of Kentucky sour mash by the neck and refilled glasses. They passed the port, huge cranes dipping into freight ships, hoisting steel cargo boxes filled with coffee beans, wicker furniture, uncut cocaine in pre-Columbian statues and heat-expired stowaways.

A fourth name tag. BRAD. He raised his drink in toast: "We're wild and crazy guys!"

Three glasses upended in unison.

Keith clenched his face and shook off the afterburn, then opened watering eyes. "That was great!"

Brad pointed at Doug. "You didn't drink yours."

"We're all supposed to do it at the same time," said Rusty.

"It's the rule," said Keith.

Doug looked at his melting ice cubes. "I think we should slow down. It's only nine in the morning. And we haven't been to bed."

The causeway tapered into a bridge. Up they went, the downtown financial buildings to the south, blinding glass and bright white concrete, the postmodern condos on Brickell, the ancient Everglades Hotel, Freedom Tower, Bayside market.

"Are we going to have to ban calls from his wife?" said Brad. "It's like she's here in the damn limo with us. That's the whole point of these conventions."

Rusty was de facto leader of the group, having the big ketchup-packet accounts. He grabbed Doug's knee with his right hand. "We all have to go through our little acts at home to keep the peace. But now we're on the road."

The others nodded.

He squeezed Doug's knee harder. "Now, show her!"

Doug raised the glass and grimaced. Down the bridge now, splitting the American Airlines basketball arena and the *Herald* Building, the freeway passing over the mole-people below on Biscayne Boulevard, families in rental cars locking doors and running red lights.

"On three," said Rusty. "Three!"

Doug slammed his drink back. Part of it went the wrong way,

and he made the wide-eyed expression of someone who'd just backed over three Harleys at Daytona.

The guys: "Hooray!"

Rusty poured again. "That calls for a drink."

Doug fidgeted nervously. He looked out the back window at the rising sun scattering light through faded blue girders of a stacked interchange. He turned around; his glass was full again.

Keith was tearing apart his wallet. "Somebody stole my money!"

"When?" asked Brad.

"I'm not sure. I just know I had a whole bunch of twenties, and now they're all gone."

"You idiot," said Rusty. "You spent them at the strip joint last night. I mean, this morning."

"Maybe a couple, but I couldn't have gone through all of it. Someone ripped me off!"

"Right, and someone ripped you off in New Orleans and Nashville and again in Houston. It's a regular crime wave."

"Exactly," said Keith, turning his pants pockets inside out.

"How come none of the rest of us gets ripped off?"

"That's what makes it so baffling."

"It's not baffling; it's exquisitely simple. Every time we go to a strip joint, you get stopped at the exotic-dancer roadblock and they make you pay the stupidity tax. In your case it's quite steep."

"Chauffeur!" yelled Brad. "Turn up the radio. And go faster!"

The driver twisted the knob on Lenny Kravitz and hit his blinker. The black stretch waited for a Ferrari to blur by, then accelerated into the obnoxious lane of the Dolphin Expressway.

The next round was waiting. "On three . . ."

Drinks went down. Keith called off the search for his missing money and began making flatulence sounds with his hands and otherwise clowning around for the amusement of the gang, because it was his job, being the fattest. Rusty held the bottle of sour mash to the skylight. "It's empty."

"Covered," said Brad, pulling an emergency fifth from a satchel of trade-show mustard samples. He began spilling as the limo approached the Miami River and angled up a drawbridge over a low-drafting Haitian-bound sloop full of stolen bicycles.

"On three . . ."

"We should slow down," said Doug. "We'll be too drunk to make the training seminar."

The others laughed.

"What's so funny?"

"We're not going to no dipshit seminar," said Rusty. " 'Making the Most of Face Time.' Fuck face time!"

"We'll get in trouble," said Doug.

"Didn't you ever go on senior skip day?" asked Keith.

"No."

"Well, you're with the varsity now," said Rusty. "Drink up."

The limo eased into a toll booth.

". . . Are you gonna go my way . . ."

"How much farther to the airport?" Brad yelled over the music.

The driver turned down the radio. "Five minutes."

"Hey, there's the Orange Bowl," said Doug. He fell back in his seat and saw Keith pull a burlap gunnysack from his briefcase.

"What's that for?"

They laughed again.

"Time we got even with Dave," said Keith.

Brad pulled coils of braided nylon rope from a shopping bag. "He's going to get a surprise at the airport."

"What are you guys planning?" said Doug. "This looks like trouble."

"All those little practical jokes Dave keeps playing on us . . ." said Keith.

"Exploding ink pens, loosening the lids on salt shakers, buttering toilet seats," said Rusty.

"Leaving phone messages to call back a new customer, Mr. Lyon . . ." said Brad.

". . . And it's the phone number for the zoo," said Keith. "Payback's a bitch."

Doug trembled. "I have to call my wife."

Rusty grabbed the cell phone away from him and tossed it to Keith, who tossed it to Brad.

A GUARD WAVED the limo through a gate at the executive airport on the west side of Miami International.

"I have a bad feeling," said Doug.

The stretch rolled across the tarmac in the morning sun. Fuel trucks, guys with orange batons, a flight tower.

"There it is!" said Rusty.

A whispering Lear made a ninety-degree turn on the runway and taxied to the chocks. The chauffeur swung the limo toward the passenger door, where they were flipping down the stairs.

Rusty tapped the driver on the shoulder. "No, pull around the back of the plane."

"What?"

"We want to surprise him with the limo and everything." He handed the driver a twenty. "Just do it."

The Lear's door opened. A man in a dark double-breasted suit stepped onto the top of the stairs. He stopped and smiled as Miami hit him in the face. Palm trees, warm breeze, sticky sense of desperation. He raised a McDonald's soda cup and sipped through a straw.

From the back side of the plane, they could only see the fold-down stairs; nobody getting off. "What's he waiting for?" said Rusty.

"Open the door quietly," said Keith, gripping the mouth of the gunnysack.

The man from the Lear finished savoring his first breaths of paradise. He took another sip from his soda cup and started to descend the stairs, the idling jet turbines winding down.

When he got to the bottom, he heard a slapping drumroll of clumsy, drunken footsteps. Before he could turn around, a sack went over his head and down to his hips.

"This is a kidnapping, motherfucker!"

The man thrashed, but the gang was too strong, even hammered. They hustled him to the limo and shoved him in back.

Brad slammed the door behind them.

The chauffeur turned around. "What the hell's going on?"

"Don't worry," said Rusty. "We know this guy. It's a practical joke."

"Surprise!" said Keith, pulling off the gunnysack.

"That's not Dave!"

"He's got a gun!"

Bang, bang, bang.

"I've been hit!"

"Grab it!"

Rusty dove for the pistol. The two men struggled, crashing into a box of prison-grade relish trays. Convenience-store coffee stirrers went flying. Somebody got bit, hair yanked.

Bang, bang.

Rusty jumped back and stared in awe at the gun in his hand like it was some kind of *Star Trek* future-weapon. Smoke filled the rear of the limo.

"What the fuck's happening back there!" yelled the chauffeur.

Brad winced, grabbing his shoulder, blood running between his fingers and down his wrist.

"You okay?" asked Rusty.

Brad nodded.

Doug and Rusty waited a moment, then leaned toward their motionless victim, lying on the floor of the limo in a bed of nondairy creamer, two red stains spreading across his chest.

The chauffeur was turned around in his seat now, kneeling and stretching for a better view. "Jesus Christ! Do you know who that is?"

They shook their heads.

"Tony Marsicano!" yelled the chauffeur. "Oh, my God! Fuck! Fuck! Fuck!"

"Who's Tony Marsicano?" asked Doug.

"Fuck me!" shouted the chauffeur. "You've just killed us all!"

Rusty gestured gingerly with the gun. "It was an accident! I just went like this. . . ."

Bang.

"You shot him again!" yelled the chauffeur.

"It's got a hair trigger or something."

A side window shattered. Keith fell forward lifeless with a gunshot in his back.

"Where'd that come from!" screamed Brad.

"Sniper!" shouted Rusty, pointing at the roof of the small executive terminal. The chauffeur threw the limo in gear and hit the gas.

Men in black suits and mirror sunglasses poured out of the terminal, guns drawn. Some ran after the limo, others toward a waiting sedan.

More gunshots. The salesmen ducked. An opera window shattered, glass spraying their hair. An unsuspecting fuel-truck driver with Walkman earphones came around the corner of a hangar on the jet's back side, choking off the limo's escape. The chauffeur stomped the pedal all the way, aiming for an opening of light between the truck and the plane. The limo's right quarter panels scraped down the side of the tanker; the left edge of the limo's roof ground sparks along the underside of the jet's fuselage. The chauffeur punched the limo through and pumped the brakes out of a fishtailing slide on the runway. The chasing sedan tried to stop but spun out, slamming sideways into the fuel truck.

The salesmen peeked out the rear window. Men scattered from the sedan before the tanker exploded in an orange-black ball of jet fuel, catching the Lear on fire, the pilot wiggling out his window and falling to the runway.

The chauffeur continued accelerating. More gunfire raked the limo. The back window blew, the trunk popped. A security guard ran into the middle of the road and blocked the service exit, waving both arms for them to stop.

Doug cowered and wept on the floor of the vehicle, covered with glass and blood and mayo, pressing buttons on his cell phone. "I have to call my wife."

The guard dove out of the way as the limo crashed through the chain-link gates, which flew open and bounced back against the sides of the stretch. The driver made a skidding left turn in honking traffic and headed back toward downtown Miami.

Doug put the phone to his head.

"Honey, I'm in trouble."

1

Tampa—1996

A BEARDED MAN in rags stood on the side of a busy noon intersection, holding up a cardboard sign: WILL BE YOUR PSYCHIC FRIEND FOR FOOD.

A Volvo rolled up. The bum leaned to the window.

"People are out to get you. Vaccinations will be rendered obsolete in coming years by superaggressive bacteria. Your memory will start playing tricks. Tackle those feelings of hopelessness by giving up."

The driver handed over a dollar. Serge stuffed the bill in his pocket and waved as the car pulled away. "Have a nice day!"

The traffic light cycled again; an Infiniti pulled up.

"Today is the day to seize opportunities and act on long-term goals. But not for you. The House of Capricorn is in regression, which means the water signs are ambiguous at best. Meanwhile, Libra is rising and out to fuck you stupid. Stay home and watch lots of TV."

A dollar came through the window.

"Peace, brother."

The light ran through its colors. Serge knocked on the window of a Mitsubishi. The glass opened an inch.

"Put off making that crucial life-decision today because you'll be wrong. Stop and notice the small things in life, like pollen. Wear something silly and give in to that whimsical urge to kick people in the crotch."

A dollar came through the window slit. Serge waved cheerfully as tires squealed. Next: a cigar-chomping man in an Isuzu. Serge bent down.

"The word 'smegma' will come up today at an awkward moment. Begin keeping a journal; write down all your thoughts so you can see how stupid they are. Don't be rash! Blue works for you!"

"Hey, what kind of a reading is that?"

"Top-of-the-line," said Serge, holding out his hand. "Where's my money?"

"I'm not paying you."

"Come on, ya cheapskate!"

"That was a lousy reading!"

"Okay, let's see what else I got." Serge placed the back of his hand to his forehead and closed his eyes. "Wait, I'm getting a strong signal now. A transient will take down your license plate, track your address through the Department of Motor Vehicles, come to your house at night and kill you in your sleep." Serge opened his eyes and smiled. "How was that?"

The silent driver held out a dollar.

"Oh, no," said Serge, "that was my special five-dollar prediction."

The man didn't move.

"No problem," said Serge, pulling a notepad from his pocket. "I'll just jot down your plate and come by later to get the money."

The man pulled a five from his wallet, threw it out the window and sped off.

Serge picked up the bill, kissed it and waved. He looked around and smiled at his chosen surroundings: drive-through liquor stores, robbery stakeout signs, bus benches advertising twelve-step programs, billboards for deserted dog tracks and talentless morning radio. A sooty diesel cloud floated by. Ah, the great outdoors! Serge turned and headed away from the street. Back to the swamp. It was a small swamp, but it was his swamp, nestled in the quarter-loop of a freeway interchange in the part of Tampa where I-275 dumps Busch Gardens visitors off for thrifty motels and breakfast buffets and encounters with local residents that make the Kumba inverting three-G roller coaster look like a teeter-totter. Serge pushed back brambles and shuffled through underbrush until he popped into a clearing at a hobo camp. Smudge-faced men tended a small fire in the middle of the cardboard boomtown, empty quart bottles randomly strewn everywhere, except on the southeast quadrant, where bottles formed strict geometric crop patterns in Serge's "quart-bottle garden."

Serge sat down at the fire. The other guys scooted closer to him. Serge began handing out money.

"How do you make so much?" asked Toledo Tom.

"Why do you just give it away to us?" asked Saratoga Sam.

"Why don't you have a nickname?" asked Night Train O'Donnell.

"I'm a simple man, with simple needs," said Serge. "I'm on an Eastern ascetic journey right now, trying to shed material wants."

"How did you get to be homeless?" asked Whooping Cough Willie.

"Oh, I'm not homeless," said Serge. "I'm camping."

They laughed and passed a bottle.

"No, really. I love camping, ever since I was a kid. I used to go to the state parks, but cities are much more dangerous and fun."

"But your beard . . . ?"

"Your smelly clothes . . . ?"

"Begging on street corners . . . ?"

"That's for the cops. If you're a fugitive and want the police to leave you alone—if you want *everyone* to leave you alone—go homeless-style. No eye contact, nothing. It's like being invisible. Even if you get in some kind of scrape, you're too much trouble to be worth the paperwork. They just tell you to move along or drive you to the city limits, not even fingerprints."

"You're hiding from the cops?" asked Tom.

"Ever since I escaped from Chattahoochee."

"You escaped from Chattahoochee?" Sam said with alarm.

"A few times."

"Isn't that where they keep the crazy people?" asked Willie.

"Oh, like you guys are a group photo of solid mental health," said Serge.

"What were you in for?" asked Tom.

"I killed a bunch of vagrants."

They began crab-walking backward from Serge.

"That was a joke! I was kidding! Jesus!"

They slid forward.

"Of course, how do you really know when someone from Chattahoochee is kidding?"

They stood up.

"I was kidding *that* time," said Serge. They sat back down. "But do you really know for sure?"

They took off running in crooked directions.

"Guys! It was a joke! I thought if anyone could appreciate irony . . . !" Serge stood and made a megaphone with his hands. "I'm just joshin' ya! I'm pulling your leg! . . . Or am I? Ha, ha, ha, ha, ha!"

A rustling came from the woods on the far side of the camp. Men burst into the clearing.

"There he is! That's the one who threatened me!" said the Isuzu driver.

"Uh-oh." Serge got up to run, but three cops quickly tackled him facedown.

Serge turned his head sideways and spit out some dirt. "I predict you will soon be seated in a Dunkin' Donuts."

A TALL REDHEAD in wire-rim glasses and conservative gray suit tapped a pencil. She looked up at a stark wall clock hanging against institutional cinder blocks with fifteen coats of high-gloss latex, then over at the man sitting across from her.

"You know, not talking says a lot, too," said the psychiatrist. "And it's usually not good."

Serge swayed in his beige straitjacket, humming.

"I know you're angry to be back at Chattahoochee," said the doctor. "That's natural."

Serge hummed louder.

"I'll bet you're angry about a lot of things. Why don't you tell me about it?"

"But I'm not angry."

"Yes you are."

"Couldn't be happier."

"The first step is to recognize denial."

"I'm not in denial."

"That's a denial."

"Things are looking up."

"How can you say that? You're sitting there in a straitjacket forced to talk to someone you clearly hate. I can tell by your body language."

"It's the cut of this jacket. I've asked them to take it out."

"Why won't you admit you're angry?"

"Because I'm not," said Serge. He looked up at the diplomas on the wall. Alix Dorr. "What kind of spelling is *Alix*?"

"My mother used an *i* to make it feminine, but it didn't work. I still get all kinds of junk mail for men's magazines."

"And this makes you angry?" said Serge.

"Interesting," said the doctor, leaning over and writing.

"Will you stop that!"

"If you'll admit your true feelings—"

"Look, from your angle over there, I can see how this predicament doesn't look too festive. But I'm a glass-is-half-full kind of guy. I have my health, there are some books I still want to read. I can't help it if I have a naturally high positive charge. In a resting state, I'm extremely buoyant."

"You're lying to yourself."

"I'm telling the God's honest truth. It's all your frame of mind. Every second I'm alive, it hits me like a thunderbolt: 'Holy fuck! I'm still breathing! What a great day!' So in your book that makes me sick?"

"No, the physical violence makes you sick."

"I already explained. Some people just don't obey the rules, have no respect for the social contract."

"So you have to beat them?"

Serge grinned. "But I'm happy when I beat them."

The doctor wrote something.

"Is it better if I'm angry when I beat them? Will that get me out of here sooner?"

"How about you don't beat them at all?"

"Oh, right, like *that's* an option."

The doctor wrote something else and looked up. "Have you ever killed anyone?"

"That's for me to know and you to find out."

"This could go against you. Maybe increase your stay."

"I'll take my chances."

"Why are you so uncooperative this time?"

"Because last time I trusted you and opened up. Next thing I knew, my release was on indefinite hold and you were injecting me with all kinds of crap that made my brain feel like honeycomb and gave me the sensation I was in Spain."

"You have chemical imbalances."

"I like me."

"There's nothing to feel guilty about."

"I don't."

"It's hereditary. Your grandfather had the same thing, long history of dissociative behavior. I have his file here from the VA. . . ."

"Let's stick to you and me."

"You don't like to talk about your grandfather, do you?"

Serge looked away and whistled.

"Is it because he committed suicide?"

"He did not commit suicide!"

"You're angry now."

"*I got sunshine . . . on a cloudy day. . . .*"

"We'll call it accidental, how's that?"

"It was no accident. He was murdered. And someday I'm going to find out who."

"So you're carrying this anger around with you? And you plan to unleash it on the person you suspect of killing—"

"I ain't gonna deliver a Candygram, if that's what you mean."

The doctor tabbed back in her manila file. "You said in our last session that his death had something to do with missing gems?"

"I don't think, I *know*. And someday I'm going to get to the bottom of it. If I can only track down those diamonds I'm sure it will lead to the killer. I've decided that as soon as I get out of here, I'm going to launch a far-reaching investigation by a blue-ribbon panel. Of course, I'll be the only person on it, because I hate panels."

"Same thing in your grandfather's file: an obsession with some make-believe jewels. I find that very intriguing—the same delusion."

"You never heard of the Museum of Natural History job in '64? Murph the Surf and the Star of India?"

The psychiatrist shook her head as she wrote. "You give your figments some imaginative names."

"Damn it, check the microfilm in any library! It drives me nuts when people don't believe me just because they haven't done their homework."

"And that makes you angry?"

"I'm not talking anymore." Serge began swaying again to the soundtrack in his head. "I've had it with doctors."

"Like the one you put in the hospital?"

"Oh, I see where this is going. You're all in a fraternity."

"No, I just want to understand."

"Then help *me* understand. What is it about doctors that makes them think they're a superior species? First they demand a special title in front of their names, and next they're treating everyone else like the subterranean Morlock race from H. G. Wells."

"So you broke his skull?"

"A man can only take so much. Every time I had an appointment, it was at least an hour before I could see him. Every single time. I can't tell you how crazy waiting makes me. I'm a very punctual person. If I have to be somewhere, I synchronize my watch to the second with the Time Channel."

"Why didn't you just get another doctor?"

"You fuckin' guys! You have no idea what it's like on this side of the little paper smock. You ever been in one of those managed-care Sam's Clubs? You can't just let your fingers do the walking. Then I read this article, and I almost hemorrhaged when I found out there are medical seminars teaching doctors how to manipulate a patient's wait—they've actually done cost studies on how long people will tolerate the lobby, when to move them to the examining room, and how long they'll wait there. Which is longer than you'd expect because, after all, ho! ho!—you're in *The Room!* Then they instruct doctors to chop up the wait some more by sending in the nurses for blood pressure and other tap dancing. And you're thinking, Hey, foolish to leave now—this is almost like actual treatment!"

"What triggered the attack?"

"I saw a thing on Fox News about this horrible new disease that has no symptoms. And I thought, Shit, I've got that! So I rush in for an appointment, and I tell the woman at the desk that we don't have any time to waste. I'm showing none of the symptoms of the new disease on TV. . . . Sure enough, it's another whole hour before I get to the examination room, and the nurse comes in and Velcros that rubber thing around my arm and starts pumping her little turkey-baster bulb. I glance at my arm, then squint at her and whisper, 'I know what's going on here,' but she just acts innocent and says, 'What?' And finally, when he's good and ready, the doctor comes strolling in all smiles. I say, 'Doc, my appointment was over an hour ago.' He keeps smiling and says they got behind and then starts opening my chart. I reach out and snap the chart shut and say, 'Not so fast, Kildare. I'm on to your game.' I tell him he can't treat people this way. I describe my disease and the microscopic pictures I saw on television of these horrible alien-looking things with all these legs and suckers that were going condo in my pancreas. Then I demand he cut his patient load in half immediately and start attending patients in a more timely fashion. And you know what? He laughed at me!"

The psychiatrist pointed with the eraser end of her pencil. "And that's when you head-butted him, resulting in the cranial fracture?"

"Hey, he was the doctor. He knew the medical risks better than me."

"What about the creatures in your pancreas?"

Serge grinned and turned red. "Boy, am I embarrassed! I missed the top of the TV segment. Turns out they're common parasites we all have. They're actually good for us."

The psychiatrist nodded and scribbled. "This is excellent. You're opening up."

"That's opening up? . . . You tricked me. I'm not saying any more."

"I think it's a mistake. You were starting to make progress."

"That's my point. I poured out my heart the last time I was here, and you lengthened my stay. Then you turned around and released Crazy Luke, who kept his mouth shut the whole time."

"You didn't think that was fair?"

"Jesus! On his first day out, he chopped off all those people's heads!"

"Psychiatry is an imprecise science. That couldn't have been foreseen with any certainty."

"You've got, like, a million degrees and you couldn't see that coming? Every frothing lunatic in this hospital would have told you he'd do it!"

"Why do you say that?"

"Because he never stopped talking about it! All day and night: 'Yep, gonna chop me some heads off.' *You* try to sleep with that kind of shit coming through the walls."

"Nobody told me."

"Did you need a diagram?" said Serge. "His name was *Crazy Luke,* for heaven's sake! Didn't that tell you anything? That's 'crazy,' as in insane. What did you think the context of 'crazy' was? Like glue? Like he worked really well?"

"Now you're getting your anger out."

Serge deliberated a moment. He took a deep breath. "All right. Since you've already made up your mind to keep me in for the max, I'll tell you what makes me angry. Tire ads."

"Tire ads?"

"Like, I'll see an ad in the paper: 'Tire Blowout!' And it'll say, 'Name-brand tires from nineteen ninety-five!' So I get eighty dollars together and go in there, maybe a few extra bucks for tax. But when I arrive, they start talking about balancing, alignment, stems, disposal fees, and just like that we're over a hundred and fifty. But the best part is, I can't even get the nineteen-dollar tires. 'Oh, no, I won't let you buy those. They don't last at all if you do any regular driving.' And if you really stand firm and demand to see the ones from the ad, they bring out these little lawn-mower tires. And you say, 'What is this, a joke?' And they say, 'See?' So now I'm into the twenty-nine-dollar tires, 'which had those terrible *Road & Track* tests where the treads separated and crash dummies were ejected all over the place.' So we move up to the thirty-nine-dollar jobs, but they're no good either. They don't channel water or something when it rains and go sliding into gas pumps. Of course you don't want that, so you move up again, and again, and by the time it's all over, you're driving away on five hundred dollars of new rubber, scratching your head and thinking, 'How in the fuck did *that* just happen?'"

"Interesting," said the psychiatrist, flipping to a fresh page. "What else?"

"Phone companies that say they'll show up between one and five, subcontractors who don't show up at all, drivers who stop side by side in the road to chat, a pop group's third farewell tour, those smug young professionals and their chardonnay, the quiet voice of golf announcers, Orkin bug-sprayer uniforms with military epaulets on the shoulders, asshole popular kids in high school now making a fortune in Gap ads, the whole El Niño thing . . ."

"I see. What do you—"

". . . gated communities, canned laughter, sesquicentennials, Members Only jackets, little Napoleons on school boards, the inexorable drumbeat of genocidal horror throughout human history, the final episode of *Seinfeld*, that I can't get my head around why water *expands* when it freezes, struggling to get a pizza box into the trash, remembering to set the clocks back, right lane must turn right, 'MasterCard—It's everywhere you want to be' . . ."

"Thank you. I'd like to ask—"

". . . bankers' hours, sellers' markets, horned dilemmas, vicious circles, conspicuous consumption, hidden costs, private clubs, public opinion, live callers, the death of courtesy, new spellings like 'lite' and 'thru,' old spellings like 'shoppe' and 'olde,' celebrity breakups, celebrity breakdowns, celebrity TV chefs, conservatives in general, liberals in particular, youth oriented beer commercials that extol the social advantages of being drunk and stupid, lawsuits by rejects who can't perform simple tasks like drinking coffee without putting themselves in the fucking emergency room, the daily double-wide news item on the fatal stabbing over the last drumstick in the bottom of the KFC bucket, ads for hopelessly lame cars that use high-energy rock songs and quick-cut photography so you can't get a very good look at the vehicle, the '72 Olympic basketball final, the colorization of *The Maltese Falcon*, the tags in the backs of my T-shirts, the seams across the toes of my socks, 'Would you like to take our survey?' 'Would you like fries with that?' 'What would Jesus do?' 'No shit, Sherlock' . . ."

SERGE IMMEDIATELY LAUNCHED a medication strike, which resulted in a gripping fixation on the wacky sitcom *Hogan's Heroes* running in syndication in the dayroom. He began addressing the staff as Schultz and Klink, calling his fellow patients LeBeau and Newkirk. He answered all question by bolting upright: "I know *nothing!*"

It was infuriating for the staff, and they bit their lips not to laugh. Serge organized his colleagues into a method-acting troupe, re-creating episodes that immediately degenerated along impromptu plotlines, actors wandering away talking to themselves, Serge running around like a hyper sheepdog herding them back to the stage. "Come on, guys!" The patients straying again, driving imaginary cars, flapping wings, beating off, the staff cracking up in the back of the room.

Serge didn't give up. He couldn't resist the layered black humor and bad taste of putting on a sitcom about a German war camp in a home for the criminally insane. Also, it was perfect cover for his escape tunnel, which was the "fake" tunnel used for the show's production. He built a tiny cardboard-box "barracks" out in the exercise yard and got the tunnel started about three feet each day before the regular afternoon collapse triggered by Serge's determination to force screaming claustrophobes into the hole to "face your fears."

The tunnel wasn't remotely a secret. In fact, it was high entertainment for the guards, who gathered each afternoon for the daily escape attempt. The digging was not going well. The same problem. Too many different agendas. Guys screaming at dead relatives in the fourth dimension, defecating, eating little rocks, Serge pulling on two wiggling legs sticking out of the collapsed tunnel: "Have you out in a second!"

A month after the onset of his *Hogan's Heroes* phase, Serge went around to everyone in the dayroom and informed them the tunnel was finished; this was the day of the Great Escape. He told all the guards, too. "Schultz, you've been a good friend, so you have a right to know. I'm escaping today." Then he gave each of them a big, tearful hug. "I'm going to miss you, buddy."

"I'll miss you, too," they said, trying to keep straight faces. The escape was obviously preposterous. The tunnel had never gone more than a few feet; the fence was fifty yards away. The guards even went out in the exercise yard and checked to make sure. "Nope," said one of them, crawling backward out of the cardboard box, pointing at a spot on his tape measure. "Only three feet."

That afternoon's turnout was the biggest ever. Amused guards from all wards and stations gathered as patients loosely filed out of the building in their pajamas and formed a line at the entrance of the cardboard box. Some brought luggage.

The first patient got inside the box. It began to vibrate. His hand reached back out the flap. "Flashlight!" The box shook some more. Then muffled screaming, the others patients pushing the cardboard away and grabbing a pair of kicking legs sticking out of the dirt.

And while the guards were laughing and pointing, Serge went out the front gate in a laundry truck.

2

Miami—Present

A LARGE AUDIENCE milled on the front steps of Jackson Memorial Hospital. Reporters, undercover cops, bodyguards, onlookers. Uniformed police on hand for crowd control. A TV personality spoke into a camera on the edge of the gathering. It was overcast, cold.

FBI agents Miller and Bixby sat across the street in a Crown Victoria with blackwall tires. Miller adjusted the zoom on a Nikon; the motor drive whirred as the shutter clicked through a series of close-ups.

"Recognize anyone?" asked Bixby.

"Not yet, but we'll have the boys back in Virginia look 'em over."

"If they know they're being photographed, why do they show up?"

"Tradition."

"Look at all the press, like he's some kind of celebrity."

"He is," said Miller. The zoom went out. Click, click, click.

Miller had a flattop haircut. He was the sixty-four-year-old veteran, which meant patience, sarcasm, and set ways about music. He'd seen it all, from the big gem heist back in '64 to Ted Bundy, Adam Walsh, and the bloody shoot-out off Old Dixie Highway. Bixby had just graduated from the academy. He was enthusiastic and very smart. He was also young, which meant he was stupid.

Steam rose from twin beverage holders in the Crown Vic. Miller's side held a plain Styrofoam cup filled from a thermos prepared at home by Mrs. Miller. Bixby's had a Starbucks.

The younger agent studied the hospital entrance with binoculars. "What's the public's fascination with this guy?"

"America has always loved its villains," said Miller, reaching into a brown bag, unfolding the butcher paper around a BLT.

Bixby took the molded plastic lid off a tray of sushi. He saw Miller looking at his lunch. "What?"

"Nothing," said Miller, but to him it was yet another small sign that Bixby was going to find some way to fuck up his pension.

Bixby quickly put down the tray. "Something's happening."

The crowd across the street pressed forward as the hospital's front doors opened. A nurse pushed a wheelchair out the entrance. The chair held a frail old man with a hearing aid. A flat golf cap sat on his head, a plaid blanket over his legs. TV people held out microphones on long poles. Dark-haired men with black gloves and black overcoats pushed them back.

"Mr. Palermo, how's your pacemaker?"

"I feel like I'm twenty," responded the old man. "What do they say nowadays? I'm going to Disney World!"

The reporters laughed.

"Mr. Palermo, what about the indictments?"

The old man chuckled. "Prosecutors are politicians. Their polls must be down."

Laughs again.

"But what about your crime syndicate? Meyer Lansky once

said you guys were bigger than U.S. Steel. Is that still true today?"

The old man slowly smiled. "Meyer was a family friend, that's all. I don't know anything about any crime syndicate. That was something you guys made up to sell papers."

The men in the black coats shoved a path through the crowd for the wheelchair.

"Mr. Palermo . . . !" "Mr. Palermo . . . !"

A white Cadillac with spoke wheels arrived at the curb. A man with thick arms whispered something in Mr. Palermo's ear. The old man nodded and turned to the press. "Now, if you'll excuse me, I have a funeral to get to."

"Mr. Palermo . . . !"

Bodyguards blocked the media. "No more questions." The nurse pushed the wheelchair up to the Caddy, and Mr. Palermo got in. TV cameras and microphones pressed against the tinted back windows as reporters yelled more unanswered questions. The Cadillac pulled away.

Across the street a Crown Vic started up and pulled into traffic. It began to rain.

Orlando—Present

SIX FAMILIES RODE a squirmingly slow, powder-blue gondola through a dim grotto.

"It's a small world after all . . ."

Children pointed with glee at the clusters of tiny, brightly colored, singing people. Little Chinese people, Italian people, Russian people, Hawaiian hula people.

"Look, Mommy." A small girl pointed.

Two full-size men appeared ahead in the darkness, running along the wall, through the plastic Alps and little Germans in lederhosen.

"Coming through!" yelled Lenny. He and Serge high-stepped over miniature windmills and tulips and cheerful, swaying Dutch people, disappearing around the bend.

It was quiet again, except for the narcotic, piped-in music.

"It's a small world after all . . ."

The boat reached France. More commotion. Two breathless

security guards hurdled the Eiffel Tower. They stopped beside the boat. "Which way did they go?"

The little girl pointed again.

"Thanks." The guards disappeared around the Taj Mahal.

"... *It's a small, small world.* ..."

Serge and Lenny jumped the turnstiles and burst out the exit into sunlight.

"I told you!" said Serge. "You can't smoke dope in Disney. They make you run."

"They seemed so friendly when we arrived."

"Now I can't get that fucking song out of my head."

They stopped at the Fantasyland crossroads and looked around for an escape route.

Guards climbed through giant teacups. "I think they went that way."

"Follow me," said Serge.

They ran past an exhibit entrance and up a service alley where employees in *Lion King* costumes were walking back out to work, talking about the dental plan.

There was a plain metal service door. Serge tried it. Unlocked. "Quick! In here!"

The pair felt their way in the darkness.

"I can't see a thing," said Lenny.

"Use your lighter."

Lenny lit a joint.

"That's not what I meant."

"It sensitizes my optic nerves. And settles my stomach. This place is not relaxing at all. . . . Oops." There was a clattering sound on the floor, followed by a metal clang and a distant liquid plunk.

"Don't tell me you dropped the lighter."

Lenny got on his hands and knees. "I think it fell through some kind of grate."

They continued stumbling and feeling their way, led only by the glow of Lenny's joint.

"What is all this stuff?"

"I think I found a couch," said Lenny. "I need to rest."

"I found a mannequin," said Serge. "Must be prop storage. Where are you?"

"Over here." Lenny waved his doobie like a tiny homing beacon. Serge joined him on the sofa.

Serge and Lenny. Opposites. Bad chemistry. They had hooked up a few years earlier following Serge's final escape from Chattahoochee and were now living together in South Florida to cut costs. A scheme here, a scam there, trying to stay off law-enforcement radar while Serge continued his investigation into the missing diamonds and his grandfather's death, which was chronically derailed by Serge's clinical passion for travel and Lenny's relentless pot habit. That's how they had come to the current moment. Serge wanted to visit the Magic Kingdom and resume his lifelong anthropological chronicle of the theme park with complete sets of photographs every few years to catalog changes in exhibits, visitors' attire and ever-shifting political subtexts of the parades. Lenny wanted to get high and eat onion rings.

"Whew," said Serge, catching his breath. "That certainly was an interesting little adventure."

Lenny patted the cushion he was sitting on. "Wonder what they use this couch for."

Suddenly a lurch. Then hydraulics and a mechanical hum. Finally the low rumble of machinery and the feeling that something very large was starting to move.

"What the . . . ?"

Curtains rose in front of the pair as an audience of three hundred rotated and locked into place.

Serge looked around. "Excellent! We're in the Carousel of Progress. I *loved* this ride when I was a kid. But I've never seen it from up here."

Stage lights came on, Lenny caught red-handed with the joint. The audience murmured and gestured at the stage.

"We're trapped," said Lenny. "What do we do?"

"Act robotic." Serge began moving his arms in jerky fashion.

The Carousel of Progress was a revolving exhibit depicting technology of various twentieth-century periods. Serge examined the furnishings and gauged the era. He haltingly tilted his head, turning to Lenny on his right, then toward to his "wife," the female animatronic robot on his other side.

"Well, Betty," Serge announced. "It's now the sixties, and it looks like little Johnny has turned into a pothead."

Some of the audience laughed. Others went to get security. A din of conversation rose from the crowd.

"What's going on?" someone called out.

"I'll tell you what's going on!" said Serge, breaking from robot persona and walking to the front of the stage. "Change. Change is what's going on. It can be good. And it can turn on you. I remember when the Carousel of Progress first debuted at the 1964 World's Fair in New York. After it closed, they relocated the carousel to California and then here. The concept was inspired: this big round stage cut into five pizza slices twenty years apart, a huge wheel of a theater rotating the audience around it. Back then it was *General Electric's* Carousel of Progress, and the last of the five chronological sets was Progress City, a domed, Orwellian, climate-controlled Stepford-land powered by GE's own nuclear power plant. A schmucky retro view of the future. Man, it was so cool!"

"I remember that," said someone in the audience. "I was a little kid."

"Me, too," said someone else.

"It was great!"—half the audience nodding now.

"I think we *all* remember," said Serge. "This was the perfect exhibit, and they had to go and muck it up! Progress City is gone. They've replaced the last set with a perpetually updating scene featuring the latest in consumer electronics, Grandma trying to figure out the friggin' DVD. If I want that, I can go to the mall. . . . Me and my dependency-challenged friend are with the

Progress City Liberation Front, and we're here to demand restoration to its original historic state. We're taking over this exhibit! Who's with me?"

Serge began chanting and punching a fist in the air in cadence with each word: "Bring—back—Progress—City! . . . Bring—back—Progress—City! . . . Bring—back—Progress—City! . . ."

A few people joined in, then a few more, mostly smiling and laughing.

". . . Bring—back—Progress—City! . . ."

A door in the back of the hall opened. "There they are!"

Guards charged up the aisle.

"Uh-oh." Serge and Lenny took off across the stage, opening a door on the side of the set. It led through the partition to the carousel's next set, then the next, the guards right behind them, traveling back in time, the forties, the twenties, turn of the century—Serge knocking over props to block the guards' path, icebox, gramophone, gas lamps, Zenith cabinet radio.

They ran off the rear of the stage and out the exit to another service alley, Snow White and the dwarfs eating tuna sandwiches and smoking. Security was right behind. They chased them all over the park: the Country Bear Jamboree, Swiss Family Robinson Tree House, Pirates of the Caribbean, Serge looking back— "I can't believe they're still there"—past the Tomorrowland stage, the Jungle Cruise, Cinderella's castle, the pair opening up a lead at the Haunted Mansion and finally losing the guards outside Hall of the Presidents, blending into the giant mob of teens assembling for the Disney Channel filming of 'NSYNC's dance-tribute to the bicameral legislative system.

4

4

Miami—Present

AN ENDLESS PROCESSION of black sedans moved south on the Florida Turnpike, evenly spaced, under the speed limit. Just before noon. Headlights on.

The cars stacked up on an exit ramp west of the airport. Red and blue lights flashed as motorcycle cops zipped by in the breakdown lane to clear the intersection. The convoy wound its way up 117th Avenue and turned in the entrance at Our Lady of Mercy Cemetery.

Mourners got out. Large men helped old women by the arms. People began making their way to an open-sided tent across the lawn.

A sleek black Cadillac Seville pulled through the gates and parked. A group of men assembled outside the car, looking around, hands clasped respectfully in front of them. One opened the back door. A broad-shouldered young man got out. Jet-black hair, rugged Italian features. The suit was Milan.

A Crown Vic with blackwalls sat under an oak tree across the street from the cemetery. Agent Miller crouched and aimed his camera at the Lincoln. Bixby's binoculars peered over the dashboard. "So that's Tony Marsicano. The heir apparent."

"Just waiting for Carmine Palermo to keel over." Miller squeezed the shutter as a ring of bodyguards escorted Tony over to another Cadillac. An old man slowly emerged from the backseat. Tony leaned and kissed his hand.

"How gay," said Miller.

"You know, at the academy they taught us you're not supposed to say things like that anymore."

"What they teach at the academy will get you killed out here."

"I'm just saying—"

"You'll shut your mouth and you'll like it."

Bixby shrugged and raised his binoculars. "Why the big turnout? I thought this guy was a small fish."

"Must have something to do with the stones," said Miller. "Rico Spagliosi was the only fence still alive from the big job back in '64. The last living link to the diamonds that never turned up. Now he's taking the dirt nap."

"Is it true Tony was the only one in Rico's hospital room when he went?" asked Bixby.

"Wasn't that convenient?"

"Tony said he had no last words."

"I'm not buying that aluminum siding."

A high-mileage Datsun with press passes dangling from the rearview pulled up and parked in front of the Crown Victoria. A photographer got out, set up a large tripod and began taking telephoto pictures.

Miller straightened up from his crouch. "I really wish they wouldn't do that."

A RUSTED-OUT YELLOW '67 Mercury Cougar with Tampa plates and no air-conditioning sped south on Interstate 95.

Serge was driving with his knees, writing on the clipboard in his lap, taking photos out the windshield at half-mile intervals in his continuing lifelong project to photograph the entire highway system of Florida. Spiral notebooks poked out from the overhead visor. Post-it Notes covered the steering wheel, dashboard, and Serge's legs. A voice-activated digital memo recorder was duct-taped to a shaved spot in the middle of his chest.

"How much farther to Miami?" asked Lenny.

Serge looked up at the AAA Florida road map glued to the ceiling. "Just passed the Lantana exit. Hour, give or take."

"Lantana? Home of the *National Enquirer*?"

Serge nodded. "The British poop squad."

"Did you see those horrible pictures of Bob Hope they ran a couple years back?"

"Tabloids are the great equalizer," said Serge. "No matter how much you accomplish in life, right near the end they Photoshop your picture so you look a thousand years old."

"How much farther?" said Lenny.

"You just asked that."

Lenny glanced at the joint in his hand. "Must be the pot. Time changes."

"What does it do, turn into shapes?"

"You're thinking of acid."

"My bad," said Serge.

Lenny stubbed out his roach, then unfurled a Baggie in his lap and pulled out a pack of papers.

Serge rearranged the sticky notes on his legs, shook his head, changed them back. He began jotting on a clipboard.

"How much farther?" asked Lenny.

"I'm trying to write."

Lenny flicked a seed out the window. "What are you writing?"

"Nothing with all this chatter."

"Sorry."

"It's not your fault. I'm having difficulty organizing my notes. I'm trying to come up with a system."

"Looks like you already have quite a system."

"That's the whole problem. I have too *many* systems." Serge peeled a yellow square off the dash and stuck it to his forehead.

Lenny twisted the end of a fresh joint in his mouth. "What kind of notes?"

"Grand concepts, minute details, ironic observations, nagging questions, hard truths, pipe dreams, celebrity tidbits, groundless accusations, notions of grandeur, worst-case scenarios, pointless trivia, pithy ad jingles, harebrained schemes that just might work!, scientific theories forever changing the way we look at the element cesium, economic theories proving all money is worthless and we should be hoarding pipe cleaners, visions for a new society where all people are finally equal and that's where the fighting begins . . ."

"Watch out!" yelled Lenny.

Serge slammed on the brakes with both feet to avoid rear-ending an Oldsmobile containing four short, white-haired people going thirty-five in the left lane.

"Boca Raton," said Serge. "Forty-five minutes to Miami."

Lenny plucked a yellow square off the dashboard. " '*Cracker Jack toy decline—national metaphor*'?"

"Remember how you used to find an actual prize in Cracker Jacks?"

"I got a compass once."

"Me, too. And way, way back near the beginning, they actually had die-cast metal soldiers. Now, *that* was a prize."

"I swallowed it."

"Today all you get is a little piece of paper that just leaves you feeling hollow inside and wondering when it will all finally stop!"

"My parents found it in the toilet, pointing north."

Lenny lit his joint. Serge spoke into his digital recorder. Time passed. Serge could feel it passing. It passed like the thief Serge knew it to be, except at other moments when it was the rude rent collector, or the relentless auditor, or Mrs. Cleatus Goolsby, two-time tri-county rhubarb bake-off queen. Serge smiled cynically and nodded. Yes, that's how it was with time. You never knew. He turned to Lenny.

"You see, life's all about possibilities. Opportunities are everywhere, except most people are locked into rigid routines and mortgages and clipping coupons and aren't even looking. But I see possibilities in everything: tangible objects, memories, thin air. It's at once a blessing and a curse. I started putting it all on this clipboard, but it wasn't as convenient as the Post-it Notes, which are easily lost and need to be backed up with the digital recorder, which must be transcribed into the notebooks, and before I know it, I'm right back where I started."

Lenny exhaled a big hit. "That's how The Man keeps you down."

Objects began flying by on both sides of their car—Jaguars, Isuzus, Escalades—weaving through traffic at eight-five. A vanity plate: 2RICH4U.

"Fort Lauderdale," said Serge. "Thirty minutes to Miami."

"Why do you like Miami so much? You didn't grow up there."

"That's the point. I grew up in West Palm. Miami was the shining city on the hill, like Oz; I-95 was the Yellow Brick Road. I saw this thing on CNN where some tourists in Italy get faint and go into 'art shock' when they see all the statues and ceiling paintings. That's what Miami does to me. Whenever I cross the Broward line, I get all jelly-like inside. And just forget about the Grove or the Gables. If I'm walking the Miracle Mile and come upon a building made of coquina rock, you could lose me for hours. I'll just stare at one of the walls about three inches from my nose, slowly caressing the fossilized texture with my fingertips, reading the permanent biological history in the imprints of tiny sea organisms from long ago, imagining their thoughts and dreams."

"That happens to me on orange blotter," said Lenny. "What are you doing now?"

Serge was changing the order of the sticky notes on the steering wheel. "Prioritizing the *Master List*. The most important factor is window of opportunity."

"What's that?"

"Like when concert tickets go on sale."

"Is that where we're going?"

"No, I hate concerts. They never let me take in my equipment."

"I keep getting hit in the back of the head with Frisbees."

"Yeah, fuck that noise."

Lenny licked a finger and dabbed the side of his joint where it was burning too fast. "So what's on this Master List of yours?"

"Let's see. . . ." Serge picked up the clipboard. "Okay, now, don't hold me to this, because the Master List is subject to change without notice: Develop and test-market my new line of South Beach energy drinks, complete rehabilitation and release of endangered Loxahatchee marsh mouse, solve mystery of grandfather's death, recover fortune in missing diamonds from America's largest gem heist, cripple the Mob in South Florida, embarrass Castro on the global stage, help chamber of commerce with image crisis, restore respect for the brave men and women of the U.S. intelligence community, lure the *Today* show to Miami for local pride/economic boost, participate in my times like Robert Kennedy (depending on weather), and accomplish it all through the launch of my new-economy, clean-burning, earth-friendly venture-capital business that involves spiritual growth, historical appreciation and the Internet."

"What kind of business?"

"That's the only blank."

"Pretty cool. How'd you come up with all that?"

"By diligently recording everything that pops into my head. Always remember: Your thoughts are God's gift to you, divinely bestowed by the all-knowing life force of the cosmos that's been running through everything since the first stars were born. Every one of your ideas is special. Every one is sacred."

Serge began plucking sticky notes off his left leg and crumpled them into a ball.

"Why are you doing that?"

Serge tossed the ball over his shoulder into the backseat. "Those were stupid ideas."

A Fiero began passing. Something down the side of the car caught Lenny's attention. "Are those bullet holes?"

Serge glanced over. "Nope. Bullet-hole decals."

"Decals?" Lenny leaned and strained his eyes for a better look, then sat back. "You're right. They're a bunch of stickers. But it doesn't make any sense. What's the point?"

"I know," said Serge. "I couldn't believe it myself when I first saw them. What a country! What an *economy!* Hopelessly fake bullet holes you stick all over your car to make sure everyone knows you're not getting laid."

A horn blared. Serge looked over. A low-riding Buick Regal whipped out from behind and shot by on the shoulder. Gold hubcaps. A South American flag swinging from the rearview. The passenger gave them the finger; the driver waved a Tech-9. They accelerated away.

"We're in Miami."

DARK SEDANS CONTINUED through the entrance at Our Lady of Mercy. Graveside chairs filled up. Some late flowers arrived.

The Crown Vic with blackwalls remained across the street. FBI Special Agent Miller trained his camera. Click, click, click.

Agent Bixby tapped him on the shoulder.

"Not now." Click, click.

A yellow '67 Cougar pulled up behind them.

Bixby tapped him again. "Someone just parked behind us."

"I don't care." Miller twisted the zoom out to three hundred millimeters. Click, click, click.

Bixby stared at the Cougar through his binoculars. "Something's not right about these guys."

Miller ignored him. Click, click, click.

Serge and Lenny filled Bixby's field of vision.

Lenny inserted the nub of a joint in locking hemostats. "I don't understand what we're doing here."

"I told you: to witness history. Carmine Palermo is the last of his breed, larger than life." Serge raised his own telephoto camera. Click, click, click. "All the others died years ago. You may never get a chance to see this again, especially with his failing health." Click, click, click.

Bixby tapped Miller on the shoulder again.

"What!"

"Now they're taking photos."

"So?"

"And one of them is smoking dope."

Miller shook his head with disdain. "Newspaper people."

Lenny tapped Serge on the shoulder. He pointed with his surgical roach clip at the car parked ahead of them. "Those guys are taking pictures, too. And one of them is looking back here with binoculars."

Serge glanced up and waved, then stowed his camera. "Probably FBI. You might want to hold the drugs lower." He began sliding off his pants in the driver's seat.

"What are you doing?"

"Changing for the funeral."

"But we're not invited."

"Rule Number One: Everyone is always welcome to show respects." Serge grabbed a paper bag from the backseat and handed it to Lenny. "Put these on."

Soon they were standing next to the Cougar in black suits.

"I feel weird," said Lenny, scratching at his collar.

"Tuck in your shirt."

"Who's this dead guy anyway?"

"Rico Spagliosi. The last surviving fence from the '64 gem heist. Never indicted."

"They have food at this thing?"

"Don't embarrass me," said Serge, working on Lenny's tie.

Lenny pointed across the cemetery. "Who's that guy?"

"Now you made me mess up. Hold still." Serge glanced over his shoulder. "Tony Marsicano, godfather-in-waiting." Serge finished the Windsor and stepped back. "That'll have to do."

Agent Bixby slowly scanned his binoculars across the cemetery grounds. He stopped and adjusted focus. "Hold on. What have we got here?"

"What is it?"

"Someone new at the party."

"I see them," said Miller, zooming in with his Nikon.

"Hey, those are the two guys from the car behind us," said Bixby. "I told you something wasn't right."

Miller held down the shutter release for a rapid series of the two men, one furtively smoking something, the other genuflecting at the grave of Jackie Gleason.

"Look, now they're going over to Tony."

"This is very interesting," said Miller. He pressed the shutter again, this time letting the whole roll unwind. Click-click-click-click-click . . . "Rico croaks with Tony in the hospital room, and suddenly we have these new players dropping by for a chat."

Serge stepped in front of Tony. "Mr. Marsicano?"

"Who the fuck are you?"

"Just a concerned citizen. My deepest sympathies about Rico."

Bixby refocused his binoculars. "Look at how the tall one is talking to Tony. They seem to know each other."

"Of course they know each other," said Miller. "Look at the anger in Tony's face. That kind of bad blood has to go way back."

Serge leaned down to kiss Tony's hand.

Tony yanked it away. "Get the fuck off me!" He spun to his bodyguards. "Who let these guys in?"

A group of bent-nose men in black turtlenecks shrugged with overplayed not-guilty expressions.

"You idiots! Get them out of here!"

"Let go of me!" yelled Serge. "What are you doing?"

Miller quickly reloaded another roll of Kodak. "Whoa! Whoa! Look at this! They're getting into it! The tall one just broke free from the goons."

"I can't believe he shoved Tony like that," said Bixby. "Doesn't he know who he is?"

"Tony just shoved him back." Click, click, click.

"And he just shoved Tony again. Incredible."

"This new guy looks pretty important. Better run a check on him when we get back."

"Now the goons have him restrained by the arms. Tony's punching him in the stomach."

"Wow! Did you see how he just kicked Tony in the nuts?"

"These guys are dead for sure."

"Or maybe Tony's dead, depending on what organization they're with."

"Oh, no! They going for their guns!"

Miller and Bixby jumped from the Crown Vic, reaching for shoulder holsters.

"Hold it," said Miller, grabbing Bixby by the arm. "Calmer heads are prevailing. Tony's making them put their pieces away. That kind of judgment is why he's rising so fast in the Family."

The agents climbed back in their car and took more pictures as five goons gave Serge the bum's rush down the cemetery's driveway. "Watch the threads! Watch the threads!"

They sent him sprawling in the street. Then Lenny tumbled by.

The pair pushed themselves to their feet and swept dirt off torn suits. Lenny picked little pieces of gravel out of his red palms. "They gave me road rash."

Serge grabbed a sleeve where it had separated from the shoulder. "I loved this jacket."

They got back in their car and pulled away from the curb.

"Wonder what that was all about," said Bixby.

Miller wrote down the license plate as the Cougar drove by. "Bet anything it had something to do with the stones."

5

TONY MARSICANO WAS arguably the brightest member of the Palermo organization, which is how he found himself in charge of the Orlando operation at such an early age. Only thirty-five, but on his way.

Tony was the new generation, more corporate than Hollywood creation. No cartoon accent or idiom. He still had the big shoulders, which were handy in a pinch, but he muted them with subdued business suits, gabardine instead of sharkskin. Of course, his young–Paul Newman looks didn't hurt either. Tony carried a briefcase and was fluid in conversation. What really set him apart: He smiled a lot.

The Orlando territory mainly meant prostitution on Orange Blossom Trail and some drugs. It had never been a lot of money, and even that was drying up, although nobody was ready to write it off just yet. There had been ecstasy and heroin surges in the late nineties, but the overdoses got a lot of press and police cracked down. Tony had been in town only a week when he thought up the counterfeit theme-park tickets, which he sold in bulk to the time-share booths in Kissimmee. The time-share people learned they'd been had, and they made a lot of noise, but a couple of condo fires made them strangely quiet. The Palermo bosses loved that one. Tony kicked a big tribute back to Miami. There was no limit how far he could go.

Next: immigrant smuggling. The feds were watching the Florida shoreline for Cubans and Haitians sailing north in boats, and I-75 for Mexicans driving south to the inland migrant camps around Okeechobee and Immokalee. Nobody was thinking Eastern Europe. And they definitely weren't watching the Disney corridor.

It started on a Friday. Tony was reading his newspaper in a busy coffee shop on Highway 192, the outer economic ring of theme-park galaxy, where those who couldn't afford to stay in Disney proper commuted from a constellation of budget motels, franchised food, and off-brand roadside attractions providing supplemental bargain fun. Tony gazed out the window at a deep-discount souvenir hut shaped like a giant orange. Darkness fell on the strip, rows of flashing-lightbulb marquees stretched to the vanishing point: room-rate specials, all-you-can-eat buffets, medieval jousting shows, three-for-ten-dollars T-shirts that are never in stock, help wanted. Tony soon noticed he was having trouble getting his order taken. A lone waitress scurried around the room, setting plates in front of diners, then switching the plates, people losing patience, the waitress picking up all the plates again and running back to the kitchen, past another "help wanted" sign at the cash register. Tony went back to his paper, an article on the boom in new motel construction. Tony always read stories about anything that required concrete. Suddenly a crash. Tony jumped. An armful of broken plates lay at the feet of a sobbing waitress. Tony looked down at sharp pieces of porcelain mixed with hash browns and ruptured omelettes. And Tony saw the future. The south-Orlando service industry was expanding exponentially; the local labor pool was not. Hotel beds weren't getting made, rows of shellacked alligator heads gathered dust on gift-store shelves, unserved diners got up and left. Tony decided to fix that, for a price. He got false documents and began flying them in from Romania and Czechoslovakia, landing with the tourists at Orlando International. This time not even the local establishment kicked. They were blown away back in Miami, and Tony promptly became Mr. Palermo's personal protégé. Was this kid smart or what?

But Tony's real talent lay in the heist. The big score. Because that's where his heart was. Underneath all the poise and polish, Tony was a traditionalist. He grew up at the knees of the old guys, the tales from the glory days when a job was a work of art, not the messy smash-and-grabs these punks pull today. Then, afterward, they'd all get dressed up and go out on the town, where the restaurants and nightclubs treated them like movie stars. Even the singers onstage stopped and acknowledged them. Tony couldn't get enough of the stories. Years later, as an adult, he'd visit the retired crews in Miami Beach, bring over some groceries and cook up one of the old family dinners, fresh sausage, garlic. Then he'd shut up and let them talk. The Wells Fargo job, the Bank of the Americas job, the Panama gold transfer, the Star of India. It was about more than technique; it was about history. That's how Tony had come to be at Rico Spagliosi's bedside when he passed. For a few days, that hospital room had become the most popular place in Miami. Everyone was trying to get in, maybe work Rico for a tip on the missing gems, maybe trick it out of him under the sedatives. Tony couldn't have cared less about that. What mattered to Tony were all the hours Rico had spent with him when he was just a little squirt, teaching him magic tricks and lock picking. That's why Rico told the nurses to let Tony in, but not the others.

Tony learned that preparation was everything, and Tony became the best. It also became a dilemma for the Palermos. Tony was so indispensable running things on the organizational level that they didn't dare risk getting him popped on a job. You don't send generals into battle. But every now and then, a score came along that was so incredibly lucrative and complex, with so much to gain and so much more to go wrong, that they couldn't afford to send anyone except Tony.

Tony could do it because Tony could blend. He talked like an English teacher and thought like an insurance adjuster. He read books and magazines, which meant he could mingle. He read people, which meant he could charm.

Tony was reading *Forbes* early one Monday. He was reading it in the oak-paneled, overly air-conditioned reception area on the tenth floor of one of Orlando's newest office towers near Church Street Station. Home of Strauss & Levy Accounting. A woman sat behind the reception desk. Tony smiled at her. She smiled back, then looked down, a blush. Tony got up and strolled around the waiting room killing time, idly inspecting door frames and telephone outlets.

The receptionist's phone rang. She answered it, "I see," then hung up. She cleared her throat. "Excuse me, Mr. Davis . . . ?"

"Yes?" said Tony Marsicano.

"I'm sorry, but there must be some mistake. Mr. Culpepper is out of town today. I don't know how you were given an appointment for this morning."

"I'm sure somebody got it wrong at my office," said Tony. "No big deal,"

"Maybe someone else is available." She picked up the phone.

"That won't be necessary." Tony checked his wristwatch. "I have to be somewhere. Do you think I could use the men's room?"

"Absolutely, Mr. Davis." She buzzed him in.

Tony walked down the hall, casually glancing through open office doors, men in starched shirts and suspenders on phones. Tony tried the knob of any door that looked too small to lead to an office. He opened one, a closet with a bunch of wires and fuses. He leaned to read something on a junction box: SENTINEL.

"Can I help you?"—a man's voice with a clear but deniable edge of accusation.

Tony pulled his head out of the closet and turned. "Looking for the men's room."

"Last door on the right." The man glared, but Tony gave an easy, offhand smile and strolled away.

Two hours later a real-estate agent met Tony outside the commercial scrum of a decaying strip mall in Winter Park. Tony rented seven hundred square feet next to a yogurt parlor that would soon be something else.

Three hours after that, a representative from Sentinel Security and Alarm arrived. They shook hands.

"You handle Strauss and Levy, don't you?"

"We're not supposed to discuss clients."

"They're the ones who recommended you. I have some friends in tax law. Said they've never had any regrets about Sentinel."

"Thank you."

"I want the same system they have."

The rep looked at the empty storefront. "I think you might want something a little more modest."

"We're going to have rare coins and precious metals. I'd rather err that way. Maybe a few less sensors because of floor space, but I want all the same features."

The next evening Tony read *Newsweek*. He was reading it on the toilet outside the second-floor cafeteria in the building that housed Strauss & Levy. He sat cross-legged, a paper sack in his lap. When his Rolex said eight o'clock, Tony lowered his legs.

The main elevator opened on the ground floor of the office tower. A night watchman sat in the circular black-marble guard station in the middle of the reflecting black-marble lobby floor. He saw a man he didn't recognize who wasn't supposed to be there. And where was his badge?

The guard started getting up to intercept, but Tony walked straight toward him instead. And smiled. "How's it going"— Tony glanced at his name tag: CHARLES PAVLIC—"Charley?"

"Fine. Where's your—"

"Charley, you like barbecue?" Tony held up the paper sack he had been carrying in his right hand. "Great sandwich. Never touched. Never even opened. Got too busy up there." He handed the bag across the guard desk. "And there's some beans and potato salad in there, too."

"Thanks, Mr. . . ."

"Davis." Tony reached over the desk to shake. "Tony Davis."

"Mr. Davis. You need to be wearing a—"

Tony saluted and headed out. "Have a good one."

It went like that three nights a week for three months. Pizza, fish and chips, steak sandwiches, shrimp salad. Sometimes Tony would pull up a chair, tuck a paper napkin in his collar and chow down at the guard desk with Charley. By December they were old friends.

"Got him a train set," said Charley. "Already practiced setting it up so I won't run into anything Christmas Eve."

"He's gonna love it."

"I hope so, but all he's been talking about is the new Xbox, whatever the hell that is."

"Some kind of game system, I think."

"It's the big thing at his school. He's obsessed with it. I went to the store, but you know how much they're getting for those things? I can't believe the other parents are actually buying them."

"Train sets were good enough when I was growing up."

"Me, too," said Charley. "I sure hope he isn't disappointed."

"Kids don't know how good they have it today."

"You said it."

Another week went by, Charley filling up on Tony's late-night deliveries from the putative seasonal office overflow: eggnog, fruitcake, Hickory Farms cheese wedges.

Charley Pavlic drew the short straw and had to work Christmas Eve. Tony got off the elevator with a coat over his shoulder and a shopping bag in his hand. He smiled and set the bag on the guard desk and headed for the door. Charley stood and reached into the sack.

He pulled out an Xbox.

"Mr. Davis!" he yelled across the lobby. "I can't. This is too—"

But Tony was already pushing open the exit. "Merry Christmas, Charley."

"Merry Christmas, Mr. Davis."

6

THE YARD WAS overgrown in front of the modest blue ranch house, sitting in an entire neighborhood of overgrown yards in the shadow of the I-95 interchange near Pompano Beach. A rusty '67 Cougar screeched up the driveway. Serge and Lenny jumped out in their scuffed and torn funeral clothes.

Lenny was first through the front door. "Mom, we're home!"

"Wipe your feet!"

"We did!"

They sprinted down the hall. Back to the friendly confines. Lenny's room. Lenny was forty-eight and still lived at home with his mom. The current reactionary administration would have you believe it was because he still smoked dope, and they would be right. Serge also lived with them, because he *wouldn't* take his drugs. They shared Lenny's childhood bedroom. Tiny furniture, baby blue walls with clouds, posters: MOD SQUAD, ROOM 222, Bob Griese dropping back in the pocket. Lenny had the top bunk.

Serge tossed his clipboard onto the dresser and headed for a small hamster cage on top of his four-drawer research filing cabinet.

"How is he?" asked Lenny.

"Back to full strength," said Serge, feeding a furry little critter with an eyedropper through metal bars.

"Little fella sure seems hungry."

"That's a good sign," said Serge, refilling the dropper. "I never thought we'd see this day. He was in pretty bad shape when we found him."

"Kind of lucky I suggested we go in the woods to smoke that joint, huh?"

"That was my suggestion. I keep telling you, you can't just fire up at the rest stops. They have security now. And all those children were watching you."

Serge bent down and looked the creature in the eyes. "Feeling better today, Mr. Vonnegut?"

"He *should* feel better," said Lenny. "You've taken good enough care of him the last five months. Feeding him by hand, reading to him at night, walking around with him in your shirt pocket all the time . . ."

"For body warmth. Very important." Serge opened the cage and placed his hand inside. The animal ran up Serge's arm to his shoulder and climbed down into his pocket. "You can't leave anything to chance when rescuing a threatened species."

"What kind of rat is that anyway?"

"It's not a rat. How many times?" Serge picked up his clipboard and held it out to Lenny, tapping the spot next to Master List Item Number Five: "Endangered Loxahatchee Marsh Mouse, close cousin of the blue-tongue vole." Serge looked down in his pocket and took a deep breath to steady himself. "I guess it's time. No use postponing the inevitable." He uncapped a pen and crossed Item Five off the clipboard.

"You're really going to release him after all the work you've put in?" said Lenny, pointing at tiny eyes peeking out of Serge's pocket, whiskers twitching. "Look how you two get along. He sure is going to miss you."

"You have to be cruel to be kind."

A plump, older woman with a gray beehive appeared in the doorway. "What happened to you? Look at your clothes!"

"It's nothing, Mom."

"It doesn't look like nothing. Were you in some kind of fight? Did somebody hurt my Lenny?"

"No, Mom," said Lenny. "We went to a funeral."

"I've been to a lot of funerals in my life and never come back looking like that! Who did this to you? I'm going to call them right now!"

"It's not like that. You can't call."

"I most certainly can!"

"You don't understand—"

"Lenny, this has got to stop!" she said, arms crossed tightly. "You take off all the time. I don't know what you're doing, where you're going. If I didn't know Serge was there to watch out for you, I swear I'd have three heart attacks. Now, what's this boy's name?"

"Mom, I'm trying to tell you, you don't want to—"

"Tony Marsicano," said Serge.

"Serge!" said Lenny.

"Is he in the phone book?" asked Mrs. Lippowicz.

"Unlisted," said Serge, walking across the room to his history filing cabinet. He flipped through files and pulled out a piece of paper. "Here's his phone number."

"Thank you."

"Where'd you get that?" asked Lenny. "Nobody knows those numbers."

"Court file from his last arrest," said Serge. "A single determined person with a knack for research can find out anything."

"Is this Tony some kind of bully?" asked Mrs. Lippowicz.

"The biggest," said Serge.

"Mom!"

"Maybe I should talk to his parents," said Mrs. Lippowicz. "What's his family like?"

"The Palermo Family?" said Serge. "All thugs."

"I thought you said his name was Marsicano."

"It is," said Serge. "But it's the Palermo Family. Marsicano is the name of Tony's crew. That's how it works."

"Crew?" said Mrs. Lippowicz. "Does he have a sailboat or something?"

"More like a yacht. And a private jet, some nice cars . . ."

"So he's a spoiled bully?" said Mrs. Lippowicz.

"You could put it that way."

"Well, someone needs to stand up to him."

"Mom! Don't—"

"Your mom is a lot smarter than you give her credit for," said Serge, turning to Mrs. Lippowicz. "I'm behind you all the way. Lenny needs to be more careful. And more thankful he has a mother like you."

Mrs. Lippowicz put her hands on her hips and looked sternly at her son. "Why can't you be more like your nice friend Serge?"

Serge turned to Lenny and grinned.

"I have an important phone call to make," said Mrs. Lippowicz, marching toward the kitchen.

Serge pulled a folder from the file cabinet and trotted down the hall. Lenny caught up with him at the front door and grabbed his arm. "What did you just do that?"

"Because this whole codependency thing with your mother creeps me out. Thought I'd shake the cage a little." Serge checked his shirt pocket. "You ready, Mr. Vonnegut?"

They hopped in the Cougar and headed south on the interstate. Five full, fast lanes. Dense traffic weaving and darting without contact like a school of bait fish, palm trees going by, basketball courts, warehouses, graffiti, Canadian-whiskey billboards targeting minorities, digital time/temperature sign: 99°. Lenny checked his wallet. "I'm broke again. I still have some weed, but it won't last forever. We need to come up with another money idea."

"I'm still working on the concept for our new business." Serge opened his file folder on the steering wheel, going through papers. Cars honked.

"Business?" said Lenny. "That sounds like a job. Let's just get money."

"The number-one rule in life: Anything where you're your own boss isn't really a job."

"Bosses are mean to me," said Lenny, rolling a joint in his lap. "They always want me to go faster."

"I'm with you," said Serge. "Did you see where they had to hospitalize all those conventioneers in Miami? All because of what their bosses told them to do?"

Lenny shook his head.

"A Fortune Five-Hundred company had a big unity retreat or some stupidness down at one of the high-priced resorts. They hired this motivational firm to come up with activities to pull everyone together. So they threw a big open-bar party on the beach, built this barbecue pit and made the entire management team walk on hot coals."

"Nobody's that dumb."

"Made all the papers. The consultants got the idea from one of those reality shows. Supposed to build teamwork and esprit de corps. Then they go back to the office on Monday and, next to walking on hot coals, running a company is a snap."

"What happened?" said Lenny.

"Top of the organizational chart is laid up in Miami General with blistered feet. Stock's off twenty points."

"They actually paid for that?"

"A lot," said Serge. "I'm no professional consultant, but near the top of my recommendations would be: Do *not* make your employees walk on hot coals."

"So you want to start a consulting company?"

Serge shook his head. "I need something that parallels my

interests. You know the saying: 'Do what you love and you'll always be happy.' "

"Who said that?"

"Charles Manson. No, wait. He said, 'Kill all the people in the house.' Who am I thinking of?" The marsh mouse grabbed the top of Serge's pocket with tiny hands, watching the road ahead.

Serge tapped the clipboard with his NASA antigravity pen. "But what business can possibly tie all these things together?"

Lenny leaned across the seat for a look at the clipboard. "I don't think it can be done. Those items are all over the place. See? You've got energy drinks, the CIA, Castro, the *Today* show, the Mafia, not to mention your grandfather's death and some missing diamonds. If you ask me, it's impossible."

" 'Impossible' isn't in my vocabulary," said Serge.

"It's my middle name," said Lenny, lighting a pin joint. "I'm trying to live a disappointment-free life."

"First you break a giant task into components," said Serge. "The most challenging items are solving my grandfather's death and finding the lost gems, but look here . . ."—he drew a line— "either one breaks the other loose . . ."—more interconnecting lines, some dotted, some solid—"after that, Item Two falls into place, which makes Number Seven a natural, and by then Three and Six couldn't be easier . . ."—two loops, three arrows—"the others practically take care of themselves and there we have it."

"Our car seems to be slowing down," said Lenny. "Or someone put PCP in my dope."

"Fort Lauderdale International's coming up. I'm decelerating to time my pass."

"That jet sure is low," said Lenny, watching an inbound Northwest DC9 drop its landing gear and clear ten lanes of interstate traffic, then the highway fence, touching down on the main runway with twin puffs of black tire smoke. "Looked like the wheels were only a few feet above the cars."

"I like the jets to fly right over the car to make me feel alive," said Serge. "The whole vehicle vibrates like it's going to blow the rivets and send you sliding down the highway in nothing but a bucket seat. It's great!"

"But why slow down?"

"Increases our chances. One lands every other minute. If you're short, you can always speed up. But if you're too far ahead, you can't back up in the middle of an interstate. Actually, you can, but it's really, really dangerous."

Lenny pointed. "Here comes one now."

They looked west at the toy-size plane in the distance. The Cougar continued slowing, fifty miles an hour, forty-five, forty, more cars honking, whipping around both sides.

"Why the sudden interest in your grandfather?" asked Lenny.

"The funeral. I was determined before, but now it's all-consuming. Ever since I saw Rico's obit in the paper, it's the only thing I can think about. Nobody really knows what happened back in '64. I've had an epiphany and decided to completely dedicate my existence to a full-court press for the truth. All else is now irrelevant. Everything in my life up to this point has been bullshit, and everything afterward will just be epilogue."

"What's 'epilogue'?"

"Bullshit that comes later."

"So how are you going to start looking into his suicide?"

"He did not commit suicide! Don't you ever say that word!"

"Okay, okay. Jeez . . . So where do we start? Police reports?"

"That's for amateurs. True archival research requires firsthand interviews with any living eyewitnesses. I've done it dozens of times, tracked down people involved with some long-forgotten Florida event, then dropped by their homes for tape-recorded interrogations."

"You don't call first? You just go up and knock on their doors?"

"It's better that way—catches them unrehearsed for historical accuracy. But sometimes they mistake me for one of all the nuts running around Florida and try to close the door. You just have to be firm and push it open. They're usually old, so it's not too hard."

"Don't they call the police?"

"That's why you have to yank the phone out of the wall. But the guys we'll be looking for this time were all friends of my granddad, so that shouldn't be necessary."

"Friends?"

"Great bunch of guys, a regular social club." Serge leaned forward and held his camera over the dashboard, pointing up through the windshield. The marsh mouse burrowed deep into Serge's pocket as a deafening jet roar rattled the car. Serge clicked the shutter.

On the opposite side of the interstate, a black Cadillac Seville headed north on 95. Tony Marsicano was in back on the phone, covering one ear with his hand, straining to hear above the Continental 737 passing overhead.

". . . I see. . . . I see. . . . No, ma'am. . . . Yes, ma'am. . . . I see. . . . No, ma'am, it won't happen again. . . . You, too. . . . Good-bye." Tony hung up.

One of his lieutenants saw the bewildered look on Tony's face. "What is it, boss?"

"I just got the strangest phone call."

Back in the southbound lanes, Serge accelerated and returned to normal speed. Lenny tossed the end of his joint out the window into some dry weeds. "Who was in this gang anyway?"

"Let's see. Besides my grandfather, there was Chi-Chi and Moondog and Greek Tommy and Coltrane and Mort the Undertaker. All pieces of work. Chi-Chi got mixed up with the CIA and the Bay of Pigs and became terminally bitter. Moondog was the great-great-grandson of a slave from Macon who lived in Overtown's famous Sir John Hotel. Greek Tommy was Italian. I thought Coltrane was the funniest, but now I realize he was just drunk all the time. On average, Mort the Undertaker had the best disposition, all the more remarkable considering he worked in retail. He did the books for the gang's betting parlor, which was a front for the unlicensed barbershop in the back room. . . . Every one of them a great guy. Always a million laughs. . . ."

Miami Beach—1963

"Kick him again!" yelled Chi-Chi.

Greek Tommy kicked him. "Where's our fucking money?!"

The man curled into a ball on the floor and moaned.

"Hit him with something!"

Moondog swung a shovel. "Where's our fucking money?!"

The moaning stopped. They formed a circle and leaned for a closer look.

"Is he dead?"

"Just unconscious," said Chi-Chi.

"Stuff's coming from his mouth."

"It happens."

"I don't know about this new violence stuff," said Mort.

"We all agreed," said Chi-Chi. "We're losing too much money."

"Nobody takes us seriously," said Coltrane.

They stared down again. Nothing moved.

"So what do we do now?" asked Mort.

"I'll get the car," said Chi-Chi.

A screaming pink '58 convertible Cadillac Eldorado turned off Collins Avenue and rolled up the alley. Jumbo tail fins, white leather interior, Chi-Chi behind the wheel in his straw hat. The back door of the bookie joint opened. The others glanced around, then hoisted a limp form into the trunk.

Chi-Chi slammed the lid and dusted his hands together. "I need a drink."

One hour later. A whistling man in a yellow guayabera strolled down the sidewalk on the east side of Collins. Hotel after hotel, towering, new, expensive. Then the breaks between the buildings, bright blue sky over the Atlantic, white gulls suspended stationary in the breeze. He turned and bopped up the steps of a building with deco numbers over the entrance: 9701. A valet held the door. The man circled a glass-enclosed atrium of palm trees, kept going along the lobby's curved walls with a mosaic of bold hieroglyphics under a row of art moderne hanging lamps. A Friday. An envelope in his hand.

The man was trim, tall, clear brown eyes, short dark hair beginning to gray on the sides. He had the unassuming good looks of an unassuming tennis pro and walked with a spring in his step that suggested a cheerful outlook and bundled energy just under the hood. He came to the entrance of a dim room, the Carioca Lounge. Wiggling black and white stripes on the floor, garish mirrors, whorehouse curtains, a grand piano. From the ceiling hung a fluffy, kidney-shaped object that served no purpose but to make you look up. Five men in straw hats and guayaberas sat perched on five tall stools at the bar.

"Hi, guys!"

They turned around.

"Sergio. You're late," said Chi-Chi. His shirt had a pattern of outrigger canoes. A collection of moist, chewed toothpicks sat on a napkin next to his newspaper. "We were all supposed to meet you-know-where."

"Got hung up waiting for these," said Sergio, holding up the envelope.

"What's in there?" asked Greek Tommy.

Sergio grabbed a stool. "Photographs. Can't believe it only takes three days now to get your film developed."

The others crowded for a closer look as Sergio spread the pictures on the bar in sequential order: a long line of black cars on Collins, then a snazzy convertible with a handsome young man in the backseat. Other men in dark sunglasses stood on the running boards.

"You got pretty close," said Moondog.

"I could practically reach out and touch the motorcade."

"Doesn't seem like much security."

"They must know what they're doing."

Mort picked up one of the snapshots. "He sure seems young to be president."

Sergio pulled a final photo from the envelope, waited an appropriate duration for drama, and laid the trump card on the bar.

"Wow," said Tommy. "He's looking right at you and waving."

"Probably remembers me," said Sergio.

Chi-Chi took the toothpick from his mouth and examined it for remaining life. "What are you talking about?"

"Back when we knew each other."

"You did not know Kennedy!"

Sergio nodded. "Double-dated."

"Horseshit," said Chi-Chi. "Why do you always lie like this?"

"He stayed right up there on Monday," said Sergio, pointing toward the ceiling. "The helicopter landed in the park just over the bridge to Bal Harbour, and the motorcade rolled south on A1A to this hotel, where the Secret Service had already swept the penthouse and inspected elevator cables. This hotel is also where I hung out with Dave Garroway when the *Today* show did remote broadcasts in the lobby by the atrium, which architect Morris Lapidus wanted to fill with monkeys until I raised some maintenance issues."

Chi-Chi turned a page in his newspaper. "You know, for a moment I almost cared."

Mort pointed at the paper. "Anything good in there?"

"The *Wabash Cannonball* crashed in St. Louis. And the Birdman of Alcatraz died."

"How old?"

"Seventy-three."

"Not too shabby."

Chi-Chi stood up and adjusted his hat. "I think we better go check on our friend."

They headed down the sidewalk.

"I still don't know about the rough stuff," said Mort.

"What's not to know?" said Chi-Chi. "Who ever heard of a sports book that doesn't make you pay?"

They turned the corner and stopped cold. "My car!" yelled

Chi-Chi. The trunk lid was popped open, a big pointy crease poking up in the middle of the hood like a circus tent.

They ran to the Cadillac and checked the trunk.

Empty except for the fully extended tire jack.

Chi-Chi tried to close the lid, but it wouldn't latch. "It's fucked up."

They sulked back into the lounge and climbed on stools.

"Bartender," said Sergio.

The bartender came over.

"Have any matches?"

The bartender reached in a bowl under the counter.

"Do the matches have the name of the hotel on them or just advertising for a correspondence school to learn TV repair in your spare time for fun and profit but that really just takes your money?"

The bartender held up the pack: AMERICANA HOTEL.

"Good."

The bartender tore out a match to give Sergio a light.

"Don't smoke," said Sergio. "Just want the pack."

The bartender set it on the bar.

"Can I have a different pack? You tore out a match. It has to be intact, for the collection."

The barkeep stared at Sergio a moment, then fished another pack out of the bowl before going back to his TV at the other end of the bar.

Sergio stuck the matches in his shirt pocket.

"I got a joke," said Coltrane. "There was a man from Nantucket who sucked it. Wait, I already fucked it up. Okay, knock-knock. . . . Bartender! Refill!"

The bartender didn't answer.

"Bartender!"

Still no answer.

"Has he gone deaf?"

"He's watching something on TV."

Coltrane got off his stool and walked to the end. "Bartender."

"Shhhh!" said the bartender.

"What is it?"

Soon they were all gathered around the set, watching the live news report out of Dallas.

7

Present

MR. VONNEGUT PEEKED out Serge's pocket. An hour into the Everglades, the yellow '67 Cougar took Exit 14 off Alligator Alley and pulled into a truck stop at the Miccosukee Indian Reservation. Semi rigs and airboats. Serge got some rubber wading boots out of the trunk and handed a pair to Lenny.

A tribal police car sat in front of the restrooms. A Micosukee law-enforcement officer was in the driver's seat finishing a sausage biscuit when he noticed the two men coming toward him in rubber boots. He rolled down the window.

"Good afternoon," said Serge. "I would like permission to go deep into the swamp over there to release an endangered species." He pointed at the bulge in his shirt pocket. "Now that he's back to health, I'm forced to return Mr. Vonnegut to his native habitat, because anything else would be wrong. I could have just disappeared into the mist with Lenny, my research assistant here, who promises not to smoke dope, but I decided to ask first because I've read all about Wounded Knee and wanted you to know I'm completely behind your 'nation' out here, even if it is kind of pretend. I didn't want you to think something weird was going on."

The officer stared a moment. "No campfires, hunting, or alcohol?"

Serge shook his head. "This is a church."

"Knock yourself out." The officer rolled up the window and got back to his air-conditioning.

Serge and Lenny walked to the edge of the parking lot and started climbing through reeds and sawgrass.

"Anything around here I should be concerned about?" asked Lenny, pulling his left foot out of the muck with a sucking pop.

"Nope. My granddad used to come here all the time. Never a scratch."

"So what do you think happened to him anyway?"

"Many possibilities. I overheard a lot of stuff as a kid that I probably shouldn't have. Mental-health problems, run-ins with the mob." Serge snapped off the top of a reed and slowly inched around behind Lenny. "There was even talk he was killed by a jealous ex-boyfriend in a love triangle." Serge held the reed in one hand and bent the top back with his other. "But the big theory revolved around the stolen gems. Right after the museum job, Granddad quickly became a suspect. . . ." Serge let go of the top of the bent reed, flicking a wolf spider off Lenny's collar.

"What was that?" said Lenny, feeling the back of his neck with both hands.

"Nothing."

They started walking again.

"So why'd they suspect he had the gems?"

"Granddad was running with the wrong crowd, and police started pointing fingers at the usuals. Others say he was framed by the real thieves who wanted to throw everyone off the trail. But the main reason he was suspected was the same thing that started all the nasty suicide speculation. You see, Granddad was a little . . . how should I put it? Crazy." Serge slowly moved his right hand toward the water. "He was always claiming he knew famous people, participated in historic events. They said he was a pathological liar, but I think he was just a great storyteller. After the '64 heist, he started running his mouth about that. Maybe it was one story too many." Serge's hand splashed into the water behind Lenny, then came out flinging something by the tail. The water moccasin twirled end over end through the air and into a distant bough. Lenny turned around quickly. Serge grinned. They started walking again.

"So you think he was making it all up?" asked Lenny.

"Who knows? Sounds far-fetched, but you had to understand the times. Miami Beach back then was F. Scott Fitzgerald country. Bars hopping all night, cabarets. Bookmaking and prostitution winked at. The mob running amok. And, thanks to Castro, we had the largest CIA field office in the world. Next to all that, anything's possible."

The bog sucked one of Lenny's boots off his foot; he reached back to retrieve it. "I never knew. . . ."

"That's because today it's all *South Beach! South Beach! South Beach!* Nobody goes up past Arthur Godfrey Road, which is Forty-first Street if you're keeping score at home." Serge reached into the water and felt along the bottom for a rock. "They all stay down on Ocean Drive, a bunch of skinny European guys walking around with little tennis-ball covers over their nut sacs. Sinatra would not approve." Serge reached back with a stone and skipped it across the water's surface and into the log in front of them. The log blinked and submerged in retreat. "The air crackled with electricity, Ann-Margret and Judy Garland headlining in the Rat Pack Deco hotels. And just when it seemed it couldn't get any more exciting, the Museum of Natural History in New York was hit, a host of world-class gems plucked from their smashed cases. The investigation focused—where else?—Miami Beach!"

"They won't let you try them on first. You have to buy them," said Lenny. "The tennis-ball things."

"It's a common misconception that all the gems were recovered," said Serge. "True, they got back the big ones: the Star of India, the DeLong Ruby and whatnot. But they never found about a dozen of the diamonds. Given the total take, everyone counted their blessings. The missing stuff was only a fraction. But that was four decades ago. Today they're worth a ransom."

"Can we stop now?" asked Lenny, looking around the swamp, no sign of human anything.

"Okay, we'll rest at that palm cluster over there. That should be far enough so Mr. Vonnegut can't follow us back and get run over by a tour bus."

They arrived on dry land a minute later. Lenny waited off to the side as Serge said his tearful good-byes. He cupped Mr. Vonnegut in his hands and gently placed him on a large fungus bulb growing out the side of a fallen tree. Serge stepped back. The mouse hopped down and ran to him.

"Remember," said Lenny. "Cruel to be kind."

Serge wagged a finger in the mouse's face. "Bad Mr. Vonnegut!" He set the mouse on the fungus again and stepped back.

The mouse prepared to jump down again. Just then something large leaped from the sabal palms and landed on the log. Then it jumped back into the brush.

"Where did that fucking panther come from!"

"MOM, WE'RE HOME."

Serge was still red-eyed and sniffling as they came through the front door, blowing his nose in a hanky.

Mrs. Lippowicz was knitting. "Lenny, there's some mail for you and Serge on the table."

Lenny began walking to the table. Serge ran past him bushytailed, forgetting all about the marsh mouse. "I love mail! Mail is the best! Mail is hope! Mail is a mystery! Look! A box! That's a good sign. Always good to get a box! Envelopes can go either way. But bad news rarely comes in a box. Only goodies!" Serge seized it off the table, tumbling it in his hands, putting it to his ear and shaking. "No noise." He sniffed it. "No odor." He checked the return address and postmark. "Don't recognize them." He set the box back down and rubbed his palms. "God, I love mail! Especially mail I don't recognize! It could be anything! Opportunity, a big adventure, a whole new chapter in life about to unfold! I love this moment! I hope it's not a product sample. Ooooh, that would be bad! I get all excited and it's a fucking mini Tide detergent. Do you think that's what it is? I'm sure that's what it is! Now I'm depressed. It's got to be Tide or some female-hygiene product. God, I hate it when they do that! I'm furious just thinking about it. Damn those people to hell! . . . Wait, why am I getting upset?" He smiled jubilantly and raised the box high over his head. *It's mail!*

Serge began biting through packing tape—"Please, please, please . . ."—tearing wildly at cardboard flaps.

"What are you expecting?" asked Lenny.

"I don't know. I send away for so much stuff." A side of the box finally gave way. Serge pulled out a videocassette. He read the title, then signaled touchdown with two arms in the air. "Yessssss!"

"What is it?"

Serge ran down the hall.

When Lenny got to the bedroom doorway, Serge was reaching up in the closet's top shelf, pulling down old board games. Mousetrap, Shenanigans, Clue, Battleship, Mystery Date . . .

"My sister's," Lenny said quickly.

"That's why I love your room," said Serge. "It's like it's frozen in time. My guess would be the exact moment you started smoking pot."

"How'd you know?"

Serge found a plastic box in the back of the shelf behind the Major Matt Mason accessories. He carried it to the dresser and removed the lid. He stepped back with a breath of pride, staring at a long row of videotapes and DVDs. The last slot was empty.

Lenny came up alongside. "Another tape for your archives?"

"The most important one of all," said Serge. "This finally completes the Miami Collection."

"How long have you been working on it?"

"Forever." Serge ran his hands over the titles like touchstones. "This last one was the toughest of all. I've been searching the far corners of the Internet for months. Paid an arm. The hardest one previously was a copy of the cable documentary on the Star of India job with lots of great black-and-white newsreel footage."

"From the History Channel?"

"No, A&E. I can't watch the History Channel."

"I thought you'd love that."

"Had to finally admit I just don't have the control. I call it the Heroin Channel. If they're running one of those technology shows on the brief but exciting life of the ballpoint pen, I can occasionally break away for a snack. But when they get deep into the Chinese dynasties, Dr. Livingston, Magellan's circumnavigation and Hitler's Henchmen, that's the ball game. Next thing I know, I've been squatting in the same spot in front of the TV for days without food or sleep."

Lenny looked in the box. "I didn't know there were so many with local connection."

"Absolutely," said Serge. "Here's the A&E tape, Hitchcock's *Notorious*, the pilot for *Flipper*, *Goldfinger*, the Clay-Liston fight, *Surfside 6*, the Beatles' first visit, *Some Like It Hot*, *A Hole in the Head* with Sinatra, Robert Conrad and Don Stroud in *Murph the Surf*, the Jets and the Colts, *The FBI Murders: In the Line of Duty*, etcetera, etcetera." Serge affectionately inserted his newest video into the final slot.

"Wait a second." He stopped and yanked the tape back out. "This is a very special occasion. We have to celebrate. Go get some of that rainy-day cash from the wallets we beat out of those people."

"Field trip?" said Lenny.

8

TONY MARSICANO BROUGHT his own underboss when he came up from Miami, a loyal lifelong friend, the one they called Two-Tone Bob. Bob was like a younger brother to Tony; he trusted Bob with his life.

Bob got off his cell phone. "Mr. Palermo just sent the new guys up."

"Good, we can use the help."

Bob went to the airport to pick up the fresh crew, the one Mr. Palermo had sent to keep an eye on Tony. That's how Mr. Palermo had gotten to be Mr. Palermo. Distrust the people you trust the most. Two-Tone Bob drove the new guys out to the address Tony had given him. They pulled onto an empty street just after midnight and parked behind Tony's Cadillac. Tony was already waiting outside the car.

They met, shook hands. Tony pointed. "I want you to break in that place."

The new guys looked across the street at a vacant storefront in a strip mall. The crew's captain, Sammy Scarpotto, scratched his head. "I don't get it. It's empty. Who's it belong to?"

"Shut up!" snapped Two-Tone. "Don't ask questions! Tony told you to do something—just do it!"

"It belongs to me," said Tony.

Now Sammy was really baffled.

"I want to test the security system," said Tony. He gave Sammy the override code in case it went off.

Sammy didn't see the point but told the other guys to get to work anyway.

Tony and Two-Tone got back in the Caddy. Tony pulled out a stopwatch. His hunch about security at Strauss & Levy had been on the money. It wasn't much of a system, because it was just an accounting place. Not a very big target. Basic wiring to protect the computers. Still, it took the crew only three minutes to trip one of the motion detectors, and Sammy couldn't get the override entered in time.

Tony's cell phone rang. The alarm company. "I accidentally set it off myself." He gave the password.

Sammy led the others back to Tony's car. "Sorry."

Tony reset his stopwatch. "Try again."

Two more alarms, but Sammy was able to punch in the code each time. On the next try, the crew made it without a hitch.

Tony clicked his stopwatch.

The crew came back out to the cars. Sammy smiled proudly. "How was that?"

"Do it again," said Tony.

Five more times without an alarm. Sammy was getting annoyed, but Two-Tone kept him in line.

"That's enough," Tony finally said. He picked up a rock and threw it through the front window of his own store. The new guys were beginning to think Tony was a little loopy.

"Get in the cars and follow me."

They drove to the dark end of the street, turned around and

killed the lights. The alarm company called Tony's cell phone again. He didn't answer, just stared at the stopwatch.

Four minutes and eighteen seconds later, a police cruiser rolled into the strip mall. Then a Cadillac.

"I'm the owner," said Tony, shaking hands with the officer.

"Probably juveniles," said the cop. "We've been getting a few like this."

"I've got some plywood inside. I'll cover it up until I can get the glass company out here in the morning." They shook again, and the cop left.

The other cars turned on their headlights and drove back to Tony.

Sammy got out. "What are we practicing for? I haven't heard anything from Miami about a score."

"I told you to watch your mouth!" said Two-Tone.

"It's my own idea," said Tony. "I haven't told anyone yet."

"Kind of like the counterfeit tickets?"

"Kind of."

9

STEVE AND MARLENE Kensington of Lancaster, Pennsylvania, stood at the railing on their ninth-floor balcony. Arms around each other in white silk bathrobes—embroidered hotel crests over the pockets—gazing contentedly out to sea. Shafts of sunshine occasionally broke through a light cloud cover and danced in the Atlantic. Their tenth anniversary. Marlene snuggled into Steve and closed her eyes. "Remember when we first came to Miami Beach?"

"How could I forget?"

Steve had been a wrestler at Penn State, now a probate attorney, but the physique was still there. Marlene was a foot shorter, thin and delicate, and Steve was careful when he squeezed her.

She opened her eyes to take in the intoxicating azure view. "I love the Eden Roc."

"Couldn't stay at another hotel."

Marlene's gaze slid from the ocean back to their balcony and the glass-top table with a bouquet of red roses, folded-over *Miami Herald* and two empty room-service brunch trays with trace evidence of eggs Florentine.

She snuggled into him again. "Let's never go home."

"Okay."

A knock at the door.

"Who can that be?"

Steve padded across the suite in slippers, checked the peephole and opened the door. A pair of grinning men in tropical shirts and khaki shorts entered with two bottles of Dom Perignon, a giant welcome basket of citrus and marmalade, a sterling bucket of caviar. And a videotape.

Marlene came in from the balcony. The men began uncapping champagne.

"Honey, what's all this?" she said, then turned her head with a coy smile. "Is it another one of your surprises?"

"No," Steve said with his own puzzlement. "I have no idea what's going on."

"You're in Room Nine-nineteen," said the tall one, twisting the wire off a champagne cap and placing the bottle between his knees. "You know what that means?"

"What?" said Steve.

"This is the Lucille Ball Room! Surprise!" Pop! The plastic stopper flew past Marlene and off the balcony. "You win! All this stuff's for you! Anyone for some bubbly?"

"Wow, the Lucille Ball Room," said Marlene, taking a glass from Serge. "This is really special."

Steve broke into his own big grin and shook his head. "Isn't this just like the Eden Roc?"

"Oh, it's a great hotel!" said Serge, filling Steve's glass.

"So, like, what? Did Lucy used to stay in this room?" asked Marlene, unwrapping orange cellophane from the gift basket. "Is that what this contest is about?"

"Oh, no, even better," said Serge, opening the mahogany doors of the suite's entertainment complex and inserting his video in the VCR. "This room was immortalized in one of her show's episodes. We're going to watch it."

"You're kidding!"

"Would I kid?" Serge grabbed the remote. "Just have a seat on the couch."

"This is so neat," said Marlene, sitting down with Steve, taking him by the arm again.

The vintage black-and-white show opened with an aerial shot of the Eden Roc, then went inside one of rooms, where the two couples were on Florida vacation, ordering room service. *"That's right,"* said Lucy. *"Room Nine-nineteen . . ."*

"Did you hear that?" chimed Marlene. "She said our room!"

"It gets better," said Serge. "Lucy and Ethel challenge Ricky and Fred to a fishing contest so they can win a shopping spree. Both sides decide to cheat and buy giant tuna that they hide in their bathtubs, and of course the fish get switched, setting the stage for big laughs. Whew! They just don't make 'em like that anymore!"

Sure enough, the TV episode began unfolding just as Serge had described.

They were all laughing on the couch, and Marlene said it reminded her of a classic fishing episode on *The Honeymooners* and—

"Shhhhh!" said Serge. "Damn. Now, look what you did. You missed the key part where Fred asks Ricky where the fish is. That's crucial to the linear tension. I'll have to rewind." Serge angrily hit the remote.

The Pennsylvania couple was knocked off balance. Their heads backed up an inch. They turned and looked at each other. Steve noticed Lenny out on the balcony, surreptitiously toking a joint cupped in his hand.

He turned to Serge. "Uh, what exactly is your colleague doing out there?"

Serge looked toward the balcony, then restarted the tape and settled back on the couch. "I know, I know. It's kind of sad. At least it's not the hard stuff."

Steve glanced at his wife, then Serge again. "Forgive me for asking . . . but are you with the hotel?"

"The hotel?" said Serge, eyes glued to the TV. "Oh, no. We're not with the hotel. Why?" Suddenly, he jackknifed over with laughter and slapped Steve hard on the knee. "Look! Look! I love this! They're both walking backward with their big fish, about to bump into each other on the landing!"

"Honeyyyyyyyy . . ." said Marlene, scooting back to the farthest corner of the couch. "What's going on?"

Steve looked at Serge again. "What *is* going on? Who are you guys?"

"We live around here. I'm really into this stuff. Just got this tape today. It completed my Miami Collection, so of course I had to watch it in this room."

Steve jumped to his feet and went for the phone. "I'm calling security."

"You don't want to do that," said Serge.

Lenny wandered in from the balcony. "What's going on?"

"Nothing that can't be resolved with dialogue and respect," said Serge.

"Out!" Steve grabbed Lenny by the arm. "Get moving!"

"Let go of him!" said Serge.

Steve shoved Lenny, who stumbled toward the door.

"Hey, asshole!" Serge shoved Steve.

Steve shoved Serge back, slamming him into a wall. The former wrestler took a quick step forward, cocking his right fist for the knockout punch. A chrome pistol flew out from behind Serge's back. The barrel landed in the middle of Steve's face.

Steve froze. Marlene began shrieking like a stepped-on weasel.

"Tell her to shut the fuck up!" yelled Serge.

Steve stared cross-eyed at the gun barrel pressed to the bridge of his nose. "Honey, could you please lower your voice?"

The shrieks became whimpers.

"That's better," said Serge.

"Take anything you want," said Steve. "This watch is fourteen karat. There's money in the room safe."

"I don't want your stuff."

"Then what's this about?"

"I want to watch TV."

He marched Steve back to the couch at gunpoint. "Have a seat."

Serge sat next to them and restarted the tape. The couple didn't take their eyes off him.

"Not me!" said Serge, waving toward the TV with the gun. "You're missing Lucy!"

10

TONY MARSICANO SAT cross-legged on a toilet in the second-floor restroom of an Orlando office tower, staring at his wristwatch. He lowered his legs.

Elevator doors opened on the ground floor. Tony got out and waved toward the guard desk. Charley Pavlic waved back. "You sure work a lot of late hours, Mr. Davis."

"That's what happens when you're the computer guy."

"Wish I knew more about computers."

"Wish I didn't. They dump *everything* on you. I have to fix this big server problem by Monday. Could be here all night. . . . There they are."

Charley looked over. Four men in blue technician uniforms arrived at the building's entrance with toolboxes. Tony walked over and pushed the horizontal bar that opened the glass doors. They headed for the elevators. "Charley, we're going to be ordering out in a couple hours. Want anything? Chinese place."

"That's all right. I brought something."

They all got in the elevator. "I'll surprise you anyway," said Tony. The door closed.

Tony's plan was perfect; his help was not. Despite arduous rehearsal, someone tripped the alarm two minutes after they picked the lock on the inner office. A painful siren whooped.

"Who did that?" shouted Tony.

They all shook their heads.

The telephone rang. The alarm company. Tony didn't have the password. He unplugged the phone and clicked his stopwatch. The sweep hand began ticking. The siren wailed. The others stood around.

"What the hell are you doing?" Tony yelled. "Look like you're working on computers!"

"How do we do that?" asked Sammy.

"Just go over and fuck with them! Jesus!"

Tony opened the outer office door as Charley got off the elevator, unsnapping his holster.

"Charley! Do you know how to shut this goddamn thing off?"

It was the first time Charley had seen Mr. Davis anything but magnanimous.

"Don't you have a code to punch in?" asked Charley, resnapping the holster.

"Yeah," said Tony. "But it would help a little if they gave me the *correct* code. And I'm sure the alarm company is trying to call right now. But the computers are all wired through the phones, and we had to take the whole system down for the work." The siren blared on. Tony grabbed his ears. "I'm getting a fuckin' migraine. Now I'm going to be here till dawn!"

Charley hesitated a second, then trotted for the elevators. "I'll take care of it, Mr. Davis."

Tony walked to the office's plate-glass windows overlooking the Orlando skyline and Space Mountain in the distance. He looked at the stopwatch. Four minutes. He stared down at the street; two police cruisers pulled up. Under his breath: "Come on, Charley. Get back down there!"

Cops ran into the building. Tony checked his watch again. Five minutes. He called across the office to Bob, watching the elevators. "The numbers changing?"

"Nope. Still on *L*."

The siren abruptly cut out. Tony peered down out the window again; two tiny police officers got back in their car and drove away. Now it was even better than if they hadn't tripped the alarm—the whole system was shut off. Tony ran from office to office until he found what he was looking for in one of the partners' suites. A steel-reinforced, fireproof filing cabinet with combination lock. It was a tough filing cabinet, but it was still just a filing cabinet, child's play for the crew's safe man. The top drawer popped in thirty seconds. The safe man went to open it, but Tony blocked him with his hand.

"Everyone leave the room."

They left.

"You, too," he told Bob. "It's for your own protection."

Bob looked a little hurt, but he nodded and obeyed as he always had.

Tony pulled the drawer open, and there it was. He removed the prize and stuck it in his briefcase. Then he took a seemingly identical item from the attaché, replaced it in the drawer and locked it back up.

The elevator opened in the lobby. Tony walked over to the guard desk. He leaned on the counter as if he were in no rush at all, thanking Charley for the help and apologizing for his temper. Bob walked up behind the guard. He pulled a pistol with a silencer from his toolbox and placed the barrel an inch behind Charley's head.

Tony looked up. "Noooooo!"

Charley spun around quickly. Bob whipped the gun behind his back.

"What?" said Charley, then turned back to Tony. "What's the matter?"

"Just remembered we missed something. I'm going to have to come back tomorrow. I'll miss the football game."

Charley laughed. "That *is* serious."

"Good night, Charley."

"Good night, Mr. Davis."

11

A '67 MERCURY Cougar drove south on Collins Avenue.

Serge sat in the passenger seat with his clipboard. "Something tells me that couple back at the Eden Roc weren't big Lucille Ball fans."

"Can't expect everyone to dig your history stuff. . . . What are you doing?"

"Writing my daily letters."

"Letters?"

"Someone has to carry on the legacy of Lincoln. It's a lost art form. Everything today is e-mail, bunch of cute abbreviations—'BTW,' 'LOL.' It's killing the language. Not to mention handwriting."

"Who do you write to?"

"Depends on my mood. Captains of industry, opinion makers, people in the spotlight. Today I'm writing the president."

"You can just write the president?"

"Oh, sure. But George has lots of screeners, and only a tiny percentage of correspondence actually gets to him. That's why this has to be a kick-ass letter. It's absolutely imperative he hears my ideas, or some big mistakes are about to be made. But he seems real nice on TV, and I think I can reach him. If I'm lucky, it could lead to a permanent job."

"What about me?"

"You can be my assistant," said Serge, folding the piece of paper. "You'll even get a credit card."

"Really?"

Serge nodded and licked the envelope. "That's how Washington works." He got out a second sheet of watermarked stationery. "Next I'm writing another letter asking Katie Couric to bring the *Today* show back to Miami Beach. Then I'm going to pen my macroeconomic treatise for the *Wall Street Journal*. I've always wanted to be published in the *Journal*."

"What about our business?"

"That's still a problem." Serge reached under the seat for an out-of-print copy of *The Life and Times of Miami Beach* and began flipping through the pictures. "We need to find people who are on the same page. If only there was a way to work history and cultural appreciation into my grandfather's investigation . . . Wait! That's it!"

"That's what?"

"Our business. It just came to me."

"What is it?"

"Brand-new. Doesn't have a name yet because I just invented it. You'll simply have to watch it unfold."

"When does it start to unfold?"

"Right now. Make a left."

Lenny turned and parked in front of a tiny but bustling Cuban storefront specializing in cigars, lottery tickets, espresso and Western Union. Two old men in straw hats emerged from the store knocking back shots of bitter coffee, throwing tiny paper cups into a wire trash basket. Others relaxed on a sidewalk bench, talking fast in Spanish.

Serge got out of the Cougar and stuck quarters in a metal box for a Sunday *Herald*. He flipped to the lottery results, then went inside and filled out a megajackpot card.

The clerk stopped and stared at Serge's card. "You sure you want these numbers?"

"Positive."

"It's your dollar." The clerk stuck the card in his machine; a ticket popped out.

Serge retrieved a large orange duffel bag from the Cougar's trunk and headed down an alley toward the beach.

"What your angle?" asked Lenny, running up alongside.

"Human nature." Serge turned the corner onto Ocean Drive. He handed Lenny the newspaper and lottery ticket. "Excitement and greed always overrule rational thought. Then we'll have the money and equipment to crack the Star of India case and find out about Granddad. Did I ever tell you how the surfers pulled off the heist?"

"Yes."

"It started in the fall. The trio visited the museum like tourists and cased the joint. Then they came back after dark. One of them kept circling the museum in the getaway car while the others scaled the side of the building like mountain climbers and got in through an unlocked window."

Lenny's eyes kept darting back and forth from the paper to the Lotto ticket. "All the numbers match . . . but . . . you just . . . how did . . . ?"

"Like I said, human nature. The big thing everyone focuses on are the drawing numbers. Then they're all pumped and just make a cursory check of the date on the ticket, which of course precisely matches the date of the newspaper. . . ."

Lenny nodded enthusiastically.

"But today's newspaper reports results from *yesterday's* drawing; the ticket is one day too late. Easy mistake in the excitement of the moment. . . . Then the surfers sat in wait and timed the night watchman's rounds and made their move with glass cutters and tape, wiping out the contents of the rare gem room, which had dead batteries in the alarms. They flew back to Miami in the morning."

Lenny stared at the ticket. "So are we rich?"

"Gimme that." Serge snatched it away. They entered an ultra-chic sidewalk café. Tank tops, leather, egos. Sexy men and women in flavors not seen by the rest of the country.

Serge handed Lenny the duffel bag. "Now, here's what I need you to do. . . ."

A waiter met Serge with a menu.

"Table for one."

The waiter began leading Serge but stopped when he realized the customer wasn't with him anymore. He looked back.

Serge stood in the middle of the tables, mouth open, eyes bugged, lottery ticket in one hand, newspaper in the other. He began jumping up and down. "I won the lottery! I won the lottery! I can't believe it! Twenty million dollars! All mine! I'm rich!"

Heads turned. Lenny walked up like he didn't know Serge, who showed him the ticket and newspaper. "See? All the numbers match!"

Serge stomped his feet and ran in a circle. Conversation swept the crowd. He yanked a tall German blonde up from one of the tables and began manic ballroom dancing. "I won the lottery! I won the lottery! Yipeeeee!"

"He's right!" yelled Lenny. "I can't believe it! It's the winning ticket! It matches the newspaper!" He showed the waiter, whose heart began to pound as his eyes went down the line, matching number after number. He came to the end and looked up, color gone from his face. "It's the winning ticket."

Serge was dancing with another woman now. "I won the lottery! I won the lottery! I—" Suddenly he stopped. He slowly turned around. Faces stared back at him. Half the men looked like Boris Becker. He held out an arm like a traffic cop. "No, I can't take the money. It'll change me. It'll completely ruin my life." He handed the ticket to the waiter. "Since all of you fine people were here to share this special moment, I want you to have it. Divide it up as you see fit." Serge walked away with his newspaper.

The waiter stared in shock at the ticket. There was a pause. A couple slowly got up from a table, then another. They looked at the ticket in the waiter's hand. "The numbers match!" The rest began getting up until a crushing circle surrounded the waiter, arms reaching, voices louder. Someone got pushed. Another shove. "Watch it!" The knot of people congealed around the ticket, shuffling left, then right. A shirt got ripped. A woman went down with a scream, feet on her back, and finally a full-scale people-pile like the winning team after the final out of the World Series.

Serge and Lenny moved quietly through the tables, filling the duffel bag with purses, cell phones and laptops.

12

December 31, 1963

CROWDS LINED THE sidewalks and balconies of Biscayne Boulevard, ready to ring in the new year. Some wore glittery "1964" novelty sunglasses. A thumping, roaring sound came up the street. Floats, high-school bands, baton twirlers. Drums and tubas. The thirty-first King Orange Jamboree.

On the other side of the bay, strings of headlights trickled down Collins Avenue. Montereys, DeSotos, Comets, Corvairs. Whitewalls and hood ornaments. Stumbling rivers of people jammed the sidewalks.

The back door of a bookmaking parlor opened. Men glanced around the alley before hoisting a limp body into the truck of a pink Cadillac.

Chi-Chi slammed the lid. "Coltrane, you got rid of the tire jack, right?"

Coltrane nodded.

"Let's get a drink."

They zigzagged from the Bamboo Room at the Hotel Roney to the Pagoda in the Saxony. A flying cork hit Moondog in the side of the head behind Murray Franklin's. The latest chart-toppers blared out open nightclub doors. "Wipe Out," "If I Had a Hammer," "Da Do Ron Ron." By nine o'clock the gang was halfway in the bag. Tommy and Mort still had their party hats, but the rubber band had broken on Moondog's. A Chevelle nearly hit Sergio crossing Nineteenth Street as he examined the night's haul of matchbooks. Coltrane walked around with two lit sparklers sticking out the top of his straw hat until Mort noticed it catching fire.

Chi-Chi threw an exhausted toothpick in the gutter. "We better go check on you-know-who."

They weaved back up the street to the bookmaking joint. Chi-Chi approached the Cadillac and stuck his key in the trunk. "Bet he's ready to pay now."

"Must be scared shitless," said Greek Tommy.

Chi-Chi raised the lid.

A glint from a long piece of swinging metal.

Chi-Chi grabbed his shoulder and went to the ground. "Fuck!"

More metal flashes.

Moondog hit the pavement. "Owwww! Shit!"

Greek Tommy went reeling off, crumpling against the side of the building. "My arm! I think it's broken!"

The others jumped back in shock. The piece of metal clanged to the ground. The man ran off into the night.

"Where'd he get that fucking tire iron?" said Tommy.

"Coltrane!" yelled Chi-Chi. "I thought you said you got rid of the jack!"

"I did. What? Is the iron part of it?"

Just before midnight, the gang decided to make a last stand in the Driftwood Lounge, bandages and all. They headed up the steps of the Nautilus Hotel. A woman staggered down toward them, swinging an almost empty bottle of champagne by the neck. She blew her noisemaker at Tommy, then fell off her high heels and took a frightful spill down the rest of the stairs. She stood up, put her boobs back in her clothes and stumbled away.

The gang moved single file past illuminated nautilus shells on the lobby walls, then into the lounge. Sergio ordered. Six champagnes and a matchbook.

The crowd on the bandstand counted down to zero. Balloons fell. Happy New Year.

Six men toasted.

Sergio set his glass down. "Man, am I glad to get the hell out of 1963. I mean, what a downer. I'm still numb from Dallas."

"It's a new year. Cleanses everything," said Mort. "That's what it's all about."

"I know it's a new year, but it doesn't feel any different," said Tommy. "I still have that kicked-in-the-gut feeling. I can't believe they killed the president."

"Believe it," said Chi-Chi. "Now nobody's safe."

"Is that supposed to make me feel better?" said Sergio.

"Last day I remember like that was Pearl Harbor," said Tommy.

Moondog drained his plastic champagne flute. "December seventh and November twenty-second. Sure hope we don't get any more dates to remember in our lifetime."

"I think Mort's right," said Sergio. "This is a cleansing. This year could be the beginning of a whole new era, major changes in society. . . . I gotta hit the can."

They shot the breeze, complained about business, talked family. Sergio returned. He said his daughter and son-in-law in West Palm were going through tough financial times. She had to take a sales job at Burdines on the weekends. It looked like Sergio was going to be doing a little baby-sitting in 1964.

"That's a very nice thing to do," said Coltrane. "That's real stand-up of you. . . . I gotta hit the can."

Coltrane was washing his hands in the men's room when he saw a plastic bottle in the trash. "Oooo, prescription medication!" He retrieved the bottle and shook it. "Almost full!" He read the name on the label.

They were debating Arnold Palmer's chances at the Masters when Coltrane returned. He called Sergio aside.

"I found this in the wastebasket."

"So?"

"It has your name on it."

"I threw it away."

"I'm no expert, but I've heard of this medicine. Major psychiatric stuff. If you're taking it, it pretty much means you need it."

"It's a new year, and that's my resolution. I want a fresh start."

"How long have you been taking this?"

"I don't know. Twenty years?"

"Twenty years! You can't just stop!"

"I just did. I've been on it so long, who knows what I'm really like? *I* don't even know."

"Hope you realize what you're doing."

"I'm feeling better already," said Sergio. "I think this is going to be a big, big year."

13

Present

"MOM! WE'RE HOME!"

"Where have you been?"

"Out."

Serge and Lenny ran down the hall with their duffel bag. They dumped the contents on the bottom bunk.

"Perfect," said Serge. "Everything we need to start our cottage industry. Lenny, you skim the wallets for cash and segregate the cell phones. I'll get our computer department up and running. Where's your phone jack?"

"Behind the desk."

Serge began tapping the keyboard of a stolen laptop. He clicked an annoying desktop icon to establish an Internet connection with a free trial offer.

"What are you doing?" asked Lenny.

"Building our website."

Lenny turned a Gucci purse inside out. "Sounds like work."

"Patience," said Serge. "It's not so easy since the dot-com collapse. The days are gone when you could just throw together a half-ass site, get showered with venture capital, buy time slots on *Everybody Loves Raymond,* and watch the stock go ape."

"We can't?"

"No, the New Economy turned out to be something a lot different than everyone expected."

"What?"

"Pornography."

"We can get pornography on that thing?" said Lenny. "My turn!"

"Not yet. I'm still working on our flash intro. . . . What just happened? I lost my connection."

The phone rang in the living room. Mrs. Lippowicz answered.

Lenny dug in another purse and pulled out a vibrator. He turned it on and began rubbing his cheek. "Hey, look. One of those facial massagers."

Serge began tapping again, reestablishing a connection. Lenny grabbed a chair and sat down next to him, rubbing his chin with the humming wand.

Serge was loading wallpaper when his keystrokes locked up. "We lost the connection again. What's going on?"

The phone was ringing in the living room. Mrs. Lippowicz answered.

"Telemarketers," said Lenny. "It's dinnertime. They bug Mom like crazy ever since that one guy sold her all those plastic Japanese frog lanterns in the yard."

Serge logged on again. He lost the connection again. "Son of a bitch!"

He got up and went down the hall.

Lenny ran after him. "What are you doing?"

"Putting a stop to this." Serge entered the living room. "Mrs. Lippowicz, I couldn't help but notice you're plagued by solicitors. Would you mind if I handled the next call?"

"Why, thank you, Serge."

They all sat on the couch and watched *Full House*.

Lenny leaned over. "The little girl's really twins, you know."

"That's how they get around child-labor laws," said Serge.

"You know everything."

The phone rang. Serge answered. "Hello? . . . No, let me save you some oxygen before you read your whole script. . . . Stop talking. . . . Let me say something. . . . You're still reading the script. . . . *Shut up!* . . . Thank you. I want to inform you that this is now a business number, so get on your little telemarketing computer and make a notation not to call this number anymore because . . . You're reading the script again. . . . I'm not remotely interested. . . . Because carpet cleaning with sound waves is an idiotic idea. . . . You're still reading. . . . No, you've just changed scripts. . . . You've changed to the script you read after the person says they're not interested. . . . I'm hanging up. . . . I have to hang up. . . . Now you're reading the 'I have to hang up' script. . . . I really have to hang up."

Serge hung up.

The phone rang.

"Hello?"

Serge got a look on his face as he set the phone back in its cradle.

"What is it?" asked Lenny.

"He called back just to hang up on *me*."

"Wow. That's really got to piss you off."

"And because I don't know his phone number, there's nowhere for my anger to go."

"Hold on," said Lenny. "I know a new feature that gives you the last number that called in." Lenny hit star and a couple of buttons. He listened and looked at Serge. "The number's blocked! And we just spent seventy-five cents!"

"Son of a bitch!"

Serge grabbed the phone and dialed again.

"Who are you calling?"

"The phone company . . . Hello, yes, I'd like to file a complaint against a telemarketer. . . . No, I don't know that. . . . I tried, but they had the number blocked. I figured since you're the phone company you could look up— . . . What do you mean there's no way to do that? . . . I'm sorry, but I'm finding that very hard to believe. . . . You've got a bunch of satellites in orbit, and yet you can't circumvent your own blocking feature? . . . Okay, so they're probably out of state, so how does that make it more difficult? . . . Look, if they're out of state, they have to pay long-distance. My number has to be recorded to someone's account so you know where to mail your bills, or do you just send them anywhere, launch them out into space on the wings of hope? . . ."

Serge listened a moment. He put the phone down.

"What happened?"

"Said I had a bad attitude. Then she hung up."

They went back to Lenny's room. Serge got on the Internet again. A website popped up. Serge surfed to another, then another, then a few more, then online directory assistance. Serge stopped and folded his hands in front of him in thought.

"What is it?"

"I've found the heads of several telemarketing companies, but they're all unlisted."

"Maybe they don't want to be bothered by phone calls."

Serge began tapping again. A new site popped up. *Florida Secretary of State.* He clicked the "Corporations" button.

"How does that help?" asked Lenny.

"Companies are required to file personal addresses and phone numbers of their officers." Serge pointed at the bottom bunk. "Hand me one of those cell phones."

"But how will you know they're the same company that called us?"

"I won't. But they set the rules. They pick us at random, so do we. . . ." Serge punched a number into the phone. "Hello, how are you doing this evening? . . . No, this isn't a solicitation call. . . . This is an *anti*solicitation call. . . . If you think telemarketers are dick-brains, please press one now—"

Click.

"Probably has Caller ID. Hand me a different phone."

Lenny fetched a compact blue model. Serge dialed. "Hello, we're conducting a survey. When do you like telemarketers to call? A: When you're taking a shit. B: When—"

Click.

"Hand me another." Serge dialed. "Tired of your wife fucking your friends—"

Click.

Serge dialed again. "Hello—"

"I'll kill you, you bastard! I'll find out who you are and smash your brains out with a brick! You're fucking with the wrong person! . . ."

"Mr. Jamison, this is Detective Swayback with the police department," said Serge.

"Oh."

"We've received word that a dangerous mental patient may be heading to your house. He's suspected of killing several people with a really big ax after phoning them numerous times pretending to be a telemarketer."

"He's been calling all night!"

"Lock all your doors and windows. We're on our way."

Serge hung up and smiled at Lenny.

"But how does that stop solicitors from calling our house?"

"It doesn't, but it makes me feel better. That's the number-one rule in life: Always do what makes you feel better at all times."

"That's three number-one rules now."

"Rule Number One is that Rule Number One is whatever you want it to be at any time based on self-interest, blinding rationalization and petulance. At least that's the code everyone in this country seems to be operating under."

Serge returned to website construction.

Lenny opened his bedroom window and lit a joint.

"How'd you learn how to build web pages?"

"Nothing to it. I just cut and pasted from other e-business sites."

"Like what?"

Serge held up his clipboard. "Mortgages Made Easy, Bankruptcy in a Box, Sell Your Products in Togo, International Brides from Developing Countries, International Brides from Nondeveloping Countries (medical waiver), Runaway International Bride Tracking Service, Bleeding Gums? No Problem!, Clip Art for Inmates, Credit Repair for Cokeheads, Offshore Casinos That Never Pay, Make a Six-Figure Income by Mistreating Others, Tiny Home Video Cameras for Security and Peeping—"

"Is this going to take much longer?"

"If you keep bothering me."

"I think I'll take a nap," said Lenny, climbing onto the top bunk. "I'm sleepy from the weed. Wake me when we're ready."

Serge tapped on the keyboard with his right hand and picked up a cell phone with his left. "Hello? Mr. Jamison? . . . No, this isn't Detective Swayback. This is Lieutenant Muldoon at the police department. . . . That's what I need to talk to you about. . . . Whatever you do, I want you to remain calm. . . . Are you sitting down? . . . Good. The serial killer is going by the name Detective Swayback. And we've been able to do a phone trace. . . . Mr. Jamison, the calls are coming *from inside your house!*"

MIDNIGHT, LENNY'S EYES fluttered open. Serge's face was two inches away. Lenny jumped. "Ahhhhhh!"

"Good, you're finally awake."

"How long were you staring at me like that?"

"An hour, more or less. Finished the website."

Lenny hopped down from the bunk and pulled up a chair. Serge handed him the mouse.

"What do I do?"

"See the 'Okay' button?"

"Yeah?"

"That means 'okay.' Click it."

Lenny clicked the mouse. The screen went black.

They began hearing faint musical horns, growing louder, becoming the opening score from *2001: A Space Odyssey*. The Miami skyline took form out of the predawn darkness, then a burst of light, the music switching to allegro tympanic synthesizer as time-lapse photography shot the sun out of the Atlantic into a quick twelve-hour arc across the Florida sky, clouds zipping back and forth, interspersed with flashing still images: cocaine seizures, machine-gun seizures, exotic-animal seizures, people jumping into the sea from overloaded immigrant smuggling boats, police in riot gear, chalk outlines, pools of blood, sheet-covered bodies, prostitutes in hot pants, shirtless men in handcuffs, syringes in storm drains, hurricane-leveled trailer parks with sad-faced pets walking through debris . . . then sunset and blackness over the city.

"Pretty cool," said Lenny. "Where'd you get the idea?"

"The Action Five News intro."

A final bright explosion filled the computer screen, dissolving into a set of turquoise-and-pink neon letters: *Serge & Lenny's Florida Experience*.

"You put your name first," said Lenny. "We didn't discuss that."

"You slept. I made the page."

"I still don't know what business it is."

"You've seen all those new specialty travel tours? Ghost tours, notorious-crime-scene tours, celebrity-home tours, literary tours, cemetery tours, architectural tours, seedy-underbelly tours, drug-sampling tours along the Vietnamese-Laotian border . . ."

"Which are we?"

"All of them."

"Even the drug tour?"

"Normally I'd say no, but it's part of the underbelly, so morally I must include it."

"This is what you've been planning the whole time? A travel service?

"Yes and no. The tour business is just a subsidiary of our ten-tacled conglomerate designed to achieve all the objectives on my clipboard through the implementation of a plan so complex, dominating and unfathomable that I weep in awe of its scope. The tour is just the tip."

"What's the rest of the plan?"

"Can't tell you. Each facet is compartmentalized on a need-to-know basis, in case they torture you."

"Somebody's going to torture me?"

"Possibly, but the good news is you can't tell them anything," said Serge. "Not even *I* know the whole plan."

"How is that possible?"

"I planned it that way. It will all become apparent as it starts unfolding with the flood of customer e-mail hitting our website in the next few seconds."

Serge clicked the mouse over to their Internet mailbox. The two stared at the screen. And stared.

"Where are all our customers?" asked Lenny.

"Something's wrong," said Serge.

They kept staring.

"The site's not working," said Lenny.

"The customers must be having trouble deciding from our incredible selection of option packages. They're probably going into choice shock." Serge stood and stretched. "That has to be it. I'll get some sleep and check the mailbox in the morning before our first tour."

Lenny took a seat at the computer and began tapping. "I'm pretty rested from my nap. I think I'll do some surfing before I turn in."

*   *   *

"SERGE! WAKE UP!"

"Wha—What is it?" He sat up in bed, a crease from the sheets on his cheek. He looked at the bright bedroom window. Morning.

"I think we got a bunch of e-mail!"

Serge swung his legs over the side of the bunk bed and trudged to the computer, hair standing up. He clicked open the website's mailbox.

"It's completely full," said Serge. "I knew it!"

They high-fived, and Serge began scrolling with the mouse.

"How much money do you think we'll make? ' asked Lenny.

"Uh-oh, keep your pants on," said Serge. "It's all spam."

"Spam?"

"Junk e-mail. That's another thing about the Internet. It's an incredible technological revolution, but at a price. Every time decent folks log on, they're forced to realize there are division-strength armies of really twisted motherfuckers out there, doing all kinds of sick shit they couldn't have remotely imagined if it weren't for spam. Just look at these subject headers: 'Wild women, wild horses,' 'Barely legal teen facial cum shots,' 'Ever been fisted?,' 'Got Porn?,' 'Double-Dong Lesbo Action,' 'Ass Ventura: Crack Detective' . . ."

"Look," said Lenny. " 'All-natural penis extender.' There's a picture of a bowling pin."

". . . Except even this seems a little extreme, considering we just opened an account. . . . Lenny, what kind of websites did you visit last night?"

Lenny turned red.

"Well?"

"I sorta stuck my head in a lesbian chat room. Just for a minute."

"What name did you use?"

"Pamela."

"Just great. We'll be wading in cyber-sewage for weeks."

"I met a nice girl," said Lenny.

"What was his name?"

"*His?*"

"Lesbian chat rooms are just a bunch of fat guys in under-shorts eating bratwurst and logging on as Candy and Fawn."

"But that would be lying."

"You had virtual sex, didn't you?"

Lenny covered his ears. "I'm not listening anymore. Blah, blah, blah, blah, blah . . ."

Serge stared back at the screen and ran a hand through his hair. "Why isn't the site working? Have we skipped a critical step?"

Lenny uncovered his ears and lit a joint. "What do we do now?"

"Of course," said Serge. "We forgot to send out press releases."

"But you're a fugitive. Remember how all those reporters were looking for you?"

"You ever see how a newsroom operates?"

"No."

"If you're ever in hiding and want to be aggressively ignored by the media, send out press releases."

Serge spent the next hour dispatching electronic notices to all major South Florida news organizations. Then he prepared to close out the computer program.

A modulated voice from the laptop: *"You've got mail."*

"Hold on. What's this? A new e-mail. And it looks legit."

"Open it!"

Serge read the message and smacked Lenny on the back. "Our first customer." He picked up a cell phone and dialed the number on the screen. "Hello? This is Serge and Lenny's. We just got your e-mail. . . . Tomorrow morning? Let me see if we have an opening. . . . Yes, we can work you in. . . . How's ten o'clock sound? . . . Good, you know the rendezvous point from the web-site? . . . See you then."

Serge hung up. "We're in business."

"This calls for a celebration," said Lenny. "Let's party."

"No time. I have to rush-order some magnetic signs and make an exhaustive supply run." Serge pulled cash and credit cards from their haul of wallets. "And tell your mom we'll need to borrow her van. We won't be able to fit all the customers in the Cougar."

"This is getting exciting."

"They'll never look at Miami the same again."

14

TONY MARSICANO AND Two-Tone Bob had a late celebratory dinner at Del Frisco's. A bottle of burgundy. This was the best time, right after a job. They always had the veal.

"A toast," said Bob, holding up a glass of merlot. "To whatever the hell it was we stole."

Glasses clinked.

"You understand I have my reasons for not telling you," said Tony.

"I know, I know," said Bob, sawing meat with fork and knife, sticking a piece in his mouth without changing the hand the fork was in. "It doesn't bother me."

"Do we need more wine?"

Bob nodded, chewing. Tony snapped his fingers for the waiter.

Bob got up and tossed his napkin on the table. "I gotta take a leak."

"I have to make a phone call," said Tony.

They headed the same way out of the dining room and parted in the hall. Tony went to a pay phone and set his cell phone on top. For the important stuff, Tony only used pay phones.

Bob emerged from the men's room a little drunk. He heard Tony's voice. It was around the corner. Bob was about to walk right out, but he stopped and listened.

Tony finally hung up. Bob appeared.

"There you are!" said Tony, putting an arm around Bob's shoulders as they went back to the table.

The new bottle of wine arrived. Bob waited until the waiter left. "How come you wouldn't let me deal with the guard back there?"

"Not this time. The job had to be totally undetected. Otherwise what I took becomes worthless."

"Now I'm really curious. You sure you can't tell me?"

"Let's just say you can transport it totally undetected and it launders money completely."

"Because you're taking it with you when you leave on Friday?"

Tony's expression changed.

"I heard the phone call," said Bob.

"I have to go away for a while," said Tony. "I only kept it from you because it could get you in trouble."

Bob lowered his gaze. "I can't believe you're going to testify."

Tony reached across the table and grabbed Bob by the wrist. "I would *never* turn against the Family. You know that. But they have some bad stuff on me—I got no choice. So I offered them some of our competitors. Hell, the Palermos should give me a medal. I'm going to do what the Family hasn't been able to for five decades."

"If you've already struck a deal, weren't you risking it with tonight's job?"

"Just the opposite—it was no risk at all, a free shot. If I get away with it, I'm rich. If they catch me, they ignore it. It just falls on the immunity side of the balance sheet that they erase with my testimony. There's absolutely no way I'm going into the witness program on their pitiful allowance."

"Then I guess that answers the question about the stones. You obviously don't have them."

"What stones?"

"The missing ones from 1964."

"Who's saying that?"

"Everyone. Shit, are you completely out of the loop up here? That's the big talk back in Miami. You were the only one Rico allowed in his hospital room before he died. Everybody just assumed."

"That was loyalty."

"So you're actually going to walk away from it all on Friday?"

"No. Right now."

Tony set his napkin on the table and stood. "Let me get a good look at you." Bob got up, and Tony grabbed him by the shoulders; they hugged. Tony tossed a couple hundreds next to his plate. "Take care of yourself."

Bob stayed at the table and watched Tony walk all the way across the restaurant and out the front door into the warm Orlando night, the last time he would ever see him. Bob went to the pay phone.

"Tell Mr. Palermo he was right. Tony's working with the feds. . . . Just left a minute ago. . . . Goes into the program Friday morning at ten. . . . I heard the phone call. He's meeting them at Miami Executive Airport."

15

FOUR MIDDLE-AGED MEN in Michigan State alumni jerseys strolled down Collins Avenue on a quiet Miami Beach morning. A tall one, a skinny one, a bald one, a short one. They came to Four-teenth Street and made a left. They walked another half block and turned up an alley. They stopped and looked around. Grime.

"Are you sure this is the place?"

The tall one nodded.

"It can't be right," said the bald one. "Why would they want to meet here?"

"Guess it's supposed to be part of the experience."

"Are you sure about these guys? Where'd you find them?"

"On the Internet."

"Oh, great!"

"No, really. They had an impressive website."

"Anyone can put up a website."

The bald one watched a burly cockroach scurry up a wall covered with peeling dance-club flyers. "Let's get out of here. I don't feel safe."

The skinny one jumped. "What was that?"

"What?"

"That sound."

"You're imagining things."

"There it is again. It's coming from that Dumpster."

"I heard it that time, too."

They took cautious steps forward and peeked over the lip of the metal bin.

The garbage exploded. A mangy old man jumped up.

The alumni jerked back.

"I was here first!" said the bum, climbing out of the bin. He slammed his hand loudly against the steel side. "Dibs on everything in here."

"It's all yours," said the bald one.

The bum opened his hand to reveal a crumpled fast-food burger wrapper. "My lucky day. A whole bite left." He popped it in his mouth.

"Oooo! Gross!"

"Oh, excuse me," said the bum. "Did that upset you? I'm so sorry. I forgot all about my reservation at the *Four Fucking Seasons!*"

"I didn't mean it that way."

"I know how you meant it. Gimme a dollar."

"Don't give it to him," said the skinny one. "It will only support his addictions."

"C'mon, ya pampered prick, gimme a fuckin' dollar. I'm not going to buy malt liquor. I want an espresso." The bum pointed at the Cuban lunch counter across the street.

"In that case I guess it might be okay." The bald one slowly pulled a bill from his wallet with lingering indecision.

The bum snatched George Washington out of his hand. "Don't

be so damn melodramatic. It's only a dollar." The bum looked both ways and ran across the street to the lunch counter.

"At least we got rid of him."

"Are you sure this is where we're supposed to meet? It's taking forever."

"Just hold on—we're a little early."

"Ten more minutes and that's it."

"Don't look now."

The bum trotted back across the street, wiping his mouth on the back of his sleeve. "You waited for me."

"We're waiting for someone else."

"You think I'm just a bum, don't you? I can see it in your eyes. But I used to be somebody. You look around at all these homeless people on the street—every one of them used to be somebody. And I'm going to be somebody again." The bum pulled a stained wallet from his back pocket. "Check this out." He flipped it open to display a pink-and-white Florida lottery ticket in the transparent ID sleeve. "I'm going the be rich Sunday morning. This is my week; I can feel it!"

"If you didn't spend the dollar on that ticket, you could have bought your own espresso."

"What is your fucking hang-up with the dollar? You don't see me getting all bent out of shape about money, do you? God has blessed you with so much, yet you're so self-absorbed and ungrateful. Shame on you!"

"Sorry. I guess you're right."

"It's okay. Gimme another dollar."

"Why?"

"I need a beer."

"I thought the money wasn't for beer."

"That was the last dollar. But now I'm all wired from the caffeine. You did this to me. This is *your* problem now. You can't take me to the ball and expect me not to dance."

"I don't think I'm going to give you any more money."

"It's just a dollar, for chrissake!"

No response.

"Tell you what," said the bum. "Pick a number between one and ten."

"What for?"

"Just pick a number already! You know, you're a very difficult person to talk to."

"Four."

"All right, since you were so nice giving me the other dollar as well as the *next* dollar you're going to give me, this is what I'll do. Next week after I win the lottery, I'm buying me a candy-apple red Rolls-Royce. Always wanted one of those. But right after that, I'll come by and give each of you four thousand dollars. That's right, four thousand. No need to thank me—that's just the kind of person I am. You have my word. Yes, sir, when you see that red Rolls coming down the street, you'll know it's going to stop and a man in a fancy new suit will jump out and hand each of you four big ones!"

"I want to change to seven," said the short one.

"You idiot! He's not going to win the lottery!"

"Why not cover bases?"

"Because you're encouraging him!"

"Sorry, contest's closed," said the bum. "Gimme a dollar."

Tires screeched. A black Dodge van skidded up to the opening at the end of the alley.

The bum turned. "Oh, no. Not *those* guys!" He took off running and dove back in the Dumpster headfirst.

The bald one squinted. "I think that's them."

The four started walking toward the van, reading the magnetic sign on the side as they got closer: SERGE & LENNY'S FLORIDA EXPERIENCE . . . NOW FEATURING MOTELS OF THE TERRORISTS!

The passenger door flew open. A lanky man in dark aviator sunglasses jumped out. White sneakers, untucked floral shirt, .38 shoulder holster. He jerked his head around, then began urgently waving the four men toward the van with a windmilling motion of his arm.

"This is going to be so cool," said the tall one. "That fake gun really looks real."

"Hurry up!" yelled Serge. "This isn't a joke!"

The men each paid Serge fifty dollars as they climbed in the van. Serge slammed the side door shut and jumped back in the passenger seat.

"Hit it."

Lenny punched the gas and patched out, skidding around the corner of Washington Avenue. A moment later two police cruisers with sirens and flashing lights came flying up the alley, sending a trail of paper trash into the air. They stopped at the corner. One of the officers got out and looked around. He reached back into the car for the radio microphone.

The bum stood up in the Dumpster, annoyed at all the racket. He watched the police cars turn off their lights and drive away peacefully. He ducked back down in the trash. A merry humming emanated from the bin. The bum found half a bagel from Einstein Brothers. He sniffed it, took a bite. Suddenly a screech, doors slamming. The bum popped his head up again.

The black van was back at the end of the alley. The side door flew open. Four men in Michigan State jerseys scrambled out. They handed four guns back to Serge and began running away as fast as they could.

"Wait! Come back! I can explain!" yelled Serge.

"You're a madman!"

Serge pointed angrily. *"You can't handle the truth!"*

16

FOUR ELDERLY MEN in plaid pants and flat Scottish golf caps sat in a row of wheelchairs. The chairs rested near the box-seat railing at the horse track in Hialeah. Blankets in their laps. Four body-guards in back.

A gourd-shaped man in size-too-small Sansabelts waddled down the stairs from the venerable clubhouse. He stopped next to the old man at the end of the row and caught his breath.

"Mr. Palermo, we just got a call from Orlando. Afraid it's bad news." He leaned over and whispered in the old man's ear.

Mr. Palermo nodded.

The man stood back up. "What do you want us to do about it?"

Mr. Palermo made a slight motion with his hand. The man bent over again. Mr. Palermo spoke into his ear as a pack of race-horses thundered by the railing. Jockeys in yellow, scarlet, teal, orange.

The Sansabelts man stood up and nodded.

Mr. Palermo leaned forward trying to see the end of the race, but they were already leading a horse over to the winner's circle. He sat back and opened the program in his lap.

There was a beeping sound. It came from the pocket of a bodyguard. The guard pulled out an electronic device the size of a cigarette pack. "Mr. Palermo, time to check the pacemaker."

The old man nodded and took the device from the guard. He held it to his chest and pressed a button. The box automatically dialed a computer at the hospital. Data flew back and forth a few seconds. The box displayed a green light. The old man handed it to the guard again and smiled at what he'd lived long enough to see. "Technology. Amazing."

"Yes, it is, Mr. Palermo."

The old man raised an unsteady arm and pointed across the track, toward a sea of pink in the infield, hundreds of the track's trademark flamingos around a glistening lagoon.

"Those birds—I wonder how old they are," said the old man.

"I don't know, Mr. Palermo."

"I've been coming here since the track opened in 1925. I was a child. Did you know it was Florida's first major sports facility?"

"I didn't know that, Mr. Palermo."

The old man nodded. "Big social scene. Everyone came—Churchill, Truman, Kennedy. I remember Amelia Earhart making her national farewell here in 1937 before she flew away, never to be seen again. But the birds never fly away. There's no cage. Why do you think they don't fly away?"

The bodyguard shrugged. "Maybe they've gotten comfortable."

The old man nodded once more. He reached his right arm out again and moved it generally over the two hundred manicured tropical acres. "Still beautiful, like I remember." Then he moved the same arm up toward grandstands dotted with the occasional person here and there. "But they don't come anymore. There's no tradition."

"No, there isn't."

"Is it because of the cocaine?"

"I don't think so, Mr. Palermo."

The last race of the day ended. The air was cooling. Four bodyguards began wheeling four wheelchairs.

Sansabelts walked beside them. "Mr. Palermo, who do you want me to give the job to?"

The old man held up a hand for him to stop. "We'll talk in the car. You'll ride with us to the Fontainebleau. . . . You play cards?"

The man shook his head.

"Too bad."

Everyone was silent as the phalanx of chairs rolled toward a line of waiting limos. Sansabelts got in the backseat with Mr. Palermo.

"You sure you don't play cards?" asked the old man. "We play gin at the hotel."

"I've heard a lot about those games. They're legendary."

"The younger guys—none of them want to play gin. I blame the cocaine."

17

A BLACK VAN with magnetic door signs pulled up the driveway of a ranch house in Pompano Beach. Serge and Lenny moped as they came through the front door.

"How was business today?" asked Mrs. Lippowicz, knitting a religious toaster cover.

"Our customers ran away," said Lenny.

"Serge, you got a phone call," she said.

Serge jumped back. "Cops?"

Mrs. Lippowicz chuckled. "Why on earth would the police call?"

"Gave to their ball once. Now they won't leave me alone."

Mrs. Lippowicz made a loop with a big needle. "Some reporter from the newspaper. She mentioned a press release. I left her number on the fridge."

Serge grabbed Lenny. "This could be our big break!" He ran in the kitchen and snatched the number from under a pizza-delivery magnet.

Three hours later Serge and Lenny sat in a booth in the back of a dark bar. Across the table was a rookie lifestyles reporter in unfashionably large glasses and a green beret, jotting personal shorthand in a steno notebook.

"This is great!" said Serge. "We're really going to be in the paper? I've never been in the paper before. At least not in the light I'd like. Remember to tell them about the website. And the customized tours—that's important. Mix and match your stops, doesn't matter to us. Grave sites, famous hotel rooms, infamous crime scenes where you can still see blood if you look close enough, historic bars . . ."

"Like this place?" asked the reporter, bending over her pad.

"*Fox's?* Are you kidding? This place is 'the bomb.' That's what you kids are saying these days, right? I mean, look at the joint, stuck forever in the 1940s when it opened. Ultradark lighting, smoke, Mike Hammer vibes, neon martini glass over the door, red vinyl booths—the kind of place Joe Pesci might walk in any second, located on an up-for-grabs stretch of South Dixie Highway, cutting across the underside of the state below Miami, desperately tapering toward the Keys like a doomed escape route. The death of hope." Serge inhaled with pride. "Smells like . . . Florida!"

"So you decided to capture all that with an offbeat travel service?"

"What do you mean 'offbeat'?" said Serge. "In my world this is straight up the middle."

The reporter kept writing.

"Why? Is it better to be offbeat?" asked Serge. "You understand the media end of things better than we do. Will we get more customers that way?"

"Maybe."

"Then we're offbeat." Serge turned. "Lenny, we're offbeat from now on."

"Cool."

A waiter arrived with two sodas for the reporter and Serge, a White Russian for Lenny.

"What are your last names?"

"No last names," said Serge. "It's just 'Serge and Lenny's.' We're trying to build a mystique, like, 'Who *are* those guys?'"

"You also said something about solving mysteries?"

"Don't forget that part," said Serge. "That's the most important facet that distinguishes us from all the cheap imitation offbeat tours."

"How does it work?"

"While visiting all the best points of interest, we're also in the process of trying to figure out some of the area's oldest unsolved crimes. You get to see live, real-time casework, meet unsavory characters, even carry your own gun."

The reporter chuckled. "You don't mean real guns."

"Is that not good?" said Serge. "Again, I'm new at all this. Maybe that's what spooked those customers. Lenny, no more guns for the customers."

"This thing has milk in it," said Lenny.

"It's a White Russian."

The reporter was getting a kick out the guys. She began smiling. "Tell me about one of the mysteries your customers might see."

"Cold case, strange death. I'm thinking murder." Serge reached in his wallet and pulled out a yellow newspaper clipping, January 2, 1965. He handed it across the table. The reporter read the headline: ECCENTRIC STORYTELLER DROWNS IN NEW YEAR'S EVE PARTY TRAGEDY. A photo of a cop on the beach holding the shiny, dripping 1965 party hat.

"Doesn't mention anything about foul play," said the reporter. "A lot of drinking on New Year's Eve, old guy goes for a swim in the ocean. Stuff like that happens all the time." The reporter noticed a thumbnail mug shot of the victim. A resemblance. "You related?"

"My grandfather. Namesake. Sergio. Heard all kinds of stories over the years. I just *know* he didn't drown. Someone punched his ticket. He was always shooting his mouth about who killed Kennedy, when they were going to invade Cuba again, what the CIA was up to. Who knew the truth? He led a complex life, played with too many matches. He had big plans, but maybe they were too big. Or maybe he talked too much. He belonged to this gang, real hard-boiled cases. . . . What's the matter?"

The reporter was laughing. "That's pretty good. Is it like a noir script you've memorized for the customers."

"What are you talking about?"

The reporter stifled her laughter and went back to her note-book. "Okay, stay in character. I kinda like it."

Serge looked at Lenny. "What's she talking about?"

Lenny shrugged with a white mustache.

The reporter reached in her purse and took out a Canon Sure Shot. "Mind if I get a picture?"

"No problem," said Serge. He put an arm around Lenny's shoulder. "Smile, Lenny."

Flash.

"Mind if I get one?" Serge pulled out his own camera without waiting for an answer.

Flash.

The reporter bent back over her notebook. "Tell me more about your granddad's gang."

Miami Beach—1964

Eleven in the morning. Ninety degrees on the beach. Five men in hats and guayaberas entered the Aladdin Room at the Algiers. Drinks arrived. The bartender made change.

"Check it out," said Greek Tommy. "I got one of the new half-dollars." He held up a silver coin with the profile of JFK.

"That sure was fast."

"Did you read where Miami might get a football team next year?" said Mort. "Supposed to be the Dolphins or something. Danny Thomas is involved."

"Look who finally decided to finally show up," said Chi-Chi.

Sergio walked in the bar holding a small boy by the hand.

"Who's this shaver?" asked Tommy, pinching the boy's cheek.

"I'd like you to meet Little Serge, my grandson. He's from West Palm Beach."

The gang: "Hi, Little Serge."

"Pull my finger," said Coltrane.

Sergio let go of Little Serge's hand, and the boy began running laps around the bar as fast as his tiny legs could churn.

"Look at him go," said Tommy.

"Sure has a lot of energy," said Mort.

"They named him after me," said Sergio. "That makes me eponymous."

Little Serge ran by.

"What's he doing with you?" asked Moondog.

"My daughter's working Burdines this weekend, so I said I'd take him."

"What about his dad?"

"Has to play jai alai. It's the height of the season. So it's just me and Little Serge all weekend! . . . Hey, Serge, ready to have some fun?"

Little Serge ran by.

"What sort of stuff are you doing with him?" asked Tommy.

"I'm teaching him about Miami."

"What about it?"

"Like Overtown," said Sergio, snagging Little Serge by the arm on his next pass. "Remember me telling you about the curfew where black people have to go back to the mainland? Isn't that fucked up?"

Little Serge nodded. Sergio let go. The boy took off.

"Jesus, what are you talking to him like that for?" said Chi-Chi. "He's only three."

"Actually two, but tall for his age," said Sergio. "I want to prepare him. It's a Darwinian furnace of injustice out there. The sooner he accepts that, the happier he'll be."

Little Serge stopped running and tugged on Sergio's shirt.

"What is it?"

"Can I have a fucking soda?"

"Sure you can."

"Listen to how he's talking already!" said Mort.

"I know. Isn't it amazing?"

Moondog leaned down and gave Little Serge a light poke in the tummy. "I'm crazy about kids."

"Me, too," said Tommy.

"Sure is a cute little fella," said Moondog, crouching down in a playful boxing pose. "Despite the dubious lineage."

Chi-Chi checked his watch. "It's time. We have to go to the place."

A pink Cadillac convertible cruised down Collins. Buddy Holly on the AM. The car was crammed, six men in straw hats and guayaberas, not talking, arms resting on the tops of the doors, staring ahead in dark sunglasses as the warm Miami air flapped through their shirts. Little Serge bounded from lap to lap in the backseat.

"What's black and white and red all over?" asked Coltrane.

Little Serge shook his head.

"A wounded nun!"

Chi-Chi nodded toward the curb. "There's the asshole now."

The others looked over at the sidewalk. A gangly man in an untucked lime shirt and tortoise sunglasses walked past a telegram window. The Cadillac pulled alongside. The man saw the car and took off.

Chi-Chi hit the gas and stayed with him. "Manny! Stop! You're only making it worse!"

Manny didn't stop. He crashed into an old Cuban woman, groceries flying, bread stepped on. People shouted and cursed. The Cadillac screeched up and jumped the curb, cutting off Manny, who darted down the alley. The gang vaulted out of the car without opening the doors. Sergio carried Little Serge.

Manny tried to escape over a chain-link fence, but Greek Tommy caught him from behind, grabbing him by the belt. Manny's fingers tightened their grip through the holes in the fence. "No! Please don't! I promise I'll pay!"

"He won't let go!" yelled Greek Tommy.

The others grabbed the man's legs and pulled. They had him out horizontal, crying, still clutching the fence. "No! Oh, sweet Jesus! I have a family! I'm begging!"

Sergio stood off to the side, covering Little Serge's face with his hand. Little Serge grabbed the hand and parted the fingers.

Chi-Chi took off a shoe and bashed Manny's fingers with the heel. There was a loud scream when he let go, and they all went tumbling. Then the stomping began.

Another set of tires screeched at the end of the alley. A black Cadillac skidded up next to the pink one. Doors opened, thick men in seersucker got out and headed down the alley.

The biggest one stopped in front of Chi-Chi. "You have our money?"

"That's what we're doing now."

"Mr. Palermo wants his money. You run a sports book in this town, you pay tribute."

"I know. Just give me a minute." Chi-Chi kicked the man on the ground. "Gimme the money!"

"No more time. You're already late." The big man stepped forward and pulled a blackjack from his pocket. "Where do you want it?"

"Now, hold on!" said Chi-Chi. "If you're going to hit anyone, hit Manny"—pointing down—"He's the one with your money."

"I have to hit you."

"But we're just the middlemen. You'll get your money quicker if you hit him."

The goon shook his head. "Tried that once. Messed up our accounting." He looked at the guy on the ground. "Scram."

The man ran away. One of the goons took Little Serge by the hand and walked him to the side of the alley. The others formed a circle around the gang and closed in, the goons' shadows slowly falling over their faces.

Present

The young lifestyle reporter flipped another page, writing furiously. "Did you get any of this story from actual events?"

"Story?" said Serge. "What do you mean? It's all true."

The reporter looked up and stared.

"No, really, that's how all the trouble started. It got even worse after they teamed up with Lou. Man, Lou! Don't even get me started there. Lou's how the gang found themselves mixed up in the famous Star of India heist from '64."

"Never heard of it."

"You're joking, right? The Murph the Surf case?"

She shook her head. "What was it?"

"Just the biggest jewel heist in U.S. history! Dominated the papers for weeks. The story had all the elements: daring crime, surfing playboys, chic locale, wild sex parties with priceless jewels thrown in swimming pools, frolicking babes diving in after them. Then the net closes. Jealous boyfriend tips the cops. Surfers busted. But police are more concerned with finding the gems. They cut a deal and bring one of the suspects back to Miami to retrieve the rocks from his fences."

"I think I have enough for now," said the reporter, closing her notebook.

"That weekend the surfer and the cops zigzag all over Miami—we follow the exact route on Tour Option Twelve. The surfer makes a bunch of calls from pay phones to his underworld associates: 'Give the stones back, or I'll turn you in, too.' They arrange the handoff, but it only results in a frantic series of near misses, everyone too jumpy. On a false lead, the cops even put on scuba gear and dive in Biscayne Bay to check dock pilings. . . .''

The reporter pulled the strap of a purse up over her shoulder. "That about wraps it up."

". . . Meanwhile, the press stakes out the surfers' apartments, where beach bunnies are holed up, peeking through the blinds. The detectives stumble into the bunny nest with their suspect. The press pounces. The cops bolt, the reporters follow, the chase is on! The gumball rally winds all over the county, all night. Everyone even stopped and met up in a couple of bars before running back out to their cars trying to get away from each other again. The cops finally ditch their wheels, run across a parking lot and jump in a cab to get away. In the wee hours they recover the Star of India and a bunch of the other stones from an out-door bus-station locker on Biscayne Boulevard. But a dozen of the diamonds remain missing to this day, and I'm going to find them!"

"Good luck." Car keys jingling.

"Here—write this down in your notebook. I'm announcing a special offer today that you'll only get from Serge and Lenny's Florida Experience. Whoever is with us on the tour when we recover the stones gets a cut." Serge leaned back in the red vinyl booth and beamed with self-satisfaction. "How's that?"

"I don't think anyone else is making that offer."

"I didn't think so."

18

THE FABULOUS FONTAINEBLEAU.

Flamboyant, extreme.

The era's most famous architect, Morris Lapidus, unveiled her in 1954. The critics were horrified. The public came in waves.

So did the celebs. It was Frankie's place, and Dean's, and Jerry's. Elvis chose it for his welcome-home-from-the-army TV special.

It was the King Kong of Miami Beach. Twelve hundred rooms in fourteen stories forming a quarter circle around twenty acres of pools, gardens and cabanas. Attention to every detail, to make sure it was excessive enough. They painted a mural on the side of the hotel—*of* the hotel. No place was bigger in the fifties.

At the dawn of the new millennium, no place was bigger than South Beach. But that was thirty blocks below the Fontainebleau. The stars stopped coming. It wasn't Gwyneth's place, or Rosie's, or J.Lo's.

But not everyone forgot. The hotel still held a warm spot for the old diehards, the keepers of the flame.

A Thursday afternoon. A panting man in Sansabelts banged on the door of one of the hotels' massive penthouses. A weight lifter with a shoulder holster answered. The man stepped into a luxury suite the size of a blimp hangar, full of sun and sea from the spacious glass. In the middle of the room was a green felt table, four men in wheelchairs, four bodyguards. Drinks, cigars, a pile of playing cards. Gin.

The man caught his breath and approached the table with a newspaper under his arm. "Mr. Palermo, I think you want to see this."

He unfolded the paper and held it in front of the old man, open to the feature article about a peculiar new tour service. Mr. Palermo slipped on reading glasses and leaned his head back to make out the type. He took the glasses off and looked away. "Tell me what it says."

"It's about a travel company these guys are starting in Miami. It's got a picture of them."

"I didn't know we were against tourism?" said Mr. Palermo. The other card players laughed.

"Mr. Palermo, look at this." The man held out another newspaper. "This was the story on Rico Spagliosi's funeral, the one with all the photos we were so sore about."

Mr. Palermo nodded.

"Remember how one of the pictures was of that guy nobody knew who got in the scuffle with Tony?"

Mr. Palermo nodded again.

"Here's that picture. And now here's the new picture from the article on the travel service. It's the same guy."

"So an unstable citizen is driving a tour bus? So I should kill him for shoving Tony a couple times?"

"There's more. In the travel article, it says the guy's investigating the missing diamonds from the '64 job. Says his grandfather might have even gotten whacked over it."

Mr. Palermo folded his hands in his lap and stared out the window at the sea. "You don't think it was a coincidence that this man who is talking to the papers about the gems also just happened to show up at Rico's funeral?"

"No, do you?"

The old man smiled. "There are no coincidences."

"Mr. Palermo. We still haven't found Tony, and he's supposed to meet the feds tomorrow. Now this. Things are getting—"

Mr. Palermo raised a hand. The man stopped. The room was silent except for ice cubes as Mr. Palermo picked up a glass and took a slow sip of Cutty Sark. He set the drink back on the card table.

"Call our friends in California."

"Yes, Mr. Palermo."

The old man held out his right hand, making a dubious shaking gesture. "And find out more about this *offbeat* travel thing."

19

T HE FOUR MEN had been drinking for some time. Serge could see that as he swung the limo up the driveway of a strip club in a west Miami Quonset hut. He had gotten their e-mail through his website that afternoon. Serge rented the limo when the customers said they were high rollers and didn't do vans. They would pay extra.

The disheveled clients swayed on the sidewalk in the midnight wind. A line of cabbies from seventeen different nations had already picked up the scent. The limo raced up to the curb, and Serge jumped out. "Back off, boys. Let the big dog eat."

He held the limo's rear door open as the men stumbled inside. "Thank you for choosing Serge and Lenny's for all your offbeat travel needs. Welcome aboard . . ."—he read convention name tags as they got in—"Keith . . . Doug . . . Rusty . . . and Brad. This is one trip you'll never forget."

Serge got back into the driver's seat and looked over his shoulder. "What kind of place you want to start with? I know them all. Just name it!"

They said a bar.

"We can go to bars anytime. Miami is your oyster. A million better opportunities. Besides, we have our own bar." Lenny smiled on cue at the men. He sat opposite them in the back of the limo, wearing shorts and a tuxedo T-shirt, shaking a jigger of martinis. He leaned forward. "Psst, wanna buy some weed?"

"Weed?" said Doug.

"Lenny! Behave!" Serge laughed nervously. "He's just kidding. It's part of the underbelly. You're paying for that. . . . So what'll it be? Historic crime scene? Heroin shooting gallery? Celebrity grave?"

A bar.

"Suit yourself. A bar it is. But it'll be a great, historic bar."

Serge faced forward and put on a baseball cap with thirty-three enamel pins from South Florida tourist attractions and a blinking I ♥ MIAMI light on the visor. He turned the ignition. "We ride tonight!"

The limo worked its way through a desolate industrial stretch of town near the river. Half-submerged shopping carts, crime lights, people sleeping in boxes. He turned west on Seventh Street. "Please direct your attention to the crumbling art deco building on the right next to the half-completed highway ramp. It was used for exterior shots of police headquarters in *Miami Vice*. If you look closely, you can see the scowling ghost of Edward James Olmos in the upstairs window. . . ." He drove another block and turned right on South Miami Avenue, pulling up to an old concrete building shy of the river. They looked out at the vintage neon sign.

TOBACCO ROAD

LIQUOR BAR

'TIL 5 A.M.

"Here she is," said Serge. "Oldest bar in Miami-Dade County. Established 1912."

"I don't know . . ." said Doug.

"It's an institution!" said Serge. "Used to be a speakeasy where Capone hung out when he was down here working on his tan. Now an intimate blues joint."

"It's not topless," said Brad.

"The last place we were at, the girls had little stickers on their nipples," said Keith.

"Do you know a place that doesn't have stickers?"

Serge jumped out and opened the back door and began grabbing guys by the arms. "Get in there! Live the history!"—pushing them toward the door.

They climbed a tight staircase in clandestine red light and found two cocktail tables near the front. The singer belted an uncanny Muddy Waters. The men waved down a waiter. "Is there a titty bar nearby?"

A TWO-MAN FBI sniper team sipped coffee on the roof of Miami Executive Airport. Black jumpsuits, black baseball caps. The pair watched a twin-turbofan Gulfstream land. Bankers got out. The plane taxied to a hangar.

The snipers went back to debating the Dolphins secondary. Two more corporate jets touched down. One of the agents was opening the coffee thermos when a walkie-talkie squawked. The other answered it. He looked up at the horizon. "We're on."

A tiny spot appeared in the western sky. The snipers used binoculars and rifle scopes to comb the runways and nearby buildings, then a perimeter sweep of the underbrush on the opposite side of the mesh fence around the tarmac. The Lear grew larger and dropped landing gear, lining up its approach from the Everglades.

Four FBI agents in suits and dark sunglasses came out the glass terminal doors directly beneath the snipers. They stood between potted palms and folded their arms. The jet's rear tires touched simultaneously, the nose came down, then a whoosh of braking thrust-reversers. The Lear slowed to a stop, rotated at the end of the pavement and rolled back to the terminal. Someone kicked chocks under the tires. A small staircase flopped down from the hatch.

The waiting was always the worst, and now it was over. The agents began to untense with the plane safely down and engines off. The happiest was the agent in charge.

"Look sharp," said Miller. "Nothing can go wrong now. Just drive the witness back to headquarters, and it's promotions for everyone." He turned to Bixby. "This is going to be the crowning moment of my career. Remember this day. You're going to see history."

The jet door opened. Tony Marsicano stepped onto the top of the staircase, feeling like a million, not a care in the world, sipping soda through a straw. He started down the stairs.

The spotter on the sniper team scanned his binoculars slowly across the runway. Something caught his eye. "What's the . . . ?"

A black limo rolled up behind the plane. A magnetic sign on the door: SERGE & LENNY'S FLORIDA EXPERIENCE.

Before anyone knew what was happening, some guys had a gunnysack over Tony's head and were hustling him back to the limo. The sniper peered through the scope. "I can't get a clear shot. I'll hit the witness."

The agents down on the runway pulled their pistols. Miller jumped in front of them and spread his arms. "Don't shoot! You'll hit Tony!"

The limo's back door slammed shut.

"I have a shot now," said the sniper.

"Take it!"

The limo's back window shattered.

"To the car!" yelled Miller.

Four agents jumped in a Crown Vic, and tires squealed. The sedan swung around the back of the plane, gaining on the limo.

Bixby grabbed the dashboard. "Fuel truck!"

"Shit!"

From the rooftop the sniper team saw it all coming apart—agents scattering from the crashed Crown Vic, the pilot jumping from the plane, the fuel truck blowing with a fireball higher than where they were. They squeezed off a few last shots as the limo crashed through a gate and disappeared toward the city.

20

Miami—February 10, 1918

SERGIO GONZALES SURPRISED the world tonight.

He entered it quite prematurely in the back bedroom of a Coconut Grove bungalow. María and José proudly watched their six-pound son asleep in his crib, bathed in crisp moonlight filtering through palms and entering the open window on a bare breeze.

In the first weeks, the curious-eyed child slept so much it worried his parents. He would make up for that in time.

At the outset of the 1900s, the Grove was not the artist-hive, out-of-sight-real-estate market of today. It was frontier. Mosquitoes, no AC. The Gonzaleses' parents arrived from Cuba on an illegal steamer in the confusion of the Spanish-American War. Much soon changed. The Flaglers, Fishers, Tuttles and Brickells were living people, not causeways and bridges. In every direction: dredging, new streets, railroad spikes.

It was a hectic contrast to Sergio's family and their quiet village. They were fishermen, working the shallows of Biscayne Bay. When it was time, Sergio would take to the business, quickly developing hard calluses handling net and rope. But not catching fish.

In 1920, just after the Eighteenth Amendment passed, the villagers noticed a lot of new boats crowding their waterways, all these skiffs and powered dinghies. The Cubans braced for competition, but the other boats bypassed the fishing grounds, instead zipping into hidden mangrove tributaries and coves. They seemed to prefer running at night.

Soon the whole village became rumrunners. Sergio started riding along at age six; they taught him how much booze could draft which channel on what tide. In 1928 a man from Chicago bought a house on Biscayne Bay. Actually, he bought two houses—he lived in the one set back on the property, and the rum boats snuck into a secret dock underneath the one built right up against the water.

Sergio saw Al Capone only once, at a distance. They were delivering another load of Cuban rum. Sergio's father pointed out the gangster to the young boy. "You see that man on the seawall? He is an important man. Very smart and powerful. Watch him carefully—he has what it takes to make it in America."

Sergio watched. Capone was in the final stages of venereal disease, and the boy saw a bald man in a urine-soaked bathrobe giggling to himself and swatting imaginary insects. But Sergio accepted his father's wisdom on face and decided he still had much to learn about this new land called America.

Sergio was a respectful son, a diligent student and a ferocious trumpet player. Near high school graduation, things began to slide. It wasn't an all-out collapse, just pimples of odd behavior initially dismissed as youthful enthusiasm. It wasn't called "streaking" at the time, and people weren't nearly as amused. Then trouble with the trumpet. The first song Sergio learned was "Taps." He wouldn't let it go. Played it all over town, all hours.

Sergio got a ride home in the back of a police car after performing sixteen straight renditions next to a wedding on the beach.

Sergio's solid grades got him a scholarship at the new school opening up in nearby Coral Gables. Everyone called it "Cardboard College" because of mellow construction standards. Officially it was the University of Miami. The school promptly set about establishing a reputation for football.

In 1936 Miami proudly held its coming-out party, the first annual Orange Bowl game. The Magic City was ready to take its place as America's next great metropolis. The eyes of the nation were on a South Florida football field as the University of Miami hosted Bucknell.

Late in the first half, Bucknell held a narrow lead and kicked off to Miami. Sergio fielded the ball on the ten-yard line and made an unbelievable run up the right sideline to midfield. It was more unbelievable because Sergio wasn't on the team. Three cops tackled him.

No denying it now; Sergio was different. There were other quirks, some quaint, others very much not. Sergio would take a seat in a crowded restaurant and start clinking the side of his water glass with a spoon, like he had an announcement to make, or a toast. When the other diners became quiet and gave Sergio their attention, he'd look down and read the menu. Conversation resumed, minutes passed, Sergio began clinking his glass again, and so on until police gave him another ride home.

The judicial system didn't have mental-health treatment back then. They made you dig ditches. Sergio was hip deep in a gulley along the Tamiami Trail when the Japanese bombed Pearl Harbor and blasted him out of that ditch and into a sailor's uniform.

Almost overnight the military transformed Miami Beach into a subtropical Parris Island. A row of PT boats docked along Bayfront Park, a hundred luxury hotels became barracks, platoons marched on golf courses, Sergio did hundreds of jumping jacks on the beach. But then, he'd been doing that for years.

One day a photographer for *Stars and Stripes* asked Captain

Sergio to pose next to his PT boat. Then MPs arrested Sergio for impersonating an officer and threw him in the brig.

This time he got the help he so clearly needed. A military doctor prescribed a regimen of mild antipsychotics that cooled him out, and the VA continued refilling prescriptions after the war. Sergio became, as they say, a model citizen. Society didn't hear anything more from him for another twenty years.

West Palm Beach—1961

"The Fastest Game on Earth."

Sergio read the words on the cover of the thin program in his lap.

There was a loud crack like a rifle shot. Sergio looked up. A small, rock-hard ball ricocheted off the wall at a hundred miles an hour. Sergio's eyes followed it as a player in a yellow number-seven jersey dove and caught the ball with the curved basket on his hand. The player rolled once on the floor and came up with a mighty underhand swing.

"Watch out!"

The player in front of Number Seven hit the deck as the ball sailed through the space where his head had just been. The ball kept going, higher and higher, ending up in the padding above the wall with an impotent thud. Point lost. Number Seven lowered his eyes and trudged back to the bench as the next set of players took the court.

The crowd booed and ripped up betting stubs. "Who said you could play?" "Get outta town, ya bum!"

Sergio loved jai alai. He also loved his daughter. She was his only child. And just like Sergio himself, Gloria had made a surprise entrance into the world, but in a different way. Shortly after the war, a Collins Avenue burlesque dancer named Vavette tracked Sergio down to a tiny apartment in Surfside. She was a sucker for officers' uniforms, and there had been a brief but scorching tryst with a PT-boat captain. Then she learned Sergio wasn't an officer and summarily dumped him. Four years later she dumped Gloria. Dropped her off on Sergio's doorstep before hopping back in the passenger seat of a ragtop Valiant and speeding away with a lounge singer who looked like Sal Mineo.

Sergio watched the convertible disappear, then looked down at the big brown eyes staring back up at him. It was the best day of his life.

They became inseparable. He took her everywhere. The zoo, the beach. And jai alai. Fifteen years quickly passed. Through everything, she was always Daddy's girl.

The next game started at the West Palm Beach Fronton. Sergio leaned over to Gloria in the seat beside him. "Watch the one in the yellow jersey. The crowd doesn't like him, but he's the only one with any intensity." Sergio checked his official 1961 season program, running his finger down the entries until he came to Number Seven. "Testaronda."

Sergio and Gloria reflexively jerked their heads back as Testaronda dove for a shot and crashed headfirst into the screen in front of them.

"Boooo!" "Get off the court!"

Next round. Number Seven charged the service line and caught the pelota on the fly for what should have been an easy, dribbling drop shot. Instead he gave it all he had, like he did every time. He was so close to the wall that the ball was back to him in a split second, right in the stomach. Players and trainers rushed to the curled-up player on the floor.

"You stink!" "What a loser!"

Sergio stood and faced the jeering crowd. "What do you know? He's got heart!"

"Sit down, you old fart!"

"Daddy, sit down."

Sergio plopped into his seat and folded his arms. Gloria was leaning forward with concern. "He's hurt."

"He'll shake it off. He's tough."

"I hope he's all right."

Sergio watched her a moment. He hadn't seen this look before. He'd always taken it for granted that she was Daddy's girl, but now he realized for the first time that eighteen really wasn't a girl.

Sergio stood up. "Let's get something to eat."

"I want to watch jai alai."

"I don't like jai alai anymore."

"What's wrong?"

"Nothing. I'm hungry."

Sergio was quiet as he drove his Nash Rambler a few blocks to the Cesta Inn, a popular postgame pizza joint with beer posters in Spanish and action photos of jai alai players on the wall. They went inside and found a table. Sergio grabbed a newspaper left behind on one of the chairs.

A steaming pizza soon arrived. Gloria began picking things off a slice.

"But anchovies are the best part."

"They're too salty."

The front door opened.

"What are you looking at?" asked Sergio, turning around. The players had arrived.

Sergio popped one of Gloria's cast-aside anchovies in his mouth. "Playboys."

"I think Number Seven's cute."

"He can't play worth a darn."

"That's not what you said—"

"I say a lot of things."

The players came by the table, twenty, twenty-one years old, athletic builds, stylish slacks, smoldering Latin features.

Gloria had always been a shy youth, but it was out of her mouth just like that. "You played great today."

"Oh, thank you," said Number Seven.

"Is your stomach okay?"

"Just a big red spot."

"Do you get hurt a lot?"

"Yes."

"What kind of name is Testaronda?"

"Fake one. I'm really Pablo. Pablo Storms. Pleased to meet you." They shook hands.

The other players had taken a large table in back, and they called for Pablo.

"Just a minute." He turned to Gloria. "Would you like to join us?" Then, to Sergio, "I mean, with your permission, sir."

"Can I, Daddy?"

"Sure, go ahead. I wanted to read the sports anyway."

"Thanks, Daddy."

Sergio held the sports section up to his face, glaring over the top at the table of jai alai players and his daughter.

It was a quick courtship, lots of hand-holding sunset walks along the beach, Gloria occasionally turning around and waving at her father, walking ten yards back.

They were married on the fronton court before the daily double. The best man handed Pablo the ring in the bottom of his cesta. Sergio had since resigned himself. Deep down, he really liked Pablo, especially the intensity part, and he gave his daughter away with brimming pride.

Gloria came off the court and threw her bouquet into the cheap seats. Then she gathered up the train of her wedding gown and settled into a front-row seat as Pablo dedicated the next game to his bride.

The wedding night was unforgettable. Gloria applied ice to her husband's swollen right eye.

"Didn't you see the wall?"

"I thought I had another five feet."

Gloria instantly became pregnant. Soon, another curious-eyed infant boy entered the world. Gloria never had a second thought what to name him.

Sergio sat in a chair in the corner of his daughter's hospital room, cradling the newborn in his arms. "Hello, Little Serge. I'm your granddaddy."

Little Serge grew like crazy. He ate everything in sight, which he immediately burned off in a constant series of heart-stopping moments. His exhausted parents stood over Serge's bed each night as he slept hard from another full day of perpetual motion. He had inherited the combined intensities of Sergio and Pablo, and the results were exponential. He was obviously destined for something special. But what would that be? His parents thought of the future. They tried to image how Little Serge would apply his energies as an adult.

21

Present

EVERYONE JUST CALM the fuck down!" Serge yelled at the terrified tour customers screaming and crying in the back of the blood-splattered limo. "I've been here before. It'll all turn out fine if we keep our heads. Except for Keith, who's already dead, thanks to the sniper. Can't fix that. But the rest of you, take my word: If you do everything like I say, someday you'll all look back on this and laugh."

Doug continued weeping on the floor with his cell phone, telling his wife he wanted her to come get him. He began describing the limo.

"Lenny, take the wheel," said Serge. Lenny began driving from the passenger side as Serge climbed over the seat and snatched the phone from Doug's trembling hand. He slapped him back and forth across the face. "Snap out of it! Be a man!"

Serge put the phone to his ear. "Hello? Is this Doug's wife? . . . Never mind who I am! I've been listening to your calls all morning, and I want you to get the fuck off this man's back! Do you have any idea the kind of pressure he's under? People are dead! His life is in extreme danger, and the last thing he needs is your gutless yammering! If he survives, he'll call you when he's good and ready. Good-bye!" Serge hung up and began beating the phone on the wet bar until it started coming apart. He handed the biggest piece back to Doug. "My advice is to get rid of her ASAP, or you'll be in adult diapers before you're fifty."

"Want me to keep driving?" asked Lenny.

"No, Lenny. Let's just crash." Serge surveyed everyone still alive in the backseat. "Okay, first rule of crisis management: Don't panic. Second: Damage assessment. We're doing a hundred on the Julia Tuttle Causeway over Biscayne Bay in a shot-up limo with a couple of smashed windows, blood streaks on the others, a trunk lid flapping up and down and two bodies in the backseat"—Serge stopped and looked out the windows at the rest of the traffic—"which means we're pretty well camouflaged. What else? Oh, yeah. One of the dead guys is a top mobster, so the contracts on us are going out as we speak. And we killed him in the commission of a kidnapping—well intentioned as it was—which brings the death penalty in the Sunshine State. Am I forgetting anything?"

There was a moan.

"And Brad's been shot." Serge put his hand on Brad's back. "Brad, try to move your arm."

Brad looked away, moved his arm and screamed.

"Brad, don't move your arm. . . . Lenny, get me another cell phone."

The limo swerved into oncoming lanes as Lenny grabbed a Motorola off the floor and tossed it over his shoulder. Serge caught it and punched in a number. "Hello? Doc? It's Serge. . . . Yeah, I have a little situation. . . . A shoulder situation. . . . No, the situation did not go all the way through. I think the situation is still in there. . . . Good, I'll call back in two time units when I know the address of the banana. . . . Bye."

Rusty gave Serge a weird look. "What kind of doctor were you calling?"

"A pretty good one from what I hear."

"It didn't sound like a real doctor," said Rusty. "That's not how the conversations go when I talk to mine."

"There are all kinds of definitions for 'real,'" said Serge. "Right now we're *real* desperate. We can't go to a traditional hospital because they're required by law to report gunshot wounds. Does that sound fair? I mean, I can understand if you walk into an emergency room waving a gun and saying you just shot someone yourself. Then they pretty much have to call the authorities. But we're talking about the person who's *been* shot. You're already a victim, and now you have to explain things to the police. Maybe you don't feel like talking to them. I don't think you should have to explain a preference like that. Unfortunately, the way the law reads, if you want any privacy, you're compelled to go outside normal channels. And thanks to elitists at the AMA, it's gotten a bad name."

"What's gotten a bad name?" asked Rusty.

"Surgery on the secondary market."

"Stop the car!" Rusty shouted. "This is nuts! Drop us off right now!"

"No can do. Between the cops and the mob, you're dead out there, which means it'll lead back to me, and then I'm dead. I'm afraid I can't let that happen." Serge reached behind his back and produced a giant chrome .45 automatic.

Everyone screamed.

"Calm down! I'm just getting this ready. I'm not going to shoot you." Serge gestured at Rusty with the gun. "Look, I know how you feel, but a regular doctor is out. Besides, if you're going to get shot, you couldn't have picked a better place. We've got a whole network of great doctors in South Florida who've had just one or two itty-bitty little problems in the operating room. It's amazing how politicized hospital boards are now. So they're forced to set up more modest practices and pass the savings on to us." Serge pulled a booklet from a pocket behind one of the seats and tossed it to Rusty.

"What's this?"

"Our provider network. Go ahead, keep it. You might need it someday." Serge inspected the limo's interior again. "And those two bodies need to go. They'll only invite questions."

"My arm's getting tired," said Lenny.

"I'm coming back up."

Serge climbed forward into the driver's seat and took over the wheel. He aimed down Collins and made a right on Fourteenth Street, then a quick left, moving slowly up an alley, glass bottles popping under the tires. He stopped at a Dumpster.

"Lenny, gimme a hand," said Serge, dragging Keith's body out of the car by the ankles.

"You're just going to leave Keith in a Dumpster?" said Rusty.

"That's what they're there for. And while we're here, let's clear some of the trash out of the backseat. It's starting to look like a pigsty." Serge rounded up some mustard packets and Tony's smashed McDonald's soda cup and threw them in the Dumpster.

Then Lenny and Serge grabbed Keith by the hands and feet and got a swinging motion going. "On three! . . ."

Keith went into the bin with a deep metal thud. Then Tony.

Then an argument, the guys debating whether to make a run for it or stay with Serge.

"He's gotten us this far!"

"He's insane!"

"But we don't know this city! He does!"

"I'd love to stay and chat," said Serge. "But right now we have to get this car off the street and hole up somewhere until the doctor arrives and we can figure a few things out. Everyone back in the limo."

"Serge," said Brad, "the car looks awful. We can't keep driving like that."

Serge stepped back and rubbed his chin. "You really think so?"

"Serge!"

"Okay, if it'll make you feel better. You've been pretty cooperative up to now, considering everything."

He took off down the alley on foot and turned the corner.

"Don't leave us!"

He was back a few minutes later with a shopping bag from a Cuban sundries store on Washington. He pulled out masking tape and Glad trash bags, which he ripped into sheets and taped together to cover the limo.

"How are we going to drive it like that?"

"That's not for driving," said Serge. "That's to buy time. Stay here."

"Don't leave us!"

Serge left them.

"The guy's a psychotic!" said Doug. "Let's get out of here before he comes back. Now's our chance!"

"And go where?" said Brad, holding a blood-soaked towel to his shoulder.

"The police."

"Tell them what?"

"It was an accident."

"I'm more afraid of the mob," said Brad. "Let's stick with Serge until we can get out of town. Then we dump him."

"He's a lunatic!" said Doug. "Just ask his friend!"

They looked at Lenny. Lenny nodded.

"I'm with Doug on this one," said Rusty. "The guy's certifiable. This can only get worse. We have to get you to a doctor."

"I'm the one who's fuckin' shot!" yelled Brad. "And who's brilliant idea was that? Who said, 'Let's get even with Dave. It'll be a barrel of laughs'? If you didn't notice, they were shooting at us back at the airport! With real bullets! The only reason we're still alive right now is Serge!"

"Okay, okay, since you want to play the I'm-the-one-who's-shot card, we'll do it your way for now," said Rusty. "But the next thing that goes wrong—"

A motorized roar came down the alley. They turned. Serge

raced up on a Kawasaki 500, a shopping sack from a hardware store in his lap.

"Where'd you get that?"

"They rent these top-line bikes now, especially in youth destinations like Miami Beach."

"You rented it?"

"Way too expensive. Hot-wiring is much cheaper." Serge dumped the shopping bag's contents on the plastic-covered hood of the limo. Scissors, black spray paint, chrome car-bumper touch-up paint, pencils, ruler, stapler. He went to the Dumpster and pulled out some cardboard boxes. He sat down on the ground and drew templates on the boxes with the pencils and ruler. He picked up the scissors.

The others gathered around as Serge snipped away in concentration. He finished cutting and began folding, talked to himself: "Insert tab A in slot B, fold flap C . . ."

"What the hell's he doing?" asked Doug.

"Going completely crazy," whispered Rusty.

"I heard that." Serge finished folding and stapling his creation. Then he made a second one. He set them down in the alley and rattled the can of black spray paint, giving each two full coats. He pulled a newspaper out of the Dumpster, cutting shapes and taping them to the cardboard for detail work with the chrome paint. When he was done, he gestured proudly. "Ta-da!"

"That's not going to fool anyone," said Doug.

"Not if they're perfectly still and you're standing right over them, like we are now," said Serge. "But check this out. . . ." Serge put one of the contraptions on his shoulder and mounted the motorcycle. He took off to the end of the alley and turned around. Then he raced back and passed the group. He made another skidding spin at the other end of the alley and returned.

"What did you think?"

"Not a chance," said Rusty.

"It looked real to me," said Brad. "I bet it works."

"Of course it'll work." Serge yanked the plastic sheets off the car. "Lenny, I'm going to need you to climb up and lie right here. Doug, are you okay to drive?"

Doug nodded.

"Good. Everyone else in the car." Serge kick-started the Kawasaki. "Let's get this show on the road!"

TOURISTS ALONG COLLINS stopped and pointed. Others took snap-shots. Police up ahead saw what was going on and wondered why they hadn't been informed. They cleared pedestrians from a crosswalk.

The bullet-pocked, blood-flecked limousine continued a steady thirty miles an hour up the street, people running to the curb for a better view.

Serge rode alongside the limo on the motorcycle, aiming in the driver's window with his shoulder-mounted, twin-reel, profes-sional Hollywood movie camera. Made of cardboard. Lenny was on his stomach on the limo's hood, aiming his own camera through the windshield.

22

F BI HEADQUARTERS, MIAMI, Florida. White shirts, black ties.

Special Agent Miller was under fire. He had been responsible for taking Tony Marsicano into protective custody, and the business at the airport now hung over his pension like a midway mallet.

Files and teletypes covered Miller's desk, the corkboard on the wall full of overlapping index cards and photos. Agents began arriving for the morning shift in fresh shirts. Miller and Bixby had never left. Ties hung loose, hair mussed, perspiration stains in the middle of their backs. Cold Maxwell House in the bottoms of FBI coffee mugs.

Twelve hours earlier it had looked hopeless. No leads, just two bodies in a Dumpster and the magnetic signs on the limo, which were obviously fake. The mob was always disguising their vehicles like plumbing and cable-TV trucks. They checked the phonebook anyway. No "Serge & Lenny's," just as they'd suspected.

Then the big break. A routine search of local newspaper archives on the Internet.

"Come quick!" yelled Bixby. It was the article on the new off-beat travel service. "The guy in this photo looks familiar. And the article mentions the gems."

Agent Miller came over and stared at the grinning picture of the two men. "I don't believe it."

"What?"

Miller knocked over coffee running to the filing cabinets. He thumbed manila folders until he came to one with PALERMO on the tab. Miller dumped the file on the desk. Black-and-white photos flew everywhere. Bixby picked two off the floor. "What is it?"

Miller riffled through the pictures. He picked one up, stared at it a second and slapped it down hard on the desk. "I knew it!"

Bixby picked up the picture. "Hey, it's one of the surveillance photos we took at Rico Spagliosi's funeral."

"That's why he looked familiar. Because he is! That's the same guy who got into it with Tony. I told you that was no coincidence."

Miller and Bixby kicked a junior agent off the computer with the new facial-recognition software. They scanned in the surveillance photo. It was a grainy, long-range shot. The search came back with two thousand possible hits. *Incomplete data.*

"What about the license from the Cougar at the funeral?" asked Bixby. "We ever run that?"

"Shit." Miller raced back to his desk and retrieved his notebook. He typed the tag into the computer. Registered to one Lenny Lippowicz, last known address: a burned-down shotgun shack in Tampa. Miller logged on to the website for the Hillsborough County property appraiser and input the street address. Owner of record: Storms, Serge. Then he cross-searched the name with the two thousand possible hits off the photo.

Forty seconds later a single hit from the FBI database in Quantico. An old arrest mug of their boy popped up on the screen.

Serge A. Storms, suspect in four South Florida homicides, wanted for questioning in nine more. The computer spit out a thick rap sheet.

Miller flipped the pages. "Holy Mary!"

"All those murders . . ." said Bixby.

"Must be a button man for the Palermos," said Miller. "They had him whack Tony."

"We have to inform the local police," said Bixby. "This now goes way beyond the Marsicano case."

"Not a chance," said Miller. "Do you know what kind of embarrassment this would be for the Bureau? The protection program will lose all credibility. Besides, this is Miami. Who knows what police are on the Palermo payroll?"

They dove back into the case with renewed vigor. Miller worked the phones, Bixby the computer. Another pot of coffee. The sun started coming up. Arriving colleagues hung jackets on hangers.

"Another all-nighter?" asked one agent.

"Shhhh, he's concentrating," said another. "He's rereading the part in the manual that says we're supposed to protect witnesses, not kill them." They walked away laughing.

"Miller!" yelled Bixby. He pointed at the computer screen. "They have a website."

"Must be for coded communications."

"It's got lots of cool pictures. . . . And there's a number to call for reservations."

"So there is," said Miller, flipping open his notebook.

The fax machine started up.

"I'll get it," said Bixby.

He came back to Miller's desk with a torn-off piece of thermal paper. "You're not going to believe this."

"What is it?"

"A personal letter from Serge."

"Let me see that." Miller put on his glasses and snatched the fax, a copy of a red-flag letter the Secret Service had just turned over to the Bureau:

Dear Mr. President, The Mac Daddy W, Scourge of the Axis of Evil etc., etc.

The White House
1600 Pennsylvania Avenue
Washington, D.C.

What a first term! Fuck! I thought I was watching Independence Day *there for a while. And who would have thought you'd rise to the occasion after all those things they said about you? What the hell did they mean, "not smart"? Don't they understand that's the crucial part of your genius? The United States has lacked a credible deterrent for too long. Until you came along. And a brilliant strategy it is, giving off the impression you don't think things through all the way. Guess what? It's working! Even our allies are jittery. Well, I say, take it up a notch! Next time one of those pissant potentates starts with the saber rattling and bad-mouthing us like he even has a country for any reason other than we let him—storm into the press-room and pound the podium, yelling that he's embarrassed you in front of your squeeze (Laura) and must apologize and dis-arm immediately. If that doesn't do it, start struggling with the National Security guy who carries the nuclear football in his briefcase. They'll be shitting themselves for weeks. Of course, it will all be carefully orchestrated, and Colin and Condoleezza will restrain you while Rumsfeld dives in the audience, attack-ing reporters ("Look what you're doing to him!"). Then you break free, run to the microphone, and point menacingly into the CNN camera: "How'd you like me to pour you a nice big cup of Shock and Awe, motherfucker?!" . . . Right, I know what you're thinking. You can't say "motherfucker." But why not? These are crazy times demanding new ideas. And I'm just the guy. I know you've been disconnected from the street your entire life, so that's where I come in. This is about primal posturing, and nine out of ten alpha males from my 'hood prefer "motherfucker" to "evildoer." It's simply a matter of proportion. After all, we drop those 10,000-pound daisy-cutters that immolate the primary radius, suck all the oxygen out of the air and kill everything else by rupturing individual cells with sonic concussion. (By the way, how do those things work? I've been slapping together my own home version but can't get past the trigger mechanism.) So, in conclusion, if invasions and assassination are back in play, I think you can say "motherfucker" a few times. Think about it (but not too much, ha ha ha). . . . I know, I know. You're worried about the press. They've been so unfair. You let me take care of that. A few well-placed "visits" will quiet that kind of biased talk in a hurry, because it's hard to type with two thumb casts. As you can see, I have lots of fresh proposals that you're probably not hearing from your oil-gorged yes-men. I'm down here in South Florida patrolling the perimeter, conducting my own counter-espionage sweeps of the drug-binge motels on U.S. 1 and hanging out at Miami International looking for all those strangers offering to pack our luggage. But I can be up there at a moment's notice. I'll understand if you don't think we should be seen together, so I've been studying satellite photos and various websites and have discovered a tiny fissure in White House security. I can slip in undetected and meet you late some night in the Lewinsky Room. Meantime, always remember: You're a Bush. That still carries a lot of weight, even for Jeb, who especially needs it with his weeny-aggressive disorder and that weird-shaped head. And just think: After your upcoming landslide reelection, only four more years until you're barred by the Constitution from another term and free to get back to full-time heavy drinking. Heaven knows you deserve it. I knew you were one of us when I read about the DUI. The press got all wadded up again, but America understands. I'm riding down Collins*

Avenue right now and my driver is drinking. Smoking dope, too. I heard about the coke, so I'm just assuming you're into weed as well. I'll have Lenny bring the good stuff when you call. Until then . . . you da man!

> Your faithful agent in the field,
> Serge A. Storms

P.S. Did you recognize my writing style? It's Lincoln!

23

A TEAM OF valets rushed down the driveway of the Sheraton Bal Harbour, hoping for the huge tips that traditionally come from film crews.

Lenny and Serge quickly collapsed their cardboard movie cameras and stowed them in the trunk as a herd of men in white shorts arrived with the clapping of sneakers on pavement.

"You're really shooting a movie?"

Serge nodded.

"What's the title?"

"*Death of a Valet.*" Serge handed him the keys. Another kid in shorts got on Serge's motorcycle. He handed each a ten-spot.

"Thanks!"

Serge pointed at the big brass luggage carts by the front door. "We're going to need a whole bunch of those. Got all kinds of film gear."

The hotel staff began unloading suitcases, steel boxes, VCRs, stereos, giant boat coolers and a large green molded plastic case with JOHN DEERE on the side. The luggage-cart convoy followed Serge into the lobby.

"Know what this place used to be called?"

Nobody answered.

"The Americana! One of the most famous spots on the strip . . . Hey look! They still have the skeleton of the old terrarium in the lobby, only they took out the glass."

An Irish flight attendant with strawberry hair and a cute little blue cap sat on the curved couch around the atrium. She smiled when she saw Serge and held up two fingers. Serge nodded. She winked and headed for the reception desk.

"What's going on?" asked Rusty. "Who was that?"

"Bridget. We should be in our room in just a few more minutes."

"Who's Bridget?"

"Our discount ticket. Whenever I'm in town, I call her to check into hotels for me and get the airline-employee discount," said Serge. "I operate a professional travel outfit. Just because we're running for our lives doesn't mean we stop thinking about value."

"What was she signaling with two fingers?"

"Two adjoining rooms," said Serge. "Or she wants a curveball."

Serge walked up to the desk and began talking to the agent handling Bridget's check-in.

"Know what this place used to be called?"

"I just know it's the Sheraton."

"The Americana!" Serge gestured across the lobby at the atrium. "Morris wanted to put monkeys in there."

"Uh, can I help you with something?"

"Yes! Bring back the *Today* show! Dave Garroway used to film it right over there. I'm already working on that myself, personally writing Katie Couric, but the form letters I'm getting back give me the impression they're mistakenly throwing my correspondence in the nut pile."

Serge turned and pointed at the ceiling, addressing the bell-hops forming a line behind him with the carts. "President Kennedy stayed on the top floor after the motorcade brought him here November eighteenth, four days before Dallas. And over there is where they filmed the wedding of Lisa Kudrow and Billy Crystal in *Analyze This*. Of course, that was much later."

The receptionist handed Bridget her magnetic keys. She headed for the elevators.

"Follow that flight attendant!"

The bellhops were winded when they finally pushed the carts into the tenth-floor oceanfront suite. Serge handed out more ten-dollar tips. "Here sonny, buy yourself some crack." He marched across the room and onto the balcony. "What a view!"

Bridget joined him. She put her arms around his neck. Serge grabbed her wrists and pulled them away. "Control yourself! I'm working!"

The guys glanced at each other.

There was some arguing they couldn't hear. Bridget stomped back into the room with tears.

"Oh, all right," Serge called after her. "Then will you leave me alone so I can get some work done?"

Serge went in the bedroom. Bridget brightened and trotted after him. The rest of the gang ran to the doorway.

Serge drew the blinds open wide, then stood in the middle of the room and looked around in thought. He pulled the king bed away from the wall, spun it ninety degrees and pushed it across the floor until the headboard was against the balcony window. "Okay, Bridget. That works for me."

He noticed the stack of heads in the doorway. "Would you mind?" Serge walked over and slammed the door. They put their ears against it.

They didn't hear anything at first, then Serge's voice. But what was he saying? It was a monotone, rattling a long tangent in even cadence before suddenly breaking into quick drama like a Univision soccer play-by-play man. Then a sultry Irish female voice: *"Yes! Yes! Yes! Yes! Yes! . . ."* Finally piercing shrieks.

A few minutes later, Serge opened the door and saw a bunch of ears. The guys wandered away and picked up magazines.

Bridget came back in the main room, hair frazzled, beret crooked, staggering with a dazed, codeine grin. She passed the guys, opened the front door and left.

The gang stared in awe at Serge, tucking in his shirt.

"Man, the hoops these days to get a travel discount." He headed for the TV set. "Everybody settle in and relax. Nobody can find us here."

A knock at the door. Serge spun and pulled a gun. "Who the fuck!" He crept across the room and checked out the peephole. He stuck the gun in his waistband and undid the chain. "Lenny, you might want to hide your dope."

"We're carrying drugs on us, too!" said Rusty.

"It's all right. Lenny's a bishop in the Coptic Church." Serge opened the door. "You might as well come in."

Two more women. They stormed into the suite. Tall, exotic, even more striking than Bridget. One an athletic young Lena Horne, the other a statuesque Scandinavian blonde.

Lenny grabbed his heart. "City and Country!"

"How dare you ditch us on the side of the road like that!" yelled the blonde.

"It was for your own good," said Serge. "You were out of control! All you wanted to do was get high and fuck!"

The guys glanced at each other again.

"How'd you find us?" asked Serge.

"Lenny's mom told us."

"Lenny! You told your mom we're at this hotel!"

"I called her from the lobby. You know how she worries."

City and Country sat cross-legged on the floor in front of Lenny. "Got a joint?"

"Sure." He reached in his shirt pocket.

"Just wonderful," said Serge, throwing up his arms. "The All-Hemp, All-the-Time Channel is back on the air!" He began opening boxes and luggage, removing file folders, electronic components, the Miami Collection.

Rusty slid up next to Serge and glanced at the women. "City and Country?"

Serge grabbed the big hotel TV, turned it around in the cabinet and went to work with pliers. "Traveling companions from past misadventures. We had to dump them—they were irresponsible." Soon, coax and RCA cables ran everywhere, his towering audio-visual Mission Control taking shape.

"What are you doing?" asked Rusty.

Serge handed him a file folder. "Check out the dossier."

"Dossier?"

"For our tour. I've got all these archival photos, Xeroxes from library microfilm, ticket stubs, letters, highlighted maps—"

"Serge! Jesus! Forget the tour!"

"Forget the tour? *Forget the tour?!*"

Lenny passed the joint to Country. "Uh-oh. You shouldn't have said that."

"Forget the tour?" Serge pulled the gun from his waistband. Rusty and the others put their hands up and leaned back as the gun barrel swept past them. "We never forget the tour! The tour continues!"

Lenny snagged some beers from one of the boat coolers. "Serge, you're scaring them."

Serge looked down at the gun in his hand. "Yikes! How'd that get there?" He tossed the pistol on the couch and stuck a video in the VCR.

"Dig this. It's Alfred Hitchcock's *Notorious* from 1946. There's Cary Grant and Ingrid Bergman in that convertible riding along the moonlit Miami waterfront. Notice how peaceful and empty it is. Just palm trees and water, no development yet, if you can believe it—"

Another knock at the door. Serge jumped and grabbed the gun

again. He checked the peephole, opened the door and jerked someone into the room. "Glad you could make it. He's in the bathroom."

"Who's that?" asked Rusty.

"The doctor for Brad's gunshot."

The doctor came out of the bathroom with an extension cord and handed it to Serge. "Can you plug that in?"

"I noticed the doctor was wearing a Corona T-shirt," said Rusty. "I mean, he does have medical training, right?"

"Oh, absolutely." Serge stuck the plug in a socket. "Licensed and everything. At least used to be. Ten years a spotless record, then he amputates one wrong leg in a Tampa hospital and the papers blow it *way* out of proportion."

The sound of power tools came from the bathroom, barely drowning out the screams.

Serge yelled over the noise. "Doc, want a beer?"

The machinery stopped, but the screaming didn't. "What did you say?" shouted the doctor.

"Beer?"

"No thanks. Just had one." The machinery resumed.

Lenny got up and changed the TV to a local station, a news crew broadcasting live from the airport.

"Lenny, I'm doing a presentation."

"Sorry, thought you'd finished. . . . Hey look, we're on TV!"

A reporter teased to the big shoot-out at the airport that would be coming "right after these commercial messages."

Everyone crowded around the set. Commercials for the car show, the boat show, the computer show, a new restaurant with Old World charm. Then the news.

An aerial shot of the Miami skyline at dusk with a busy highway interchange in the foreground. A computer-generated explosion detonated in the middle of the picture. Out of the smoke came a glowing numeral five. Urgent, fast-paced music.

"Welcome to Action Five News! And the Action Five News Team, with your anchors Natalie Rojas and Blaine Crease, and featuring the Action Five investigative team—'If you can't find something out, we'll try!'—plus Andy with sports, Bing with the weather and Captain Bob on traffic. . . . And now Natalie and Blaine!"

"Good evening," said Natalie. "Our top story tonight: An early-morning melee erupted at a South Beach drag show when patrons discovered one of the female impersonators was actually a female. The woman, who suffered minor abrasions and goes by Jerome Mendelson, told police that society wasn't ready to accept a male transvestite trapped inside the body of a woman."

"Can I get a diagram of that story?" Blaine chuckled, then pivoted to another camera. "More bodies were unearthed today as authorities continued questioning neighbors about the man who lived alone in this modest frame house in Homestead with his two dogs and several thousand wind chimes and had no prior record except noise complaints. . . . Natalie?"

"In other developments, one of the peripheral figures in the Elián González saga is back in the news tonight." A picture of one of the fishermen appeared on the screen. "Blaine?"

"Thanks Natalie, dozens were hospitalized today when fighting broke out downtown between large groups of Cubans and Italians over the rights to Latin Appreciation Day. And on the domestic front, is there a common substance in your home that could kill you in the next few hours? We'll tell you at eleven!"

Picture cut: "I'm Andy De Laporte at the sports desk. When we come back: What will last weekend's arrests mean for the Dolphins' playoff hopes?"

Picture cut: "Don't forget about this big mass of cold air at the top of the map that could ruin everything."

Picture cut, helicopter whapping sound: "And if you're taking the Don Shula home tonight, don't."

More commercials. An attorney specializing in bedsores: "Because it's just wrong . . ."

Lenny nudged Serge. "When are they going to get to our story?"

"They always save the best for ratings. . . . Shhhh! They're coming back!"

Blaine shuffled papers and looked up. "The Baby Jennifer custody case took a turn for the complex today when a second Baby Jennifer case was discovered in South Florida, bringing the total number of parents to sixteen. . . . Natalie?"

"Thanks. And at the airport, it was another day of chaos . . ."

"This is us! This is us!" said Lenny.

The station went live to the smoldering, charred husks of a Learjet, tanker truck and FBI sedan being hosed down by men in yellow hazmat suits. The gang listened to the voice-over with the latest details.

Serge whistled with respect. "Wow, you killed a mob boss *and* a government witness!"

Doug and Rusty stood in front of the TV, getting woozy as an FBI spokesman described the massive manhunt under way.

"Serge, please bring us someplace and drop us off," said Rusty.

"Are you kidding? You'll be picked clean!"

"We'll take our chances."

Doug gestured toward the entertainment center. "You're obviously busy with your special videos and all—"

"Don't forget the gems," said Serge.

"That's what I mean. We'll just be in the way. We're going to head down to the lobby now and get a cab."

"Not a chance," said Serge. "I would never do that to you."

"Serge, I'm begging."

"Exactly. You're desperate—your judgment's clouded. But we're used to this. Been here a million times. Notice how normal we're acting."

Lenny unrolled a Baggie. "Serge, you got any old albums in one of your boxes? Preferably a two-record set."

"Just CDs."

"How do they expect us to de-seed dope?"

Doug grabbed the arm of a chair. "I have to sit down."

Serge patted him on the shoulder. "You're in good hands."

The doctor came out of the bathroom, wiping hands on a formerly white towel, now pink.

"Well?" said Rusty.

The doctor shook his head. "I lost him."

"What do you mean you lost him?" yelled Doug.

"Did everything I could."

"It was just a flesh wound!" yelled Rusty. "What kind of doctor are you?"

Serge stepped between them. "One who makes house calls on the weekend and deserves just a little more gratitude." Serge looked at the doctor and shrugged. "Everyone expects miracles."

"Listen, Serge, you think I can get cash this time? My bank's been a little funny lately about checks."

"No problem."

The television showed a family tree of the Palermos, then some grisly assassination photos from sidewalk restaurants.

Doug grabbed his chest. "I can't breathe. Having trouble breathing."

"Doc, I think he's having a panic attack."

"Two beers," said the doctor, tucking twenties in his billfold.

Serge snapped his fingers. "EMT Lenny, get the trauma kit and stabilize the patient."

"Right." Lenny gripped a joint in his mouth, opened the boat cooler again and fished a pair of Heinekens from the bath of melting cubes.

"You guys are insane! You're going to get us killed," said Doug, opening his mouth wide like a sea bass to get oxygen. "I can't take it anymore!"

The doctor reached in the cooler for his own beer and headed out the door. Rusty ran in the bathroom to check on Brad.

Doug began breathing in the plastic bag that came with the hotel wastebasket. He took it away from his face. "Serge, we can go to the police. If we tell them everything, maybe they'll put us in a protection program."

"Right," said Serge. "Tony Marsicano was in a program, and a lot of good it did him."

Doug began crying. "They're going to kill us!"

"Nobody's going to kill anyone," said Serge, sitting down next to Doug and putting his arm around his shoulders. "Remember, we still have the big advantage. The main thing going for us is that nobody knows who we are. Neither the FBI nor the mob. Now that we're out of the limo and safely in this hotel, there's no way they can connect us. We're home free!"

Serge's cell phone rang.

"Hello? Serge and Lenny's . . . Yes, we were at the airport today. . . . Who wants to know? . . . Yes, I've heard of the Palermo Family. . . . How'd you get this number? . . . From the magnetic sign on the side of the limo? I guess that was money well spent. . . . Kidnapping? No, that was just a big misunderstanding. . . . Calm down, threats never solve anything. . . ."

Doug stared blankly at Serge, growing faint. Serge saw his expression and gave him a big smile and a thumbs-up.

Rusty walked slowly out of the bathroom, eyes fixed, shallow breaths. "I can't believe it. Brad's really dead. The doctor was right."

Serge covered the phone. "I told you he was a good doctor."

Rusty collapsed on the floor. Doug ran in the bathroom and threw up.

". . . Calm down," Serge said in the phone. "Stop shouting. . . . Lower your voice. . . . I'm not going talk to you anymore if you don't lower your voice. . . . You're shouting again. . . . No, I wasn't involved personally. I was just the driver. . . . That was my customers' doing. . . . Yes, they're right here. . . ."

Serge walked over to Rusty and held out the phone. "It's for you."

Rusty wasn't responding, just making himself into a fetus on the floor, so Serge held the phone to his head. Rusty listened and began sobbing. Doug staggered out of the bathroom with spit-up on his shirt.

Serge took back the phone. "You finished? We were just about to watch a movie. . . . Where's Tony now? . . . How should I know? . . . We let him out of the car as soon as we realized our mistake. . . . Believe whatever you want. . . . I already told you to lower your voice. . . . Lower your voice. . . . Fuck you, too." Serge hung up.

Rusty and Doug stared in shock.

"Don't worry, he'll call back. That's the only language they understand."

Doug put his hand to his mouth and ran in the bathroom again. Rusty passed out. Serge slapped him lightly on the cheeks until he came around.

"Good news and bad news," said Serge. "Which first?"

No response.

"Okay, bad news first. Remember that big tactical advantage of anonymity I mentioned earlier? Well, we can pretty much forget about that. . . . The good news? I have a plan!"

Serge went over to the sofa and picked up his pistol. "First, we get back some leverage. . . . I can see by that thoughtful look in your eyes that you're asking, 'But, Serge, how on earth do we do that?' I'll tell you. By kidnapping one of *them*."

Doug ran for the door to escape, but Serge caught him from behind before he could unbolt it. He was wiggling and kicking pretty good as Serge lifted him up and carried him back into the room.

"Look," said Serge, "I'm not any happier about this than you are. We're only still alive because they want Tony back, which is obviously out of the question. As soon as they realize Tony's dead, our bargaining position is weakened considerably. We need a Palermo that's still breathing to trade for our lives."

Serge got on the phone to a second limo-rental company. ". . . Here's where I need it delivered. . . ."

THE NEW LIMO was even longer than the first. Lenny aimed it down Washington Avenue. Serge sat in the passenger seat writing on his clipboard. He looked over his shoulder. "Everybody okay back there?"

City and Country said they were getting hungry. Doug and Rusty stared without blinking.

"Sorry about herding you into the car at gunpoint. You were dragging your heels a bit."

Lenny played with the radio. "If we're going to kidnap someone, we should have ski masks."

"Right, Lenny. Why don't we just pull over at one of Miami's many ski shops?"

"What about pantyhose?"

"Miami has those."

The limo swung into a Walgreen's.

24

1964

LOU WAS IN the diamond business. Quite by accident.

A canary yellow '61 Cadillac convertible raced south on Washington Avenue, a postcard of every excess Miami Beach had come to represent. Behind the wheel, an immense man in charcoal pinstripes. A pinkie ring hung over the side of the car. All the maître 'd's in the finest restaurants knew him on sight. Al Lorenzorelli, also known as "Big Al," "Fat Al," "Third-Helping Al," "Let Me See the Dessert Wagon Al."

But nobody was looking at Al as the bright yellow car rolled through the intersection at Lincoln Road, past the club where Desi Arnaz was discovered moonlighting from his job cleaning parakeet cages. Nobody was looking at Al because they were all staring at his passenger. Al's bowling trophy. A tall bottle-blonde with Nancy Sinatra hair wrapped in a leopard scarf. Dark cat's-eye sunglasses in ruby frames. White go-go boots. A tight mustard Pucci-print top and equally snug avocado slacks that matched her dangling costume avocado earrings. Chewing gum and smoking filterless Lucky Strikes, watching her ice-cube-size engagement ring sparkle in the Florida sun. Lousiana Rhodes, the gun moll from Fort Lauderdale. Lou.

The light turned red at Fifteenth Street, and the Caddy rolled to a stop. Big Al squeezed Lou's knee with his right hand and leaned over for a kiss. Lou's hand shot up to block him. "Watch the fuckin' makeup!"

Al's hand came off her knee. He reached across his chest to deliver a cracking backhand across her smart mouth.

Before he could, tires screeched. Three shiny black Cadillacs boxed in the yellow one. Men jumped out with tommy guns.

"Tony Spumoni says hello." They opened up with a deafening fusillade. Metal shell casings clanged to the ground. Blood spurted everywhere. Louisiana shrieked in horror.

"My clothes!"

Doors slammed. Cadillacs sped off.

Louisiana was still cursing as she snatched her zebra purse off the seat, slammed the passenger door and nearly broke a heel climbing to the curb. The car was such a bloody mess that the men on the sidewalk could barely keep their eyes on Lou, all curves and gams, stomping out her cigarette and marching angrily up the street toward a pawnshop.

Roy "The Pawn King" leaned over his glass countertop, reading *Hollywood Confidential*. Bad Boy Robert Mitchum was at it again. Roy had a street face like Karl Malden. A white, short-sleeved clerk shirt. Thin, oily hair combed back. Dandruff.

Bells jingled. Roy looked up. "Lou, good to see you." He noticed the red splatter on her clothes and more on her cheeks. "Another engagement called off?"

"These fucking guys! They're animals!" She strained to pull the ring off her left hand and tossed it. The ring bounced on the glass counter, and Roy used his stomach as a goalie before it could go off the edge. "How much?" asked Lou, popping a bubble with her gum.

Roy stuck a jeweler's glass in his eye. Lou lit another Lucky Strike.

Roy removed the magnifier. "I'm a small operation. All I can give you is ten. But I have to tell you it's worth a lot more."

"I'll take it," said Lou, blowing smoke rings toward a shelf full of trombones.

"Lou, I'm worried about you. This is the fourth time in six months."

"It's not like I'm *trying* to do it. These guys have absolutely savage tempers."

"You're starting to get a reputation," said Roy, sticking a key in the cash drawer. "Nobody wants to go out with you."

"Al did."

"Of course he did. He was the size of a piano."

"That's just like men," said Lou, scratching an armpit. "They act like barbarians, and *I* get the bad rep."

Roy handed her Kleenex and a mirror for the blood on her face.

"Thanks, Roy. You're a sweetie."

"It's the type of guys you pick. I have this cousin, Ralph. Real quiet, prepares taxes—"

Lou shook her head. "I need a dangerous man. Otherwise I can't get turned on."

Roy chuckled. "That's my Lou." He counted out money. Another set of smoke rings went toward a stack of hi-fi record players. Long, hot-pink nails tapped on the counter.

Roy slid the cash in a brown envelope and handed it to Lou, who stuffed it in her purse and pulled out a flask. She twisted off the cap and took a pull.

"You're making a pretty good living at this," said Roy. "If I didn't know you better . . ."

"Roy, for chrissake, I'm in fuckin' mourning! I just became a widow or something."

"When's the funeral?"

"Don't know yet. He's still out there in traffic."

"How do your nerves handle it? I'd be shell-shocked."

Lou took another pull and stuck the flask back in her purse. "I'm holding up."

"I mean, you were with Rocky DiPesto when they stabbed him with ice picks, and Benny Sardines when they put that bomb in his lunch box, and Little Ricky 'Don't Call Me Ricardo' when they tied him down in the quarry and ran over him really slow with a steamroller. Feetfirst."

"That was a rough one," said Lou, stubbing out her cigarette. "On the other hand, that's also how I got to meet Vito 'The Noodle' Lombardini. Can't tell you how sexy he looked up there working those steamroller controls."

"And who would later be found decomposing in an underwater grate at the sewage plant."

"Sexiness is all timing." Lou got her flask back out and raised it for another shot. Just a couple drops left. "Damn."

"The Deuce is open."

"That's what I was thinking. Thanks for everything, Roy."

A pair of white go-go boots swaggered up the sidewalk. Pairs of men's dress shoes stopped and turned as the boots went by. Wolf whistles. The boots made a left at Fourteenth and crossed the street toward a lounge on the corner with the alley.

Lou pushed open the door under a green-and-orange neon sign from 1926. CLUB DEUCE BAR.

It was bright as noon outside, barfly black inside around the double-horseshoe counter. The way Lou liked it. She leaned against the juke with her left arm, avocado ass cocked, Lucky Strike in her lips like Lauren Bacall. She dropped a dime in the slot. "Twist and Shout."

A man's voice: "Great selection."

She turned around.

Broad shoulders. Perfect suit, million-dollar smile. "Name's Vince."

She offered her hand to shake. "Lou." He bent down and kissed it instead. She saw the gun bulge under his jacket. Her heart fluttered. *Rrrrrrrrrow!*

Vince was the consummate gentleman. He bought her martinis, lit her cigarettes with a pearl lighter, held the door to the men's room when they went inside for a quickie.

Two punching bags in suits stood outside the restroom door, standing guard for Vince. Lou sat atop the toilet tank in her black lace bra, legs hoisted. Vince proposed mid-orgasm.

They dressed and returned to the bar. Vince pulled the diamond ring off his pinkie and slipped it on Lou's left hand as they left the Deuce arm in arm. Two men were waiting on the roof.

ROY "THE PAWN King" handed Lou another Kleenex. "You got some more blood by your nose."

"This is getting ridiculous," said Lou.

"I thought they just dropped safes on guys' heads in cartoons."

"Me, too," said Lou. "Believe me, it's not something you want to see twice."

Roy checked the latest ring under his jeweler's glass. "How does five sound?"

"Fine." She struck a match and lit a Lucky.

Roy pointed at the ashtray on the counter. "You already have one going."

Lou stubbed them both out. "Maybe it *is* getting to me."

"I'm telling you, Lou, you need to meet someone who's not in the outfit."

"You might be right."

Bells jingled. They looked toward the front door.

25

Present

THE COLLEGE FOOTBALL teams were announced for the upcoming Orange Bowl. Big press conference. Buffet, open bar, crepe-paper streamers in team colors. The next day the Miami Chamber of Commerce blew a gasket. The reason lay in the middle of a conference table, the morning paper.

It was that snotty, know-it-all, thinks-he's-so-cute sports columnist from New York, Mick Dafoe. Were they forgetting anything? Oh, yeah. Prima donna.

Every year, the same thing. The Orange Bowl rolled around, supposed to be the biggest national publicity windfall for the city. Every year, the chamber went all out to put on the best face, painstakingly covering up every local disgrace.

And every year, like clockwork, Dafoe penned his annual column mercilessly ridiculing the city in the name of morning-coffee entertainment. Then the column was picked up by the wires and reprinted across the country.

This year's offering was the harshest yet:

"And now, with apologies to David Letterman, the Miami Chamber of Commerce's Top Ten Rejected Tourism Slogans. Drumroll, please.

"10. Miami: It's like a whole other country. Really.

"9. Return to paradise—your flight back home.

"8. English, Schmenglish.

"7. The kind of elections that make you forget about our riots.

"6. Home of the Fighting Miami Relatives.

"5. Gateway to Little Haiti.

"4. Cocaine: It's not just for breakfast anymore.

"3. Come for our friendly people, stay for our penicillin.

"2. *Fear Factor*, 24/7.

"And the number-one rejected slogan by the Miami Chamber of Commerce:

"Krome Avenue Detention Center is for lovers."

The chamber wasn't laughing.

"I'm complaining to the publisher!"

"I'm writing a letter to the editor!"

"I'll strangle him with my bare hands!"

The media-savvy image consultant told them to take it easy. They were approaching it all wrong. "You never pick a fight with people who buy ink by the barrel."

"So what do we do, then? Nothing?"

"No," said the consultant. "Schmooze him. It works with most reporters, especially sportswriters. They usually roll over for a hot dog and commemorative tote bag." He laid out the plan—spare no expense with an offer for a free "advance research" trip. Fly the writer down early on a private jet, put him up in the finest hotel, take him to the best restaurants, then a "souvenir" shopping spree, all ostensibly to show off the side of the city he's apparently overlooking. It can't miss.

The chamber staff got on the Internet, looking for a tour service that would give Dafoe the best possible take on the city. An assistant scrolled down the screen. Something called Serge

& Lenny's caught her attention. She thought a second, then kept going until she found someone a little more mainstream.

Mick Dafoe was sitting in his New York office throwing pencils into acoustical ceiling tiles when the gold-embossed invitation arrived. He began laughing. Sure he'd take the trip. Then he'd destroy them in another column. And they would be paying for it all. This was too good!

THE CHAMBER OF Commerce called out the troops. Hundreds of smartly dressed people waited on the edge of the runway at Miami Executive Airport. There was a high-school band, a red carpet, balloons, giant Stalinesque photos of Dafoe on sticks for the crowd to wave. A white courtesy van sat near the terminal: "Sunshine Tours."

The Lear came into view. Everyone straightened up.

The jet landed and rolled to the red carpet. The crowd erupted in rabid ovation when Dafoe appeared in the door, smiling smugly, a Yankees baseball cap on his head backward. The giant signs waved furiously as Mick made his way down the stairs.

The chamber president's chest was puffed out. "This'll make him forget all about the crime rate."

Dafoe reached the bottom of the steps and headed across the carpet. A limousine with a magnetic sign on the door pulled up. Serge and Lenny got out wearing pantyhose on their heads. The same pair. Dafoe heard the commotion and turned around. "What the . . . ?" The conjoined twins threw a gunnysack over his head and hustled him into the limo. They sped away.

The volunteers' cheering dribbled off, the signs with Dafoe's giant face falling by their sides. The chamber president sagged. "Why do we even bother?"

26

FBI HEADQUARTERS, MIAMI.

Miller and Bixby were pushing into the third day on catnaps, caffeine and career fear. Fatigue took its toll. Mistakes made, details forgotten, simple tasks becoming needless imbroglios. The other guys were worried, not making fun anymore.

Miller snapped a pencil in frustration. Bixby jumped. The fax machine went off.

They ran for it. Miller tore the sheet off the spool and began reading.

Bixby looked over his shoulder. "What is it?"

"Another letter from our boy."

"What's it say?"

"Shhhh! You'll get your turn."

Miller's lips moved as he read through to the bottom. His eyes narrowed in puzzlement. "What the hell does that last part mean?"

"Let me see," said Bixby, grabbing the page.

Katie Couric

NBC Studios, Peacock Central
New York, New York

Dear Ms. Couric,

I understand you are extremely busy with all your guests and everything. And an amazing lineup it is, at least at the top of the hour. But as you get further into the program, when we reach the segments on quack medicine and bizarre self-recovery books for the totally screwed-up, I can see that pained expression on your face—what a bunch of weirdos!

That's why I've been patient. But I've sent you at least two dozen letters now without a single reply except the early form letters and that photograph of Al Roker with the forged signature. Did you really think I would fall for that? I took it to a handwriting expert, which was the bill I also submitted, but no response there either. So I have to ask myself, What the hell is going on?

First, let me apologize for the third letter. I'll take the blame for that. You should see all the outgoing personal correspondence to muckety-mucks I have to contend with each morning. That white powder was from the doughnuts I was eating. Hoo-wee! I can just see the scene I created! I was thinking it might have gotten me on some kind of list, so I wanted to clear that up right away and let you know I'm a serious businessman. As I said before, I represent the Miami Beach Renaissance and History Task Force. It's just a one-man operation right now. I don't want to misrepresent our clout and count my friend Lenny just yet, because he still has some substance problems he needs to conquer before we get him on board your show.

My generous offer is essentially the same. You relocate your program from New York to Miami Beach, and I promise I'll give you a hundred-and-ten-percent. It may not sound like much, but don't underestimate me. Others have.

Besides, Miami Beach is a natural for Today. Dave Gar-

roway broadcast from the Americana forty years ago, and I think we all have more than a little obligation to the past. Miami Beach helped make Today *what it is; it's only right to repay the favor. I've been in touch with the mayor's office and have total commitment of his resources. What do you say?*

Look, let's not kid ourselves here. Good Morning America *has been eating your breakfast lately, and I'm sure neither one of us is happy with* that *development. I mean, Diane Sawyer and Charley Gibson! You must be throwing up around the clock over that galactic miscarriage of justice. But it's been building for some time now.* Today *has been plagued by four decades of missteps so monumental and mind-numbing that they can only be attributed to blanket incompetence or deliberate sabotage.*

Just ask yourself the following questions:

Why was the genius of Hugh Downes squandered on Concentration?

Who leaked the Bryant Gumbel memo?

What, if anything, does Gene Shalit bring to the table?

Which writer came up with the feature you have every year, 'Where in the fuck is Matt Lauer?' or whatever it's called—fire the guy.

Who told Willard Scott to go after the hundred-year-old viewers? You can't find their ratings share with an electron microscope.

What happened to Jane Pauley? Was it something to do with Doonesbury's *editorial slant? You can tell me if it was, and I'll take steps.*

And then what the hell happened to Deborah Norville? People were changing chairs so fast, I thought my cable company had shuffled all the channels again.

Of course, that last departure was necessary to pave the way for the Katie era. I know you didn't have anything "official" to do with it. But, between you and me, good move. You did what you had to. I've lived in the South and, believe me, her type is nothing but trouble.

In short, you need to start taking chances. A major shakeup is in order, and I'm your man. If you think Bryant's memo scorched some britches, wait till you see mine.

You can make an appointment by calling me, or I can just come up to New York for a surprise visit. I saw you once up in the Rainbow Room atop the GE Building, but I didn't get a chance to introduce myself before the misunderstanding with the staff that resulted in me being offered the option of leaving on my own or with help. Everyone's so friendly up there!

Waiting by the phone,

Katie Fan Numero Uno
Serge A. Storms

P.S. We'll soon be arriving in the Beatles' room, so you can reach us there.

LENNY DROVE WITH a six-pack between his legs as they made their second getaway from Miami Executive Airport in as many days. Serge sat in back with the prisoner. He pulled the gunnysack off.

"Hey, this doesn't look like Johnny Palermo," said Serge, covering Mick Dafoe with a pistol. "Lenny, are you sure you got the right airport?"

"There's more than one?"

"You idiot!"

"Sorry."

"Wait. I know this guy from somewhere. But where?" Serge studied his face, then flickered with recognition. "Yeah, I remember now. He's that smart-ass sports columnist. . . . Man, I love your stuff! The other guys crank out fish-wrap tripe, but you're like a daily dose of literature!"

Dafoe's eyes stayed on Serge's pistol.

Serge noticed him looking at the gun. "Since I'm a fan, this won't be necessary."

Dafoe didn't know what to think, whether to be scared or

angry. He spoke tentatively: "Did the chamber put you up to this?"

"The chamber?"

"Chamber of Commerce. Is this a practical joke?"

"No, this is real." Serge turned to Lenny. "Real *stupid!*"

"I said I was sorry."

"Wanna hit?"

Dafoe turned around. A hand was offering him a lit joint. Dafoe was about to say no when he noticed the hand was attached to a drop-dead Scandinavian named Country, seated next to the equally stunning City.

Dafoe looked back at Serge. "What's going on?"

"It was supposed to be a kidnapping," said Serge. "But *somebody* can't read a map!"

"You're not kidding, are you?" said Dafoe.

"Don't worry, you weren't the target. Supposed to be a mobster."

Country tapped Dafoe on the shoulder. "Want a hit or not?"

"I guess I could do a *little* hit." Dafoe took a drag and handed it back to Country, who inverted the joint in her mouth and blew City a shotgun.

Dafoe didn't mind seeing that. "Are you two lesbians?"

"No."

"Darn."

Lenny reached between his legs and popped a couple beers off the six-pack ring. He put one in the driver's beverage holder and held the other over his shoulder. "Your friend want a beer?"

"Yes, that's a great idea!" said Serge. "How about a beer for the greatest sports columnist in the world?" He popped the top and handed it to Dafoe. "Welcome to Miami!"

Serge got out a polishing rag and went to work on his chrome .45. "Yes, sir. I don't think most people can grasp the level of your brilliance. They don't know how to read anymore, completely missing the allegorical references and subtle symbolism, like that hilarious time you called Baseball Commissioner Bud

Selig a syphilitic pimp for allowing the world-champion Marlins to be cannibalized for spare parts."

"Thank you."

"So Whitmanesque!" Serge noticed Rusty and Doug, catatonic. He slapped each of them on the knees. "Hey! Don't you know who this is? It's Mick Dafoe, the famous sports scribe! Isn't that exciting? This makes my whole day! . . . Lenny! Tunes!"

"Roger." Lenny grabbed a Soup Dragons CD, the first of several excellent selections.

"*. . . I'm free to do what I want, any old time . . .*"

Country passed Dafoe the joint again, down to a nub. "I'll roll you another." She pulled out a pack of Job 1.5s. Dafoe had never seen this side of Miami. He had another drag as the stereo changed songs.

"*. . . Don't you love her madly? . . .*"

"Relax," said Serge, passing him another beer. "You're among friends."

Dafoe accepted the can and reassessed his situation. A few minutes ago he'd just touched down in Florida, standing in the doorway of his airplane looking out at that chin-tucked crowd, utterly dreading the relentless chitchat and glad-handing on the cocktail circuit of local shakers with spinach dip in their teeth. Then suddenly he's plucked off the runway and thrown in the back of a stretch limo, where he was now sitting with a beer in one hand, a joint in the other, listening to the Doors, ogling two hot babes personally rolling him more doobies while some guy tells him he's practically the best writer who ever lived. Dafoe looked out the window at the palm trees and rippling blue water and windsurfers in T-backs going by at ninety. He took another hit and nodded: I'm starting to come around on this city.

Country finished rolling and expertly twisted the end in her mouth. She handed it to Dafoe.

"Say, can I sit over there between you two?"

"No."

"Darn."

The limo suddenly lurched. "What was that?" said Serge. It lurched again.

"Lenny, what are you doing?"

"It's not me. Something's hitting us."

Serge looked out the back window. A van rear-ended the limo again, then swung out and pulled along the driver's side.

Serge lowered his electric window.

The passenger in the van lowered his. "Give us back our customer!"

"No way!"

The van sideswiped the limo.

"Give us back our customer!"

Serge pulled his head in the window and speed-loaded the magazine of his .45.

Lenny glanced in the rearview. "Who are those guys?"

"Sunshine Tours," said Serge. "They think they're *so* offbeat."

Serge finished loading and stuck his head out the window.

"Last chance!" yelled the van's passenger. "Give us back our customer!"

Serge answered by shooting out the right front tire, which quickly came apart, strips of belted rubber sailing into windshields of other cars. The van swished back and forth on the rim before veering off the road.

Serge leaned farther out the window and fired a parting shot into the radiator. "Who's offbeat now, motherfucker?"

The phone rang.

"Serge and Lenny's . . . Yes, I remember our last conversation. . . ." Serge covered the phone and smiled at Rusty and Doug. "I told you they'd call back." He uncovered the phone. ". . . Look, remember last time when I told you we didn't know where Tony was? Well, actually we killed him. . . . Because we didn't like his looks! What difference does it make? . . . We shot him. He went quickly, didn't suffer. . . . I thought I told you about raising your voice. . . . Hey, Spanky, you may have time to gab, but I'm trying to run a small business here. . . . If you don't like it, then stop calling me! Fuck yourself!" Serge hung up. "There, done. We can cross that item off the to-do list."

Rusty and Doug didn't look so good. Serge clapped his hands sharply. "Wake up!"

The phone rang.

"Serge and Lenny's . . . You again? . . . What do you mean, you don't care about Tony? I thought that's what this was all about. . . . Oh, it's the *gems* you really care about? . . . You'll let us live if we give them to you? . . . Yep, we got the gems. . . . Sure, you can have them. . . . Just let me take care of a couple loose ends, and we'll meet. . . . Thank you. . . . No, thank *you.* . . . Well, I shouldn't have gotten upset either. . . . Talk to you soon. . . . Hug the kids. Bye." Click.

"W-w-why'd you tell him we have the gems?" asked Doug.

"Because it's what he wanted to hear," said Serge. "That's the number-one rule in life: Always tell people exactly what they want to hear at all times. It's the lubrication of society; otherwise the world would grind to a cracked-cylinder halt. 'Betty, love your hair.' 'Great report on the merger, Dick.' 'Yeah, I got the gems.' "

"But we don't have any gems," said Doug.

"Then we better find some, don't you think?"

"And we trade them for our lives?"

"Hell, no! I'm keeping 'em!"

"But they're going to kill us!"

"Reality check: They're going to kill us anyway. You can't trust the mob. And you definitely don't want to start doing business with them. They won't ever let you go. Blood vendettas, *omerta,* magazine subscriptions . . ."

Doug and Rusty became faint. Serge slapped his hands together again. "Come on! We have some gems to find! Who wants to be a millionaire?"

27

1964

THE GANG WAS holding court in the lobby bar of the Deauville Hotel. Guayaberas, straw hats, bandages and slings. Chi-Chi read the newspaper, February 17.

"Where's Sergio?" asked Moondog.

"Late," said Chi-Chi, turning the page.

"Anything good in there?" asked Tommy.

"Buy your own paper."

"Come on."

"Jack Ruby goes on trial today."

A car honked outside. And honked.

Chi-Chi looked up from his paper. "Who's making all that racket?"

More honking. They went to investigate.

Sergio was parked at the curb in a sporty new convertible they didn't recognize. Little Serge bounced up and down in his lap hitting the horn.

"What are you doing?" asked Chi-Chi.

"Teaching him to drive."

"Don't you think you're rushing him?"

"He already steers great," said Sergio. "Made it over the causeway all by himself. I just worked the pedals."

"What kind of car is that?" asked Moondog.

"Called a Mustang. Not even supposed to go on sale for two months, but I know a guy at the dock. Isn't she sharp?" He opened the door and got out. "I don't know why they haven't been making them like this all along."

"How much?" asked Chi-Chi.

"Twenty-three hundred."

Mort raised his eyebrows at the amount. "That's a lot of money for something that size. I'd want one of those new Cadillacs. I like to stretch out."

A car door slammed across the street. A woman's voice: "You!"

"Uh-oh," said Sergio.

The woman waited for traffic to clear, then strutted across Collins. The men could almost hear brassy burlesque music as they watched those legs and hips, a triple-scoop of Rocky Road packed in tight, glittery turquoise pants. Stiletto heels, jade Bakelite bracelets clacking together. Chewing gum.

"Where have you been!" she yelled.

"I, uh, with my grandson."

"You were supposed to pick me up an hour ago!"

Sergio looked at his watch. "That late?"

"Button it!"

The guys glanced at each other. What a loud, pain-in-the-ass piece of trash! They were in love.

"Aren't you going to introduce us?" asked Chi-Chi.

"Yeah, who's your friend?" said Greek Tommy.

Sergio lifted Little Serge out of the car and set him on the sidewalk, and he immediately ran out into traffic. "Guys, this is Louisiana Rhodes. You can call her Lou."

"Don't call me shit!" She stuck two fingers in her mouth and made a loud, shrill whistle that stopped everything. "Serge! Get out of the fuckin' street!"

Little Serge's ears perked. He ran over to Lou and reached for her hand. She walked him into the bar.

Sergio turned to the others. "And she's great with kids."

They went back in the lounge.

Lou tossed her zebra purse on the bar and lit a filterless Lucky. "Somebody buy me a drink."

The guys crashed into each other getting money to the bartender.

Little Serge began a long series of somersaults across the floor.

"Did anyone see the Beatles last night on *Sullivan*?" asked Sergio.

"I thought they were on last week," said Tommy.

"They were, but that was from Sullivan's New York studio. Last night they broadcast from this hotel."

"I didn't hear about that," said Tommy.

"From the Napoleon Room," said Sergio. "They're staying up on the eleventh floor right now."

"They need haircuts," said Chi-Chi. "They look like girls."

Lou did a shot of whiskey and slammed the empty on the bar. "I think they're cute."

"They're pretty cool guys," said Chi-Chi.

"Nice, too," said Sergio. "I was telling them—"

"You do not know the Beatles!" said Chi-Chi.

"We were partying pretty late," said Sergio. "Met them at the Peppermint Club on the causeway, but they started getting mobbed, so I suggested we head to the Castaway. More private."

"Look, there's something in the paper about it," said Tommy, pointing over Chi-Chi's shoulder at an article in the *Herald* with a photo of a chimpanzee wearing a wig.

Mort got the bartender's attention. "Turn up the TV."

News on the black-and-white set. A segment about a brouhaha

at the weigh-in for the big championship boxing match. The wide-mouthed face of Cassius Clay filled the screen.

"I hope he loses," said Mort. "He's too obnoxious."

"That's just an act," said Sergio.

Chi-Chi scooted up next to Lou and tried to form a rare smile, but it came off dyspeptic. "Do you know anything about boxing? It's pretty exciting once you learn some of the basics. I can tell you all about it."

Lou yanked a notebook and pen from her purse. She clenched the cigarette in the corner of her mouth. "Okay, what kind of odds you giving?"

"On the fight?" said Chi-Chi.

"No, dipshit, the weather. Of course, the fight . . . Come on, speak up. What's the vig?"

"Why?" asked Chi-Chi. "What's going on?"

"I'm not here for my health," said Lou. "I'm going to straighten out your sports book. You guys are a fucking joke on the street. From now on I give the orders."

"You're muscling in?"

"If there was any muscle to muscle in on," said Lou. "Who's off by the most?"

"That would be Joey Asparagus," said Tommy. "Owes us six large."

"That money could really help us," said Mort.

"Guys!" said Chi-Chi. "I started this book!"

"Shut up!" said Lou. "You're a silent partner now." She wrote something, then stood. "I know where to find him."

They headed for the lobby. There was a loud commotion. A large female mob shrieked and jumped up and down in front of the elevators. The doors opened. Four mop-top heads bobbed through the crowd to some cars waiting at the curb. The crowd ran outside and chased the cars down the street. Sergio and the gang piled in Chi-Chi's pink Cadillac.

An hour later the Cadillac cruised over Biscayne Bay on the

Rickenbacker, the Platters on the AM, Lou behind the wheel. Banging from the trunk: "Let me out!" They came over the crest of the bridge, and Sergio pointed. "There it is, Little Serge! There's the gold dome! The one I was telling you about!"

Lou eased off the causeway on Virginia Key and pulled into the parking lot of the Miami Seaquarium. They unlocked the trunk and got Joey Asparagus out. Lou had a crowbar in one hand, pistol in the other. She poked the gun in his back. "Move!"

They headed for the elevated monorail at the entrance.

28

LENNY AND MICK Dafoe wheeled a stuffed shopping cart across the parking lot to the waiting limo. They popped the trunk. Serge stood lookout as the two transferred purchases into boat coolers.

"Remember," Mick told Lenny, "one cooler for alcohol, one for grub."

Lenny jammed a bottle of vodka down in the ice. "Mick's going to show me how sportswriters set up shop on the road."

"Are you two bonding or something?" asked Serge.

They nodded. The coolers were soon full, and Mick added a top layer of ice, carefully sculpting the cubes around the provisions with his hands. They all stepped back in admiration.

Serge whistled. "Look at all that shit."

"This is just the mandatory stuff," said Mick, pointing at respective contents. "Jack Daniel's, Finlandia, Grolsch, Budweiser, limes, salt, cheese cubes, jerky, olives, three kinds of chips, three kinds of dip, eight-piece supermarket fried chicken, foot-long subs, mixed nuts, Ritz Crackers, pepperoni, pearl onions, hot sauce, shot glasses, multipurpose bar tool, playing cards, *Playboy*, Sominex, NoDoz, Alka-Seltzer and"—patting his shirt pocket—"cigars."

Lenny reached in a drugstore bag and pulled out a pair of twenty-nine-dollar portable black-and-white TVs from China. "I thought I knew how to party. But it's like there's this whole other level."

They climbed back in the limo and headed over the Kennedy Causeway. Serge grabbed his camera and pointed it out the window. Click.

"A picture of the Crab Shack?" asked Lenny.

"Used to be the Peppermint Club. That's where the Beatles hung out when they came down for the Sullivan show in '64."

"How do you know that?"

"Good scavenger hunt last month. Went to the main Miami-Dade library in the Cuban section of downtown. Found a write-up in the *Herald*'s microfilm about what the Beatles did when they were here. But of course the Peppermint is gone, so I went to Special Collections and pulled the library's old 1964 cross-street index for the address."

"Impressive."

"That's what I thought, so I drove out to the restaurant and went inside. You'd think everyone would want to know about my discovery."

"They didn't?"

"Not only that. They said I would have to leave. That I was *bothering* the customers."

"They doesn't sound very polite."

"Crab shacks are a different culture."

A cell phone rang.

"Serge and Lenny's. . . . Agent Miller? . . . With the FBI? . . . I was wondering when you were going to call. . . . No, we're not with the Palermo Family. We're a travel service. . . . No, I didn't kill Tony Marsicano. One of my customers did. But it was self-defense. I saw the whole thing, so you can close the case. . . . Sure, he's right here."

Serge held out the phone. "It's for you."

Rusty was busy with a breakdown, so Serge had to hold the phone to his head again. Rusty began crying.

Serge took the phone back.

"You upset him. I hope you're happy. . . . Look, the tour is getting behind schedule, so unless you have something else . . . What do you mean, I won't get away with it? Get away with what? . . . Why does everyone think they have to shout on the phone? . . . Lower your voice. . . . I'm not going to listen to talk like that. . . . Fine, fuck you, too."

Serge closed the phone. "Everybody yells."

Lenny reached Sixty-ninth Street and angled up the drive of the Deauville Hotel.

"Here we are! Everybody out!" said Serge.

They quickly settled into their new room. City and Country staked out a patch of floor and packed a dragon's-head bong. Mick and Lenny opened boat coolers and set up the mobile bar/snack command post on a dresser. Serge anchored the third corner of the triangle, the TV turned around, pliers and wires, assembling the multimedia studio. Rusty and Doug sat at the edge of a bed in the center of it all, feeling the room starting to spin.

"We've entered the Beatles phase of your tour," said Serge. "I can't tell you how hard it was finding the specific rooms the Fab Four stayed in when they came to Miami Beach in '64. This one was Paul and Ringo's." He swept his arm around the interior of the suite. "Do you feel it? They actually breathed the air in this room! Of course, it's different air now, but we can use our imaginations."

Serge turned the TV back around and held up a video. "This is out of print, very hard to find. A behind-the-scenes documentary of the Beatles' first U.S. visit." He stuck the tape in the VCR. Old black-and-white footage came on, a pack of racehorses coming down the homestretch at Hialeah, a man springing off a high dive into a pool. The announcer's voice: *"And now from the stage of the Deauville Hotel, here he is—Ed Sullivan!"*

Two portable TVs were going on the other side of the room. The Florida State game and the Notre Dame game. Lenny broke out the fried chicken. Mick filled shot glasses and flipped open his cell phone. "I'm going to teach you how to win some money. . . . Hello? Zippy? It's Mick. Gimme a dime on USC, take the points. . . ." He covered the phone and pointed at one of the sets. "Lenny, the Irish just scored. You have to do a shot."

"And a hit," said Country, passing him a joint.

"Sports are cool!"said Lenny.

Serge snapped his fingers in front of Rusty and Doug. "Pay attention." He nodded toward the big TV. "When you mention the Beatles on *Sullivan,* most people think of the New York show. But for the second broadcast a week later, they performed live from this hotel, when they actually pulled a bigger home audience." The footage cut to the young Brits clowning in their hotel room. "Notice how it exactly matches the interior of this room?" Serge swept his arm around the suite: City and Country toking, Lenny coughing his brains out.

"You okay?" asked Mick.

Lenny nodded. "So that's what a boilermaker is."

"The Irish just scored again."

Serge slapped the TV screen. "Beatlephiles and the hotel staff concur they stayed on the eleventh floor, but I couldn't nail the precise room. This balcony scene was the big clue. The breakwater you see indicated the room was on the east face. From there the investigation progressed rapidly. I did a frame-by-frame Zapruder analysis of the video, and here it is, the magic bullet." Serge hit pause. "Right there! You can count two more balcony railings to the north. So it's the third room from the end, number eleven-fourteen, our room, and Inspector Serge solves another one of History's Mysteries!" He restarted the tape, McCartney on the balcony throwing crackers to seagulls. "Notice they haven't changed the balcony." Serge pointed out the glass doors, where Mick and Lenny were at the railing smoking cigars, raising drinks in the air and shouting.

"Wooooooooo! Miami!"

"Wooooooooo! Beatles room!"

Rusty finally snapped and jumped to his feet. "This is an insane asylum!"

"Exactly!" said Serge, pounding the TV cabinet with his fist. "That's what I keep trying to tell everyone. Life makes no sense! The world is a madhouse! Once you accept that, you can start being happy. Expect logic and fairness, and it's nothing but a heartbreak."

"No!" Rusty screamed back. "Right here! You! These people! We're going to be killed, and you're just fucking around!"

"Have faith in the Master Plan. You'll see."

"There is no fucking plan! Look around this room! What does any of this have to do with . . . *anything?*"

"Everything has to do with everything else. It's all interconnected. Didn't you listen to 'The White Album'?"

29

AGENTS MILLER AND Bixby walked down a bright hallway. Visitor badges clipped to their pockets. Nurses went by.

The agents stopped at a guard station under an Orwellian sign: MIAMI-DADE MENTAL HEALTH. A series of electric locks clicked. A thick metal door opened.

"Who is this guy again?" whispered Bixby.

"Agent Mahoney," said Miller. "Found him in the case file. He almost caught Serge a few years back. Used to work for the state as a profiler. Tracked Serge to Tampa in '97, then picked up his trail again when Serge infiltrated the governor's campaign in '02. But the stress was too much. He began to obsess, tried to get inside Serge's mind. Now he's a drool-farmer in the silly house."

They approached a locked door. A doctor in a white jacket checked their laminated visitors' passes, then punched a code into the keypad.

It was a windowless room. Fluorescent light. A thick Plexiglas partition cut the room in half. On the other side, a man was pacing. Tweed jacket, fedora, necktie with coconuts. Talking to himself: "Need to run down the Chinese angle on the shylock's mazuma before the twist cops a roscoe and squirts metal at the brunos. . . ."

"Excuse me," said Miller. "Time for a word?"

"You a news-fink? My trap's zipped."

"From the Bureau."

Mahoney nodded. "G-men."

"It's about Serge."

"Regular wiseguy. Didn't dance straight. Ran with a wrong-number dizzy for the juju."

"Juju?" said Bixby.

"Muggles," said Mahoney.

Miller turned to Bixby. "Marijuana." He looked back to Mahoney. "What's the last you heard?"

"He was mixing with some trouble boys on the flimflam, putting screws to a Peterman after the box job."

"How'd you hear?"

"Jawed with him on the Ameche."

"Ameche?" said Bixby.

"Blower," said Mahoney.

Miller turned. "Phone."

"The new skinny?" asked Mahoney.

"He's back in town." Miller pulled the Katie Couric letter from his jacket and slipped it through a slot in the safety glass. "Wanted to see what you made of this."

Mahoney read the letter and began smiling. "Underwood jockey. Regular Spillane."

"We haven't been able to figure out that reference to the Beatles' room," said Miller. "I hope we're not into some kind of Helter Skelter trip."

Mahoney looked up. "Deauville Hotel, Room Eleven-fourteen."

Miller and Bixby ran out the door.

* * *

COUNTRY WAS GETTING on Serge's nerves. She kept rubbing his crotch while he was trying to load guns.

Serge pushed her away. "Will you stop!"

She wouldn't.

Doug and Rusty gawked. Their lives were still in danger, but they were still guys. They couldn't believe Serge. First Bridget and now this. Serge looked at them and shrugged. "You can't reason with the stoned. It's like trying to train a Pet Rock."

Country kept rubbing.

"You got five minutes," said Serge. "Then will you leave me alone?"

She grinned and nodded. They headed to the bedroom. Serge opened the curtains and pushed the bed over to the window. He walked back and slammed the door on the collection of faces.

Serge got on top. He started moving, then stopped.

Country looked down. "Is something wrong?"

Serge stared out the window. "I've got total visibility to the horizon, but cloud cover is casting shadows. I need full sunlight."

They waited. Clouds began to part. Sunlight broke through and bathed the South Florida coast. Serge slipped on his polarized fishing-guide sunglasses for proper enhancement of cyans and magentas.

Country looked down again. "There we go."

The bed began squeaking as Serge established a rhythm: "Cape Florida lighthouse . . . Freedom Tower . . . Crandon Park . . ."

"Fuck me harder, you lunatic!"

"The Flagler obelisk . . . Hibiscus Island . . . Southeast Financial Centre . . ."

Down on the beach, a small child pointed upward. "Mommy, look at the funny man doing push-ups in the window." The mother whisked the tot away.

". . . The gold Seaquarium dome . . . the converted Pan Am city-hall building on Dinner Key . . . the Aquatronics condo on

Brickell with the cutout . . . Oh, my God! A seaplane! . . . It's banking over the Orange Bowl to land in the bay! . . ."

Country shrieked at the pain-pleasure threshold. She became paralyzed, quivering helplessly like she'd touched a high-tension wire.

". . . A twin-engine Grumman Mallard N1208 refitted with the new turboprops! . . ."

"Faster! No, stop! It hurts! No, don't stop! . . ."

". . . It's splitting the Marriott and Bank of America for the belly landing! Here it comes! . . ."

". . . Stop! No, fuck me! No, Stop! Don't stop! . . . Ahhhhhh-hhhhhhh!"

Serge finished, rolling off her onto his back. "And another safe landing."

It was quiet for a bit. Serge opened the bedroom door; guys scattered.

"You people need to go out on a date or something." Serge strapped on a shoulder holster. "Start folding up the tents. This feast is moving."

He herded the gang into the elevator on the eleventh floor of the Deauville.

"But we just got to the room," said Lenny.

"This one's getting too hot," said Serge. "Everyone who's ever been caught always stayed just a little too long."

The doors started closing, then bounced back open.

"One of the boat coolers won't fit," said Lenny. "Not enough room with all the people and luggage carts."

"Everyone squeeze back," said Serge. He got out, crouched down on his knees and pushed the cooler hard. People inside groaned. "Almost there." The doors started closing again, and Serge jumped up on top of the cooler. The elevator shut all the way as the doors of the next car opened. Miller and Bixby got out.

Serge's elevator headed down. He stood atop the cooler, faced the others and spread his arms. "The Year of Our Lord Nineteen Hundred and Sixty-four. A watershed time—for the nation as a whole and Miami Beach in particular, but with very different implications. For the country, the birth of an epoch, America coming out of assassination funk, finally facing its own social skeletons in a decade of unprecedented upheaval before maturing to greatness. For Miami Beach, the last hurrah. The peak years of the fifties already far behind, Hotel Row on the skids. But Miami Beach still had one last year left in her, one that would be bigger than all the others combined. You wouldn't believe the confluence of colossal names and seismic events that rocked the world in 1964—all from just a few blocks along the strip here. The Beatles were just the beginning, but you'll be learning about the rest in coming days, thanks to your wise decision choosing Serge and Lenny's Florida Experience for all your historic travel needs."

The elevator opened. Serge jumped off the cooler.

"The basement?" said Lenny.

"Always leave by the basement," said Serge. "Avoids a lot of unnecessary explaining. Plus, I'm meeting someone."

"Who?" asked Lenny.

"A link to the old days. Maybe put us in touch with the right people. I made some calls from the limo trying to reach him at his business, but he'd been bought out by a national chain. They said he came here."

The Deauville's basement was a low-ceilinged concourse of modest retail shops under the lobby. All empty. Serge led the gang down the north corridor, then shepherded them to one of the storefronts.

"A barbershop?" said Mick.

"Doesn't look like much today," said Serge. "But check out the ancient customer photos in the window. There's Mickey Rooney in that bib and Liberace getting a trim. This is Perry Como, and the one over there is Robert Goulet, who forgot the words to the national anthem."

Serge went inside.

Three barber chairs. Two empty, the other holding a white-haired barber reading the newspaper. A broom leaned against the counter. The barber heard them and stood. He set his paper on the counter and walked around behind the chair he'd been sitting in. "Who's first?"

"We're not getting haircuts," said Serge.

The barber's brow crinkled. "Then how can I help you?"

"Roy, it's me, Little Serge. Sergio's grandson."

Roy's eyes opened wide. "Little Serge!" He ran out from behind the chair and gave Serge a big hug.

"Rusty and Doug, I'd like you to meet Roy. Roy 'The Pawn King.' He might have some information that could help get us out of this. He's the reason we came to this hotel."

"I thought it was because you were obsessed with the Beatles," said Doug.

"Please! Give me a little more credit. It was part of the Master Plan."

Roy held Serge by the shoulders. "Great to see you! . . . But how'd you find me?"

"Tracked you down through Pawn Nation. At first they kept hanging up. I talked to like ten employees until I found one who knew where you'd gone. . . . Roy, the old pawnshop, Jesus! How could you?"

"They offered me an obscene amount of money. Besides, I was getting too old for all the cokeheads bringing in stolen crutches and hearing aids. . . . So tell me, what are *you* doing here?"

"Conducting a travel tour, looking for gems, working on a mystery, layin' low, lovin' life, livin' large—"

"Slow down! Slow down! Damn, you're just like your grand-dad!"

"You know where I can find anyone from his old gang?"

"The whole place has gone to hell. Most of the old-timers couldn't take it and moved out. The last one I heard still hanging around was Coltrane. He was working with some of the new boxers down at the Fifth Street Gym."

"I didn't know Coltrane knew anything about boxing."

"Doesn't. He just gets drunk and walks around the gym yelling. But they like him over there, kind of a mascot. Why do you want to find them anyway?"

"Set the record straight on my grandfather's death. I'm absolutely sure he didn't kill himself."

Roy put a hand on Serge's shoulder. "I know it's hard, but do yourself a favor: Let it go. You don't want to be asking around about that."

Serge shook his head. "Can't do it."

Roy looked Serge over again and took a resigned breath. "You're just like him."

"Thanks, Roy."

"That's a compliment."

"I know."

MILLER AND BIXBY wore latex gloves, combing Room 1114 of the Deauville Hotel. Others from the Bureau had been called in. The room was full of people in dark suits scribbling notes, filming with video cameras. Photo flashes went off every other second. Agents carted away boxes full of tagged evidence: roaches, beer empties, pizza boxes, loose bullets, condoms, sticky notes, bloody bath towels, empty box from a Beatles documentary.

"What the hell was going on in this room?" said Miller.

Brad's body came out of the bathroom in a rubber bag.

Bixby removed more Post-it Notes from the wall and dropped them into a sterile Baggie. "There must be hundreds of these things."

Miller plucked one of the yellow squares off the nightstand: "*Analyze* Raging Bull *Florida scenes (freeze frame). Find address of LaMotta's old Miami Beach nightclub.*"

A junior agent came in the room with an urgent fax. "Just got this from city hall." Miller grabbed it and put on his reading glasses.

Dear Mayor of Miami Beach,

As you might recall from my last correspondence, I'm president of the Miami Beach Renaissance and History Task Force, and I have good news! Are you sitting down? I've been in touch with the Today *show, and they are right on the verge of relocating from New York to Miami Beach. So everybody needs to look snappy, and pronto!*

I haven't actually heard from Katie herself, but I did receive an autographed photo from Al Roker as a signal of his readiness to make the big jump south, which I am enclosing as an advance token of my appreciation.

Not having received a reply to all my other letters, I am taking your continued silence as tacit approval to proceed with my operation. I understand that plausible deniability is essential for your scandal-ridden administration, and you'll need to distance yourself while I grease some outstretched NBC hands and take the network advance teams to the "right" clubs, if you know what I mean. But here's the lowdown: My personal time is completely volunteered, although expenses are starting to add up. Ten thousand should get us through until the ink is dry. You know that third garbage can at the Metro Zoo by the cage with the little monkeys, where if you stand too close they hit you with poop? I know it, too (wink). Meanwhile, I'll keep you regularly apprised through the usual back-door channels. See you on TV!

Your faithful citizen,

Serge A. Storms

P.S. I'll also need some stationery with your official letterhead and a concealed-weapons permit. If anyone asks, I don't know where I got them, okay?

Agent Miller took off his glasses. "Where the hell are they?"

30

WHERE THE HELL are we?" asked Lenny, leaning over the limo's steering wheel.

"Still a ways to go," said Serge, chugging a bottle of water in the passenger seat.

"How do you know this Coltrane will be there?"

"I don't." Serge set a briefcase on his lap and opened it. "But we have to start somewhere." He pulled out a large brown envelope from a local print shop.

"What's that?"

"My labels." He showed Lenny a sheet of self-adhesive stickers.

"What for?"

Serge killed the water. "Watch this." He wiped the plastic bottle dry on his shirt, then wrapped one of the stickers around it. "My own new brand of energy drink. The kids are buying this stuff like crazy in the clubs. Somebody out there is making a killing. I want it to be me."

"A lot of big companies are in that market," said Lenny. "It'll be hard to break in."

"That's what my secret formula is for." Serge unfolded a wrinkled piece of paper from the briefcase and handed it to Lenny. "Do you think you can get me these drugs?"

"Sure, but they're illegal," said Lenny. "I though you were against drugs."

"I am. But this is a *health* drink."

Rusty tapped Serge on the shoulder. "We'd like to get out of the car now."

Serge shook his head. "You're still obsessing on the negative. We need to break that worry cycle." He tucked the briefcase under his arm and climbed over the seat into the back of the limo. "You've just entered the Muhammad Ali phase of the tour."

Serge reached in the briefcase and pulled out an eight-by-ten black-and-white of a young Cassius Clay clowning around a boxing ring with John, Paul, George and Ringo.

"After they played the Sullivan show, the Beatles hung out a few days and visited Clay's training camp. Clever segue, eh?"

Blank faces.

Serge stuck a tape in the limo's VCR. "This is rare footage from the closed-circuit feed of the Clay-Liston fight. Very hard to find." He extended a telescoping pointer and tapped a spot on the side of the TV screen. "See these guys? That's trainer Angelo Dundee, sidekick Bundini Brown and the soon-to-be Muhammad Ali. A Catholic, a Jew and a Muslim. The way it should be in this country, tighter than brothers."

"What about Protestants?" Lenny called back from the front seat.

"I hate fucking Protestants."

"But, Serge . . ."

"Kidding, Lenny. . . . Now, watch the screen closely everyone . . . Mick, since you're the expert, would you like to do guest commentary?"

"Wha . . . ?" said Mick, passing the Lucite dragon bong back to Country.

"Sorry. I didn't realize you were busy turning your brain to window caulk. . . ."

Lenny glanced in the rearview. "Mick, you're smoking my special blend. One part Saskatoon skunk weed that makes you see God; one part Maui-Wowee rad resin weed that makes you see the Devil; one part brown Mexican shake 'n' bake that just makes you dizzy."

"Okay, study Clay's footwork, wearing Sonny down with surgical jabs, barely being touched—shocking the star-studded crowd at the Miami Beach Convention Center, which should be going by right about . . ."—Serge didn't look up from the TV as he tapped the window with his pointer—". . . now."

Rusty and Doug saw the convention center pass by.

Serge let the tape run and climbed back up front. "We're almost there."

"I still can't see it," said Lenny.

"I told you, it's right there on the corner of Fifth and— Oh, my God! Stop the car!"

"What's the matter?"

Serge grabbed the dash, staring in horror at a parking lot and some new boutiques. "It's gone! The whole building! They tore down the Fifth Street Gym!"

"They're always putting up new things around here," said Lenny.

"But this place was a shrine. Those great stained-glass windows, the wooden floor consecrated with sweat and blood, the echo of Dundee's voice in the walls. Someone must pay!"

"What do we do now?" asked Lenny. "This is where Roy said Coltrane would be."

"The building's gone, but the boxers aren't. They had to migrate somewhere. I need to find some Yellow Pages."

* * *

SERGE AND THE gang stood on the corner of Seventh Street, two blocks away, staring up at a garish purple sign. WORLD-CLASS SHOWGIRLS.

"A strip joint?" said Lenny.

"Beside it. That little doorway leading to the upstairs loft."

They entered a cold, dank concrete hallway with a single naked lightbulb. Serge took out a pocket camera and hit the shutter. The flash lit up a mural of Muhammad Ali. He turned to the other wall and raised his camera again. Flash. An autographed boxing poster for a 1992 light-heavyweight bout, Francisco Harris versus "Marielito" Mickey Rourke.

They trotted up the stairs.

It was a busy room, hot and musty from exertion. Grunting, shoes shuffling, pop-pop-pop on the bags, gongs going off every three minutes.

Serge scanned the room: nobody he recognized. He was about to tap a trainer on the shoulder when he heard a crash behind him in the men's room. He turned around. There was another crash, like a stack of metal dustpans falling, then a bunch of fluorescent-light tubes bursting. The door opened.

Serge stepped forward. "Coltrane?"

A large man in overalls stumbled toward him. "That's my name, don't wear it out."

"Coltrane, it's me, Little Serge. Sergio's grandson."

Coltrane's eyes narrowed, then spread. "Little Serge! Great to see you! Pull my finger."

"Maybe later."

"I'll do it," said Lenny. "What happens? . . . Ewwwww."

"What are you doing here?" asked Coltrane, uncapping a flask.

"We need your help."

"Tell me while we walk. A fighter's waiting for me."

"I'm looking into my granddad's death," said Serge. "I wanted to know what you remembered. And where I might find the other guys."

They arrived at the corner of a sparring ring. Coltrane hit the

flask again and leaned over the turnbuckle: "Jab with your
right, kid. Your right!" He turned to Serge. "Then you want his
diary."

"Diary? What diary? I never heard about any diary."

"Kept it religiously. A little black one. If someone killed him,
their name's probably in it."

"So you believed him? You think he really got the jewels?"

Coltrane glanced around. "I wouldn't talk about that if I were
you, even now. . . . The left, kid! Lead with the left!"

"Know where I can find this diary?"

"Not a clue."

"Damn."

"But Moondog does."

"Really? You wouldn't happen to know where I can find him?"

"Sure, he's still living in Overtown. Got his number somewhere here in my wallet. . . . You realize you'll be stirring up bad
history."

One of the fighters came over to the corner and pulled off protective headgear.

Serge's neck snapped back. "You're a girl!"

"This girl will kick your ass," said Coltrane. "Carolina, meet
Serge. Serge, this is Carolina Garcia-Aguilera."

Serge extended a hand. "Nice to meet—hold it, not the famous
Cuban-American writer!"

"That's her," said Coltrane.

"What are you doing boxing?"

"Stress," she said, unlacing a glove with her teeth.

"Why don't you spar?" said Coltrane.

"I couldn't," said Serge.

Coltrane grabbed a dirty towel and threw it over his shoulder.
"Why not?"

"She's one of my favorites. You know, brain damage and all. I
want her to be able to write more books . . ."

"Wussy," said Carolina.

". . . but I could go a round or two."

They suited Serge up. Coltrane called instructions from the corner. "Get ready. Here comes the bell. . . ."

Ding.

There was bright light at the end of a tunnel, a voice beckoning: *"Serge . . . Serge . . . Serge . . . Are you okay . . . okay . . . okay? . . ."*

They sat him up.

"Oh, my God, I'm so sorry!" said Carolina.

"What happened?" said Serge. "Did I win?"

"How many fingers am I holding up?" asked Coltrane.

"Twelve."

31

1964

THE SHRILL SCREAMS were unnerving. The gang stared in shock out the crowbar-jimmied door of the monorail at the Miami Seaquarium. Thirty-five feet below: a man writhing on the ground with legs bent in unnatural directions.

Lou sat down and lit a Lucky.

"Jesus! I can't believe you just threw Joey Asparagus out of the monorail!" said Chi-Chi.

"You want to get paid, don't you?"

"But this is the Seaquarium! . . . Look! A crowd's already gathering."

"That's the whole point. We need some talk on the street."

Sure enough. The street began chattering. The betting parlor on Collins got crowded with people rushing in to pay up, some taking second mortgages.

But not all. Lou led the gang on a merciless reign of terror, doggedly tracking down the remaining deadbeats who had cleared off the beach and were hiding out on the mainland. The gang was as frightened as the victims when Lou got down to business. She has handy with a sap and knew her way around a shiv. There were pistol-whippings, kneecappings, cigarette burns and chicken heads left on doorsteps in the part of town where that sort of thing held sway.

The guys were more than uneasy with the violence, but the increased cash flow limbered up their consciences. These were the good times. Piles of greenbacks all over the betting joint, the gang laughing, thumbing through wads of twenties, smoking cigars, buying new suits, getting the best tables in restaurants. The bulge meant increased tribute to the Palermos. Cops were put on the dole. Everybody was happy.

The gang was a little snockered the night they stumbled down a dock on the Miami River, climbing aboard the fifty-foot sail-boat where Lou had requested a late-night rendezvous. They giggled their way across the deck. Then they heard whimpering.

The sound grew louder as the guys worked their way across the stern. They came around the back of the cabin and froze.

"Lou!" screamed Sergio. "Don't! There's got to be another way!"

"For the love of Christ!" yelled Chi-Chi.

"You've gone too far!" shouted Mort.

"Shut up, you pussies! We're not running a charity!"

Lou stood at the starboard railing. In front of her, sitting naked with legs hanging over the side of the boat, was Frankie Clams. Lou had her gun in his back. Frankie's feet were encased in blocks of freshly dried concrete.

Lou pushed the barrel into his spine. "See what you get when you fuck with us?"

"Lou! Before it's too late!" said Greek Tommy.

"He's into us for ten large!" yelled Lou. "What do you want me to do?"

"I swear I'll pay!" said Frankie.

"Is that why you were hiding in a washing machine?"

"Lou! We didn't bargain for this!"

Lou pushed Frankie hard with the gun. His sweaty butt slipped on the side of the boat. He screamed. His frantic wiggling made him slip some more.

The slippage stopped. Frankie was dangling right on the edge now, crying too hard to make words.

"Lou! We're begging you!"

Lou set the gun down. The gang sighed with relief.

Then she unceremoniously shoved Frankie overboard.

Splash.

They ran to the railing. Frankie was thrashing around. In three feet of water.

Lou leaned over the side. "Pay up by noon tomorrow or we do it again at high tide!"

THE NEXT DAY, a minute before noon. Someone began feeding ten grand under the front door of the bookie parlor; then they heard feet running away.

Lou picked up the money and licked her fingertips.

Celebration time. No more dives for the guys.

The gang arrived in the prestigious Pompeii Room at the Eden Roc.

The seats at the bar were all taken. The patrons saw Lou approaching, and then seats were available. The gang settled in, and the opinion factory opened for business. The Warren Commission was hiding something, the Vietcong wouldn't last six months, Queen Elizabeth II was pregnant, but who cared?

"Liston takes Clay in two," said Chi-Chi.

"Will not!" said Sergio.

"Look at the size and power difference," said Chi-Chi.

"None of that counts anymore," said Sergio. "I've been watching Clay train at the gym. He's invented this whole new form of boxing that's going to shake up the world. He told me his plan is to get Liston overconfident."

"You do not know Cassius Clay!" said Chi-Chi. "Jesus! I can't tell you how old that's getting!"

"I was hanging around the gym a few weeks ago. They needed a sparring partner."

"Wow! You sparred with Clay?" said Mort.

"He did not spar with Clay!"

"Almost beat him."

"Stop!"

"I'll prove it," said Sergio, standing up. "We're going to go see him."

The guys paid their tabs. Chi-Chi hopped off his stool. "This I gotta see."

They piled in the new Mustang and Chi-Chi's Cadillac and headed thirteen blocks south to the Fifth Street Gym.

"We can just go inside?" asked Mort.

"Of course," said Sergio, opening the front door and heading up the stairs. "This ain't no celebrity hangout. It's a real fighters' joint."

They climbed to the second floor. Two bantamweights exchanged uppercuts in the ring. A young fighter from Louisville was off to the side, working on the speed bag. Sergio knelt next to Little Serge and pointed across the room. "See that man over there? That's the legendary trainer Angelo Dundee. And the fighter next to him won an Olympic gold medal in Rome four years ago. He's going to be the next heavyweight champion."

"Okay, you were able to find the gym," said Chi-Chi. "I'm amazed enough at that. Doesn't mean you know him."

"Watch this." Sergio waved across the gym. "Hey, Cassius!"

Clay slowed his punching rate and looked across the gym in puzzlement, then went back to his workout.

"See?" said Sergio.

"See what?" said Chi-Chi.

"He looked at me."

"Of course he looked at you. You called his name. He had no idea who you were."

Moondog tapped Sergio on the shoulder. "Who's the guy over there in the glasses? He looks familiar."

"Malcolm X. Another real nice fellow." Sergio turned and threw a fist in the air. "Malcolm! Bro!"

There was light pedestrian traffic on Fifth Street when the door of the gym flew open and Sergio came tumbling down the steps.

MOONDOG NURSED A Harvey Wallbanger in the corner booth, sitting with the only white people in the club. Dim red light, loud music, laughter.

Moondog pointed with a swizzle stick. "You got quite a shiner there, Sergio."

"Who would have thought those guys at the gym could get so rough? They were wearing bow ties." Sergio took a little black book from his shirt pocket and scribbled something.

"Can't believe you were right about Clay winning tonight," said Moondog.

"It was a sure thing. Sonny's a bone-crusher, Clay's a boxer. The boxer always wins."

The house band launched into a number by the Coasters. Lou stubbed out a cigarette and got up. "I see someone I know."

"This place is really jumping," said Sergio. He looked to his side. "You having fun, Little Serge?"

Little Serge nodded, holding his Shirley Temple with both hands.

Moondog signaled a waitress for another round. Sergio grabbed the pack of matches out of the ashtray and turned it over: THE KNIGHT BEAT. LIVE MUSIC. OVERTOWN. Little Serge finished his drink and jumped out of his chair. He ran down an aisle, then back to the table, then down the aisle.

"Should he be doing that?" asked Moondog.

"Has a little trouble sitting still," said Sergio. "He'll tire eventually."

"You and the kid sure are spending a lot of time," said Moondog.

Little Serge crawled under someone else's table.

"It's up to two or three days a week," said Sergio. "At first I thought it was going to cramp my style, but I'm having a blast! He's just like his granddad, loads of natural charisma. You should have seen how the strippers took to him the other night."

"Now he's out on the dance floor," said Moondog.

"He likes to dance."

"He's not dancing. He's just running real fast in a little circle."

"It makes him happy. The others seem to be getting a kick out of it."

Sergio was drowned out by wild applause sweeping the room. The dim lights lowered even more. A soft spotlight came on, and an emcee announced the main act. Little Serge ran back and jumped on Sergio's lap.

A handsome young man took the stage and grabbed the bulky steel microphone off the stand.

"Sergio, uh, I don't know how to bring this up," said Moondog. "I don't want to meddle, especially when it's another's man's..."

Sergio slowly bobbed his head as he watched the performer. "What is it?"

"It's Lou," said Moondog. "I mentioned her name to a few of the fight guys. There are some pretty wild stories circulating."

"Like what?"

"Everyone she dates ends up dead. She's getting quite a reputation."

"Oh, *that*. Lou told me all about it. A bunch of coincidences. Said not to listen if I heard any of the talk."

"Darling, youuuuuuuuuu send me . . ."

"If you ask me, she's nothing but trouble," said Moondog.

"We're in love," said Sergio. "She wants to get married."

"Then what's she doing dancing with that guy?"

Sergio strained his neck toward the dance floor. "You mean

Desmond? They're old friends. She told me all about him, too. Strictly platonic."

Moondog watched Lou platonically tongue-wrestle Desmond in front of the bandstand.

Sergio looked around the room. "The women really like this singer. Listen to that shrieking. It's like back at the hotel with the Beatles. Who is he?"

". . . *Youuuuuuuuu send me . . .*"

Moondog stirred the cubes in his drink. "New guy. Sam Cooke or something."

32

Present

FOUR MICHIGAN STATE alums sat at the bar in the Hotel Franklin, the door open to the beach air and sidewalk scene. Clocks for different international cities on the wall: Tokyo, London, Cairo. A green financial ticker ran under the TV set.

"Gimme a dollar."

They turned.

"Uh-oh."

Action 5 News came on. A report out of Orlando.

TELEVISION VANS CONVERGED on the courtyard outside a towering office complex in downtown Orlando. A stage and a microphone. The audience was already in place. A big, happy press conference about to get under way.

Elevator doors opened on the ground floor of a modern steel-and-glass building. Television lights came on. A dozen armed guards precision-marched through the lobby, escorting a man in a gray suit, Brian Levy, cofounder of Strauss & Levy Accounting. Levy held a metal box by the handle. It was handcuffed to his wrist. The marketing people had told him to do that. He stopped at the main guard station to shake hands with security officer Charley Pavlic, for the benefit of the cameras.

Levy arrived at the stage and made some brief remarks, thanking his employees, the press, and all the good people at McDonald's. "Now, the moment you've been waiting for . . ." One of the guards gave a command into a walkie-talkie.

Twin columns of motorcycle cops came around the corner, leading a convoy of ten identical armored cars. More police held up traffic as the trucks backed up to the courtyard, forming a perfect row. The drivers kept the engines running. The guard on the passenger side of each vehicle got out, walked to rear bumper and stood at attention.

"Eenie, meenie, miney, mo!" Levy pointed at one of the trucks. The guard unlocked the gun-ported doors, revealing thousands of McDonald's paper soda cups ready for shipping to restaurants across the country.

Levy opened the metal box on his wrist with a big gold Hamburglar key and took out an identical cup. He held it in the air. "The one-million-dollar winner of McDonald's Instant-Peel Contest, with thousands of other instant prizes including jet skis, minibikes, Bic Macs, fries and Happy Meals. See stores for details. Good luck, America!"

Levy climbed in the back of the truck and tucked the cup among the countless stacks. He got back out, the guard closed her up, and ten armored cars departed in different directions, police motorcycles escorting them onto entrance ramps of various highways heading out of Orlando and across the U.S. of A.

FOUR MICHIGAN STATE men finished watching the news and left the bar.

"C'mon, give me a dollar," said the bum, bringing up the rear.

A limo with magnetic signs drove by. It picked up speed and made a right turn for the causeway.

"Where are we going now?" asked Lenny.

"To meet Moondog," said Serge. "I called the number Coltrane gave me."

"You reached him?"

"He was in the middle of eating farina and watching the new *Family Feud* with Louie Anderson. Remind me never to retire."

Serge gunned the limo across the Miami River on Northwest Second Avenue. They passed under a sign: OVERTOWN.

"Why are you slowing down?" asked Lenny.

Serge was baffled. "This can't be the eight-hundred block. Where did everything go?"

Lenny looked out the window. Vacant lots, weeds, broken furniture. A single building still standing.

"I was wondering why Moondog wanted to meet in the Lyric Theater instead of the Famous Chef or any of the other places I suggested."

"Looks like a bomb hit."

"That empty spot there used to be the Alexander Apartments, one of the places Muhammad Ali lived in the early sixties. And on that other block was the Sir John Hotel, where the famous underwater *Life* magazine photos of Ali were taken in the pool. Man, the future is just one heartache after another. Little Broadway wiped out like it never existed."

"Little Broadway?"

"You say Overtown today and people go, 'Oh, yeah, blighted black area.' But forty years ago this was one of the most culturally vibrant places in the country. All the white vacationers in Miami Beach staying in their fancy hotels—oh, they loved to go see the great African-American headliners in the nightclubs, but then the entertainers had to race back to Overtown to beat the Jim Crow curfew."

"Pretty fucked up," said Lenny.

"That's what my grandfather used to say. But, man, did this place jump in the wee hours. After performing on the beach, all these world-class acts would come and play late-night sets along this little strip here. Can you imagine going door-to-door among these intimate cocktail lounges and seeing Count Basie, Nat 'King' Cole, Louis Armstrong, Ella Fitzgerald and Sammy Davis Jr.?"

"The Candyman can."

Serge parked the car at the curb in front of the vintage-1914 theater. "Then they decimated the neighborhood with the interstate, and now we have this. . . ." He looked over his shoulder at Rusty and Doug. "Can I trust you two not to run away?"

Rusty and Doug stared petrified out the window at the neighborhood around them.

"Good." Serge and Lenny got out and walked to the entrance.

Serge grabbed the knob, then stopped. "I almost hate to look."

"Won't it be locked?" asked Lenny.

"Nope. It's on the local preservation tour, but nobody comes, as usual." He turned the knob. The front door creaked open.

Serge gasped like Christmas morning. "Restored! Thank God! Aged wood grain in the armrests, accurate upholstery . . ."

The place was empty except for an old man sitting alone in the front row. Serge trotted down the aisle.

"Moondog?"

Moondog had put on a little weight, looked like B.B. King now.

"Little Serge?"

They hugged.

"Last time I saw you, you were this high. Hyper little sucker . . . Sorry about your granddad."

"That's what I wanted to talk to you about. Coltrane says you know something about a diary."

"What diary? Coltrane's drunk."

They sat in adjoining theater seats and faced each other.

"I was hoping I could find out something about what happened. The police version doesn't make sense. I'm thinking his death had to do with the gems."

Moondog looked around quickly, then leaned. "You don't want to be bringing that up. Trust me on this one."

"Know where any of the other guys are?"

"Last I heard, Chi-Chi got a little feeble, ranting about CIA safe houses and Castro. They put him in a home. Don't know where. Greek Tommy was living over one of those nightclubs on South Beach. Used to be the old bookie parlor."

"Address?"

"Up on Fifteenth. That new place, 'Plus Twenty-Four'. . . . Wait—did you say diary?"

"He always kept it. Coltrane said—"

"You mean that little black book?"

"You know about it?"

"Oh, that thing? Sure," said Moondog. "Wrote in it all the time."

"That's what I've been talking about!"

"I didn't know it was a diary. Thought it was a shopping list or poetry or some shit. Always kept it in his shirt pocket. Unless he had his special box with him. Then it went in there."

"Box?"

"This old wooden box where he kept all these souvenir matchbooks and stuff. He was pretty weird about it."

"Now I remember," said Serge. "He used to show it to me. All kinds of junk in there, sterling alligator spoons, orange gumballs . . ."

"And a citrus sipper," Moondog said with a smile.

"That's right, the citrus sipper. Classic Florida roadside keepsake. You jammed it in an orange so you could get juice all over your shirt. My folks only let me use it if I was wearing a bathing suit and standing in the ocean."

"Last time I saw it, the book was sitting in the box right under that sipper."

"Any idea where it might be?"

"I know exactly where it is. It's—"

A gunshot rang out.

Moondog tumbled off his seat with a hole in his back. Serge grabbed him. "Moondog!" Still breathing but in no condition to talk. Serge looked up at the balcony. A puff of smoke.

"Lenny, take care of Moondog!" Serge pulled a pistol and ran out of the theater. He spun around in the middle of the street.

Nothing but the limo.

＃ 33

T

WO MIAMI CULTURES are battling it out for the heart and soul of South Beach.

The ruthlessly chic nightclubs start at Sixth Street on Washington Avenue and continue north a dozen blocks. The themes change as often as the owners: Madonna, Ron Woods, Sean Penn, people facing grand juries.

It is an unforgiving culture of youth, the fashions and fitness intimidating, the beat exciting, the mood *now*. Some clubs don't even open until after midnight, and the action goes on until brunch, a withering brand of fun requiring constant, quick refueling from tiny storefronts wedged between the nightspots, all specializing in pizza by the slice, bottled water, and instant-personality energy drinks like Red Bull, 180, KMX, SoBe and LoIQ.

These shops alternate with a second type of modest business selling groceries and pressed sandwiches to the much older and wiser Cuban population. The kids come from far and wide and represent the pulse of the moment. The Cubans live on the next block and have staying power.

The clash was being fought out on the micro level in a two-story deco building just shy of the pedestrian mall. Four decades ago, the ground floor was the bookmaking parlor; Chi-Chi and Greek Tommy roomed together in the upstairs apartment. The years took their toll. Chi-Chi's relatives moved him to a retirement home in Little Havana. Tommy stayed upstairs, signing a long-term lease on the ground floor with a group of nightclub investors. The new club was an instant hit. And loud. It wanted to expand upstairs. Tommy said no. Tommy wanted out of the lease. The club said no. That's where it stood. The place was called "Plus 24."

"Plus 24" was the hottest of the hot new clubs. It was the hottest because of a single feature: It opened later than any other nightclub on South Beach. In the brutal battle for hipness, clubs began opening later and later into the night, not unlocking their doors until three o'clock, four o'clock, five, then dawn. Finally, in a master trendsetting stroke that stunned all involved, "Plus 24" announced it wouldn't open its doors until midnight *the following night.*

Oh, sure, if you were a square, you could just get up and go to the club that particular evening. But of course you'd look like an idiot.

The apartment had no rear entrance. In the old days, Chi-Chi and Tommy walked through the betting rooms to get to the staircase in back. It added a measure of security, and they liked that. Now it was nothing but a headache.

On a recent balmy evening, Greek Tommy drove home from the store. He was driving an electric scooter up the sidewalk, ringing a bell on the handlebars for the snaking lines of partygoers to clear the way. He had a fresh cigar in his breast pocket and another in his mouth. The basket behind his seat held a Styrofoam to-go of roast pork and moro rice.

Tommy's circadian rhythms had flip-flopped due to the bass vibrations coming up through the joists of his bedroom floor. It was just after two A.M. when the scooter rolled up Washington with Tommy and his dinner. He drove past Agents Miller and Bixby, canvassing the crowd with mug shots of Serge and Lenny. The doorman behind the velvet rope at "Plus 24" was new. He blocked Tommy's path.

"I live here. Get the hell out of my way, ya chowderhead."

The senior security man nodded; the velvet cord was un-hooked.

The scooter rolled through the ear-pounding darkness, stobe lights flashing, Tommy chest deep in dry-ice fog. "Was I insane when I signed that contract?"

Tommy made it to the back of the club and chain-locked his scooter to a hot-water pipe. He trudged up the stairs with his food and opened the apartment.

Surprise!

The room was full of people.

"Who—"

Serge grabbed Tommy by the arm, yanked him inside and slammed the door. Tommy screamed bloody murder.

"Tommy, it's me. Serge. Sergio's grandson."

Tommy stopped yelling and adjusted his eyes. "*Little* Serge?"

"That's me."

"You've grown."

"Sorry about breaking in, but we're trying to avoid some people—"

"My pork dinner."

Serge reached down and picked up the Styrofoam box, a large black footprint on the lid. He handed it to Lenny. "Heat this. And see what you can do with the presentation."

Tommy bent over and picked up a flat cigar. "You stepped on everything."

"You got another in your pocket."

"I still liked this one."

Serge helped Tommy by the arm over to a worn beige sofa.

"Tommy, I have to ask you about my grandfather. It's real important. There's a box my granddad kept. Moondog started to tell me about it just before he was shot—"

"What!"

"He's okay. He's in the hospital. But he won't be talking anytime soon."

"I don't know any box."

"Then what do you remember about his death? Lives are now at stake."

Tommy put a weathered hand on Serge's shoulder. "I know you loved your grandfather. He thought the world of you. Everyone could see that. But please let this go. You don't want to be dredging this up."

"What about Chi-Chi? Moondog didn't know where he went."

Tommy took the second cigar out of his pocket and lit it. "Moved into one of those militant-Cuban-exile nursing homes in Little Havana. Libertad Meadows."

"You think he might know about the box? My granddad kept all his knickknacks in it."

"Oh, the knickknack box! Sure, I remember that."

"You said you didn't know about a box."

"I thought you meant an important box. That one just had crap in it."

"I meant *any* box. You're supposed to disclose everything because you don't know what might be useful."

"I didn't know. I haven't done this before."

"Are you holding anything else back?"

"Like where the box is?"

"You know?"

"Of course I know. I saw it the other week when I was—" Tommy looked around the room. "Is it me, or is it getting crowded in here? Who are all these people?"

"My people. Now, quick, tell me!"

"Your people have silencers?"

"No."

Tommy pointed toward the stairs. "That guy does."

Serge turned.

"Hey, you!"

The stranger fired. Serge ducked.

A gasp.

"Tommy!"

Serge cradled the old man in his arms, a gut wound.

Heavy footsteps ran down wooden stairs.

"Lenny! Take care of Tommy!" Serge dashed out of the apartment.

It was dark and deafening in "Plus 24." Red and purple lasers slashed through the blackness over the dance floor. Fluorescent glow-sticks were twirled overhead by the ecstasy troops. Others blew referee whistles and eye-droppered unknown substances into bottled water and energy drinks. Serge ducked as the mosh pit let one get away and crash headfirst into a cigarette machine.

It glinted in the strobe light: a pistol over a man's head in the ready position as he muscled toward the door. Serge pulled his own piece and aimed, but kids' heads kept bopping into the picture. The man looked back and saw Serge. He squeezed off a hurried shot. The bullet went through a woofer, improving the music. They pressed on through the crowd. Finally, the gunman was almost to the door, no way for Serge to reach him in time. Then he'd be gone. The man reached for the knob. He turned to see how far back Serge was.

There was a deep shout, growing louder and closing rapidly like an incoming mortar round.

"Fuuuuuuuuuuck liiiiiiiiiiiiiiiife!"

The gunman looked up. The mosh diver landed on him.

THE GUNMAN DIDN'T know how much time had elapsed when he regained consciousness in the back of the parked limo. He noticed electrical tape over his mouth. He tried to move, but his hands were tied behind his back. The limo was full of people, smoking dope, drinking beer, eating ribs. City and Country waved glow-sticks. Nobody seemed to be paying any attention to the gunman until—

"You're awake!" said Serge. "Good!"

Rip.

The tape came off the stranger's mouth, and he yelled.

"It's better if you remove the tape quickly," said Serge. "At least that's the feedback I've been getting."

He stuck a gun in the man's face. "Who are you?"

The man glared and pursed his lips.

"Who sent you?"

He remained steadfast.

Serge put the gun away. "Okay, you can go."

The man braced for a skull-crack from the pistol butt, but it never came.

"I said you can go. Don't you want to go?"

The man nodded enthusiastically.

"I almost forgot," said Serge. He reached for the beverage holder on the door and grabbed a plastic bottle. "Tell me how this tastes. It's my new energy drink. I'm test-marketing it."

The man looked at the antifreeze-green fluid in the clear plastic bottle: no way!

"Lenny, he's indecisive. Help me hold him."

The man fought furiously as Serge and Lenny piled on top. Serge pressed the end of the plastic bottle to his clenched teeth, bashing the side of his jaw with a fist. "Open up. . . . *Bromo-Seltzer, Bromo-Seltzer* . . ."

The man's lips involuntarily parted, and Serge jammed the bottle in his mouth like a quart of motor oil. The hostage shut his eyes tightly as the fluid started going down, then realized it wasn't half-bad. He opened his eyes.

"Tastes pretty good, eh?" said Serge.

The man stopped resisting and nodded. He drained the rest of the bottle. Serge released his grip and untied the man's hands. "Here's a product-survey card. Postage is already paid. Just drop in any mailbox."

The man was still stunned as the limo door opened and he was let out in the middle of Club Row. The door closed.

Lenny watched through the windshield as the man backed slowly away from the car, still expecting a bullet.

"What now?" asked Lenny.

"We head over to the address Tommy gave us for Chi-Chi's retirement home." Serge checked his wristwatch. "Still a couple hours to kill till dawn. Can't just go banging on retirement-home doors in the middle of the night, which I've learned."

Lenny picked up the empty plastic bottle. "By the way, what did you do with all those drugs you had me buy for your energy drink?"

"What do you think I did? Put 'em in the drink."

Lenny examined the bottle's label, an alligator in an astronaut helmet driving a '56 Cadillac convertible on Ocean Drive. SERGE'S SOUTH BEACH ROCKET FUEL.

He turned the bottle over. "There's a list of ingredients . . . but the amounts are blank."

The gunman crossed the street to the opposite sidewalk and took shallow breaths.

"That's because I'm still tinkering with the formula," said Serge. "I decided to begin with the maximum amounts and tweak back as the response cards come in." Lenny read the list. Carbonated water, high-fructose corn syrup, phosphoric acid, D&C Yellow No. 10, FC&C Green No. 3, total polyunsaturated fat: zero grams.

The gunman stood in front of a liquor store and loosened his collar. He began fanning himself. He glanced around nervously, started scratching.

Lenny fired up a joint with the car lighter. "Sounds pretty scientific. Where'd you get the idea?"

"Started with Sprite as the base," said Serge. "The hook is the lemon-lime taste. I *love* lemon-lime. I also added some caffeine, but not too much. Don't want to drive away customers with the shakes."

The gunman stripped to his boxers and darted into traffic. He pirouetted in the street, then hit the ground, flopping like a fish. People on the sidewalks laughed. Some took pictures.

"I've never heard of these ingredients here," said Lenny, holding a toke. "Guaraná and taurine?"

"Those are the twin generators. Herbal magic from the Amazon. All the big-name energy drinks use one or the other. I use both. Again, setting the pace for the field."

The gunman grabbed his neck with both hands and opened his mouth wide, a five-alarm expression, like he was simultaneously breathing too fast and not getting enough air.

Lenny ran down the list again. "Where's the cocaine you had me get?"

"You can't put cocaine on the label," said Serge. "They'll make you take it out every time. I figured I'd use the Coca-Cola marketing strategy. Establish brand loyalty with the coke, then ease off later when people start asking questions."

The gunman clawed at the skin over his heart. He ran screaming into the liquor store—then ran back out with a bottle of grain alcohol, the owner chasing him. He began chugging to get his heart rate down. The store's owner grabbed him, trying to pry the bottle away. They fought, the man still chugging, the owner tugging his arms, half the liquor going in the gunman's mouth, the rest splashing down his chest.

"How much did you put in?" asked Lenny.

"Three grams."

"In one drink!"

"Is that too much? I don't do the stuff. It looked like such a small amount."

Lenny rolled his eyes at the limo's ceiling. "That's *way* too much coke."

"Is the quantity thing the same with chrystal meth?"

"Even worse."

"Whoops," said Serge. "Used three grams there, too."

The liquor store's owner jumped back to avoid injury when the tremors hit, the man's arms spinning like propellers. He flopped to the ground again, got back up, down, up. He made it to a streetlight, wrapped his arms around the post and squeezed with all his might to stop the vibrations. He opened his eyes and saw the limo parked across the street. He let go of the post and staggered toward it. "Help me! For the love of God! . . ."

Lenny took another hit. The roach began singeing his finger-tips. "Ow, this one's finished." He reached behind him for the electric window controls on the door.

"How much am I off by?" asked Serge.

"Roughly a magnitude of fifty." Lenny flicked the roach out the window without looking.

"That much?" Serge whistled. "Who would have thought?"

The gunman was almost to the limo when the window lowered and a glowing roach twirled out and hit him in the middle of his alcohol-soaked chest.

"How do I measure that small?" asked Serge.

"They have these scales. Electric, highly accurate. Sell them in certain *tobacco* stores, if you get my drift."

The human torch staggered off behind the limo.

"What's all that screaming?" asked Lenny.

"Probably the kids," said Serge. "They get a little noisy at this hour."

"There's a guy on fire," said Rusty.

Serge started up the limo as people ran out of stores and restaurants with extinguishers.

"I'm disappointed by South Beach," said Lenny. "Just looks like a bunch of people standing around waiting for something interesting to happen."

"And it never does," said Serge, pulling away from the curb. "It's all hype."

34

1964

SATURDAY MORNING. A modest apartment on the 1400 block of Collins. Terrazzo, boomerang coffee table, peach pastel interior paint. The island was waking up. The rising sun streamed in the wrap-around corner windows, lighting up the living-room wall and a painting of a bullfight.

Little Serge sat on the floor in his footy pajamas, watching cartoons, eating Frosted Flakes. It was a small Philco set, a little on the green side, vacuum tubes glowing in back. The Warner Brothers hour was on Channel 4—Bugs, Daffy and Elmer Fudd.

The walls were a little thin.

"Oh, Sergio!"

"Oh, Lou!"

"Fuck me! Fuck my brains out!"

Little Serge crunched cereal and watched Elmer shoot Daffy Duck in the face with a shotgun.

"You're despicable!" said Daffy.

"Your cock!" said Lou.

Serge filled his mouth with flakes.

". . . Shoot me again. Look, I'm a fiddler crab. It's fiddler crab season! . . ."

Bang.

". . . Fuck me! I'm a whore! Fuck the whore like a dog! . . ."

Serge took another bite. Elmer chased Daffy around a tree.

". . . Oh, yes! Yes! Yes! Don't stop! My pussy! What are you thinking about right now! Tell me while you fuck me! . . ."

Little Serge: chomp, chomp, chomp. Bugs tapped a carrot like a cigar.

". . . George Merrick, Charles Deering, Frank Costello, Fort Dallas, the Bayfront bandshell, Pier 5, Ba-balú, bas-relief friezes, the Shelborne, the Bon Aire, the Dunes, the Tides, the Sands, Walter Winchell, Jackie Gleason, And awaaaaaaay we go! . . ."

A minute later, the shower started. A few after that, Lou came into the living room topless, rubbing her hair with a towel.

"Little Serge, you're up already."

Serge turned and nodded, cheeks bulging, chomp, chomp, chomp. Then back to Bugs and the gang.

Sergio came down the hall in his skivvies, about to goose Lou. "Oh, Little Serge, you're up." He looked at Lou. "Do you think he heard anything?"

"He's too wrapped up in the cartoons." She lit a cigarette and headed into the kitchen.

Sergio followed. "I got the tickets you wanted. Three."

"Three?" said Lou, pouring scotch in a coffee cup and flicking an ash in the sink.

"I'm bringing Little Serge."

That evening, curbside parking filled up fast along Seventeenth Street. Brand-new Imperials, Chryslers and Cadillacs circled the block, looking for spaces. Hundreds of other people were already on foot, distinguished couples walking great distances, converging on the new Miami Beach Auditorium.

Inside, a drone of conversation covered the floor as people

filed into rows. Bright lights came on up front; men in headsets stood behind TV cameras with the CBS eyeball on the side. Someone shuffled cue cards.

Lou led six men in hats and guayaberas into the hall. She pointed at someone sitting alone in the back row. "There he is, Wheels McCoy. He always comes to these things."

They filed into the row. Lou sat down next to Wheels. He noticed her and reflexively jumped up. Lou grabbed him by the arm and pulled him back down. "Relax. This is just a staying-acquainted visit."

Wheels was only down by two Gs, but he'd been scarce lately. Lou now had a firmly established rep, and all she usually had to do was show up. Wheels would pay in full by Tuesday.

Sergio leaned to his left. "Always remember this, Little Serge. You're about to see the man deservedly called 'The Great One.'"

"When did they start broadcasting from here?" asked Tommy. "I didn't read anything."

"Two months ago," said Sergio. "He twisted the network's arm. They brought his whole production company down on a personal train."

"Why?"

"Winter golf."

Little Serge made his body limp like gelatin and began sliding out of his chair to the floor. Sergio reached to grab the boy, but he crawled out of range. He went under the row of chairs in front of them and kept crawling until they couldn't see him anymore.

"Shouldn't we go get him?" asked Mort.

"He'll be back. Just needs to burn off energy."

Chi-Chi scratched his head and turned to Lou. "Why did you call us here? If you were just going to give McCoy a warning, you could have done that yourself."

"Shut up," said Lou. "That's not why we're meeting. That's just why I picked this place. We need to talk."

The curtains parted. An announcer's voice: "From the sun and fun capital of the world, Miami Beach, it's *The Jackie Gleason Show!*"

The gang saw a startled ripple down the row where Little Serge brushed people's legs. The ripple made a U-turn and headed back.

"Try to grab him when he comes by," said Sergio.

The guys reached down, but Little Serge was too fast.

Sergio sat up. "He'll be back. . . . Look! The June Taylor Dancers."

"What do we need to talk about?" Chi-Chi asked Lou.

"We're going to expand."

"Expand?" said Chi-Chi, laughing. "We don't need to expand. I don't know what to do with all the money we already—"

Lou slapped the hat off his head. "Button it! We'll talk outside."

At the end of the show, the cast took a bow and Little Serge popped back up in his seat. Gleason walked to the front of the stage and spread his arms: *"Miami Beach audiences are the greatest audiences in the world!"*

"How sweet it isn't," snipped Chi-Chi, standing and adjusting his pushed-in straw hat. The guys headed out of the theater, debating the merits of the new cast versus the unappreciated but crucial support work of Art Carney.

Lou was walking in front. She turned and faced them in the parking lot.

"We have a job Friday."

"Since when do we pull jobs?" said Greek Tommy.

"Since now," said Lou. "I know this fence. He's coming into some stones. There's a score going down somewhere, and he's taken advance orders. But he'll only have the rocks for about six hours."

"How do you know all this?" asked Moondog.

"He told me."

"Why did he do that?"

Chi-Chi inserted a fresh toothpick. "Why do you think?"

His hat went flying again. "All of you, shut up! We'll meet at

Jake's at seven, then you'll follow me to where I'm meeting him for drinks."

"And he's going to have the stones on him?"

"Wants to impress me," said Lou, lighting a Lucky with a wooden match. "Told him hot ice turns me on."

"I don't know . . ." said Mort.

"It's an easy knockover. Probably won't even have to use our guns."

35

Present

FIVE A.M. THE limo worked its way through silent, empty streets, Van Morrison's "Moondance" on the radio. A sheen of moisture reflected lights off the black pavement. A drunk on a bicycle slammed into a garbage can in front of the library. Small-caliber fire echoed in the distance; a police-copter search beam swept down the beach. Serge pulled up to a curb on Seventeenth.

Lenny was the only passenger still awake. They got out of the car and started across a lawn. Lenny pulled a joint from behind his ear. "You think we're getting anywhere at all with this investigation of yours?"

"People are shooting at us, so that's a good sign," said Serge, reading his clipboard. "Just a little while longer until sunrise, then over to Chi-Chi's."

"So why are we stopping here?"

"Need to have a big strategy session. The Master Plan is picking up steam. Things are going to start happening in fast and extremely complex ways that on the surface will appear to make no sense."

"As opposed to up till now?"

"Exactly."

Serge stopped in front of a wire sculpture in a Ralph Kramden pose. He pulled out his camera. Lenny looked up at the dark marquee: THE JACKIE GLEASON THEATER.

Serge stuck the camera back in his pocket. "I'm going to need your undivided attention, because this gets tricky." He glanced around, then started whispering in Lenny's ear. They took a break after ten minutes.

"I don't mean to hurt your feelings," said Lenny, "but it just sounds like chaos."

"That's the way it's supposed to sound. Mathematicians have discovered that there's order to chaos. And I've decided to harness it." He showed Lenny his clipboard, covered with algebra and engineering symbols.

"What's this part?" asked Lenny, pointing.

"The awesome power of fractal geometry. Our lives will depend on it."

Lenny flicked his lighter but got only sparks. "I was never good with numbers."

"That's because of all the pot. To you the Wendy's ninety-nine-cent menu is fuzzy math."

They resumed walking across damp grass. Serge got out a pocket flashlight and scanned the ground.

"Why do you like to do this?" asked Lenny.

"Do what?"

"Creep around at night looking at stuff."

"I get lõced after dark." Serge's beam found several handprints in cement. Eartha Kitt, Leslie Uggams, Michael Mann . . . "Mann is like the Kevin Bacon of Miami, six degrees of separation. He created Miami Vice, but he also did the movie Man-Hunter with William Petersen, who went on to fame in CSI, which spun off CSI: Miami, starring David Caruso, who got his start way back in a TV series called *Crime Story*, which was created by . . . Michael Mann!"

Lenny kept flicking his Bic. "This lighter's fucked."

Serge stopped walking. "Time for the next part of the plan." He looked around and began whispering again.

"Hold it," Lenny said after five minutes. "I'm totally confused. Especially about the CIA and the FBI. You keep going back and forth from one to the other. I can't keep them straight."

"Neither can they," said Serge. "That's the key chaos element." He tapped a spot on the clipboard with a sigma and some ratios. "FBI handles domestic, like the mob; CIA handles international, like spies. They're always pissed at each other, stepping on toes, messing up operations. That's why we need to get *both* involved. The polarity and tension will give us just the leverage we need." He flipped a page on the clipboard showing the coyote aiming a catapult at the roadrunner. They started walking.

"I can't tell you how jazzed I am about *CSI: Miami*," said Serge. "I've been waiting forever for this place to get another show."

"Caruso annoys me," said Lenny, getting out matches.

"Yeah, but he's so annoying it's art."

"He also annoyed me on *NYPD Blue*."

"Then he quit the show to embark on his top-secret movie career. . . . But here's the eerie part: The farewell episode of *Miami Vice* in 1989 was titled 'Freefall,' and the premiere episode of *CSI: Miami* in 2002 was called 'Golden Parachute.'"

"I think you're the only person in the world who knows stuff like that."

"If only I could figure a way to make money off it."

"Why don't you put all this shit in a book?"

They came to more palms in cement. Serge handed the flashlight to Lenny and got down on his knees. Lenny shined the light as Serge placed his hands in the Muhammad Ali prints.

"Your hands are the same size," said Lenny.

Serge stood back up. "I could have taken Liston."

Lenny looked up at the sky. "I think it's starting to get light out. Or someone sprinkled mushroom dust in my dope."

"No, it *is* getting light. Okay, last item of business. The Master Plan's final puzzle piece. Here's what we're going to do." He looked around again, then leaned to Lenny's ear.

When Serge was finished, Lenny pulled back and made a funny face. "Castro?"

Serge slapped him on the shoulder. "Let's rock."

They made good time on the nearly deserted Dolphin Expressway. Just a few delivery trucks for the convenience stores. The rising sun peeked over the city as the limo pulled up a circular driveway and parked next to a big sign. LIBERTAD MEADOWS. Underneath were paintings of little squirrels and chirping birds and crossed rifles.

They got out and headed for the entrance.

"You're Cuban," said Lenny. "What's the deal with all the extreme anti-Castro stuff around here?"

"What's the deal? What's the *deal*? Do you have any idea what that man did to my people? I'd like to take him out myself. A while back I even volunteered for Radio Martí."

"What's that?"

"The U.S. government station that beams the message of hope to Cuba. But I had to leave. Creative differences. Since then I've been writing a series of vitriolic letters to *El Neuvo Herald*."

"*El Nuevo Herald*?"

"The *Miami Herald*'s home county is now like sixty-five-percent Latin, and they have a Spanish-language edition. Except it's not really a straight translation."

"It's not?"

"Supposed to be," said Serge. "But the publishers play to their Cuban readership. Very subtle editorial nuances in the translation, like the *Herald* will have a story about a commemorative tree planting in a park, and the same story in *El Nuevo* will say something like 'Castro fucks dead donkeys.' "

Serge opened the front door of the retirement home; they approached the receptionist's desk.

"We're here to inquire about a resident named Chi-Chi."

"Last name?" said a woman with gold hoop earrings, filing her nails.

"Don't know," said Serge. "He was a friend of my grandfather. I was just a kid. So it was first-name basis. I should have asked Greek Tommy, but I figured with a name like Chi-Chi . . . You're getting all this, right? We're into something important and dangerous, but you look like you're not a blabbermouth. I hope I'm not mistaken."

"We have seven Chi-Chis." Still filing nails.

"Straw hat?" said Serge.

"Five straw hats."

"Relentlessly irascible?"

"Orojo or Menendez."

"Former CIA operative."

"Menendez."

"Can we see him?"

"He's out now. At one of the meetings."

"Who's meeting at this hour?"

"The secret exile group planning to overthrow Castro."

"If it's secret, how do you know?"

"It's not really secret. It's been totally infiltrated by Cuban spies. In fact, everyone at the meetings is an agent."

"Chi-Chi?"

"He's the exception. The exiles send him to keep tabs on the spies."

"I've heard about them," said Serge. "Buffoons, completely incompetent, a disgrace to the intelligence community. The Cuban government is broke and can barely afford to keep them fed, so most of the agents are forced to take night jobs or participate in multi-level marketing. Can you stop filing your nails?"

She looked up.

Serge grinned. "It's a respect thing."

She looked down and started filing again.

"Thanks. This meeting place have an address?"

No answer.

Serge picked up the nameplate on the desk: JEAN SANSONE MANDELL HERZFELD.

"I think I like talking to you, Jean. I could stay here all day. What do you want to talk about? You like movies? Did you see *A Beautiful Mind*?"

She huffed and put down her nail file, then scribbled an address on a scrap of paper.

The limo turned off Calle Ocho and pulled up in front of a faded lavender ranch house with wrought-iron burglar bars. Serge and Lenny opened the gate of a chain-link fence and stepped over a Big Wheel in the yard. They knocked on the front door.

A slot opened. "Who is it?"

"Serge. I want to join the movement. Fuck Castro."

"Who's the guy with you?"

"Anglo sympathizer. But he can be trusted. Lenny, show him."

There was a pause. Serge elbowed him.

"Fuck Castro," said Lenny.

"Okay, you can come in."

The door opened. The living room was full of people in Samsonite chairs. The pair took seats near the back next to an old man in a straw hat. At the front of the room, a series of men took turns addressing the group, alternately denouncing the Havana regime in the strongest possible terms and pitching the newest line of Amway.

"Pssst! Chi-Chi! It's me, Serge, Sergio's grandson."

The old man turned. "*Little* Serge?"

"We need to go somewhere and talk. It's about my granddad."

"I have to stay at the meeting in case something happens."

"Anything ever happen?"

"Nope."

"Why bother? These guys are the clowns of the spy world. Let 'em do themselves in."

"Believe me, I'd love to."

"I was hoping you could help," said Serge. "I'm trying to find out who killed my granddad."

"You don't want to be bringing that up. Do yourself a favor—"

"Please," said Serge. "I need closure."

"Then drop it," said Chi-Chi. "I loved your granddad, despite all the crap I gave him. And you were such a great kid. But this is best left in the past."

"I'm trying to find a diary. Or a box. Please."

"I remember him writing in this little book, but I don't have any idea where it could be. I never saw a box. If anyone knows, it's Mort. They were closest. Mort handled the funeral arrangements. He'd know what happened to the personal effects."

The man sitting behind them leaned forward. "Shhhhhhhh!"

Serge turned around. "No, *you* shhhhhhhh!" He faced Chi-Chi. "Where can I find Mort?"

"Lost track a long time ago, but I can make some calls. Roy 'The Pawn King'—"

"Already tried him," said Serge.

"Then who else?" Chi-Chi said to himself. "Let me work on it. If he's still around here, I'm pretty sure I can find him."

The man behind them leaned again. "Shhhhhhhh!"

Serge stood up. "May I have your attention?" Heads turned. The room went quiet. Serge pointed at the man seated behind him. "This guy's a spy!" Serge reached and ripped open the man's shirt. Wires and little microphones taped to his chest.

The group was flustered. This had never happened before. But the other spies had to maintain cover, so they beat the piss out of him.

Serge smiled at Chi-Chi. "Do that once a meeting, and this spy thing will take care of itself."

"It'll take too long."

"I have an idea."

FBI Headquarters, Miami

Agents Miller and Bixby were at their desks eating roast-beef sandwiches out of waxed paper from a no-fooling-around sandwich shop in Kendall. A courier arrived with a small cardboard box. Miller took a swig of acid coffee, wiped his mouth, and set the mug down on a stack of dead-end leads. "I've been waiting for this." He grabbed scissors.

"What is it?" asked Bixby, wiping his chin with a napkin.

Miller cut through tape. "This is from Radio Martí down in the Keys. That propaganda we beam at Cuba."

"How does it figure?"

"That will soon be more than apparent." Miller opened the box and removed an audiocassette. He opened the bottom drawer of his government-issue gray desk and pulled out an old Radio Shack tape recorder with a missing play button, just the little metal thing sticking up. Miller inserted the tape and pressed the metal thing. The tape's sprockets began turning in the scratched plastic window.

"I got a line on this when we ran the initial computer checks in Virginia. Our buddy Serge volunteered for Martí a few years back. At first they didn't think the tape still existed. It's a recording of an experimental broadcast, one of the few made in English in an attempt to endear the Cuban people to American culture."

The agents listened as a catchy jingle rattled out of the small tin speaker, then a baritone announcer's voice: "*And nowwwwwwwwwwwww, coming at you with one hundred thousand watts of insane freedom from the fabulous United States of America, it's time for* 'The Doctor Serge Showwwwwwww'!"

"Thank you, Johnny, and good afternoon everyone. Welcome to *The Doctor Serge Show*. I'm Doctor Serge, and have we got a program for you! So give me a ring and— Wait, we have our first caller. This is Doctor Serge, how can I help?"

"Doctor Serge, I fell in love with a man last year. We were going to be married. He said he loved me. Then I got pregnant and found out he was having sex with my best friend! [*loud sobbing*]"

"Let Doctor Serge stop you right there. I've heard this one a million times. Tell me, who's the head of state?"

"What?"

"Who's the president?"

"Uh, Castro."

"It's Castro's fault."

"What should I do?"

"Overthrow him. . . . Next caller, hello, you're on *The Doctor Serge Show*."

"Hi, Doctor Serge. This is kind of embarrassing, but I have this little thing on my you-know-what, and I'm not sure if I should have it looked at. Do you think it might clear up on its own?"

"Not while Castro's still in power . . . And while we're on the subject, let me tell you about that old puss-filled Soviet whore. Why, I'd love to shove that hammer and sickle up his Marxist ass myself. He should be— Hey! You're not supposed to be in the broadcast booth! The 'On Air' light is on! What are you doing! Let go of me! I thought this is what you wanted! . . . Don't go away, loyal listeners—Doctor Serge will be right back after this station break [*scuffling sounds*]. . . . Let go of me, you Communist-radio-station apparatchiks! . . . [*voice fading*] Fuck Castro! Fuck him and his imbecile brother, Raúl! . . ."

Miller pressed the stop button. "A very sick man."

Bixby was grinning.

"What? You liked that?" said Miller.

"I chuckled in spots. You ever listen to drive time in this city?"

Miller crumpled the waxed paper around a leftover bite of sandwich and threw it in the wastebasket. "This changes everything. If he was with Martí, that means a CIA angle, which brings the whole exile community into play, not to mention the mob connection from the hit on Tony, and before you know it, it's Miami 1964 all over again, tangled up in a vast, hydra-headed conspiracy that would give Oliver Stone whiplash."

"What are you going to do?" asked Bixby.

Miller popped the cassette out of the machine and stuck it in his shirt pocket. "I'm taking this to the top."

"You're going to Webb?"

"He's got to know."

THE CARS STARTED arriving just after dark. Neighbors held up cardboard signs: PARKING $5. Streams of men poured down the sidewalk, turning in a chain-link gate in front of a lavender concrete ranch house.

Chi-Chi manned the door, screening people. Two young men in black satin shirts stepped up. Chi-Chi checked through the little slot, then opened the door and quickly waved them in.

The living room began to fill. Some took seats in the rows of chairs and watched TV; others chatted by the punch bowl. Serge wore oven mittens and removed a tray of nachos from the broiling rack. Lenny sat by the cash box with a roll of raffle tickets.

Finally, it was time.

Chi-Chi walked to the front of the room and turned off the TV with the ceramic Madonna on top. "Will you please take your seats?"

The hum of conversation dwindled as stragglers drifted back to their chairs with last-second snack plates. Serge set up an easel and blackboard.

"Thank you," said Chi-Chi. "Tonight I have a surprise. Very historic news. What I tell you now must never leave this room. . . ."

The men in the audience turned to each other and murmured. Chi-Chi began writing with chalk as he spoke. "As you all know, I'm a veteran of Brigade 2506. And I have been awaiting this day for more than forty years. . . ." He kept it up for an hour, the board filling with arrows as the invasion plans took shape. Beach landing, artillery dispersement, troop movements and, finally, the siege of the presidential palace. When he was done, Chi-Chi set the piece of chalk in the easel's tray and faced the room again. "Gentlemen, our hour of glory is upon us."

Serge began clapping hard, and the rest of the room quickly joined in.

The visitors were all abuzz as they helped fold chairs and then headed for their cars, Serge holding the door—"Good night . . . good night . . . good night . . ."—the raffle winner carrying a Lazy Susan—". . . good night . . . good night . . ." The last person left, and Serge closed the door. "I think they bought it."

Chi-Chi lit a cigar. "We'll see." He handed Serge a piece of paper.

"What's this?"

Chi-Chi exhaled a big, relaxed cloud. "Mort's address and phone number. A friend of a friend . . ."

36

1964

SIX MEN IN hats and guayaberas hunkered in Jake LaMotta's Lounge on the 2100 block of Collins.

They had come to some serious decisions. The times were a-changin'. It was long overdue and way too fast. Martin Luther King was in jail for a stink at a St. Augustine lunch counter. Doctors had just told everyone to stop smoking. The French embassy got sacked in Saigon. The Russians put a woman in orbit. The Beatles were bigger than Jesus.

Little Serge jumped off his stool and ran laps around the bar.

Sergio stuck a pack of matches in his pocket and looked up. "Holy cow, that's him! He's coming this way!"

"Who?" said Moondog.

Sergio ignored Moondog and waved. "Hey, Jake!"

The others joined in. "Hi, Jake," "How's it going, Jake?" "Great place ya got here, Jake."

The man smiled and nodded slightly as he went by.

"So that's the Raging Bull," said Tommy.

"Why was he shuffling on the front of his feet like that?" asked Mort.

"You would, too," said Chi-Chi. "Did you see the second Robinson fight? He wasn't human!"

"Inner-ear equilibrium must be wrecked," said Sergio. "Probably just has to go with visual horizon."

A commercial came on the TV in the corner, a little girl picking petals off a daisy and counting. Then a bright explosion, a mushroom cloud and a deep voice: *Vote for President Johnson on November third. The stakes are too high for you to stay home.*

"What a downer," said Tommy.

"I think that's the idea," said Mort.

"Goldwater doesn't have a chance," said Chi-Chi. "Ever since the Gulf of Tonkin."

"Did you see that new show Saturday?" said Sergio. "The one with the dolphin? NBC's running it up against Gleason."

"So what?" said Chi-Chi.

"So it means two-thirds of the Saturday prime-time lineup is shot right here in our own town. We're like the center of the universe."

Little Serge ran by.

"What's ABC got?" asked Moondog.

"*Outer Limits*."

"That show's too unbelievable for me," said Tommy.

"And *Flipper* isn't?" said Chi-Chi.

"I know it's not real," said Tommy. "Still . . ."

"Who's this new guy Brian Kelly playing the park ranger?" said Mort. "I liked Chuck Conners better in the pilot."

"He was the guy in *Branded*, right?" said Coltrane. "Gets all the buttons torn off his jacket?"

"That would really piss me off," said Tommy.

"It's supposed to," said Chi-Chi, turning a page in his newspaper. "That's why they do it."

"Anything good in there?" asked Tommy.

"Lenny Bruce is going to jail for obscenity."

"I saw Bruce being interviewed on the radio," said Moondog.

"Where?"

"Pumpernik's deli up on Sixty-seventh, by that new guy Larry King."

"King's style gets under my skin," said Chi-Chi. "You watch. His career won't last."

Coltrane looked around. "Where's Lou? She said seven sharp."

"Lou scares me," said Moondog.

"Me, too," said Mort.

"Then why are you here?" asked Chi-Chi.

"Because I'm more afraid not to show up."

"I'm with Mort," said Greek Tommy. "This job tonight doesn't feel right. We had a nice little sports book going, but this is more than I can handle."

"Lou's got a good head," said Sergio. "She can be trusted."

"Trusted?" said Chi-Chi. "She cheats on you."

"Who says?"

"Everybody. Open your eyes. She's taken up with this character named Desmond."

"Where'd you hear that?"

"Moondog."

Serge glared at Moondog.

"Sorry."

"You got it all wrong," said Sergio. "Desmond's just business. He's the fence we're going to knock over."

"Sergio, haven't you heard the talk?" said Mort. "She used to date all those dead mobsters. In fact, everyone she's ever rolled with is dead except you and Desmond."

"And Mr. Palermo," added Tommy. "Who happens to be insanely jealous."

"You better watch yourself, Sergio."

"I got a bad feeling about tonight," said Moondog.

"Let's walk away from this while we still can," said Mort.

"He's right," said Tommy. "We have to draw a line."

"This whole thing is doomed," said Moondog. "Let's get out of here."

They started standing up.

"Here she comes!"

They sat back down.

Lou tossed her zebra purse on the bar. "Where were you guys going?"

"Nowhere," said Chi-Chi.

"Liar." Lou ordered a shot, did it, slammed the glass on the counter. "Everybody ready?"

The gang crossed Twentieth Street, looked around suspiciously, then snuck in a corner doorway under a round neon sign: FIVE O'CLOCK CLUB.

They nursed overpriced cocktails at a dark table. Nobody talked. All eyes on the stage, a leggy brunette peeling off an evening glove to the tempo of a junkie's snare drum. She tossed it in the audience. The drummer picked up the naughty pace. The woman sashayed down the catwalk in a peekaboo bra, twirling the end of the feathery stole around her neck. She peeled off the second glove and flung it. It landed draped over Greek Tommy's face.

He left it there.

The dance ended without further disrobement. The gang sighed. Tommy took the glove off his head and stuck it in his pocket for later research.

"Stay alert," said Lou. "We're not here for entertainment."

Music started again. A platinum Jayne Mansfield type came out, a fan of peacock plumes sprouting from her derriere.

"This is Martha Raye's old joint," said Sergio. "Harry Bellafonte got his big start here."

"Yeah, well, that's all very nice," said Chi-Chi. "Check out this rack."

"I'm not sure Little Serge should be seeing this," said Mort.

"You're nuts bringing him," said Moondog.

"His mother's working—I had no choice. Figured I'd pay one of the strippers to watch him. Besides, this is a very historic place. I want him to get an education."

"He's getting that."

Little Serge sat back in the vinyl booth, legs not reaching the edge, big eyes watching the shaking fan of feathers going by.

Lou stood up. "There he is."

"Where?"

"At the bar by the juke."

"He looks drunk."

"All the better."

They watched as Desmond's head slowly sagged over his drink, then bobbed up, then started sagging again.

Lou opened her purse and took out a small .25 pistol. "Let's do it."

Sergio pulled a sawbuck from his wallet and flagged down a stripper for day care. The gang spread out, making a six-point formation around the bar, getting each other's backs in case some associates crashed the party. Or worse, coppers.

Lou slid up next to Desmond with a flirty smile. It didn't matter. Desmond was facedown in a bowl of Spanish peanuts. She put her arm around him. "Hey, baby. What's shakin'?"

No movement. She tugged him. Just a lump. She looked around the bar, then slid her hand down to his wrist for a pulse.

Nobody home.

The guys started looking puzzled. What's going on?

Lou's eyes darted around the lounge in suspicion. She surveyed the bar in front of Desmond: smokes, lighter, drink . . . the drink. An amber-brown liquid, good whiskey, with a small swirl of undissolved powder residue in the bottom. She snuggled up to Desmond, kissed him on the cheek, feeling through his jacket. Nothing there, or there. Wait, something down in the lining under the breast pocket.

37

Present

A PHONE RANG. A captain in green fatigues picked it up. "Hello? . . . No! . . . No! . . . I see. . . . Yes, they'll want to know right away." The captain hung up and dialed.

A major picked up the receiver. "I can't believe it!" Soon, half the phones in Havana were ringing.

Ten minutes later, a colonel with a file folder walked briskly down a marble hallway, his footsteps echoing off stucco walls, passing a row of arched windows overlooking the Hotel Nacional. He entered the office of Cuban Intelligence and saluted. More phones rang. By one A.M. a select inner circle of men with piles of gold braiding on their visors had gathered around a large oak table. A topographical map of the island hung on the wall.

A general walked to the front of the room. He drew decisively on the map with a red marker. "We just got word from our operatives in Miami. . . ." The ensuing revelation stunned the room, everyone's eyes locked on the general. Except one of the majors. His eyes shifted side to side.

The meeting adjourned. Military jeeps roared off down cobblestone streets. A major walked up a flight of steps to his villa apartment overlooking the harbor. He went in the kitchen and stood on a chair. He reached into a hollowed-out ceiling beam, removing a miniature radio transmitter and codebook.

A PHONE RANG in Florida.

A rookie case agent burst breathlessly into the office of the CIA station chief.

"Sir, you're not going to believe . . ."

Phones began ringing all over Miami. Just before dawn a conference room in Coral Gables filled with bleary-eyed men in dress shirts, backs rigid around the oak table, gazes down at the Lemon Pledge shine. They could feel the station chief hovering behind them as he paced in a spitting rage, pounding the blackboard.

"Will someone please tell me what the hell is going on!"

No answer.

"Can anybody explain this message we got from our man in Havana?"

People looked at their fingernails.

"Schaeffer!" yelled the station chief. "You're his handler!"

"Maybe the message was garbled. Or maybe they got to him."

"You really believe that?"

"No."

A piece of chalk flew. People ducked. "Shit! Everyone knows what the CIA is doing in Miami except the CIA!"

"Sir, maybe it's one of those new cells that reports directly to Washington. Maybe we're not supposed to know."

"If we're not supposed to know, then we're supposed to know! We're in the intelligence field!" The chief made another lap around the table. "Do you have any idea what we're going to look like if a few hotshots from Washington can come down and run an operation this big right under our noses?"

The men knew their station chief, knew not to say anything. Chick Renfroe. The legend. Nearing the end of his career. He had been attached to the Miami office since the beginning, running a safe house back when things were loose, crazy. Renfroe started pacing again, talking to himself. "It has to be Peterson! He's been out to make me look bad ever since that Hasenfus fiasco in Nicaragua!" The chief spun and barked at Schaeffer again. "What else was in the dispatch?"

"Nothing important, just some supply lists, a couple fake agent names, Serge and Chi-Chi—"

"Not Chi-Chi Menendez?" said Renfroe.

"How'd you know?"

"Son of a bitch!" More flying chalk. "So it *is* a Company operation! I knew it! Chi-Chi was an exile operative working with us when I ran the safe house back in '64. Insubordinate as hell. Now he's back! . . . Goddamn Peterson!"

They kept their heads down as Renfroe moved around the table with heavy steps. "Okay, what's our move? Schaeffer—you mentioned a second guy?"

"Serge—he's the mystery man. No department record."

"Probably Chi-Chi's control agent from Washington."

"Actually, we traced him to a local tour service, Serge and Lenny's."

Renfroe nodded. "Typical front. Used to set those up all the time ourselves. We once had this homes-of-the-stars deal that let us keep track of Hollywood types with questionable leanings."

"Sir, if I may," said the youngest agent at the table. The others turned. They couldn't believe he was talking.

"What is it?"

"They may not be our boys at all."

"What do you mean?"

"Sir, ever since all the domestic-security issues, the territory's gotten gray. The Bureau's been stepping on our toes."

"Of course!" said Renfroe. "The FBI! I should have seen it a mile out!" Renfroe grabbed a coat off a hanger and headed for the door.

FBI headquarters, Miami.

Miller and Bixby were in Director Webb's office.

Webb pressed the stop button on the tape recorder at the end of the Radio Martí broadcast.

"See what I mean?" said Miller. "Just like sixty-four all over again—the CIA, the mob, assassinations. They must be working with the Palermos again, probably grabbed our witness as a favor to Carmine."

Webb thought a second. He was a calm one. He put his hands together in front of his face like he was praying. "You sure this tour service is a front?"

"Definitely."

The intercom buzzed. *"Sir, Chief Renfroe here to see you."*

"Isn't *that* a coincidence?" said Miller.

"You're dismissed." Webb depressed a button on the intercom. "Send him in."

Miller and Bixby passed Renfroe in he doorway. Webb slid the Radio Martí tape under some papers and got up to shake hands.

"The Agency paying me a visit?" said Webb. "What's the special occasion?"

Renfroe took a seat and manufactured a look of concern.

"We may be stepping on each other's toes. Are you working anything in Cuba?"

"You know we wouldn't do that. It's your territory."

"Except for the exiles. You've had a lot of dealings since that Brothers to the Rescue refugee plane was shot down by the MiG."

Webb didn't say anything.

Renfroe took a theatrical breath and surveyed the mahogany desk. There was a special stand next to the pen holder, a gold tee holding a golf ball and a brass plate: HOLE-IN-ONE, DORAL, BILL WEBB, SEPT. 16, 1982.

Renfroe plucked the ball off the tee and began idly tossing and catching it in his right hand.

Webb reflexively bent forward. "That's my special—" He caught himself and sat back.

Renfroe tossed the ball in the air again. "Are any of your exile contacts planning a trip south, say, in the middle of the night, a little beach vacation?"

Webb started laughing. "That's not exactly at the top of our list. Why? Do you have something like that in the works?"

"You know I can't answer that. You running anything?"

"I can't answer that either."

"We've just been getting little bits of chatter that we may be working some of the same people and not know it. That kind of confusion can cost lives."

They both eased back in their chairs and considered each other.

"Let's talk hypothetically," said Renfroe.

"Let's."

"Say you did have something going. It would be buffered through several layers of shady little fronts, the typical cast of ex-agents and mercenaries and former military from Central America."

"If we did, we learned it from you."

"Touché." Renfroe stood and tossed the ball to Webb, who lurched and caught it like a bulb of nitroglycerin, carefully setting it back on the shiny tee.

Renfroe walked over and looked up at a framed photo on the wall, Hoover and Nixon and a much younger Webb at a Miami banquet, autographed. Renfroe held his hands behind his back as he studied the picture. "So, hypothetically of course, you working anything?"

"Hypothetically, anything's possible."

"Us, too," said Renfroe, taking the photo off the wall for a closer look.

"I wish you wouldn't—"

"Who would you use?"

"What?"

"Who would you use?" said Renfroe. "As a front. In theory."

"I don't know."

"Serge and Lenny's?" Renfroe bluffed. "You know any outfit by that name?"

Webb involuntarily glanced down at the stack of papers on top of the cassette tape. "No. What about you?"

"Not sure."

Renfroe hung the photo back on he wall. "Okay, let's keep in touch. Let me know if you hear anything."

38

A BLACK STRETCH limo parked at Collins and Twentieth. Serge stuck a file under his arm and led the entourage up the sidewalk to the corner door. SOBE SHOWGIRLS. He pulled an old photo from the folder and held it up like a teacher.

"The canopy and the landmark Five O'Clock neon sign are gone, but you can't mistake the architecture."

They went inside. Mick and Lenny ran down to the catwalk and grabbed ringside seats. Serge scanned the booths in the dark room. No Mort. Now he had to wait. Serge hated waiting. He went looking for the manager. He showed him the photos in his file.

"Yeah, I heard a few stories," said a stocky man in his mid-thirties, shaved head and earrings. "When I first got here, I found Mae West's nameplate on a dressing-room door upstairs. I took it, figured it would be worth a lot of money someday."

"Martha Raye."

"What?"

"Not Mae West, Martha Raye."

"One old star's the same as another."

"There's a little bit of a difference there."

Serge continued questioning the man, pressing him harder and harder for information.

"Think! Anything you can possibly remember! A tiny detail that might seem unimportant to you could make all the difference!"

"Listen, guy, I don't want any trouble. Why don't you just go out and enjoy the girls?"

Serge returned to the show floor and began grilling strippers. ". . . Anything you can remember! It could be critical!"

"I just started here. Want a lap dance?"

"What about your friends?"

"Are you a cop or something?"

The room became a little brighter. Serge looked toward the open front door letting in sunshine. A bent old man came in with a cane. Serge headed over.

"Mort?"

"Little Serge?"

They sat across from each other in a booth. Mort went first.

"Chi-Chi called and said you wanted to meet. But said it couldn't be at the retirement home. What's going on?"

"Many, many things. But I'll pick one. I've been looking into my grandfather's death. It was no accident."

Mort leaned forward and lowered his voice. "You don't want to be stirring that up. I know it's hard, but trust me."

"I've been tracking down the old gang," said Serge. "Somebody doesn't want me talking to them. Moondog and Tommy have been shot."

"What!"

"They're all right. They're in the hospital. I needed to get you away from your place for your own safety."

"It's that serious?"

"Afraid so. Do you know anything at all about my grandfather's diary?"

"That book he used to write in all the time? Oh, sure. I know where it is right now."

"You *do?*" said Serge.

"Absolutely. It's—"

"Hold it!" Serge shielded Mort with his body and grimaced.

"What are you doing?"

When gunfire never came, Serge uncoiled and sat back down.

"You need to go talk to Louisiana," said Mort. "I'm sure she'd love to see you after all these years."

Serge was dumbstruck. "Lou's still here? She's still *alive?*"

"Of course she's still alive. More than ever."

"I mean, her lifestyle and all."

"Here's the address." He wrote on the back of a bank receipt.

Serge helped Mort to the door and began rounding up the rest of the gang. He turned to the catwalk. "We're going now!"

Mick and Lenny took dollar bills out of their teeth.

AN HOUR LATER. A desolate stretch of Miami south of the river. Plywood on windows. Trash blowing around. An empty Metrorail car clacked along its elevated track. Neutron-bomb territory.

They kept driving until they saw signs of human life again. A liquor store with a small crowd of men sucking on paper bags under the no-loitering sign. A bulletproof sidewalk window making short-term loans for car titles. Serge spotted the semi-occupied apartment building. He pulled over in front of a newsstand specializing in out-of-town papers and multilingual beaver magazines.

He and Chi-Chi got out and went up a walkway to one of the apartments. Serge knocked on the door. No answer. He put his ear to the wood.

"Hear anything?" asked Chi-Chi.

Serge shook his head. He pulled Mort's bank receipt from his pocket and checked the number scribbled on the back, same as the one on the door.

Serge tried the knob. Locked. He glanced around, then gave it a test hit with his shoulder. The door popped open. Serge ran his fingers along the splintered frame where the dead bolt used to fit.

"Someone's already been here."

Chi-Chi followed him, stepping over pulled-out dresser drawers. "Look at this mess."

Serge pawed through old costume jewelry scattered across the floor. "This was Lou's place, all right."

They went in the bedroom. Serge opened a closet. Empty.

"I don't like this," said Chi-Chi.

"All her clothes are gone," said Serge.

"I don't see any purses either," said Chi-Chi. "Maybe that's good."

They left the unit and headed back to the limo.

"Looks like Lou left in a big hurry," said Chi-Chi.

"Or was made to leave," said Serge, stopping at the newsstand and picking up a *Wall Street Journal*.

"This is what happens when you disturb the past."

"Oh, my God!" said Serge.

"What?"

"I rule!" said Serge, waving the paper over his head. "They finally published my letter."

"Letter?"

Serge handed Chi-Chi the paper, then lifted the entire stack of *Wall Street Journal*s out of the rack and headed for the cash register. "I'm going to send copies to everyone I know!"

Chi-Chi followed him, reading. "Serge, it says here in the editor's note that the letter was being published in cooperation with national law enforcement, who are trying to locate the writer in connection with a series of unsolved South Florida murders. Anyone with any information is supposed to call the FBI."

Serge plopped the stack of papers on the counter with an irrepressible grin. "Published is published!"

Chi-Chi finished reading the paper's disclaimer and started the letter.

To: Editor in Charge

The Wall Street Journal
Wall Street U.S.A.

From: Serge A. Storms

Re: The Coming Revolution

I saw where you ran the Unabomber's Manifesto some time ago, and I had to wonder: Is this how far your paper has fallen? Are you that hard up for good expository writing these days? I read the whole essay. What a nutbar! I know where he was trying to go, but in the end it just turned into word salad. Didn't anybody edit that thing?

Okay, I'm not one to criticize unless I have solutions, so you can start by publishing my "Wake-Up Call to the Fat Cats":

How everything has changed. And how quickly. It seemed like only yesterday the sky was the limit for my stock portfolio with heavy positions in midcap techs and George Foreman Grills. Now, just a few years later, federal cheese lines are back, and the American family is busy piecing together tiny scraps of soap found around the bathroom to make new bars.

We are living in riotous times. Remember a little while ago when you corporate types told us, "Oh, you don't need a pension anymore. We'll set you up with a nice 401(k). You'll be much wealthier. Trust us."

And that wealth will be based on?

"Our profits."

Which will be determined by?

"Our accountants . . . Have a nice retirement."

And now we're sitting around kitchen tables looking at monthly statements like people staring over deck rails at an iceberg and being told they're a bit shy on lifeboats.

But remember the joy? Remember how fun it was to set up your portfolio on the Internet with a cute little program, check it each day, maybe open an Ameritrade account and become like the so-pleased people in those ads? Yes, we have arrived.

Then storm clouds. Everyone out of the pool!

The revelations hit like a series of body blows. Cooked books, bogus oversight, Enron shuffling energy contracts like a three-handed blackjack dealer and the curtain being pulled back on WorldCom to show two Dixie cups and a string. . . . Let's cut through the fog. This is what happened: Wall Street held an open house for the middle class. "Come on in! You're now one of us. You, too, can play. Everyone is empowered! Doesn't it feel good?"

Then you took all our fucking money!

I turned on the TV. Every channel was talking about all the billions of dollars in investments that have been wiped out. . . . Hold on a sec. "Wiped out"? What the hell are they talking about? No money was "wiped out." It just went in your pockets.

So I have a few thoughts I'd like to share.

First, Wall Street: I'd start carrying guns if I were you.

Your annual reports are worse fiction than the screenplay for Dude, Where's My Car?, *which you further inflate by downsizing and laying off the very people whose life savings you're pillaging. How long do you think you can do that to people? There are consequences. Maybe not today. Or tomorrow. But inevitably. Just ask the Romanovs. They had a nice little setup, too, until that knock at the door.*

Second, Congress: We're on to your act.

In the middle of the meltdown, CSPAN showed you pacing the Capitol floor yapping about "under God" staying in the Pledge of Allegiance and attacking the producers of Sesame Street *for introducing an HIV-positive Muppet. Then you passed some mealy-mouthed reforms and crowded to get inside the crop marks at the photo op like a frat-house phone-booth stunt.*

News flash: We out here in the Heartland care infinitely more about God-and-Country issues because we have internal moral-guidance systems that make you guys look like a squadron of gooney birds landing facedown on an icecap and tumbling ass over kettle. But unlike you, we have to earn a living and can't just chuck our job responsibilities to march around the office ranting all day that the less-righteous offend us. Jeez, you're like autistic schoolchildren who keep getting up from your desks and wandering to the window to see if there's a new demagoguery jungle gym out on the playground. So sit back down, face forward and pay attention!

In summary, what's the answer?

The reforms laws were so toothless they were like me saying that I passed some laws, and the president and vice president have forgotten more about insider trading than Martha Stewart will ever know.

Yet the powers that be say they're doing everything they can. But they're conveniently forgetting a little constitutional sitcom from the nineties that showed us what the government can really do when it wants to go Starr Chamber. That's with two rs.

Does it make any sense to pursue Wall Street miscreants any less vigorously than Ken Starr sniffed down Clinton's sex life? And remember, a sitting president actually got impeached over that—something incredibly icky but in the end free of charge to taxpayers, except for the $40 million the independent posse spent dragging citizens into motel rooms and staring at jism through magnifying glasses. But where's that kind of government excess now? Where's a coffee-cranked little prosecutor when you really need him?

I say, bring back the independent counsel. And when we finally nail you stock-market cheats, it's off to a real prison, not the rich guys' jail. Then, in a few years, when the first of you start walking back out the gates with that new look in your eyes, the rest of the herd will get the message pretty fast.

Have a happy . . .

S——

CRISP FOOTSTEPS DOWN a bright white hall. Dress shoes. Black.

Agents Miller and Bixby pushed through a set of swinging doors and made a hard left down another corridor. Gurneys lined the walls, patients strapped down, screaming, crying, rambling about transmitters implanted in their heads, soiling themselves. A gaunt, whiskered man on one of the stretchers looked upside-down at Miller as he passed—"Your mother suck cocks in hell!"—then geyser-vomited pea-green sewage all over himself.

Miller reached in his jacket and held something out to the man. "Mint?"

"Oh, thank you."

The agents entered the next wing. A doctor checked their credentials against a clipboard and opened a door.

Mahoney was pacing his cell, fedora and tweed jacket, but a different tweed this time. The necktie had bowling pins. A *Wall Street Journal* lay on a table, folded over to Serge's letter. "Should have strapped iron and put daylight in the hinky shamus who dropped the dime. . . ."

The agents pulled chairs up to the Plexiglas partition. Miller removed a thick set of black-and-white glossies from an envelope and slid them through the slot.

Mahoney picked up the photos and flipped through. Buildings around South Florida. Motels, diners, bars, bus stations.

"What jumps into your head?" asked Miller.

"Chicago overcoats, Harlem sunsets, a jorum of skee, a chippie with boss getaway sticks, giving a canary the Broderick . . ."

"I mean the photos."

"You want me to pick the ones Serge would pick."

"These are tour stops from his website. But there are hundreds. We don't have that kind of time."

"And you want to know where to run the rolling stakeout."

"That's the idea."

Mahoney slapped a series of photos on the table. "This one, this one, this one, and this one." Just like that. He pushed the whole stack back through the slot. "You want the ice."

"What are you talking about?" said Miller.

Mahoney just smiled.

Miller stood. "We have to go now."

Mahoney nodded. "Blow, hoof, dust, fade, breeze, slide, heel and toe, grab sidewalk, leave leather, drivin' the shoe car . . ."

BASED UPON THE photos selected by Mahoney, Agents Miller and Bixby conducted a rolling stakeout along Collins Avenue, from the twenties to the forties. They passed the Eden Roc, northbound.

"We really should alert the locals," said Bixby, filling the chambers in his service revolver.

"And let the newspapers pick my career clean?"

The Crown Vic navigated a knot of pedestrians and mopeds in an intersection.

"I don't believe it," said Bixby, turning as he watched something pass in the opposite lane. "There's the limo!"

Miller made a wide, silent U-turn and fell in two cars back at a red light.

The light turned green. The black stretch continued south, Chi-Chi and his toothpick behind the wheel. Serge was in back with his clipboard, checking numbers on buildings. Mick Dafoe talked on the phone with his bookie and watched Norwegian log hurling on ESPN2. Lenny handed him a cheeseburger from a

Jimmy Johnson's paper sack. City and Country braided each other's hair with beads. Rusty and Doug had the million-mile stare.

On the little console TV, officials held a tape measure to the end of a log. "Sven just passed Olaf," said Mick, handing Lenny a shot. "You have ten seconds."

Lenny tossed it back and turned to Serge. "Where are we going now?"

"Working on that. Have to figure out where Lou went to."

Mick handed Lenny another shot glass.

"Again?"

"Sven's in the zone."

Lenny downed the drink and looked out the window at sidewalk traffic, beach babes in thongs, bodybuilders on Rollerblades, retirees with walkers. "I can see where Florida gets its old-age reputation. We were just at a Cuban home, Mort's in a Jewish one. And we must have seen twenty more driving around."

"Florida has 'em in every flavor," said Serge. "They're like living monuments to the state's history: the retirement community of ex-CIA agents near Fort Myers, aging industrialists in Palm Beach, TV and movie people put out to pasture in Fort Lauderdale, circus midgets in an aluminum Airstream encampment south of Tampa, even a home for elderly space chimps up at the Cape."

"You're pulling my leg."

"Who would have thought they'd live this long? But it would be wrong not to care for them. They're national treasures. Same goes for the convalescent colony of 1972 Miami Dolphins."

"They can't be that old."

"It's thirty-two years since the unbeaten season. Some are getting up there. You don't hear a lot about them because they're well behaved and keep to themselves with their stamp collections and prize gardenias. But every few years, when the Dolphins are playing some NFL team deep into the season without a loss and threatening the perfect record, they wheel them out to the Miami sidelines for good luck."

"Hey, I got a good Jewish joke," said Lenny.

"I used to tell Jewish jokes, too. Before I got into history."

"What does that mean?"

"Where do you think the Jewish people in Miami Beach came from?"

"Beats me. Cuba?"

Serge nodded.

"No, really," said Lenny.

"Many *did* come from Cuba."

"I was just joking," said Lenny. "I said Cuba because of all the Cubans in Miami."

"When things were the worst in Europe, they fled any way they could," said Serge. "Many made it to the states, but others couldn't get their papers right away, some not for years. The boats dropped them in Cuba to wait."

"Now I feel bad."

"On the other hand, I always like a good joke. If it's a 'laughing with you, not at you,' then you may proceed."

Two cars back, the Crown Vic ran a yellow light, staying close. At the next intersection, the car between them made a right, putting the agents directly behind the limo and giving Bixby a clear shot inside the stretch with his binoculars.

"What's going on?" asked Miller.

Bixby adjusted the focus. "Looks like some kind of important discussion."

"Probably a life-or-death strategy session," said Miller. "This is crunch time, the intense personal danger of the moment distilling thoughts to pure clarity, communication stripped to the essentials of survival. I'd give anything to hear what they're saying."

"A rabbi is on a motorcycle . . ." said Lenny.

"Orthodox?"

"What?"

"Is the rabbi Orthodox? It's funnier that way. I need to get the picture in my head. Those Hasidic curls always leave me doubled over."

"I don't know."

"Two things you can never go wrong with in comedy: neck braces and Orthodox rabbis. Say you got a movie with a dead spot that needs a gag. Send in a guy with a neck brace. It's always priceless—he's walking real careful and slow down the street with a cervical fracture, millimeters from total paralysis, and here come the construction workers carrying a bunch of huge ladders. I'm wiping tears after that. Same with Orthodox rabbis. All they can do looking like that is be very serious and pray. Put 'em on a trampoline and it's all over."

"Never thought of it like that," said Lenny. Mick handed him another shot.

"So what's your joke?"

"Okay, the rabbi, I mean, wait, I . . . I think I'm getting a little fucked up here."

"Report in later when you reestablish contact."

"Ten-four."

Serge clapped his hands in front of Rusty and Doug. "Back to live action." He inserted a silver disc in the limo's DVD.

"This is just going to be a drive-by," said Serge. "Ever see *Raging Bull*?"

Nothing.

"Good. Remember the nightclub Jake LaMotta had in Miami Beach near the end? It's coming up. I recently located the address in the bowels of the First Avenue Library." Serge's arms pointed in opposite directions, one out the window, the other at the TV. "I'm sure it's another club now, but hopefully they've kept the history intact."

Serge's face was at the window as the limo approached Twenty-first Street. "Here comes the place now. . . ." His mouth fell open. "Oh, my God! Stop the car! Stop the car!"

Chi-Chi eased up to the curb.

A Crown Vic with blackwalls pulled over and parked a half block back.

* * *

CHICK RENFROE ARRIVED back at CIA field headquarters.

"Find out anything?" asked Agent Schaeffer.

"Nothing I didn't already suspect." Renfroe hung up his coat. "The FBI knew something, but not much. Webb tried to bluff."

"I thought you'd be mad."

"Are you kidding? This is great news. After all these years, we're finally going back to Havana."

"But if the FBI isn't behind it, who? Peterson?"

"Doubt it," said Renfroe, loosening his tie. "Don't think anybody's running it. Looks like it's coming together all by itself."

"I don't understand."

"Think of it like Miami in general. On the surface, a beautiful city: modern, sophisticated, fast-paced. But underneath, nobody's in control. Spend two days here and you figure that out. Everything happening on its own. People are always looking for conspiracies when it's usually the conspiracy of anarchy. In this particular case, the timing and conditions are just right for spontaneous combustion. Growing frustration in the exile community, Soviet collapse, Castro's advanced age, and poof—a bunch of boats start sailing south. Surprised it didn't happened sooner."

"But why so happy?"

"You young guys weren't there." Renfroe sat down at his computer and began surfing. "The sixties were a horrible time for the agency. The FBI had been the golden boys for years. Dillinger, Bonnie and Clyde, Alger Hiss, the Rosenbergs. Then what do we get? The Bay of Pigs and the Kennedy hit, newsreel footage of Oswald handing out Fair Play for Cuba pamphlets. The morale was terrible. If you were there, you never forgot it. This is our shot at redemption."

"You aren't thinking of getting involved, are you?"

"Of course not. We stay completely uninvolved. If it tanks, we had nothing to do with it. If it works, we're poised to swoop in and take credit. It's a win-win."

"I don't like the sound of this."

"Here it is," said Renfroe, scrolling down Serge & Lenny's home page. "Hand me the phone."

MILLER AND BIXBY kept an eye on the parked limo as they slipped into body armor and checked their ammunition.

"We really should call for backup," said Bixby.

"Shut up." Miller stuck his head through the hole in a Kevlar vest. "Hand me the shotgun."

Serge stepped out of the limo in a horrified trance. He looked up at the former home of Jake LaMotta's Lounge. "A Lum's Hot Dogs?"

"He's out of the car!" said Bixby.

"Now's our chance!" They jumped from the Crown Vic and ran to the edge of a building. They started up the sidewalk, pressing against the store windows for concealment, hiding twelve-gauges by their sides. Senses alert, advancing like cats.

"What's he doing now?" whispered Bixby.

Serge furiously punched the concrete exterior of Lum's Hot Dogs with both fists—"*Why! Why! Why! Why!*"—then butted it with his forehead—"*Why! Why! Why! Why!*" Blood started running.

Miller was twenty yards away, inching closer. He clicked the safety off his gauge. The cell phone on Bixby's belt began vibrating.

"I got a call."

"Don't answer it."

Bixby checked the numeric display. "It's Webb."

"Shit." They backed into the doorway of a car rental. "Give it." Miller put the phone to his head.

A cell phone began ringing in the limo. Lenny stepped out the back door. "Serge, it's for you."

"... *Why! Why! Why!* ..." He turned. "What?"

"You got a call."

"Oh." He took the phone in a bloody hand. "Serge and Lenny's."

A few yards up the sidewalk, Miller slammed the cell phone closed and tossed it to Bixby. "Politics!"

"What is it?"

"Webb ordered us not to apprehend. Wants to give the CIA enough rope to hang itself. 'Hands off Serge and Lenny.' His exact words." They headed back to the Crown Vic and stowed the weapons.

Lenny tapped Serge's shoulder. "Who is it?"

Serge covered the phone. "Joe's Dry Cleaning."

"Who's that?"

"The CIA. ... Yes, I'm back. You say you have some trousers ready? For Chi-Chi? ... Yes, he's right here. ... Just a second." Serge stuck his head in the limo. "It's for you."

Chi-Chi grabbed it. "Hello ... Who? ... Renfroe? ... Not the Renfroe from the safe house ... You asshole! Never call me!" He hung up.

The phone rang again. Serge got it.

"Serge and Lenny's ... Yes, I think I can get him to talk." Serge covered the phone. "Why won't you talk to him?"

Chi-Chi folded his arms sternly. "Those bastards screwed up the best chance we had to get Castro."

"Just hear him out," said Serge. "The country's in a whole new state of mind now. You never know."

Chi-Chi sighed and snatched the phone. "Make it snappy! ... No! ... No! ... That's the stupidest— ... No, I don't see the point. ... Look, if it'll get you off my back, I promise to at least think about it." Click.

"What did he want?" asked Serge.

"To meet."

"Great!"

"I'm not meeting that twit."

"But we have to meet, just like in the Master Plan. Remember what we talked about?"

"I'm too old for this shit."

"C'mon. It'll be fun."

39

1964

I N THE EARLY sixties, Miami had the largest CIA field office in the world, thanks to the Cuban Missile Crisis. The field office supported an array of safe houses scattered throughout Dade County.

Chi-Chi hated going to the safe house.

He cursed under his breath all the way over, driving his '58 Cadillac convertible with the top down, wearing the flat-brimmed straw hat he only took off when he showered or slept.

Chi-Chi Menendez, Mr. Cynic. Thin, five-foot-six frame. Brown eyes, beady, the whites slightly yellowed from forty-five hard years that left him with blotched, prematurely leathered skin. Some of the wear had come during training under the Company on Useppa Island near Fort Myers. Chi-Chi was one of the few members of Brigade 2506 who wasn't captured or killed at the Bay of Pigs. It was more than enough to explain Chi-Chi's bitterness. Except he'd always been bitter. It's what made him happy.

Chi-Chi made a right on LeJeune Road just before noon, rumba music from the AM. The Cadillac headed south into a neglected neighborhood of vandalized duplexes, Spanish restaurants and dejection. It parked behind an orange apartment building. The radio went silent. Trickles of perspiration ran down Chi-Chi's cheeks as he started up concrete stairs. He came to a landing and knocked on the door.

The hip-high balcony wall was a grid of decorative gardening blocks mortared together and whitewashed. Chi-Chi leaned over and saw lizards scampering through weeds and brittle, sun-baked newspapers. His teal guayabera flapped in a breeze that didn't make it cooler, just pushed the heat around.

"Who is it?"

"Chi-Chi."

"You're supposed to use your code name."

"Open the fucking door!"

Slats of jalousie glass slowly cranked open. A pair of eyes stared out at Chi-Chi. "What's the password?"

"That's it. I'm leaving."

The door quickly opened. "Come back!" A young agent stepped onto the landing in an untucked golf shirt and amber sharpshooter sunglasses. Agent Renfroe.

Chi-Chi muttered as he turned and went back up the steps.

Renfroe leaned over the railing and looked down the street. "Were you followed?"

"Yes," said Chi-Chi. "I think I saw Castro in a T-bird."

"That's not funny."

Chi-Chi entered the apartment and plopped down at the kitchen table, where a second agent was working with a thick cigar, tweezers, a coffee can of enriched gunpowder and clay sticks of plastic explosives sitting on a stack of porno mags. Agent Renfroe grabbed three bottles of Miller High Life from the fridge and joined them. A noisy electric fan sat in the middle of the table.

"Can't you guys afford air-conditioning?" asked Chi-Chi, the brim of his hat lifting as the fan rotated past.

The second agent pointed at a piece of plywood covering a hole in the wall. "Someone stole it."

"What's with the girlie magazines?" asked Chi-Chi.

Renfroe nodded toward the second agent. "Going through a divorce. It's a tough time."

Another fan was running in the apartment, pointed at a small couch in the living room where four men sat together watching TV. There was a poster of Castro on the wall over the sofa. Someone had drawn a penis on his nose. Chi-Chi squinted at the quartet.

"You know them?" asked Renfroe.

"Recognize Meyer Lansky from the neighborhood, and I've seen Sam Giancana in the papers. Don't know the other two."

"Santos Trafficante from the Tampa family," said the second agent. "And Carmine Palermo, coming up in the Miami organization."

"Why don't you just let us handle it?" said Chi-Chi. "Those guys are nothing but trouble."

"Sometimes you have to make a deal with the devil."

"The mob is what fermented the problem in the first case. All those casinos," said Chi-Chi. "Just give us air cover this time."

"No way," said Renfroe.

The other agent looked up. "We have a more refined strategy. More subtle . . ."

Chi-Chi looked at the cigar in the agent's hands. "What's that?"

"It explodes."

"Have you lost your minds?"

"Hear us out," said Renfroe, setting a small green bottle on the table.

"Aftershave?" said Chi-Chi.

"Mixed with depilatory cream."

"So it's true."

"What's true?"

"When I heard the talk on the street, I couldn't believe my ears. I said, 'Nobody's that stupid.' "

"The beard's his trademark. The embarrassment will be tremendous."

"For us."

"I told you he couldn't be trusted," said the second agent, tightly wrapping the cigar.

"Chi-Chi's solid," said Renfroe. "He just needs time. The Bay of Pigs was pretty rough."

"This isn't funny," said Chi-Chi. "We're trying to free my country."

"So are we."

Laughter from the living room. Chi-Chi leaned back and saw four men cackling on the couch, pointing at the TV. Lucille Ball trying to keep up with a conveyer belt of cream pies.

"I don't like his attitude," said the second agent, getting up from the table and leaving the kitchen with the cigar, some plastic explosives and a girlie mag.

"Where's he going?" asked Chi-Chi.

"The demolition room. For final assembly," said Renfroe.

"The demolition room?"

"The bathroom."

"Does he actually have any real demolition training?"

"Why?"

Someone had opened a fire hydrant in the street. Small children were laughing and jumping through gushing water when they heard the explosion and saw glass rain down from an upstairs bathroom window.

Present

Two men stood silently in the shallow end of a Coral Gables swimming pool. A tall one and a short one, ten feet apart, warily eying each other, water lapping pasty white breasts sagging in the bright afternoon light. Renfroe wore mirror sunglasses. Chi-Chi had Ray-Bans and a straw hat. He chewed an unlit cigar. Behind them, a waterfall and outdoor café next to an old quarried building with orange tiles. Children splashed at the other end, water rippling its way down the pool according to the laws of wave mechanics, flickering streaks of light off the masonry.

"So . . ." Renfroe finally began. "We meet again after all these years. A couple of veteran Cold War soldiers. The last of our breed. Remember the safe house?"

"My eyebrows didn't grow back for three months."

"He was a good agent. They buried him at Arlington." Renfroe stopped and took a deep breath, then grinned. "Can't tell you how great it is to be back in the game!"

Chi-Chi took the cigar out of his mouth. "I feel stupid."

"No, this is cool," said Renfroe, staring over at the Italian lanterns hanging on striped poles in the emerald-green water. "The Venetian Pool. Great symbolism, very spy-like. Reminds me of the Benecio Del Toro scene in *Traffic*."

"That's what Serge said when he picked it."

"Is he nearby?" asked Renfroe, looking around. "When do I get to meet him?"

"You don't," said Chi-Chi. "You only contact him through me. That's the way he wants it. No offense, but he doesn't trust anyone."

Renfroe broke into a smile of admiration. "I would have expected no less from a seasoned operative. So he worked for Radio Martí?"

"Not really."

"Oh, right. I get your drift."

"No, you don't."

"The better you are at this game, the harder it is to swallow the bureaucratic bullshit. All the best are like Serge, contract hires."

"He's crazy."

"You have to be, in this business," said Renfroe. "Ever since we got the first coded transmission from Havana, there's been a lot of speculation about Serge. Tell me, what's he really like?"

"Very sick. I knew him when he was a kid, and he's turning out just like his grandfather. I feel obligated to watch out for him."

"I see. Brought him along, raised in a lifetime of espionage training. So that's how he got to be so good."

"He's in need of serious help."

"You name it," said Renfroe. "Anything we can give him. We want to make sure he succeeds."

"No, that's not what I mean."

"Right. You didn't officially ask. This conversation never took place."

"What I'm trying to say—"

"Are you working with the mob?"

"No."

"They're just dying to start up the casinos again."

"We're not working with them."

"Sure, I understand. They're not involved."

"They really aren't."

"The rules have been relaxed. It doesn't bother us if they are."

"They aren't."

"And that's exactly what I'll say if anyone asks."

"Good."

"But it's really okay with us."

"Jesus!" said Chi-Chi. "What did you want to talk about? I'm shriveling up here."

"I understand you're going to invade Cuba."

"Where'd you hear that?"

Renfroe inflated his chest. "I hear a lot of things."

Chi-Chi shrugged. "I guess we might do a little invading. What's it to you?"

"I want to help."

"No chance. I remember the last time you guys got involved."

"Don't worry, we won't actually be involved. I was just wondering if there's anything you need to make sure you succeed. We'll help in any way that's not really help."

"How about some money?" Chi-Chi said sarcastically.

"How much?"

"Ten grand."

"Done."

"You're kidding."

"Anything else?"

"Uh, let me check with Serge and get back to you."

CHI-CHI AND SERGE sat at the base of a tall statue in Little Havana, eating shredded beef and rice off paper plates.

"And he offered us ten grand just like that?" said Serge.

Chi-Chi tore a piece of Cuban bread and dipped it in his black-bean soup. "He's crazier than you are. We're supposed to pick it up after we set the next meet and I bring him the rest of your requests."

"You mean I can ask for more stuff?"

Chi-Chi nodded and swallowed a chunk of meat. "He's so obsessed he'll give you anything."

"Oh, this is too good," said Serge, rubbing his palms together. "Like a genie granting wishes. Let's see, I want that and that and that and that and . . . I better get the clipboard and prioritize. Have to be sure I don't pick the wrong things. You never want to waste genie wishes. You gonna eat those plantains?"

"Have at it."

Serge shoveled them onto his plate. He got up with his food and walked around as he ate, reading the plaque on the Brigade 2506 Memorial honoring the fallen at the Bay of Pigs. He looked up at the eternal flame. "This must be a pretty special place for you."

"You have no idea," said Chi-Chi, scooping rice. "These were great men. We can never forget."

The others from the limo were gathered around the park picnic-style, eating from their own plates.

"Is the bread supposed to be like this?" asked Lenny.

"It's Cuban bread."

"I'm not saying it isn't good. It's just different. And I ordered coffee, but they only gave me a little sample cup."

Serge turned to Chi-Chi. "I had my hopes up when Mort gave me Lou's address. Now I feel like we're all the way back to square one."

Chi-Chi dug into the beef with a plastic fork. "Lou was your best shot."

"But where could she have gone?"

Bang.

A patch of dirt flew.

"What was that?"

Bang. More dirt.

Everyone hit the deck. Chi-Chi dove behind the statue. "Serge, get down! Someone's shooting!"

Serge stood with hands on hips.

Another burst of gunfire hit the paper plates, the air filling with rice and beans. The ground was strafed, a series of dust explosions at Serge's feet. "Okay, I'm getting angry!"

Chi-Chi pointed at a grassy knoll. "There he is!"

Serge took off running. "I want to talk to you!"

THE LIMO HEADED over the bay to Miami Beach, Lenny behind the wheel. Everyone in back was staring at the duct-taped hostage.

"How'd you catch him?" asked Chi-Chi.

"Superb conditioning," said Serge. "Most people think you'll break off a foot chase after twenty or thirty blocks. He never saw it coming. I ambushed him at the corner of Twenty-second and gave him a little Bruce Lee action." Serge sliced the air with lethal karate chops, swish, swish. "I'm practicing tearing out a guy's heart with my bare hands and showing it to him while it's still beating. Except I can never seem to break through the skin, so it just knocked his wind out. . . ." Serge turned toward the hostage. ". . . Lucky for *him*." Swish, swish.

"What's the plan now?" asked Lenny.

"Make the hostage talk," said Serge. "Get to the bottom of all this shooting. Maybe even find where Lou went." He ripped the tape off the captive's mouth. "Ready to talk?"

A silent scowl.

"No problem," said Serge, replacing the tape. "You'll talk at the safe house. *Everyone* talks at the safe house."

"What safe house?" asked Chi-Chi.

"The Pacino Room."

A half hour later, the limo was parked in yet another alley.

Serge got out and opened the trunk. He removed an orange duffel bag and a large green molded-plastic case. Rusty and Doug started inching backward.

Serge waved at them with a pistol. "You're going the wrong way."

He picked up his gear and pushed open the back gate between two buildings. "On your left is the rear of the famous Colony Hotel, and on your right, Johnny Rockets, the trendy burger joint." They entered a tight passage between the structures. The left side of the walkway was a row of forgotten apartments that had somehow been crammed up against the Colony. They reached the front near Ocean Drive and started up the stairs to a second-floor balcony. Serge stopped at the first room and went to work with a lock pick.

"Doesn't someone live here?" asked Lenny.

"Under renovations . . . Damn, I can't get this lock." He opened the duffel and removed a T-shirt. He wrapped his hand in the cloth and punched out one of the door's horizontal panes, quickly grabbing the two biggest pieces before they could shatter on the concrete.

Serge motioned everyone into the room and locked the door. He began unloading the duffel bag: notebooks, videocassettes, photos, handcuffs, mini combination TV and VCR. He looked up at Rusty and Doug. "Can you feel it?"

Blank looks.

"You have no idea where you are?"

They shook their heads.

Serge went in the bathroom and set the TV/VCR atop the toilet tank. "Doug and Rusty, get over here." They stuck their heads in the door. "You've just entered the *Scarface* portion of your tour. . . . Lenny, bring the hostage."

Lenny prodded the man with a pistol. Serge handcuffed his wrists over the shower rod. He stuck a tape in the VCR.

The rest of the gang was curious now. They joined Rusty and Doug in the doorway. "Watch the TV carefully," said Serge. "Here's the part where Pacino and his gang arrive on Ocean Drive in their convertible."

Lenny looked out the bathroom's porthole window. "But I thought the neighborhood in *Scarface* was a dump."

"It was," said Serge. "That's the amazing thing about this movie. It's also a documentary, capturing the early eighties' seediness when South Beach was simultaneously a geriatric slum and Wild West cocaine show—and now the convertible is making the U-turn, which gives us a clear view of the Colony Hotel and our apartment next door. And here they are pulling up to the curb across the street—that's another thing that's changed. They found a parking space—and Pacino jumps out and crosses the street. He heads up the stairs, the same stairs we just came up." Serge fast-forwarded the tape and hit pause. "And now a splendid cinematic moment that always puts a smile on my face—the famous shower scene!"

Serge pushed through the crowd in the doorway and left the bathroom, returning quickly with the big green plastic carrying case. On the side: JOHN DEERE. "I've always wanted to do this!"

He set the case on the bathroom floor and flipped the latches. Over his shoulder, the little TV was frozen on the image of a Colombian swinging a chain saw.

Rusty's eyes went back and forth from Serge to the TV. A shock of realization. "Serge! No!"

"For the love of God!" said Doug.

"Too late," said Serge. "I've got game."

He hit the play button; a vicious motorized sound erupted from the TV. The hostage trembled.

Serge bent down to his case again. "This scene is a classic!"

Rusty turned his head. "I can't watch."

"I'll watch," said Mick Dafoe.

"Me, too," said Lenny.

The noise from the TV grew louder.

Serge opened the lid and jerked the John Deere out by the handle. He pull-started the two-stroke gas engine on the first try. It roared to life. Serge gritted his teeth and swung it toward the hostage, poking it in his face. "I'll bet you're ready to talk now!"

Lenny scratched his head. "A leaf blower?"

"They were out of chain saws," Serge said out the side of his mouth, still gritting teeth.

The hostage's hair blew around.

"Serge, maybe you need a little nap," said Chi-Chi.

"I'm having the time of my life."

"It's not going to kill him."

"Yes it will."

"No it won't."

"It'll just take longer. Hours, maybe all weekend. Think of the agony."

"Serge . . ."

"What if I put it real close?" Serge placed the end of the blower an inch from the man's stomach. "See? He's getting a rash."

They began hearing sirens in the distance.

"Serge, we better get going," said Lenny.

"Just a little more time."

Chi-Chi walked up from behind and put a hand on Serge's shoulder. "We know you mean well."

SERGE RAN A red light on Biscayne.

"A leaf blower!" he said, shaking his head. "What was I thinking?"

"Just like your granddad," said Chi-Chi, reading a newspaper in the passenger seat.

"I get these ideas," said Serge. "Who knows where they come from? Next thing, they've taken over my life. Then we have all *this*. . . ." He gestured at the sticky notes covering everything. "You can't tell me that's normal."

"The first step to recovery is admission," said Chi-Chi.

"You're right," said Serge. "It's so clear now. I have to ignore this insane chorus in my head. I have to find some way to remind myself not to record all these thoughts." He grabbed the mini digital recorder. "Note to self . . ."

Rusty tapped Serge on the shoulder. "We'd like to get out now, please."

"Would never do that to you. When I give my word, you can bank on it. Besides, we're almost home free. The Master Plan is unfolding perfectly."

Rusty lost it again. "No it's not! This is no plan! You're insane! You're just aimless driving around!" He fell back in his seat and sobbed quietly. "We're all going to die!"

The basketball arena went by. Serge looked in the rearview. "Rusty, Doug. I wasn't going to tell you because I didn't want to cause needless worry. But you've held up well and deserve the truth. Everything's changed; I'm calling an audible at the line of scrimmage. I've been doing some new calculations, and it looks like we've lost every advantage. They know who we are, they know Tony's dead, they have a huge organization and own half the city government. It's hopeless—just a matter of time before the Palermos hound us down and kill all of us in slow, unspeak-able manners. We've run out of options. And you know what that means?"

They stared.

"We have them right where we want them!"

Doug and Rusty dove for the door handles, but Serge hit the child safety locks.

"They're overconfident! So now we attack *them!*"

Rusty and Doug jiggled the handles some more, then started banging on the windows with their fists.

"It's time for the big strike," said Serge. "We're going to assas-sinate the godfather, Mr. Palermo. That's where we're headed right now. I know you're not that familiar with guns, but I'm going to need you to cover me and lay down suppression fire." They pulled up to a red light. "Do you think you can handle that?" Serge turned around and saw Rusty and Doug's feet as they climbed out the sunroof and scrambled down the trunk of the car. "What got into them?"

Serge watched in the driver's-side mirror. Rusty and Doug ran up the middle of the street, waving frantically at a police cruiser.

Serge took a quick left, turning around in a pet-grooming drive-through. Rusty and Doug were getting in the police car. Serge followed the cruiser back to a satellite precinct house and parked a block short of the station, watching the gate where the patrol cars went in and out of the fenced lot.

"This is when they'll be in the most danger," Serge told Lenny. "Wherever they take them next, they'll be coming through that gate. We can't miss 'em."

"Won't they get suspicious of us sitting here?"

"Chauffeurs are always waiting in limos. This is the perfect vehicle for a stakeout."

"You think of everything."

They waited. Pot smoke filled the car. Serge showed Lenny his collection of antique Florida View-Master reels. Lenny hit the lever, and a '52 Edsel crossed the old Sunshine Skyway.

"The best is when you can actually go to the place where they took the View-Master stereographs," said Serge. "I've got this one vintage reel from the 1940s down in the Keys. Priceless shots of the Bahia Honda Bridge and Sloppy Joe's. I like to stand on the same spot as the photographer and put the left eyehole of the View-Master over my right eye, so I can overlay the images. One eye is looking at the current scene, the other the way it appeared a half century ago. I go back and forth, blinking one eye and then the other, pretending I'm a time traveler. Hours of endless fun!"

Lenny hit the lever on viewer. A 1950s model in a madras swimsuit plucked an orange off a tree in a grove. "Why do you love Florida so much?"

"Because I need nonstop stimulus. Living here is like being in a permanent studio audience for *Cops*."

Lenny hit the lever again. Mermaids. "Everyone thinks we're dumb. Flori-*duh*."

"And that's exactly what we want them to think. Then they come here on vacation all superior and off guard, and we pick them clean in a Miami minute. . . . Hold on. Something's happening."

A squad car with two people in the back rolled out the gate and turned south. Serge started up the limo and pulled into traffic.

The cruiser made a straight shot down Biscayne, then turned left on Northeast Fifth.

"They're heading for the port," said Serge.

"I didn't know they had a police station out there," said Lenny.

"They don't."

The limo shadowed the cruiser down South American Way, over the bridge, onto the island with the big ships. They crossed train tracks, passing stacks of giant cargo containers stretching football fields. Pavement changed: concrete, tar, gravel, slab, sand. They reached the isolated back part of the port, no work going on, metal containers getting rustier, a long line of huge, idle cranes.

"Look at the size of those things," said Serge. "From time to time, I see giant cranes in a variety of settings, and I always wonder: Who makes them? And where? How much do they cost? How hard are they to operate?"

"I used to run a forklift at Home Depot," said Lenny. "I could barely stay in control of those things."

"Because you were high?"

"I thought that would help my concentration. But the things are constantly making this beeping sound that gets on your nerves, so I turned the beeper off. Then they fired me. I got the prongs hung up on the top shelf one afternoon and dumped a pallet of those mosquito-repellent tiki torches on a Girl Scout troop. I'm just lucky I was in a protective cage. That is not a safe place to work."

"Don't they drug-test?"

"Sure, but I tricked them with one of those secret rubber bladders of someone else's urine taped to my stomach and a little tube running down under my—"

Serge raised a hand. "Hold that touching thought. We're getting close."

They reached the end of the island, driving slowly along the seawall. Serge made a right around another cargo crane and saw the police car pull inside a warehouse. Two men slid the large metal doors closed behind it.

"I know this place," said Serge. "It's a major smuggling dock. Mr. Palermo's a partner."

"This doesn't look good."

"Unless I'm mistaken, Doug and Rusty will be dead in a few minutes. Here's the plan. . . ."

TWO INDUSTRIAL LAMPS hung from girders inside the damp warehouse, making two bright circles on the greasy cement floor. In one circle, the police car, doors open, Doug and Rusty standing outside with two cops. In the other, three Cadillacs, a dozen broad-shouldered men in black turtlenecks positioned by the fenders, cradling submachine guns. In front of them, a wheel-chair holding an old man in a flat golf cap with a plaid blanket over his legs.

The old man made a slight motion with his right hand, like an expensive auction bid. "Pay the police officers."

One of the turtlenecks nodded and pulled two brown envelopes from his jacket.

They began hearing a noise. The crew tried to place it. An engine sound, like a stock car overrevving, the tachometer pegged, getting louder, then a screech of tires. They turned toward the sliding metal doors at the front of the warehouse. The pair of men guarding the entrance peeked through a slit, then dove in opposite directions as the steel panels buckled and broke away, flying up over the hood of a limousine, which spun out and stopped in the middle of the floor.

Serge jumped from the driver's seat and smiled. "Am I late? Did you start? Could you please repeat anything you might have already said, because I don't want to miss anything good."

Serge turned and winked at Doug and Rusty, who became faint and fell back against the side of the police car.

The Palermo lieutenants stepped forward and cocked their weapons.

"No," said the old man, holding out a hand. "Not yet."

Mr. Palermo thoughtfully appraised Serge, standing there grinning, bopping jauntily on the balls of his feet. The old man raised his chin and spoke in an understated voice. "What are you doing here?"

"Just gettin' my swerve on," said Serge.

"You've come to the wrong place." Mr. Palermo began to signal his lieutenants.

"I'm here to deliver a message," said Serge.

Mr. Palermo folded his hands in his lap. "What is this message?"

"*Luca Brasi sleeps with the fishes.*"

The lieutenants looked at each other.

"I didn't know until this day it was Barzini all along."

One of the turtlenecks leaned down to the old man. "What's he talking about?"

"He's doing *The Godfather*," said Mr. Palermo. "He's mocking us."

"Mr. Corleone is a man who insists on hearing bad news immediately."

The lieutentant stood back up and ran the slide on his Mach 10. "Mr. Palermo, let me shoot this cocksucker!"

"Cocksucker?" said Serge. "Oh, so you're homophobic?"

"What?"

"You realize that gay-bashing is the IQ demarcation line of the subzero intellect?"

"Shut up! It's just a figure of specch!"

"How long have you been a bigot? What do you have against gays anyway?"

"Nothing!"

"Are you a moron? Do you have some kind of problem with cocksucking?"

"No!"

Serge pointed dramatically. "He sucks cock! He sucks cock! You heard him!"

The other lieutenants turned their guns toward the first.

"That's not what I meant! Guys! He's putting words in my mouth!"

"Along with, say, *cocks!*" added Serge.

The other lieutenants surrounded the first.

"Enough of this foolishness!" said Mr. Palermo. He grabbed a cane off the armrest of his wheelchair and slowly stood.

Serge fell to his knees and clasped his hands together. "He can walk! Praise Jesus!"

"You talk too much," said Mr. Palermo. "You have no respect. The only reason you're still alive is you may have some information I need." He aimed at Serge with his cane. "Where are the stones?"

"The Stones? I think they're playing Philly tonight. And I must say Jagger is still moving quite well for his age."

"You tire me. You're wearing out my pacemaker." Mr. Palermo sat back down in his chair and made another small gesture. One of the lieutenants wheeled him toward the newest Cadillac.

"What do you want us to do with him?" asked one of the turtlenecks.

"Wait until I leave the building."

The crew watched the Cadillac drive out through the bright square of sunlight where the metal doors had been. They turned back and raised their weapons.

Serge muttered under his grin, "C'mon, Lenny. What's taking you so long?"

"Any last words, smart guy?"

"Hold it!" yelled Serge. "Stop! Wait!"

"What is it?"

"I'm still thinking. . . ."

They took aim.

"Okay! I got it!" Serge cleared his throat and began singing, only slightly off-key. ". . . I'll repeat myself, at the risk of being crude, there must be sixty-four ways to die in Miami. . . . There must be sixty-four ways to die in Miami. . . ."

The goons' eyebrows angled in confusion.

Serge snapped his fingers and began a little soft-shoe routine. ". . . Another shark attack, Jack; bad robbery plan, Stan; you're a DEA decoy, Roy, and now your soul's free. Fall off a bus, Gus, you don't need to be dragged much; just snort a whole key, Lee, and it's curtains for thee. . . ."

The goons looked back and forth.

". . . Mob double cross, Ross; potent designer drug, Doug; innocent bystander, Flander, just listen to me. Agree to testify, Sly; botch a bank job, Bob; Tainted seafood, Jude . . ."

The crew raised their guns again.

"... *Sudden sea squall, Paul; leaky gas heater, Peter; watch out for that machete, Eddy! ...*"

A tremendous crash. The goons didn't have time to look up as a semi container of chopped car parts smashed through the metal roof.

It missed everything.

"Nice aim, Lenny. Shit." Serge dove for the limo, dodging gunfire. Bullets raked the side of the stretch as he swung around and T-boned the police car.

Another long burst from the machine guns. The cruiser's headlights exploded. Rusty was standing between them and stared down incredulously at the line of red bullet holes across his chest. He was dead before he hit the concrete. Doug screamed. Serge yanked him into the limo and punched the gas for the exit. The hoods ran for their own cars.

Lenny jumped down from the controls of the cargo crane and ran for the warehouse entrance. Serge slammed the brakes as the limo broke into the light, and Lenny dove in with the limo still rolling. The Cadillacs were right behind.

"What took so long?" asked Serge. "You said you knew how to run those things."

"I thought it would be like the forklifts at Home Depot, but the controls were way, way more complex. Finally, I thought, Just do what you did that time you dropped all that stuff."

Serge made a hard left, throwing up a cloud of dust. He checked the rearview. Two Cadillacs emerged side by side from the cloud, guys hanging out windows shooting guns as they all raced along the seawall, the bright Miami skyline across the water in the distance.

"Lenny, take the wheel." Serge hung out his own window, returning fire.

It was a bumpy road. Nobody was hitting anything.

"Lenny, stop the car!"

"What?"

"Stop the car!"

Lenny reached for the brake with his left foot and skidded to a halt. Serge braced his shooting arm on the roof. The Cadillacs were almost on top of them, ready to plow right through the limo's trunk. Bullets from the goons whizzed by Serge's head.

"Remember *Jaws*?" Serge shouted to Lenny.

"Who doesn't?"

Serge gritted his teeth and began squeezing the trigger. "Smile, you son of a—!"

Ka-boom.

Tire pieces went flying. The two Caddies banged into each other, locking bumpers, still closing on the limo. They veered wildly, the two drivers fighting each other for control, finally swerving past the limo with inches to spare and sailing off the seawall in tandem. Two pairs of black tailfins bobbed in Biscayne Bay.

"That settles that," said Serge, climbing back in and hitting the gas. He made another tight left around the back side of the warehouse, sending up a last big cloud as they headed home.

Lenny glanced over his shoulder. "Holy shit! Where did *they* come from?"

Serge looked up in the mirror. A white van came through the cloud.

"Fuckin' Sunshine Tours," said Serge. "Will they never learn?"

"Look out!" yelled Lenny.

Serge turned and saw a big yellow object up ahead, closing fast. "Oh, shit!"

"I must have forgot to set the parking brake," said Lenny.

Serge swerved, barely missing the crane rolling backward down the incline next to the warehouse before plowing broadside into the van, sending it sideways into the bay like a Matchbox car.

Serge did a quick head count. "Doug, you okay? Mick, you good? City and Country, how's the worst generation?"

"Serge, the limo's full of bullet holes again," said Lenny. "It's even worse than at the airport."

"You're right," said Serge. "I don't think we can let it slide this time with 'It's a Miami thing.'"

They drove ten blocks and pulled up in front of Auto Parts Nation. Serge went inside and was out in three minutes with a shopping bag.

"Lenny, give me a hand."

Ten minutes later they were finished covering the bullet holes with bullet-hole decals.

"Wow," said Lenny. "It's the perfect disguise."

"They're not marketing these things right."

They headed back to the beach. Serge looked over his shoulder from the driver's seat. "By the way, hope I didn't offend anyone with that gay-baiting back at the warehouse. Sometimes you're forced to turn small minds against one another, and homophobes are the easiest to spot."

"Why do we need to spot them?" asked Lenny.

"Because they're a safety hazard," said Serge. "The frontal cortex isn't developed. You'll see them smoking while gassing up four-by-fours. And when they drink whiskey, it speaks to them."

"What's it say?"

"'Clean your gun collection.' They're the people you read about in the paper who say things like, 'Gee, the pack of Rottweilers we kept in our mobile home seemed so gentle we never thought they'd eat the children. They never did it before.'"

"I've heard of them," said Lenny.

"Besides, heterosexuals are the strangest. I should know. You want freaks? Take a stroll down hetero alley. I've personally got a whole steamer trunk full of little Freudian peculiarities that I'd rather not have see the light of day."

"What about putting gerbils in your ass? Ever done that?"

"Yes, but only the non-cruel, gerbil-safe, all-synthetic N'erbils®.

You know how I feel about animal rights. What a horrible way to go. What if some giant space alien landed and did that to you?"

"I'd stay perfectly still, just out of spite," said Lenny.

"You know, I never thought of that," said Serge, picking up his mini digital recorder. "Note to self . . ."

40

1964

A SMALL PLANE pulled a banner through the clear blue sky over the Atlantic. WELCOME TO MIAMI BEACH.

Another magnificent day in paradise. Eighty degrees, carefree, the mating reflex in play. The deck behind the enormous Fontainebleau Hotel crawled with tourists filling poolside loungers. Waiters circulated with trays of umbrella drinks. Women frolicked in the most daring new one-piece suits. Play-boys positioned themselves for sex by doing cannonballs off the three-meter board.

Five serious men in hats and guayaberas worked their way across the patio, the only people in trousers. A splash from a can-nonball hit their cuffs.

Greek Tommy heard a noise. "What's that!"

"Just a plane and some helicopters."

They looked up and shielded their eyes. A Cessna and banner

passed overhead, followed by two copters with movie cameras on the runners.

"They started filming *Goldfinger* today," said Moondog. "The new Bond flick."

"I'm just a little jumpy,' said Tommy.

"We're all jumpy after last night," said Mort.

"Was that guy really dead?" asked Coltrane.

Chi-Chi inserted a fresh toothpick. "What are you, completely simple?"

Mort looked up as the plane and copters circled again. "Then Lou had to go and steal the gems off him. That probably makes us murder suspects."

They walked past the high dive, a man doing a triple somersault into the water. Moondog got splashed again but didn't care. "I'm more worried about whoever really killed him, not to mention whose diamonds those are. Did you see the size of those things?"

"That's what scares me the most," said Mort. "I think we've stumbled into something that's way out of our league."

"We just need to stay calm and wait for Lou in the bar," said Chi-Chi. "She'll straighten this out."

They walked down a staircase into the Poodle Lounge. The wall behind the bar was thick glass with an underwater view of the swimming pool. They grabbed five stools. Chi-Chi spread out his newspaper.

"I sure wish Lou would hurry up and get here," said Tommy.

"Maybe the paper will take our minds off it," said Mort. "Chi-Chi, anything in there?"

"Still looking for those three missing civil-rights workers in Mississippi."

"They're dead."

"No shit."

"Okay, the paper's not helping," said Mort.

Another diver knifed into the water behind the bar, leaving a thin ribbon of bubbles. Someone grabbed the empty stool next to Chi-Chi. The guys turned.

"Lou!"

Lou looked like she hadn't slept. She sat down and chain-lit a cigarette.

"Lou, what's going on?"

"Tell us what to do."

She closed her eyes and rubbed her temples. "Shut up! I'm trying to think."

"Where are the gems?"

"Sergio has them. I sent him into hiding. He's our ace in the hole until I figure some stuff out."

"Where did all those giant stones come from?" said Mort. "Something's seriously wrong."

"Don't you think I fuckin' know that?"

The bartender was watching something on the TV in the lounge.

"Turn it up!" said Coltrane.

The bartender turned it up. A news report out of New York. Footage from the Museum of Natural History. Ropes dangling from the roof, smashed glass cases in the rare-gem room. A reporter with a microphone talked into the camera: *". . . Acting on a tip, authorities have traced the crime back to Miami Beach and are already making arrests."*

Lou's face fell in her hands. "Oh, no."

41

Present

A SMALL PLANE PULLED a banner through the clear blue sky over the Atlantic: WELCOME TO MIAMI BEACH.

The landmark Fontainebleau Hotel came into view. Orchestra music played. A man on the high dive did a triple somersault into the pool.

Serge hit pause on the hotel suite's VCR, suspending the diver in midair.

"This was the opening of the blockbuster 1964 hit *Goldfinger*." Serge pressed play again. "And here's where Gert Fröbe makes his dramatic entrance outside the cabanas at this very hotel. It was the third film in the series, the one that ignited the whole James Bond phenomenon."

Serge hit fast forward with the remote and trotted across their suite. It was a big one, airy and curved, following the architecture of the hotel. They were on the concave side. Lenny sat in a corner, scraping out a bong but getting only plastic shavings.

Mick Dafoe had ordered up a putter from the pro shop and tapped a golf ball across the carpet. A Frisbee sailed by. City caught it and threw it back to Country. Chi-Chi sat at the kitchen counter with a big cigar in his mouth and a pile of dominoes. Doug perspired on the couch next to the gagged hostage tied to a chair, wearing only undershorts.

"*Dr. No* and *From Russia with Love* weren't shabby, but *Goldfinger* put all the ingredients of the double-O-seven formula together for the first time. The gadgets, larger-than-life villains, Sean Connery's glib dialogue in the face of death, those Bond women with the sophomoric names, and glamorous locales—like Miami Beach!" Serge had the hostage's pants under his arm, going through the wallet. Nothing interesting. He threw it all aside and pulleyed open the balcony curtains. "Jerry Lewis also favored this place, before the French got hold of him." Serge pointed the remote at the TV and hit play. A blonde in a white bathing suit lay on the balcony, looking down at the pool with binoculars and talking into a microphone.

Serge smiled proudly at Doug, gesturing at the balcony with one arm and the TV with the other. "Get it?"

Another empty stare.

"You're in Goldfinger's room!"

A Frisbee hit the hostage in the head.

"I studied the film exhaustively, triangulating views off the balcony, then went down to the patio and traced the vectors back with a stolen surveyor's scope. Those things are so accurate now!"

Doug spoke like a peeping bird. ". . . I don't want to die. . . ."

Serge chugged a bottle of water and tossed it in the trash. "Sure, we've got a few things to tidy up, but the secret of true happiness is to enjoy the process. Rule Number One: Life is like an orgasm. It's here and then it's gone, so you better be paying attention."

A knock at the door.

Serge grabbed his pistol, rolled twice on the floor, and sprang up into a tight shooter's crouch. "Who the fuck can this be?"

"My pizza," said Lenny, opening the door. "Can I borrow some money?"

The pizza boy came in. Lenny handed him a joint. Serge put his gun on the counter and grabbed his wallet.

The pizza boy handed the joint back to Lenny, caught a Frisbee. He looked over at the bound and gagged hostage in his undershorts.

"What's with that dude?" He threw the Frisbee back to Country.

"Says it gets him off," said Serge. "What's the harm?"

"It's Miami."

Serge handed him a twenty. "You're in Goldfinger's room."

"Right. Later . . ."

The door closed.

City, Country, Mick and Lenny sat down in the kitchen nook and went at the pizza like hyenas on a limping wildebeest.

Serge was in front of the TV, working with the remote to find a particular spot. "C'mon, Doug, cheer up. You have to enjoy the moment. You're in the fabulous Fontainebleau. It's a great place. I've only been kicked out once. I was taking my contingency photos in the Tropigala Lounge downstairs, where they have a running stage show called *Latin Fever*, the last Havana-style revue in Miami. Of course it was off hours, but the door was unlocked, so I didn't think twice. And I'm walking around the empty room, not bothering anyone, taking my pictures. Security comes in. They ask if they can help me. And I say no and go about my business. But they keep following me. They ask me to go with them and say they don't want any problems. So I say, 'Well, I have a problem. I don't feel so well. I think I'm coming down with a case of . . . *Latin Fever*!' . . . Believe me, some people have no sense of humor." Serge pressed a button on the remote.

"This is the part I've been waiting for. I've always wanted to do this." Goldfinger stood over Bond, tied down on a table.

Serge walked over to the hostage and ripped the tape off his mouth. He pressed a gun to his forehead. "Are you working for the Palermos?"

The man didn't answer.

Serge cocked the pistol and pressed it harder.

Still nothing.

Serge leaned and whispered, "You're supposed to say, 'You expect me to talk?'"

The man remained silent.

Serge smacked him upside the head with the pistol. "Say it!"

"Uh, you expect me to talk?"

"No, Mr. Bond. I expect you to die!"

CIA STATION, MIAMI.

Renfroe hung up his coat, started the coffee.

Schaeffer came in. "Wanted to see me?"

Renfroe sat down at his computer. "It's going to be a long night. I just found out the mob is involved with the invasion."

"How do you know?"

"One of the exiles told me personally. I have to make sure they succeed. Put all agents on standby." He picked up the phone.

"WHAT A MESS," said Lenny.

"I don't get it," said Serge. "They did it so neatly in the movie."

Mick Dafoe poked the hostage in the head with his putter. "Is he dead?"

"Don't think so," said Serge. "Probably just passed out from the fumes."

They moved closer for a better look. The hostage lay on the bed with an uneven pattern of gold paint over most of his body, matted in his hair, dripping off his shoulders onto the sheets.

More gold paint on the side of the bed, paint overspray on the walls and curtains, a film of dried gold dust on the furniture, and gold footprints on the carpet, leading back to Serge, reading the label on the can of gold spray paint in his hand. "These things don't give nearly the coverage they advertise."

"He doesn't have enough on him?" asked Lenny.

"Not yet. See these flesh-colored spots on his legs? The pores can still breathe. You don't see those in the movie." Serge pointed at the TV and the gold woman lying in the exact same position on the bed. "I think I have another can in my duffel bag."

"I'll get it," said Lenny.

"It's by the bathroom."

Lenny rummaged. "It can't find it."

"It should be right there on top."

"It's not here."

"Jesus." Serge went over to the bathroom.

They tore through the duffel bag. "I put it right on top. Where can it be?"

"I told you it wasn't here," said Lenny.

Serge stood up. "Lenny, what's that sitting on the table?"

"Oh, the spray paint. That's the first thing I took out of the bag to give me room to look."

"How did you ever survive to breeding age?"

Serge got the metal ball rattling in the can as they headed back across the suite. ". . . must have used a drop-cloth in the movie. . . ."

They stopped in the doorway. The gold outline of a person on the bed. No person. The sliding glass doors were open. Gold handprints on the frame and another set on the balcony railing. Then screaming.

They ran out onto the balcony.

"There he is!" said Lenny, pointing toward the pool.

"He must have climbed down balcony to balcony."

More yelling. People scattered. Women grabbed their children.

The gold man staggered toward them for help, arms out like a mummy, throwing up.

"It half worked," said Serge. "Didn't kill him but made him real sick."

A MARATHON GIN game was under way in a penthouse suite at the Fontainebleau. A phone rang. A man in Sansabelts answered.

"Yes, yes, I'll see if he's here."

The man covered the phone and approached Mr. Palermo.

"Who is it?"

"Joe's Dry Cleaning."

Mr. Palermo took the phone.

"Well, if it isn't my old friends at Joe's Dry Cleaning. It's been a long time. To what do I owe this pleasure?"

Mr. Palermo's face changed. The other gin players stopped. They could tell it was important.

The old man turned away from the table and spoke quietly into the receiver. A few moments later, he hung up. The gin players were waiting. Mr. Palermo snapped his fingers. "Scotch. The good bottle."

A bodyguard opened the liquor cabinet. There was distant shouting outside by the pool.

Anticipation built around the green-felt card table. They searched the old man's face for a clue.

Mr. Palermo just smiled. One bodyguard arrived with the old scotch, another with a set of crystal glasses and ice bucket. A third looked off the balcony. "There's a gold guy down there."

Drinks were poured. Mr. Palermo held up his glass.

"Gentleman, I never dreamed I would live to see this moment. It is the one thing I thought I would have to leave to the others after me. But this day we have made peace with our old friends at the CIA." He raised his glass higher.

"We return to Havana!"

＊ ＊ ＊

SERGE AND LENNY stood on their balcony, watching the gold man. The shrieks from the patio got louder, the people down below appearing tiny like ants scattering in alarm, pandemonium spreading, tourists running every which way, crashing into each other, knocking over tables full of drinks and falling into the pool.

"I shouldn't say this," said Lenny. "But from way up here, it actually looks kind of funny."

"Where's he going now?"

The man stumbled off the patio and thrashed around in some tropical landscaping before punching through the shrubs and into a service driveway, where he was run over by a catering truck with a logo of a dancing wedding cake.

"Show's over," said Serge.

They went inside.

Mick was in the kitchen showing Chi-Chi how they play dominoes in the press box. Lenny drifted over. The table was covered with black rectangles standing on end in a complex formation of interlocking figure eights that finally ran up ramps built from playing cards and ending at a little row of shot glasses. Mick carefully set the final piece in place. "You should have seen when we played this at the Rose Bowl. The wire guy got so fucked up he couldn't file."

City and Country came through the room kicking a hackeysack.

Doug cried quietly.

Serge paced the suite with his clipboard. He circled an item on the Master Plan. "Lenny, any pizza left?"

"I think there's a slice. I got a jumbo. But it's cold now."

"That's okay. It's still good," said Serge. "Rule Number One: Pizza is *always* still good. Left out all night, under the couch, in the rain, backed over by a car. Doesn't matter. Just reheat. The most resilient food source on the planet."

Mick's finger set the dominoes in motion, tumbling and clicking around the table.

Serge tossed the clipboard aside and opened the flat pizza box. "Somebody picked all the stuff off."

"Sorry," said Lenny.

"It's still good." Serge lifted a chair and placed it on the kitchen counter. He piled more stuff on top. Footstool, telephone books, suitcase, towels. Soon, he had a teetering tower reaching for the ceiling. He grabbed the microwave oven.

The final rows of tumbling dominoes ran up the ramps and into two of the shot glasses. Mick grabbed the Jack Daniel's. "Now I get to punch you both in the shoulder and pour shots in your mouths. . . ."

Serge looked up at his tower on the kitchen counter, swaying left and right. "Come onnnnnn . . . Easy now . . ." The tower stopped moving. "There!" He climbed up on the counter with the microwave and carefully placed it at the very top, wedged against the ceiling. Then he stuck a slice of pizza in the oven and set the timer.

Mick opened an ice chest. "Who wants a brewski?" He began tossing beer cans around the room. Serge stood atop the kitchen counter and aimed the remote control at the TV, restarting *Goldfinger*. City and Country came through kicking the small leather ball, catching cans of beer as they went. Lenny began setting up the dominoes again. A fat Asian man on TV threw a razor-edged derby at Sean Connery. A can of Coors flew by Doug and broke a lamp. The microwave went ding.

"My pizza's done." Serge opened the oven. He took a big bite and yanked the slice away fast, snapping off a cheese string. He opened his mouth and breathed in and out fast. "Ow . . . hot, hot . . . burning tongue . . . ow . . ."

"You left it in too long." said Lenny.

Serge shook his head and swallowed. "Food's always better when it reminds you you're alive."

A loud thud from the ceiling.

Doug jumped up. "What was that?"

Serge hopped down from the counter again and took another

bite. "My guess would be Mr. Palermo after his pacemaker gave out."

There was a flurry of heavy footsteps from the ceiling, muted yelling.

"Mr. Palermo's in the room above us?"

Serge nodded and chewed. "Oh, yeah. Everybody knows that. His gin games are legendary—same time, same place, every week for fifty years. If you're familiar with the Fontainebleau's floor plan, you know the card table is right above our kitchen counter."

"You knew he was up there all along?" said Doug. "You were planning to kill him with the microwave this whole time?"

"Of course. It's in the Master Plan. Why did you think we're in this room? Because I was hung up on *Goldfinger* or something?" Serge took another bite of pizza and hit eject on the VCR, substituting tapes. "This is a rare copy of *Surfside 6,* one of the campiest shows ever aired. It was the Florida knockoff of *77 Sunset Strip,* starring Troy Donahue and featuring Margarita Sierra as 'Cha Cha O'Brien' from the fictitious 'Boom Boom Room' in the Fontainebleau. . . ." Serge grabbed his former hostage's trousers and began going through the billfold again. ". . . They ran a detective agency out of a houseboat parked in the waterway across the street."

Mick, Lenny and Chi-Chi were out on the balcony, raising drinks.

"Wooooooooo! Miami!"

"Wooooooooo! Goldfinger's room!"

"Wooooooooo! *Cuba Libre!*"

Serge segregated the wallet's credit cards from worthless video memberships. He turned the billfold inside out. "What's this?" A folded scrap of paper hidden under a flap. "How could I have missed it before?" He opened it. Something in code. There was a number: the limo's license plate. And another number, seven digits. Serge picked up the phone for reverse directory assistance.

He wrote down an address.

42

CIA STATION, MIAMI. Agent Schaeffer appeared in a doorway. "You wanted to see me?"

Renfroe picked up the phone. "Mr. Palermo's been assassinated!"

"What!"

"The Cubans," said Renfroe. "Preemptive strike to cripple the invasion."

"You sure?"

"Isn't it obvious?"

"What do you want me to do?"

"Things are going to start happening fast now." He handed Schaeffer a piece of paper. "Set up another meet with our field contact. I need to make a call."

A phone rang in one of the Fontainebleau's majestic penthouse suites. Two dozen men milled around in black funeral attire and shoulder holsters, eating potato salad from paper cocktail plates. A man in Sansabelts answered.

"Joe's Dry Cleaning? . . . Yes? . . . Yes? . . . What! . . . Where'd you hear this? . . . That can't be true! . . . I see. . . . I understand. . . . Yes, thank you for the condolences." He hung up.

The others were all staring at him.

"Mr. Palermo was assassinated. Comes straight from the CIA."

"I thought it was his pacemaker."

"Cuban intelligence used a new state-of-the-art microwave device."

TWO LOBSTER-COLORED MEN with white nose cream stood in the shallow end of a pool in Coral Gables.

"We have to make this quick," said Chi-Chi. "I'm seriously burned from last time."

"Everything's changed," said Renfroe, rotating in place for a visual sweep of his blind spots. "The Cubans assassinated Mr. Palermo."

"No they didn't."

"Right, good idea," said Renfroe, revolving. "The Cubans *didn't* do it. Otherwise, panic in the streets, the Havana-Red Menace in our midst."

"They really didn't do it."

Wink.

"Whatever. I have a message from Serge—"

"Were you followed? I think we were followed. But it couldn't have been me. I kept driving in boxes of four consecutive right turns to shake any tails."

"So that's why you were late."

"Something's out of place. Who are those people over there?"

"Children," said Chi-Chi. "You're paranoid."

"This is my edge. Shit's on boil now. Tell Serge he can have whatever he wants. I've got middlemen standing by in dummy businesses all over Miami."

"He wants three hundred men."

"We don't have that many."

Chi-Chi shook his head. "He wants Cubans."

"You know the exile community better than I do."

"These are all in prison."

"I don't understand."

"Remember the Mariel boatlift in 1980?"

"Who doesn't?"

"And how after all the nice, law-abiding refugees starting arriving, Castro began emptying his jails and asylums of the worst of the worst?"

Renfroe recalled with bitterness. "The bastard!"

"This invasion is going to get rough, hand to hand. We'll need the meanest, baddest sons of bitches we can find. A bunch of the undesirable Mariels are still serving long prison sentences for terrible crimes they committed here after the boatlift. Many are still only in their forties."

"But we put them in prison. Why would they agree to work for us?"

"We offer them freedom. Besides, our jails are four-star hotels compared with what they went through under Castro. They all have a serious ax to grind. We're planning two landing sites, Marianao and Guanabacoa. Then our men execute a pincer movement on the capital and catch Castro's forces in the middle like a nutcracker. His army's underpaid, out of practice and shape. You give us these guys, we can do it in our sleep." Chi-Chi handed Renfroe a watertight capsule. "The embarkation point's in there."

"Okay, I'm not promising anything, but I'll make some calls."

"I'm burned again."

"Using prisoners," said Renfroe. "Reminds me of *The Dirty Dozen*."

"Serge saw it last night. That's where he got the idea."

"It was Telly Savales's best work."

"That's what Serge said."

"I like this Serge more and more."

"Is that guy taking pictures of us?"

"What guy?"

Chi-Chi pointed through the fence at a car across the street. "Over there."

A Crown Vic with blackwalls sat at the curb. Bixby turned to Miller in the front seat. "Webb told us to back off."

Miller snapped more pictures. "He just said not to apprehend. He didn't say no surveillance."

"Twist it any way you want. It's disobeying a direct order."

"Then why don't you take your little rule book and get out of the car?"

Bixby got out.

43

1964

IT'S HARD TO categorize a place like Jimbo's. It's a bar, but there is no bar. There's a boccie court. Beer is self-serve from garbage cans full of ice inside an old shrimp packing house. Other cans hold plastic bags of smoked fish. Patrons lounge outside on mismatched furniture watching a TV sitting on the ground, starting to fritz from the salt air, surrounded by piles of rusting junk, disabled vehicles, nonrunning appliances, and a M*A*S*H-style signpost with wooden planks pointing which way.

It's hard to find Jimbo's. It opened in 1954 on Virginia Key, across the street from the Miami Seaquarium. Way across the street. Down a long gravel road, past a water plant and state preserve, back, back, until you come to a cluster of shanties around a lagoon that opens onto Biscayne Bay.

It's hard not to like Jimbo's.

"I hate this place," said Chi-Chi, turning off the highway.

"Shut up and drive," said Lou.

The pink Cadillac rumbled across the undeveloped island, hot limestone rocks crunching under the tires, rounding bend after bend of coconut palms and Australian pines.

Mort ducked as a palm frond whacked the right side of the windshield. "Where is this place?"

"Still a ways," said Lou. "One of the few places it'll be safe for Sergio to meet us after handing off the diamonds to the cops."

Chi-Chi kept driving farther back into the mangrove jungle. He followed the road around until a bleached wooden building appeared next to an old dock. The gang got out. Clay balls clacked and scattered on the boccie court. Beer tabs popped. Mullet cooked in the smokehouse. Chi-Chi stopped by the front door. "So now what?"

Lou plopped down on a ratty love seat. "Wait and watch TV until it's dark."

They began drinking Busch. Someone shouted. Everyone jumped.

Chi-Chi grabbed his heart. "Shit, what was that?"

Another shout.

They saw a TV crew down by the dock. A director yelling.

"Let's go watch," said Coltrane.

They strolled to the edge of the lagoon, standing on their toes behind the technicians. A man in a park-ranger uniform ran down the dock with two young boys in shorts. A camera rolled beside them on little rails. The trio climbed in a ranger boat. Suddenly, a dolphin popped out of the water, chattering and clicking.

One of the boys leaned over the side. "What is it, Flipper?"

A bunch of clicking, then a tail splash.

"You say Mr. Burns had a heart attack on his boat and is now drifting toward some unexploded harbor mines left over from military exercises?"

More clicks.

"And a big storm's approaching?"

The dolphin nodded.

The ranger hit the throttle, and the boat took off through a mangrove pass.

"Wow, we actually got to see them film," said Tommy.

"Big deal. It's just the same show over and over," said Chi-Chi. "Every week some people get in an impossible jam in a boat but leave a rope dangling in the water with a loop on the end the exact size of a dolphin snout. How fucking convenient."

They went back to the couch. More waiting. The sun set. Nerves wearing thin. Deeper into the night.

"I'm getting worried," said Moondog. "We haven't heard from Sergio yet."

"What if the cops find us in the meantime?" asked Mort.

"They're not looking for us," said Lou. "Just Sergio."

"Why's that?"

Lou didn't answer.

"What is it? What did you do?"

"Well, I sort of tipped them."

"Lou! How could you?!"

"Hey! I panicked, okay? They came by the apartment and grilled me. Searched the place without a warrant, the assholes."

"Why'd they come by your place?"

"They had Desmond under surveillance and saw me with him, so I had to say I was just having an affair with him, and it was really my boyfriend, Sergio, who was moving ice with Desmond."

The gang glared at her.

"What was I supposed to do? Besides, Sergio was already safely in hiding. It'll all work out. You'll see."

"I still don't get it," said Mort. "Why didn't whoever killed Desmond just take the diamonds themselves? You had no trouble finding them."

"Because they didn't know about them," said Lou. "That wasn't about the jewels. That was Carmine Palermo's jealousy again. I didn't even think he knew about Desmond."

"What a mess," said Chi-Chi, covering his eyes with his hand. "It's just a good thing Carmine doesn't know about Sergio."

Lou stared off toward the lagoon.

"Lou?" said Chi-Chi.

Lou looked down at her nails. "He sort of does. Some guys came around."

"Oh, Lou!"

"We told him you were bad news!" said Mort.

Chi-Chi squinted at her.

"What?" said Lou. "Why are you looking at me like that?"

"You know," said Chi-Chi. "There's something else."

"What do you mean?" Lou's hand was shaking as she lit a Lucky.

"I can tell by your voice. Give it."

She blew out a thick stream of smoke. "Okay, okay. The Fongs."

"The Fongs?" said Chi-Chi. "Who the hell are the Fongs? Jesus! How many people are in this plot?"

"I've heard of them," said Tommy. "That insanely violent Asian gang. Even the Palermos stay clear of them."

Chi-Chi pointed at Lou with a toothpick. "What do the Fongs have to do with this?"

"It was their diamonds. Desmond was the courier."

"Oh, my God!"

Lou was smoking rapidly. "They know the Palermos killed Desmond, but they don't know it was jealousy—they think it was the jewels. And since word's out Sergio has the stones, they think he's the one who whacked Desmond for the Palermos. It could be a war."

Five jaws hung open. Chi-Chi finally fell back on the couch and slapped his forehead. "Great. The Palermos want Sergio dead, the Fongs want him dead, the cops want him in jail for life, and you've put him in the middle of an impending gang blood-bath. Anything else?"

"I gave him the clap."

"Lou, you're a keeper."

"Hey! I love the guy!"

"Remind me to stay off your shit list."

After that, the gang began going through cans of Busch at an impressive clip. More TV. The news came on.

"Turn it up," said Tommy.

One of the boccie players twisted the volume knob. Footage earlier in the day from Miami International. The black-and-white set showed a large plane on the runway, props slowing. A mob of reporters waited outside the terminal with cameras and notepads. A staircase went up to the plane. Two detectives appeared in the doorway, holding a handcuffed man by the arms. The reporters surged forward yelling questions, but local cops held them back.

"Reminds me of when the Beatles landed a few months ago," whispered Tommy.

The TV announcer said police were mum, but "reliable sources" indicated that the surfers were cooperating for reduced sentences. New York detectives had flown in with one of the suspects to arrange secret meetings to get the missing jewels back.

The report switched to other scenes that had developed later in the day: Shaky footage taken from cars during the press chase all over town. Shots outside the surfers' pads, a young woman opening the door a crack, then slamming it. More driving around in cars, the detectives stopping and running up to ringing pay phones.

"What a farce," said Chi-Chi. "The police can't even lose the reporters."

There were more snippets as night fell: The entourage running in and out of bars. The lens blocked by cops' hands. The police and the surfers switching cars and taking off again.

"Look!" yelled Mort, pointing at the set.

Cars squealed up to yet another phone booth and blinding camera lights came on again, catching the man inside wide-eyed like a deer.

"Sergio!"

Chi-Chi's toothpick fell out of his mouth. "For the love of . . ."

The man on TV dropped the phone and ran off into the dark.

44

Present

TWO DOZEN MEN in military uniforms sat around a conference table. Conversation buzzed, the air charged with urgency. The director of Cuban Intelligence entered the room. Everyone shut up.

A man in an admiral's uniform stood and saluted. "Sir, the gunboats are in place as you requested. We should have no problem scuttling them at sea and turning back the rest with minimal loss of life, just as planned."

"Plans have changed," said the director. "We're not going to interfere. We're going to let them land."

Heated conversations broke out.

"Sir, they get a foothold on land, there's all kinds of cover they can take," said the admiral. "It's a very bad idea."

"This comes from the very top."

"It's a brilliant idea," said the admiral.

"These exiles have been pests for too long," said the director.

"It's time to teach them a lesson. What's a Miami exile's worst nightmare?"

A general raised his hand. "Anglos take back the city council?"

"You idiot!" said the director. He began pacing. "Just look what they risked getting to America. Many left with only the clothes on their backs, sailing the Gulf Stream in foolhardy contraptions. No, their worst nightmare is to be captured and jailed in Communist Cuba, never allowed to leave. That'll put the fear of God in them once and for all!"

Heads nodded in agreement.

"But what if something goes wrong and they make it off the beach? A small, determined force could get the upper hand if they reach the hills."

"We're covered," said the director. "The invasion party has been totally infiltrated by our agents in Florida. They'll be more than enough to take care of any eventualities."

The room bubbled with confidence. They stood and saluted. The meeting broke up, and jeeps roared off into the Havana night. A major went home to his waterfront apartment and retrieved a miniature radio transmitter from a hollowed-out ceiling beam.

A LIMO WITH magnetic signs wound its way to the Rickenbacker Causeway. Chi-Chi at the wheel. He turned off the highway and headed down an unpaved road past the sewage plant.

Serge was in back, a remote control in each hand.

"This is one of the early *Flipper* episodes shot right where we're going. That young actor is none other than Martin Sheen. I like to play it with the sound off, substituting the soundtrack of *Apocalypse Now*."

The young man on TV piloted a skiff along the Miami shore, a dolphin swimming beside him.

"*. . . Never get out of the boat, absolutely goddamn right.*

Kurtz got out of the boat—he split from the whole fucking program...."

Serge eventually got control of his hysterical laughing and dabbed his eyes. "Hoo! That was a good one.... Doug, you okay? You don't look so hot."

"Where are we going?" asked Lenny.

"Jimbo's."

"Jimbo's?"

"Chi-Chi knows the place."

The limo continued deeper into the sticks, coming upon a village of shotgun shacks and the hulk of a former shrimp house on the water. The packing house was faded earth tones; the shacks were done up bright Jamaican. There was a broken-down school bus painted by hippies and a Technicolor VW Beetle with flat tires. A handful of old-timers played boccie, ignoring the fashion photographers shooting swimsuit models on the porches of the Caribbean shacks. Another photo team was down on the dock, someone holding up a large white reflector screen to fill in shadows on the shirtless male model staring across the water with a purposeful gaze and firm jaw that said: I'm doing some coke right after this.

Chi-Chi parked behind two choppers. The gang got out and followed Serge past a collection of people lounging outside on musty furniture, watching basketball on a snowy old Magnavox. They reached the building. "Anyone want a beer?"

Lenny and Mick raised hands. Serge stepped through the open front door. He fished Bud Lights from an ice-filled garbage can and set two dollar bills on a piece of wood.

Serge led them over to ringside seats at the boccie court.

"Now we wait."

THE TUNA BOAT passed the jetty at the bottom of South Beach, pounding across the wake of an outbound Swedish cruise ship.

Then through a swarm of jet-skiers and around the tip of Fisher Island. It turned up the inlet with Virginia Key. The throttle cut back as the boat threaded a keyhole passage through the mangroves and into a broad lagoon. It pulled up behind a shrimp house. A Cuban jumped from the bow to the dock, shooing away a male model and tying rope to a mooring cleat. Another Cuban jumped off the rear of the boat with the stern line.

Other vessels began arriving. Bayliners, trawlers, catamarans, slipping single file through the pass and anchoring in the lagoon.

Serge and Chi-Chi went down to the dock, calling out instructions to their colleagues from the exile spy meetings in Little Havana. More boats appeared, then noise back on the land. Six gray Immigration buses rumbled down the bumpy road and up to the dock. Guards walked manacled inmates to the waterfront. Boats took turns pulling alongside the pier and taking prisoners aboard. The guards handed keys to the boat crews with instructions not to use them until they were in sight of Cuba. A convoy of Cadillacs arrived and parked beside the buses. The Palermo Family and a cadre of associates got out with a small arsenal. A Hatteras yacht with a radar dome arrived. The Palermos climbed aboard.

Soon, all the boats were full, a small armada of fishing and pleasure craft. One of the spies at the helm of a Donzi sounded an air horn, and the lagoon filled with gunning marine engines. Anchors were pulled up; the boats began chugging back out the narrow mangrove pass.

Serge sniffled and waved at the departing fleet with a hanky. *"Libertad!"*

The last boat, a little cuddy, made open water and disappeared toward the straits. The lagoon was still again. Serge flipped open a cell phone and hit some buttons. "Hello? Action Five News?"

A CONSTANT FLOW of tourists posed for snapshots at water's edge in Key West, next to the giant red-black-and-yellow concrete thimble marking the southernmost point of the continental United States. A few feet away was a metal fence, warning signs, barbed wire. On the other side sat a row of huge parabolic radio dishes all pointed in the same direction, across the Florida Straits toward Havana, ninety miles away.

One of the dishes silently picked up a thin band of the electromagnetic spectrum. A tape recorder automatically clicked on inside a dark control room lit only by red instrument panels. A military technician with top-secret security clearance slid his castered chair across the floor and put on a headset. He started writing on a pad.

A phone rang in Miami.

Agent Schaeffer burst breathlessly into the office of the CIA station chief.

"Sir, we have to call off the invasion. We just got word from Key West that it's completely infiltrated. Havana knows all about it. An overwhelming Cuban force is waiting to ambush them on the beach!"

"Son of a bitch!" said Renfroe. "I knew I should never have trusted this Serge! What did I really know about him? And Chi-Chi—that backstabbing little shit!"

"We have to call the boats back."

Renfroe looked up at the wall clock. "Too late. They're already in Cuban water, probably in sight of land. Even if they turn around, the cutters can easily chase them down. We are so fucked!"

"Sir, I have an idea. What if we get out ahead of this thing?"

"What do you mean?"

"Castro's bound to parade the prisoners on TV to embarrass us. But what if before then, we preempt him with our own press conference announcing how we've broken up a rogue exile operation? We put our own prisoners on display."

"But what about the invasion? He can still embarrass us, rogue operation or not."

"We just got word that the force is full of Cuban spies, right?

We announce that we let Castro know everything in advance and were working together to help his agents infiltrate the landing party and bust it up from the inside. We say we don't like the Havana regime, but we're not about to violate international law. What can he do? His only alternative then is to admit he had a bunch of spies in Florida."

"Brilliant. We *can* turn this around," said Renfroe. "Maybe even get commendations."

"All we have to do now is apprehend some suspects before Castro can get the jump."

"Dispatch all agents. Take down Serge!"

45

FIVE, FOUR, THREE, two, one—Happy New Year, 1965!"

Streamers flew, noisemakers blew, balloons fell from the ceiling of the Nautilus Hotel.

"Can't believe a whole year's passed since we were here last," said Tommy.

"Good riddance," said Chi-Chi.

"What's the matter with you?" asked Mort.

"That's what's the matter." Chi-Chi canted his head toward four plainclothes detectives standing against the wall, keeping watch over their table. "We can't get away from those guys, thanks to Lou."

"Has anybody seen Sergio?" said Mort. "I'm really worried."

"Not since Jimbo's," said Coltrane.

"Don't look now," said Mort.

"What?" said Chi-Chi, turning in the direction of Mort's gaze.

Four other men in silk suits were staking out their table from the opposite wall.

"Over there," whispered Greek Tommy.

They looked in yet another direction. Four beefy Asian men in derbies filed in from the lobby and took up positions by the entrance.

Chi-Chi turned back to the table. "Just great."

"Pssst!"

They looked around.

"Down here!"

"Sergio!"

Sergio was crawling on the floor, wearing a pointy 1965 party hat. He poked his head up like a periscope, ducked back down. "Move your legs. I have to get under the table."

"Please let us help," said Mort. "Lou double-crossed you. We know the whole story. We'll tell the police."

"We'll all go down together and explain things," said Tommy.

"I'll be a character witness," said Chi-Chi. "I'll tell them you're a fucking idiot."

The house orchestra began playing Martha and the Vandellas.

"Sergio, the best thing is to go to the authorities," said Mort. "We read in the papers where they're giving immunity. They recovered the gems."

"Most of them," said Sergio. "I've still got mine."

"What!"

"I couldn't make the handoff. Those reporters were always in the way. So I kept them."

"He's right," said Chi-Chi. "I read where they got all the famous stuff back, but some of the diamonds are still missing."

Mort nudged Moondog and nodded toward the detectives. "They're coming over."

They looked in the other direction. The silk suits were closing in. Then another, Asian men advancing.

"They must have seen us bending over."

"... *They'll be dancing in the street!* ..."

The table and all the drinks went straight up in the air. Sergio took off running. Everyone gave chase—cops, robbers, Chi-Chi and company.

Sergio burst through the exit door. The silk suits and Asians reached it just as it was closing.

The detectives were right behind and pulled their guns.

"Freeze!"

They put their hands up. The detectives called for backup. One of them ran out the back door and down to the moonless beach, chasing a dark figure splashing out into the surf and swimming toward open sea.

Three A.M.

The typical miasma curdled over the room. The one that arrives whenever something goes awry at a wild celebration, the liquor's shut off and cops turn on all the lights. Then hours of questioning. Euphoria rotting to hangover, bloodshot eyes, nobody that attractive anymore.

A detective wrote in a notebook. "You say he had a lot to drink?"

"I don't think he had anything to drink at all," said Mort.

"But he was crawling on the floor?"

Mort nodded.

Out on the dark beach, scattered flashlight beams cut back and forth as officers combed the shore in grids. Something washed up in a foamy wave. "Captain, over here." The officer picked up a soggy 1965 party hat.

A reporter's flashbulb went off.

46

Present

MIAMI BEACH, THE dead north end of the strip. A breezy afternoon. Broken glass in front of vacant, gray stores. Brown paper bags and newspapers blowing across the silent street. Chain link around a building that was left half sandblasted. A page of the sports section caught a gust of wind, sailing lazily over the road until it slapped into the grille of a speeding limo that bottomed out in a water-filled pothole and kept going.

Serge held a piece of paper on the steering wheel, the one he'd excavated from the hostage's wallet. He glanced down to check the address he'd copied from directory assistance. Serge looked up and ran a yellow light, the newspaper page flapping over the top edge of the hood.

"What do you think that address is?" asked Lenny.

"We're about to find out. Almost there."

Serge slowed and looked out the side window, checking for a street number in a recessed doorway with wino legs sticking out.

He faced forward again and slammed on the brakes. "What the . . . ?"

Up ahead, a pair of white Ford sedans with extra radio antennas had come out of nowhere. They quickly emerged from alleys on opposite sides of the street and pulled nose to nose in the middle of the road, blocking the limo's path.

Serge threw the limo in reverse, looked over his shoulder and began backing up at forty. Another pair of white sedans closed off the street behind him.

Serge hit the brakes again. He jerked his head around. No escape forward and back, men in starched shirts and black ties getting out of the sedans, fifty yards each way, crouching behind the cars, drawing weapons.

"Who are those guys?" asked Lenny.

"Don't turn around," said Serge. "The commissar's in town."

He looked left: a wall of boarded-up stores. He looked right: a bulldozed lot with a future construction sign and three plumes of concrete dust on the far side, kicked up by three more white sedans bouncing across the lot toward him.

Everyone was quiet in the car. Serge grabbed all the guns in arm's reach and piled them in his lap, feeding new clips, going too fast, dropping bullets. "Everybody on the floor!"

Everyone already was.

The three sedans skidded to a stop in the dirt lot, evenly spaced, forming the cross-fire perimeter. A wide, dead-open space all the way around the limo. No-man's-land.

Serge finished loading four pistols—Colt, Luger, Python, Baretta—then pulled a sawed-off from under the driver's seat and racked the pump, slamming home a red-and-gold shell.

Everything was loaded. The onboard computer in Serge's head made a status check. Green lights—all systems go. This would happen his way. He took a deep, defiant breath and calmly slipped on his polarized fisherman's sunglasses, like James Cagney would, if they had polarization back then and if he fished.

From behind the smoked lenses, Serge surveyed the sedans. The men weren't moving. This was the part where they got out the megaphones for negotiation. These guys didn't. Everything was still. Serge's wristwatch ticked.

The sweep second hand made a lap. Serge blinked hard twice, then winced and nodded with resignation. He hit the electric lever, rolling down his window. "Don't shoot! Don't shoot! I have some people coming out! They're civilians!"

He took off his glasses, turned around and smiled. "Okay, everybody, this is it. End of the tour. Thank you for choosing Serge and Lenny's."

They just looked at him.

"That means you have to get out of the car now. We have some lovely parting gifts. And make sure you keep those hands way up in the air. . . . Go on, get going."

The back doors opened. Mick, Chi-Chi, City and Country got out slowly and began walking across no-man's-land with arms raised. Doug jumped out with his own arms up, running as fast as he could. "Thank God! I'm free! I'm free! Oh, thank you, thank you, thank you! . . ." He ran to one of the sedans, opened the back door himself and dove inside.

Serge turned to Lenny in the front passenger seat. "You, too."

Lenny's eyes were getting glassy. "But, Serge . . ."

Across the street, men in bulletproof vests were running out from behind the cars and pulling the approaching people to cover.

"Nothing's going to happen to me, buddy. Always trust the Master Plan. You'll see."

Lenny tried to smile, but his lips were trembling. He gave Serge a big hug, then grabbed the door handle.

Serge yelled out the window again: "Don't shoot. I got another one coming out." Lenny emerged and headed for the sedans.

Soon, everyone was safely out of the line of fire between the limo and the semicircle of sedans. The men crouched motionless again behind the trunks.

Just Serge.

Silence.

Slow motion.

Heartbeat.

An empty plastic grocery bag from Publix billowed out in the breeze and bounced across the street, a Florida tumbleweed.

Serge took another deep breath through flared nostrils. "Okay, here we are. You always knew this day would come, so remember to enjoy it. All right, final checklist: Guns loaded. Extra clips. Bystanders cleared. Gum . . ." He popped a stick of spearmint in his mouth. "What am I forgetting?" He nodded to himself and reached for the dash. "Tunes."

The FM dial reached Y-100, the station with the dolphin billboards. Serge sang along with Eddie Money, adjusting the choke on his shotgun and bobbing his head.

"Gimme some water! Cuz I just shot a man on the Mexican border!"

CIA FIELD OFFICE, Miami.

Agent Schaeffer burst into the office of station chief Chick Renfroe.

"Sir, good news! They found Serge. We have him pinned down in North Miami Beach. Doesn't look like he's going to let us take him alive."

"Too late."

"What?"

A crestfallen Renfroe pointed at the TV set on the corner of his desk. "The invasion. Action Five News already has the story. Shit."

"But how did they find out so fast? . . . I don't see—"

"How the hell should I know? They teased to it just before the commercial break. It's going to lead the early-evening Eyewitness report. This is catastrophic. We need to have an emergency meeting and get our cover story together."

"Look, it's coming back on."

They stopped talking. The trademark Action 5 intro opened over the Miami skyline. Urgent, teletype theme music.

"... And now Natalie and Blaine!"

"Good evening," said a woman in a sharp blue suit. "Our top story tonight: History repeats itself as an exile invasion force is routed by Castro's forces on the north coast of Cuba. ..."

Renfroe covered his face with his hands. "I can't watch."

"... Here's some exclusive footage from our Eye in the Sky of the doomed flotilla crossing the Florida Straits earlier today. Initial reports indicate the operation never had a chance, with insurgents barely reaching shore before a massive and overwhelming ambush by elite Cuban commandos who clearly knew all facets of the plan in advance. Hundreds have reportedly been captured. ..."

"Ooooooh!" moaned Renfroe. "This is too painful. Shoot me, Schaeffer. Right in the back of the head."

"... But unlike the Bay of Pigs, this redux has a twist. In an inspired turn of spycraft that would make James Bond jealous, the invasion appears to have been an exquisitely brilliant covert CIA operation that worked to perfection. ..."

Renfroe and Schaeffer looked dumbstruck at each other; they scooted closer to the TV and turned up the volume.

"... In a major embarrassment to Castro and a coup that must have the U.S. intelligence community toasting tonight with champagne, the ill-fated military strike now seems to have been a diversionary tactic in a grand payback scheme. Tonight, hundreds of the undesirables Castro dumped in America during the Mariel boatlift are now back on his shore. Accompanying them was the entire contingent of Cuban spies operating in the Miami area. And as a final insult, a few dozen of South Florida's most notorious mobsters were thrown in for good measure. Immigration officials have no comment, but clearly there's little chance they'll be allowed back in the country. ..."

Blaine Crease shuffled papers on the anchor desk. "Looks like Castro has egg in his beard."

"Okay, here's now we take credit," said Renfroe. "We don't confirm anything, we don't deny anything. That's what they'll expect. Everyone will just assume. . . . Damn, that Serge is *good!*"

Their heads snapped toward each other. "Serge!"

"Oh, my God, everything tanks if Serge turns up, dead or alive," said Renfroe. "Not only do we not get credit, we look like fools."

"They could already be shooting!"

SERGE TURNED OFF the radio in the limo. The sedans were waiting. An ant walked across the dashboard. Serge heard its footsteps. He pulled the handle on the driver's door and propped it open an inch with his elbow. He grabbed the Colt in his right hand and the Baretta in his left, pointed upward at each side of his head.

"Well, this is it. . . . *Thank you . . . for lettin' me . . . be myself . . . again!*"

Serge dove out of the car and rolled on the ground, jumping up and taking cover in a storefront doorway. He poked his head around the corner, ready to fire.

"Huh?"

The nose-to-nose sedans were backing up, clearing the road. He looked the other way. The Fords at the south end of the street retreated. In the vacant lot across the street, men in starched shirts opened the back doors of their vehicles, letting everyone out. They had to pull Doug from the car by his ankles. "No! No! No! I don't want to go back!"

The three sedans quickly turned around in a series of random arcs and sped away.

The gang stood alone on the edge of the vacant lot. They started walking back to the limo.

Lenny climbed in the passenger seat and cracked a beer. "Where were we?"

Serge unfolded a paper scrap on the steering wheel. "Heading to an address."

The limo continued south. A Crown Vic with blackwalls pulled out of an alley and fell in line two blocks back. Only one person in the car.

Serge eased off the gas as the numbers on the buildings approached the address in his hand. They started seeing people again, thin traffic. The transition zone. A brandless gas station, an empty Thai restaurant with the owner staring out the front window. The limo stopped in front of a low-occupancy apartment building with curved corners, glass blocks and peeling kiwi trim. Serge checked the address against the paper. He drove around the block and parked in back.

"Hey, this is the same place where we dumped Tony's body," said Lenny. "There's the Dumpster."

"So it is." Serge reached up in the limo's visor and pulled out a small, round dental mirror on the end of a metal stick. "Lenny, you ready?" Serge turned around. "Who's not too fucked up to come with me?" Mick and Chi-Chi were doing bong hits with City and Country. "Looks like just Doug."

He came out by the ankles again.

The lock was broken on the rear door of the apartment building. A stagnant hallway, mildewed carpet worn through the middle, a row of jimmied postal boxes with no names. They headed quietly up the stairs and came to the unit on the scrap of paper. Serge put his ear to the door. No sound. He got out his dental mirror. It was an old building. Wooden floors. The doors had a good half-inch clearance. Serge stuck the mirror under the crack, getting a mouse's-eye view of the room. Nobody in sight. The ancient lock was child's play for Serge's credit card. They slipped inside.

It wasn't at all what they had expected. Serge moved bewildered through the living room, a well-kept art nouveau museum. Funky bucket chairs, boomerang coffee table, wall clock with Betty Boop's eyes moving side to side, turquoise Bakelite brush and comb on the dresser. Serge began going through the drawers, tossing aside period clothing. He opened the bottom drawer and froze.

"What is it?" asked Lenny.

Serge didn't answer. His skin tingled with little bumps. He reached in the drawer and carefully removed an old wooden box with an *S* etched on top in a verdigris brass plate. Serge's heart pounding in his eardrums as he slowly opened the lid and began removing stuff, delicately setting items in precise rows on the floor. Plastic white dolphin, Hotel Nautilus ashtray, citrus sipper, matchbooks, coasters, ticket stubs. He came to a stack of black-and-white publicity photos, all inscribed. *"To my pal Sergio"* *"To my friend Sergio."* John Lennon, Muhammad Ali, Jackie Gleason . . . He went through the pictures faster and faster. Underneath the photos was a little black book. Serge flipped to the last page.

"Little Serge, if you're reading this, keep going."

"What's that supposed to mean? . . . Oh, my . . ."

Serge dug through the rest of the box, placing more items on the floor until the case was empty. He pressed his hands flat against the bottom of the box. He took out a pocketknife and pried up the edge, removing a thin piece of wood used to separate layers of expensive cigars.

There it was. Velvet drawstring bag. Serge dumped the diamonds on the floor. Twelve stones sparkled.

The door opened behind them.

Serge spun with a gun.

"Don't shoot me! Take what you want!"

An old woman stood in the doorway with a sack of groceries in one hand, gallon of two-percent milk in the other. Dangling avocado earrings.

Serge blinked in disbelief. "Louisiana?"

"Yeah?" she said, putting down her stuff. "Who are you?"

"Lou, it's me! Serge!"

It was the woman's turn to adjust her eyes. *"Little* Serge?"

Serge nodded fast with a broad smile, and they ran together for the reunion hug. Then they held each other out by the shoulders.

"You look great!"

"So do you!"

"But what are you doing in my apartment?" said Lou.

"That's what *I* want to know. We found your address in this guy's wallet. He'd been shooting at us, which really isn't all that unusual in itself—"

Lou stepped back and grabbed her heart. "Oh, my God! That was you?"

"What is it?"

"I can't believe what I almost did! Oh, I'm so sorry! How could I?"

"What?"

"I started hearing things. People were poking around, asking questions about your granddad. It all started right after Rico Spagliosi's funeral. I thought it was Carmine Palermo's people, so I hired some guys."

"But why?"

A new voice: "I'll take those diamonds."

They turned around. Agent Miller stood in the doorway with gun drawn.

"Put the gems back in the bag and slide them over here." He pulled out handcuffs.

Serge got down and began picking up the stones. He slid the bag across the floor and into Miller's shoes. "Let's make a deal—"

Another voice: "Drop the gun!"

Everyone turned. Doug was pointing a pistol at Agent Miller. Miller slowly bent over and set his piece on the floor.

"Doug, have you lost your fucking mind?" said Serge. "And where'd you get the gun?"

"Toss me the bag," said Doug. Miller picked it up from the floor and underhanded it. Doug snatched it out of the air and stuck it in his pocket. He walked over to an old black rotary phone on the wall and dialed. "Honey, it's me. Yeah, I got the stones. . . . Better send the guys. Some FBI agent crashed the party."

"Time out!" said Serge. "Now I'm completely confused. . . . Your wife . . . ?"

Doug hung up the receiver. "That's not my wife. It's my female contact with the Palermos. Or what's left of them, thanks to you. That's how we were supposed to stay in touch during the contract on Tony."

"You mean you didn't shoot him at the airport by accident?"

"Not remotely. That was a hit all the way—just wasn't supposed to happen so fast. The Palermos saw you in the papers, suspected you and Tony were mixed up. If Tony wouldn't lead us to the diamonds, maybe you would." He patted the pocket with the jewels. "And he was right."

Serge slapped himself in the forehead. "Just hang a big 'kick me' sign on my back. No wonder my progress was so slow. A Master Plan's only weakness is another Master Plan. . . . I'm seeing it all new. Like over at the warehouse, Mr. Palermo wasn't going to kill you. That was a meeting."

Doug nodded. "They paid off the cops. But not to betray us. To deliver us. Once you said you were going to kill Mr. Palermo, we needed to get out of that limo and warn the Family. You had busted up my cell phone—"

"You guys were fucking great actors. You should get your SAG cards."

Doug pulled out his wallet and flipped it open.

"You already got one! So you're really actors?"

"Only part-time. Mostly we do contract work for families across the country when they need top-notch talent for delicate undercover operations. I'm just doing this until I get my big break. I want to be taken seriously."

"What have I seen you in?"

"Nothing you'd remember, just some commercials. I was the smiling guy in a sweater riding a bicycle past a field of daisies in that ad for prescription antidepressants. But Rusty had a small recurring role on *Days of Our Lives.* Guess they'll have to write him out. . . . Now, all of you, up against that wall and turn around."

"You're going to shoot us?" said Serge. "After all we've been through together?"

"You won't feel a thing," said Doug.

Another voice: "What the fuck is going on here?"

Everyone turned. A ratty old bum stood in the doorway with a big sack of trash.

Serge used the split-second distraction to dive for Doug's gun.

A struggle. A gunshot. Serge checked his own chest. No holes. Doug fell to the floor.

Serge looked around. Smoke curled out the barrel of the pistol that Agent Miller had picked back up.

"Gee, thanks."

"Shut up." Miller kept his pistol on Serge as he walked over and kicked the gun away from Doug's hand. He bent down and retrieved the sack of gems from Doug's pocket. He stood back up and faced Serge again. "This is the end of the road."

Serge laughed nervously. "I'll bet you want to talk about all those murders. I can explain. It's been a comedy of errors. . . ."

"I'm not going to arrest you."

"You're keeping the gems?"

"Do you have any idea what kind of pension I'm looking at?" Miller waved his gun at the bum. "Away from that door." Miller backed out of the room and tipped the brim of his hat in the hallway—"Have a nice day"—then took off down the stairs.

Serge started after him, but Lou grabbed his arm. "Let him go."

"But the diamonds!"

She smiled at Serge.

"Will someone please tell me what the hell is going on!" yelled the bum.

"This is Little Serge," said Lou.

The bum tilted his head. "Grandson?"

THE CREW DOUG had called from the wall phone was just pulling up in a fleet of Cadillacs when Miller came out of the building. "Uh-oh." He took off running.

"There he is!"

Miller sprinted down an alley. He had a solid block head start. The alley dumped into a construction site. Miller hid behind an unattended cement mixer. He knelt and dug a quick hole in the graded dirt and threw the velvet bag in. He covered it up and marked the spot with a stray orange ribbon from a surveyor's stake.

Yelling from the alley: "He went that way!"

Miller took off.

"SO THAT'S WHY you hired the gunmen," said Serge.

"I thought Carmine might have found out Sergio was still alive," said Lou. "You wouldn't believe how jealous he is."

"Was," said Serge.

"I heard. That was you?"

Serge nodded.

They ignored the distant gunshots as a brief firefight broke out before Agent Miller got riddled.

Lou looked down at Sergio's trash bag. "How'd you do today?"

"Pay dirt. All kinds of cool things. I find the best stuff on Miami Beach. It's the only place for me!"

"Me, too!" said Serge.

Sergio pulled a pizza crust from his bag and started munching. "So much has changed. I could give you a whole new tour."

"What are we waiting for?"

"Let's go!"

"We're on!"

Lou pointed at the floor. "Aren't you forgetting something?"

The pair looked down at the body, then at each other, then started nodding.

"He'll keep."

"Sure, he'll still be here."

They ran down the stairs to the limo. Lou followed at a more casual pace. Sergio and his bag of trash displaced Lenny in the front passenger seat. He opened the plastic sack and stuck his head inside. Serge turned the ignition.

"Let's see what we have in here. Ooooooooh, a matchbook. You collect matchbooks?"

Serge nodded and pulled into traffic. His granddad handed the pack across the seat. "You can have these. I already got them. What else is in here? . . . Cool!" He pulled out a crumpled soda cup. "The McDonald's Instant-Peel contest! And it hasn't been played!" He grabbed the corner of the sticker. "I feel lucky. Bet I won some fries."

Epilogue

Miami International Airport

CURBSIDE PARKING. TRAVELERS sweating for reasons other than heat. Castanet music from an unseen speaker.

People moved at an anxious clip that suggested an underlying current of drama, like a Turkish bazaar or illegal aphrodisiac market in Bangkok.

Pink and yellow sports coats. Hotel vans. Luggage wheeled quickly over the crosswalks from the Dolphin and Flamingo long-term garages. A man in a Panama hat struggled with a duffel bag of deceptive ballast. Others rushed for cabs to take them wherever they go to get the condoms out of their stomachs.

A limo screeched up. Doors opened.

Mick Dafoe got out with a gym bag.

Serge and Lenny joined him on the sidewalk and shook hands.

Mick twisted his Yankees cap around backward. "Those two chicks were hot! Why'd you ditch them at that convenience store?"

"City and Country?" said Serge. "Oh, I didn't ditch them. They wanted to be dropped off."

"But they were running after the limo."

"They're into that new exercise craze."

Mick turned and punched Lenny in the shoulder.

"Ow."

"Remember what I told you. Always take the points and the home dog after a divisional road loss, except on Astroturf."

He punched the shoulder again.

"Ow."

Mick gave Serge a quick salute. "Had a great time, saw Miami in a whole new light. . . . Just wish I could remember a little more of it."

"You were pretty busy maintaining that carefully constructed buzz." He handed Mick a couple pieces of paper. "Don't forget this."

"What's that?"

"Your Miami column. You wrote it last night."

Mick looked over the first page. "I don't remember doing this."

"Oh, yeah," said Serge. "It was something to watch. Giving it all you had, tapping a vein, pushing beyond the natural limits of artistic human endurance like van Gogh."

Mick flipped to the second page. "Wow. I write this good?"

"With the proper inspiration. I told you, you're a genius."

"But, Serge," said Lenny, "I saw you writing—"

Serge elbowed him in the stomach.

"Ow."

Mick headed for the automatic doors. He turned around to wave. The limo was gone.

FIVE OLD MEN sat on five stools at the bar. Wearing bathing suits. The water in the pool was up to their chests. They were in a cave under a waterfall. The bartender served them through a hole in the grotto.

"The Fontainebleau sure has changed," said Tommy.

"It's weird," said Chi-Chi. "Not the good weird."

"I like it," said Coltrane. "Bartender! Double!"

There was splashing behind them. Someone making his way through the curtain of water from the falls.

"Sergio!" said Mort.

Sergio had cleaned up well with the help of Lou, his grandson and some spending money. Close shave, executive haircut, new clothes, back on meds . . . somewhat. He grabbed a submerged stool.

"I nearly fainted when I heard the news," said Mort.

"The police said you drowned."

"The water wasn't even over my head. I was standing there in the dark a hundred yards offshore, watching all the commotion on the beach."

"Why didn't you ever contact us during all those years?" asked Tommy.

"I was crazy."

"We would have helped."

Sergio shook his head. "It was Lou's idea. When I disappeared New Year's, she saw it as our big chance. My death would close the case on the missing jewels and stop Carmine Palermo's jealous rampage. The only hitch was, we could never move the gems. If they ever turned up, Carmine and the cops would know I was still alive. And I couldn't contact friends or family, which Lou knew I'd do if I took my medication, so she kept me off it. She really loves me."

"So what happened to the gems?" asked Tommy.

"Someone stole them a couple days ago."

"That stinks."

"But then I won the McDonald's Instant Peel game."

"Which prize?"

"The big one. Million dollars."

"Oh, right!"

"Chi-Chi, you were in the limo," said Sergio. "Tell them."

"All I heard was a lot of yelling and you hanging out the window before they pulled you back inside."

"But I really did win."

"Still the storyteller," said Mort, smiling and putting a hand on Sergio's shoulder. "Glad to have you back."

CIA headquarters, Miami

The stereo was cranked. Everyone laughing, smoking cigars, even the female agents. The phone rang again. Station Chief Renfroe answered with delight. "No comment. You know I can't answer that. . . . Yes, that's music you hear. . . . 'Havana Daydreamin',' Buffett's fourth album, sixth if you count the Barnaby label releases. . . . Sure, you're welcome."

Agent Schaeffer arrived with the morning papers. "It a clean sweep. The *Herald*'s leading with a big headline. 'Sources: CIA Trumps Castro.'"

"*El Nuevo Herald*?"

"'Fidel Sucks Ass.'"

THE MIAMI CHAMBER of Commerce couldn't believe their eyes. They blinked a few times, but the newspaper article lying on the conference table didn't go away.

MIAMI NICE
by Mick Dafoe

I love Miami!

What was I thinking before?

I love everything about her, from Bill Baggs to Bal Harbour. It is the People's City—has to be, because the officials are always getting locked up. And I'm here to report she is in good hands.

My newfound affection for this great metropolis reminds me of words spoken long ago in the Rudolph Wilde Platz, when, on June 26, 1963, President Kennedy faced a sea of Germans and proclaimed, "Ich bin ein Berliner." Except he got the translation slightly off and actually said he was proud to be a jelly doughtnut—true fact, look it up. But that's another topic, another day.

What JFK was really getting at before he said he was pastry is that people can come together and take pride in each other. So, as all lovers of their fellowman, wherever they may live, are citizens of Miami, I therefore take pride in the words, I am a Miamian!

Walk into any Miami sandwich shop at one A.M. and check out the human menu at the lunch counter. Stripes you never imagined, all dancing to the same tune: It's cool to be different.

Sure we get some bad press—a clash here, a protest there, another boycott—but that's only the Cubans. Just kidding. We all really know it's the blacks' fault. That was another joke. See the fun you can have with tolerance? This city is out of sight on the national getting-along curve, the complete spectrum of humanity braiding together like sailors' rope. Strong. Weather-ready. Latins, Asians, Africans, Eastern Europeans, Australians, Eskimos—all united in brotherhood toward a common goal: teaching the Canadians how to multiply by fifteen to twenty percent.

And speaking of restaurants, there's the food! Stone crabs, jerk chicken, alligator tail, blackened snapper, coconuts, guava, mango . . .

And the arts! The Wolfsonian, the Lowe, the Bass, the Gusman Center, the Coconut Grove Playhouse . . .

And sports! A great major league baseball club, plus a couple of pretty decent pro football teams, the Dolphins and the Hurricanes.

I love Miami! Come at once!

Only leave the stupid Florida jokes at home. And stay on

your toes. Philadelphia may be the City of Brotherly Love, Atlanta "Too Busy to Hate," but Miami conks you on the head and shoves you in the back of a limo for an eye-popping visual tour that plays out like a rhapsody, an exquisite looping composition blurred by in a dizzying wash of palms, tiles, stucco, faces and flowers, building in heart-pounding delirium like the whirling symphonic transition from "A Day in the Life."

So what if we have all those wacky crime stories here? Consider it spicy topping, like salsa.

Salsa! The food again! I love Miami! . . . *Somebody stop me!*

And on it went. The praise more gushing and effusive until Mick finally said he owed his epiphany to his new friends at a small, offbeat tour service.

"So that's what happened," said the chamber president. "It wasn't a kidnapping after all. It was one of those novelty travel deals."

"Someone must have double-booked tour services," said the treasurer. "That's where the confusion came." He looked around at the others. "Who booked the second company? Jim, did you? Mary? Steve?"

They shook their heads.

"Well, someone certainly deserves our thanks," said the president. "We've had nothing but trouble with Sunshine Tours."

"The International Conference of Latin Mayors is coming to town next week," reminded the government liaison.

"That's right. The *Today* show will be doing a remote broadcast from the conference," said the president. "They've been inquiring about ideas for quirky feature stories to fill out the hour."

"What do you think?" asked the treasurer.

"It can't miss. Dafoe was a complete asshole. If these tour guys were able to win him over, Katie and Matt should be a piece of cake."

The treasurer pointed to a spot on the newspaper near the end of Mick's column. "Here's a website for the company."

FOUR MEN IN Michigan State alumni jerseys trudged through the hot sand on Miami Beach, checking out topless women under the guise of not checking them out. They headed back through the palm trees to Ocean Drive and waited to cross the street. A green Jaguar went by, black BMW, white Mercedes, gull-winged DeLorean, candy-apple red Rolls-Royce with magnetic door signs.

Brake lights came on. The Rolls backed up. The driver's door opened, and an old man got out. He produced a roll of bills from his pocket and peeled off four thousand dollars for each of them. He got back in and drove off.

The Rolls passed a construction site. A slurry of concrete poured out the chute of a cement mixer, covering an orange surveyor's ribbon.

Serge was in the backseat with Lenny. He had his clipboard in hand, talking to himself and checking off completed items: ". . . launch business, solve grandfather mystery, embarrass Castro, restore CIA pride, decimate mob, help Chamber of Commerce, find gems—sort of. That one gets an asterisk. . . ."

They arrived at the curb outside Bayfront Center and parked behind a semi-trailer with a peacock on the side. Police held back a crowd waving brightly colored homemade signs. An NBC camera crew moved across the pavilion toward the street, filming a smiling man and woman walking toward the Rolls.

Serge looked out the window, then crossed the last item off the clipboard. ". . . and the *Today* show. That just about wraps it up."

One of the NBC crew opened the back door of the Rolls. Serge slipped a fresh page into his clipboard and tapped it with his pen.

"What next?"

The text of this book was set in a face called Sardonic Bold, whose origins can be traced to seventeenth-century Luxembourg, where a robust typography movement . . . Hey, who are you? You're not supposed to be in here! What are you doing? . . . Wait a minute, I recognize you now. You're that guy from the *Today* show this morning! I've never seen such a disaster! What on earth were you thinking? . . . *"Shhhhhh! I'm trying to avoid some people. Is there a back way out of here?"* . . . Yeah, that door goes into 'About the author.' . . . *"Thanks."*—a typeface that saw a brief resurgence during the Age of Realism and was later revitalized in the forgings of the so-called Sans Serif Seven.

ABOUT THE AUTHOR

Tim Dorsey was born in Indiana, moved to Florida at the age of one, and grew up in a small town about seventy miles north of Miami called Riviera Beach. He graduated from Auburn University, where he was editor of the student newspaper, *The Plainsman.* From there he worked as a police and courts reporter for *The Alabama Journal,* the now-defunct evening newspaper in Montgomery, Alabama— Hey! Who are you? What are you doing in there? . . . *"Just be a minute. Do you have something I can jimmy this window with?"* . . . Hold it, you're that guy who ruined the *Today* show. I've never seen so many fire trucks and ambulances! . . . [*Glass shattering*] . . . You broke my "About the Author" window! . . . *"Sorry. Gotta run."* . . . In 1987 Dorsey joined the *Tampa Tribune* as a general-assignment reporter and later worked as a political reporter in the *Tribune's* Tallahassee bureau. He was the paper's night metro editor from 1994 until 1999, when he left to write full-time. He lives in Tampa.